PRAISE

TE

"An intriguingly brutal tale. *Terminal Event* takes readers into a realm they've never experienced before. It surges from a horrifying prologue to a spellbinding epilogue."

—Clive Cussler

"A great read. . . . A first-rate account of the fascinating investigative efforts of the NTSB."

—*Houston Chronicle*

"What a thriller! James Thayer's *Terminal Event* manages to captivate us on every page—with fascinating details of an air-crash investigation, a pair of complex, wholly appealing protagonists, a dozen unexpected twists, and a plot that speeds from start to finish like a jet plane."

—Jeffery Deaver, author of *The Blue Nowhere*

"Gripping. . . . A vivid tale."

—*The Plain Dealer* (Cleveland)

"A book you can't put down. . . . Combines the diligent and comprehensive homework of Crichton with the imagination and character development of Koontz into a suspenseful page-turner that is also a thoughtful exploration of human psychology and pathology."

—*Winston-Salem Journal* (NC)

"One book you don't want to read on a plane. . . . Heart-stopping descriptions of what happens after a plane crash. . . . The NTSB ought to give Thayer an award for showing what a tough job its investigators have."

—*The Orlando Sentinel* (FL)

"A superbly crafted thriller . . . will make airport buyers want to miss their flights."

—*Kirkus Reviews*

"An engrossing tale. . . . Mesmerizing. . . . The baffling clues left for investigators in the wake of a passenger aircraft's horrific midair explosion and crash are detailed with goose-bump realism in Thayer's chilling new novel. . . . Thayer proves a master storyteller. . . . [A] nerve-racking thriller [rooted] in solid realism."

—*Publishers Weekly*

"Gripping. . . . A page-turner and a fascinatingly well-researched look inside an NTSB crash investigation."

—*Tribune-Review* (Pittsburgh)

"A thrilling 'Event' . . . with high-voltage suspense . . . that's difficult to put down."

—*Naples Daily News* (FL)

"Thayer scores again . . . [and] gives readers their money's worth with a bang-up, surprise ending."

—*The Pilot* (Southern Pines, NC)

"A fascinating thriller . . . a genuinely engrossing novel, which contains a twist that few, if any, readers will see coming."

—*Booklist*

"A riveting detective story. . . . There are perhaps a dozen blind alleys that the investigators must go down, and the story follows all of them . . . until a seemingly insignificant fact leads to the solution."

—*The Drood Review of Mystery*

FIVE PAST MIDNIGHT

WHITE STAR

NOVELS BY JAMES THAYER

Force 12

Terminal Event

Man of the Century

Five Past Midnight

White Star

S-Day: A Memoir of the Invasion of England

Ringer

Pursuit

The Earhart Betrayal

The Stettin Secret

The Hess Cross

FORCE 12

a novel

JAMES THAYER

POCKET STAR BOOKS

New York   London   Toronto   Sydney   Singapore

A Pocket Star Book published by
POCKET BOOKS, a division of Simon & Schuster, Inc.
1250 Avenue of the Americas, New York, NY 10020

Copyright © 2001 by James Stewart Thayer

Originally published in hardcover in 2001 by Simon & Schuster, Inc.

ISBN: 0-671-03434-0

First Pocket Books printing March 2002

10 9 8 7 6 5 4 3 2 1

POCKET STAR BOOKS and colophon are registered
trademarks of Simon & Schuster, Inc.

For information regarding special discounts for bulk
purchases, please contact Simon & Schuster Special Sales
at 1-800-456-6798 or business@simonandschuster.com

Front cover illustration by Gerber Studio

Printed in the U.S.A.

To

SENIOR AIRMAN

SEAN MCDERMOTT

(1970–1998)

320TH SPECIAL TACTICS SQUADRON

UNITED STATES AIR FORCE

That Others May Live

My heartfelt thanks to:
Stephen Brock Blankenship, Andrew Bruning, Frank Dawdy, Pat Furr, Rich Givot, Jeff Jernegan, Paul Koester, Ruth McDermott, John D. Reagh III, Brenton D. Schicker, John L. Thayer, M.D., my wonderful wife, Patricia Wallace Thayer, and to my editor, Michael Korda, who put me in mind of sailing and the sea.

The sea has never been friendly to man. At most it has been the accomplice of human restlessness.

—JOSEPH CONRAD

PROLOGUE

The raft flipped over, and his brother had drowned, and Jess McKay's memories were still merciless, even after all the years. Every day since, every hour since, McKay had returned in his mind to that river, trying to nudge his memory, hoping it would play out some other way, some less shameful way, but his brother always remained dead, and Jess always remained a coward.

Mount Index, in the Cascade Range in Washington State, is a noble granite peak, rugged in all its aspects except that it is slender by local standards. Even so, the mountain doesn't deserve what gold prospector A. D. Gunn did to it a hundred years ago, which was to name it after his middle finger. Each spring Mount Index issues its prodigious snow melt to the Skykomish River, which swells and rolls with its new burden, more white than blue as it drops quickly through the wilderness toward Puget Sound.

That day, those years ago, Jess McKay crouched on a rounded boulder, speaking loudly over the rush of water. "Where'd you get the oars?"

"These're paddles, not oars." His brother didn't

look up from the inflatable raft, where he was working with a length of clothesline. "They've been in
Uncle Dan's garage for years, hanging on the wall."

"He knows we're up here? He gave them to you?"

"Not exactly." Matt McKay had studied a book on
knots, and used a bowline to secure his backpack to
one of the raft's D-rings, retying it three times until he
was satisfied. "I drove over to Dan's house and borrowed the paddles. He always keeps his garage door
open when he's away at work. He won't mind."

Small waves pushed against Jess's boulder. Mid-
stream's swift current surged over rocks close to the
surface, sending forth confused waves in all directions,
so the water washed rather than edged the river's
banks. Jess was wearing sandals, and he tentatively
dipped his foot into the water, just half his foot. The cold
seemed like a blow, and his leg instantly contracted.
This water had been snow a few miles up the slope. He
glanced at his brother, hoping Matt hadn't seen the
water defeat him. His brother was still bent over his raft.

Jess wanted to help Matt prepare for the raft's
launch, to be of some use, rather than sitting on the
boulder like a lump, but he knew from past experience that he would only earn a rebuke, something
about being all thumbs or this being a job for an adult.
Not that his big brother was unkind. Matt just never
liked folks getting in his way, not in this raft business,
not in anything. Jess had overheard his mom and dad
wonder aloud and laugh about their eldest son, saying
things like, "Matt is sure goal-oriented," and calling
him "directional." Jess hadn't bothered looking the
word up in his dictionary. He knew what they meant
because he knew his brother.

Jess asked, "How many times you going to run the
river, you think?"

"The company told me to come back when I had experience, so I'm going to load up on experience." Matt tossed Jess a life jacket, borrowed from his uncle's fishing boat, also in the garage. "A dozen times, I figure."

"How long will that take?"

"At a run a day, you figure it out."

Matt McKay was a senior at Everett High School, and had applied for a summer job at Cascade Adventures, a company based in Everett, thirty miles north of Seattle. The company took customers on guided raft journeys on the Suiattle, Skagit, Nooksack, and Skykomish rivers, all in western Washington. Cascade Adventures usually hired college juniors and seniors as guides, but the owner was impressed with Matt: his eagerness, his three-year varsity letter in football, his acceptance at the University of Washington for next fall, a solid handshake, looking him right in the eyes. "Come back and see me when your resume has something about whitewater rafting on it," the owner had said.

So Matt had purchased an abundantly used two-man inflatable raft from Cleary's Pawn on Second Avenue in Everett after arguing for thirty minutes with the pawnbroker over whether the price should be the amount on the sticker or the amount Matt had in his pocket, a difference of ten dollars. Cleary finally agreed to Matt's offer, just so Cleary could get back to lunch. Cleary didn't have any helmets, and Matt didn't have more money, anyway.

"Did you tell Mom and Dad we were coming up here?" Jess asked as he tugged at the life jacket, trying to figure out how he could fit into the contraption. Matt's car was parked up the hill at a turnout on the county road.

"What do you think?"

"Me, neither." Curtains of mist hung over the river. Jess hugged himself against the chill, then lowered his arms, thinking it undignified. "We probably should've, though. Told them, you know."

"Mom never learned to swim," Matt replied. "She's terrified of water. She'd never let us come up here. Something must've happened to her when she was a kid."

"Maybe she fell into a well," Jess suggested, wanting to contribute. He wrestled the life jacket around himself, then connected the clasps. "One of those boarded-over wells nobody has used for years. Maybe she was out walking in a field and fell in."

"That's probably it, all right." Matt's well-used tone inferred that his brother might be a dork.

Jess's English class at school was featuring a block on creative writing, the point of which escaped Jess entirely. As a homework assignment, the teacher had asked the students to stare at themselves in a mirror and write four sentences about their appearance, avoiding conclusive terms such as *handsome* or *pretty* or *repulsive*. Jess had forgotten the assignment until homeroom the next day, and had hastily written, "I am skinny. My nose has two holes. No zits today. This makes four sentences, counting this one." He didn't wonder at the *C*-minus he received on the assignment. Creative writing was for dorks.

Had he described himself more fully, he would have mentioned his blond hair, the color of straw, which often stood out randomly like straw, too. His eyes were green or blue depending on the light, and were full of life. His smile was usually slow in coming, sliding across his face, but full and welcoming and warm once in place. He thought his nose was too large, but it was straight and masterful, and added strength to his face. His jaw was prominent and uncompromising, and hinted at Jess's stubbornness, which was just beginning to manifest itself. He thought the small cleft in his chin was goofy, and every time he shaved—every five days—he left it bloody. He was growing quickly, an inch every two months, his dad swore. Jess felt like his body was just a sack of creaky, knobby bones. Once in a while Jess flexed his arms in front of a mirror, hoping those same forces of nature that were fooling with his voice would put some bulk on his biceps, but they still resembled spaghetti. On testing day at PE, he could not do a single pull-up, just couldn't get his chin up to the damn bar, not once, to the hoots of all his so-called friends, one of whom suggested the chess club. God, he wished he were big and tough, so he could give his dumb friends such a look—slit-eyed and dangerous— that they'd scatter like poultry. Jess's mom had said, "Be patient, Jess, because two years from now you won't recognize yourself." Two years from now was a century from now.

So now he was just a skinny kid perched on a boulder. He chucked a rock into the water. The river was framed by western hemlocks, with their drooping tops, as if each tree was taking a bow, and Douglas fir, some of them ten feet in diameter, bare of limbs on their lower trunks. Matt had once told Jess that the Indians had used pitch from Douglas firs for caulking their canoes. The trees formed a dark canopy, and the wedge of sky directly over the river was intense blue, not faded by a competing sun, which was still in the southern sky this time of year, hidden behind trees.

The scent of the forest was thick, a musty odor of decay and dampness that signaled this place was ancient. Moss grew along the river banks, and so did bunchberry and brambles and stinging nettles, crowded together. Behind Matt, just up the bank, a huckleberry bush had rooted in the decomposing trunk of a red cedar tree that had fallen decades ago. Clumps of deer fern grew at the base of the trees. Matt had said that after a deer loses its antlers, it will rub the raw stubs on deer fern, some chemical in the plant offering relief. Matt knew most everything worth knowing.

Still making adjustments to his raft—small things the point of which was lost on Jess—Matt looked up and asked, "You kissed her yet?"

Jess could feel color flash across his face. He asked lamely, "Who?"

"Don't give me that." Matt laughed. "The blond in the ponytail you escort from second to third period every day."

Her name was Megan Andrews, the first girl who had ever paid attention to Jess. She sat next to him in algebra, and he had been staring at her once in a while when she wasn't looking. One day she abruptly brought her head up from her book and stared back at him. Mortified, Jess had dropped his gaze. Two minutes later when he found the courage to try the smallest of glances in her direction, she was still looking at him, and smiling. After algebra that day, she had just up and joined him in the hallway, walking along with him to their next class as if it were something natural.

Jess raised his voice over the sound of the river. "I don't know who you're talking about." He was a dreadful liar.

"Megan Andrews is who I'm talking about." Matt cackled with the victory. "Nice girl, my informants tell me. She begun puberty yet?"

Jess ignored him, staring at his sandals, the water below him streaked with white foam and coursing around the boulder. He was a freshman in high school, same school as Matt, Everett High. His big brother owned the place, him and his football buddies, while Jess bumbled along, aimless and overwhelmed, doing something stupid hourly. Matt—who liked to tease him, but never in front of friends, and never meanly, not really—had confided that he, too, had felt like a moron and klutz his freshman year. It scarcely seemed possible.

Matt was golden. Everything he did, he did easily. Everything he started, he finished. Big and strong, charming, with a quick smile full of perfect teeth, blond hair, gray-green eyes, liked to tell jokes on himself, and at once likable. Matt was everything Jess was not, except the coloring and teeth. The younger brother was squeaky and shuffling, and baffled, and wore the same basketball shoes every day and liked Nintendo and played fetch with his stupid dog who had the stupid name Tramp. Matt had entered manhood, leaving Jess far, far behind.

"So, tell you what I'll do, do you a big favor," Matt called. He was using a foot pump to top off the air in the raft's tubes. "I'll take little Megan Andrews out on a date, teach her to kiss properly, give her some good experience, tongue and all. Then I'll give her back to you."

"That's disgusting."

"You won't have to break her in, you see."

"That's sick," Jess hollered. "You're sick." But then joined Matt in the laugh, he couldn't help it.

And then Matt admitted, "She's pretty cute, Megan is, she get rid of the metal on her teeth some day."

"You think she . . . ?" Jess hesitated, struggling with

the question, one of the tangled inquiries that occasionally half-formed in his mind, questions of vast import
and consequence, usually about freshmen girls, and
which Matt always answered with such profound wisdom—the truth standing powerfully revealed—that Jess
was always chagrined the answer had eluded him.

But Matt called jubilantly, "She's ready for launch."
He pushed the raft the few feet across river stones to
the water. "You're in front, Jess."

Matt had been unable to find a second life jacket,
but Uncle Dan's garage had yielded a water skier's life
ring, big for Matt because Dan was an eater, and even
though Matt cinched it tightly it hung on his hip
bones.

The raft was made of urethane tubes, with rubbing
strakes along the outside, and with a plywood deck.
It was seven feet long—five feet on the interior—with
a five-foot beam, and weighed just fifty pounds. For
safety the raft had five separate air compartments
in the tubes, and a self-bailing scupper. D-ring tie-
downs were mounted on the deck and along the top
of the tubes. The raft was Day-Glo orange, and some
prior owner had painted red and yellow licks of fire
on the bow, like on a hot rod. The starboard tube had
been patched at the waterline with a hand-sized
square of urethane, but the patch had been sealed
evenly and sanded, and looked as if it had been done
professionally.

Jess slid off the boulder, the edges of his life pre-
server bumping his chin as he landed. Brushing a
thimbleberry bush, he stepped over stones to the raft.
A Stellar's jay loosed a metallic clack from deep inside
the cover of a juniper.

His brother handed him a paddle. "The wide end
goes in the water."

Jess hadn't been parrying his brother's wisecracks all morning—not many of them, anyway—trying to build some goodwill. That's why Jess had come on this dumb trip anyway, to ask his brother if, just once— promise, he'll never ask again, and he'll be Matt's serf forever and throw in his Swiss Army knife, Jess's only possession his brother had ever paused over—if he could go on a double date with Matt. His big brother possessed that magical key to happiness and all that was good in the world: a driver's license. Jess had Megan Andrews on his mind, not rafting.

He climbed over a tube, and sat on a low wood seat. The inflated tubes surrounded him closely on three sides, and he could rest his elbows on them. He gripped the paddle tightly, laying it across the bow. The raft scraped against pebbles as Matt pushed it from shore out into the current. With a gleeful whoop, he leaped into the stern. His knees bumped Jess's back as he settled in.

The acceleration was startling. Their spot on the bank seemed to flee behind them as the raft was pulled to the center of the river and then propelled downstream. And the river instantly seemed to calm as they became part of it, moving at its pace, with ripples and bubbles escorting them quietly along. Even the wind moved with them, so it was warmer on the river than on the bank, and quieter, almost serene. The brothers dug their paddles into the water several times, but there was nothing for them to do, as the river had taken over, and it guided them unerringly, keeping them to the middle of the flow, keeping the little raft away from granite crags that hung out into the river.

The banks sped by, and the brothers passed thick braces of red alder and steep inclines covered with green salal. Granite boulders the size of automobiles appeared to have been tossed willy-nilly on the shores and into the river. When the forest on the south bank opened, sunlight swept across the river, and the boulders, studded with numberless flecks of mica, glittered and opalesced. The river was a raw wilderness, primitive and fierce, without a trace of humankind's notice or influence, as it had been since the night of time.

"Hey, Matt, what . . . ?" Jess pointed ahead, where the water appeared to end, as if it had a brim, as if Columbus had been wrong and the world were indeed flat.

"Hang on," his brother yelled.

The raft sank, and Jess with it, over a fall no more than two feet high, but Jess yelled involuntarily as their craft plunged into the whirl of water below the drop. Lifted by all its air, the raft rebounded then lunged ahead, settled, then dipped over a smaller fall, Matt laughing crazily. The stern came around, but Matt paddled briskly, setting the raft again on its course. A moment later they entered a calm, the water oily blue and circling idly, a whirlpool tucked behind an outcropping.

"That's as much fun as you are going to have in your entire life, baby brother," Matt exulted, "doesn't matter what Megan Andrews lets you do to her, poor girl."

Jess turned halfway around, and had to speak loudly, over a peculiar hiss coming from downstream. "Matt, I was going to ask you something." Maybe now was the time, Matt in control of everything and on top of the world, Jess at his mercy. Maybe Matt would dispense some charity. "You know some Saturday night? Maybe we could . . ."

"I brought you along as a crewman, not some freeloading passenger," Matt hooted, not listening in the slightest. "Your paddle is almost dry. Let's go."

The older brother swept the blade through the water, and the raft glided from behind its protective boulder and back into the current. The river was shallow here, with stones just under the knotty surface, and the raft began to buck. Jess gripped two D-rings on the bow as he rose and fell, rose and fell, his paddle forgotten across his lap. Matt whooped and pulled at the water with his paddle, his knees banging against Jess's back.

The valley narrowed, leaving only a strip of sky overhead, and the water quickened. In their eternal and tortured passage up through the earth's crust, the boulders here had been squared off, and were full of right angles, cubist piles rising against the valley walls. Jess cocked his head. A bass rumble came from downstream, and though he hadn't seen train tracks anywhere around, the noise might have been from a locomotive out of sight around a rocky bend, and their little craft was rushing toward it. Above the canyon an osprey slipped through the sky, impartial, the undersides of its wings ghostly white.

The river stalled and smoothed behind the sheltering arm of a granite monolith that jutted out into the stream and blocked the sky. The river here in the deep shadow was bayonet gray. The raft slowed, and neared the vertical bulwark of granite. Moss clung to the stone, and improbable tufts of grass grew from tiny crevices. Uprooted by high water, a tree was trapped against a stone salient, its bark flensed from the trunk during its battering run downriver, its roots half above the waterline and resembling a claw. The roar from the west was unceasing.

Now was his chance. He twisted around again and yelled over the noise, "Matt, you know someday, when you are on a date, maybe some Saturday night, maybe we could, if you wouldn't mind too much, and you'd hardly know we were in the back seat, maybe we could—"

Matt cast his face in astonishment, then held up his hand like a traffic cop. "Wait a minute, kid brother. Am I about to hear what I think I'm about to hear?"

"Well, it's just that I thought, maybe we . . ." He didn't dare utter the phrase *double date,* offering too tempting a target for Matt.

His brother got it anyway. "Something this big needs a lot of thinking, if we are talking about the four of us. And having you and little Megan with me needs some rules."

When Matt said *no,* it was always straightaway and unalterable. When he said *yes,* it was inevitably preceded by taxing banter. This sounded like *yes,* though it would take a while. Hope surged in Jess, but he knew not to press. He leaned over the tube to dip his hand into the river. The water seemed to bite him. It hadn't warmed up any, that was for sure.

The vortex of water behind the stone mass moved slowly, and the raft curled around, the peak of the sheer granite face high overhead, seeming to wheel around on an axis.

Matt pursed his lips and crooked an eyebrow, an expression of weighty and judgmental thought, entirely transparent. "Now, Jess, what if some of my football buddies see me driving you and Megan around, and—"

The raft suddenly gained a will of its own, startlingly, cutting off Matt's words, and pushing Jess back against Matt's legs as it accelerated and spun out from behind the crag into a narrow chute of water.

Matt yelled, "Hey, what's . . . ?"

The raft shot through the channel, towers of stone close on both sides, and then bounced against a slab of rock. Jess's paddle caught in a crevice and was yanked from his hands. He tried to grab it, but found only the rough canyon wall. For several heartbeats the river remained solid and blue, but at a downward angle, the granite banks holding the water too tightly, and the speed ever increasing. Then the canyon bed fell away, and the river was expelled from the walls' tight embrace. The rush of water broke apart and plunged down in a foaming tumult.

The valley below flashed in front of him, and then Jess tumbled down, the raft pulling away. He yelled, but it was chopped off when a smothering column of white water enveloped him, turning him in ragged somersaults. He was lost in a crashing spume, and falling and falling.

His arm smashed into an unseen boulder as he rolled in a universe of frothing white water, without bearings and without air and without his brother. He scraped on stones on the river bottom. Skin on his back peeled away. He forced his eyes to open, but all he could see was the blind white of the turbulence. He kicked frantically, trying to push himself to the surface, but the thrashing water hid the way, and rolled him over and over. When his lungs worked involuntarily, his windpipe filled with water. He had the vague impression he was drowning, and that he had seen the last of all he knew.

Then the river released him, and the ferment fell away, and he gagged and coughed and found that living air was all around and that he could breathe again. He shook his head like a dog, clearing his eyes. The raft was well downstream and disappearing behind a turn in the river. His knees found a surface, and he scrambled up a grade of rounded stones, climbing out of the river. He bent over, hands on his knees, gasping for breath. He wiped more water from his eyes. His back stung where rocks had ground against him. Then he remembered his brother.

He turned back to the river, catching himself when his foot slipped on moss. He called out, "Matt."

His brother was right in front of him, an arm's reach away, moving with the current, an open wound on his forehead, and blood running down his face and mixing with the river water. His flotation ring had been stripped from him and was bobbing along in the current behind him.

Matt lifted a hand toward his brother and cried out, "Jess, help. Help."

Then he disappeared beneath the surface, suddenly, as if invisible arms had dragged him under.

Breathing in huge gulps, Jess stepped along the stony shore, trying to keep up with the current that held his brother, seeing only the churning white surface. He called out his brother's name, a small noise lost in the thunder of the rapids.

And then Matt was there again, his mouth open and his eyes white all around, water breaking over him, thirty feet out into the river.

His eyes locked on Jess. "Please . . . Jess . . . help," and down he went again, covered by the furious flow.

Jess stumbled along the bank, dodging boulders and river debris, waving his arms as he tried to keep his balance on the broken ground, his life jacket dripping water onto the ground. The rapids gave way to a short expanse of calmer water, still moving, but without the white violence.

Matt emerged again, dotting the water. He screamed,

"Jess . . . Jess . . . help me. Jess." An arm flailed uselessly against the water. Something was wrong with Matt's other arm. It trailed behind him in the water. He drifted downstream toward another loud and boiling cataract. Matt's forehead had been laid open to the skull, which reflected daylight like a mirror. "Jess . . . Jess."

Then began the fifteen seconds that forever branded Jess McKay, just a fraction of a minute, and no such tiny slice of time should wreak havoc down through the years, twisting and tearing and never relenting.

Jess stood on the river bank, his hands out to his brother, reaching out to him. Jess cried out Matt's name. But Jess did not enter the water.

He was riveted by fear. He was unable to move, to take that step into the current. His legs twitched, as if some of him were ready to go. He reached for his brother, bending at the waist, but his legs would not move.

Jess knew what he had to do. Perhaps from some unbidden instinct, he knew with utter certainty that he was called upon to go to Matt, to help, to give Matt a chance when there was none other, to bring him out of the river's grip.

All he had to do was step off the bank and swim to his brother. His life jacket would keep him afloat, would surely keep both of them above the surface. Just that, just that small thing, go, and go now, jump back into the current, and reclaim your brother.

"Jess . . ." Weaker now, just Matt's chin above water.

Those wretched seconds unfolded and when Matt's head disappeared again it was for good, and the time given Jess to make his choice was gone and would never return.

Water swept endlessly by.

PART ONE

The star-filled seas are smooth to-night.

—A. E. HOUSMAN

CHAPTER 1

Snow was wicking away blood from his leg, and the red color expanded in a circle that looked like a bull's-eye, and the pilot knew he did not have long. He was no longer cold and no longer shivering, and it vaguely troubled him, but everything was vague now, and fewer and fewer things were troubling him.

Huge snowflakes flew past, coming at him endlessly, as if he were soaring through the galaxy, and so thick he could see little beyond his boots, and his boots were being covered by snow, so he supposed he would soon see nothing but white. The mountain was claiming him. In a few moments he would cease being a human, and would become a topographic feature, another small wrinkle on the side of McKinley.

At least, that's where he thought he was, Mount McKinley. His F-16 Viper had quit on him, just flamed out, and what could he have expected from an engine built in Belgium, damn them, and the fighter had begun to coast, and an instant later his hydraulics went out. The F-16's nose sank, nothing he had encouraged, and then the plane began to roll as if it were on a spit, so he pulled the lever and out he went, into the blast of air, gratified when his chute opened. At least something worked.

Snow had softened the impact, and he had landed in fine shape, he remembered, though chilled through. On the ground, the chute toppled him and dragged him along as if he were a plow, but he managed to release it, and the chute was probably in Siberia by now, where it was surely better weather.

The pilot's name was Peter Bradley, and he had until about an hour ago been participating in the Air Force's combat exercise *Cope Thunder*, flying with Navy and Marine pilots, and with pilots from Canadian Forces and the Royal Air Force. The exercise was in its tenth day, and Bradley had been flying two missions most days. Though many American flyers in Alaska for *Cope Thunder* were from bases in the Lower 48, Bradley was posted to the 18th Fighter Squadron, the Blue Foxes, flying from Eielson Air Force Base southeast of Fairbanks. The Blue Foxes' primary mission was close air support, though not so close as to be sitting on a snowbank, bleeding to death or freezing to death, Bradley didn't suppose it mattered which.

He had taken the Arctic survival course at the Cool School at Eielson, the 66th Training Squadron's introduction to cold and hunger, and they had made him plenty cold and hungry, but not like this, out here, alone and with a broken leg. At the Cool School he had learned about the lethargy and disorientation that accompany freezing to death. He wondered how long his mind had left. Would he recognize it slipping away? Would enough of his intellect remain to understand that less and less of it remained? Can the diminished comprehend the diminishing? He should have been a philosopher.

God, he would like to see his wife again. He could

fly a Viper but she was the brains in the family. He laughed weakly, his breath rolling away behind him in a streaming cloud. He could no longer feel his ears under his helmet. He was wearing a sage-green flight suit and a winter-weight flight jacket, with its twill outer shell and quilted lining and storm flap, and he might as well have been wrapped in rice paper for all the good the jacket was doing. A Snickers bar was in a pocket on the left sleeve, held in place by a Velcro flap. A Snickers would be good right now.

Bradley had climbed Mount McKinley once. Almost climbed it. The West Buttress was the mountain's easiest route, but there were no easy routes on McKinley. His climbing team—six friends from Eielson, all F-16 or A-10 pilots—took ten days to stage their ascent, and did everything right, pushing up their caches, returning to a lower elevation to sleep. Climbing high, sleeping low, acclimatizing. They got within two thousand vertical feet of the summit when a storm roared in from the Gulf of Alaska and fairly blew them off the mountain.

McKinley—none of the pilots called it Denali, lest they be magically and irrevocably transformed into tree-hugging Birkenstockers—killed easily and routinely, with its minus fifty degrees temperatures and its hundred-miles-an-hour wind. Many times, skilled climbers had been surprised by a bit of errant weather, and had been flash frozen on the mountain. That's what was happening to him, Bradley knew. Flash frozen, something the Jolly Green Giant would do to an ear of corn. McKinley was killing him, easily and routinely. He sighed, and stopped himself when it sounded too much like a groan.

He had landed just fine, he brought up the memory again. Released his parachute from the harness after a

short slide along the snow, then had taken four
steps—he didn't know in which direction as he
couldn't see anything because of the falling snow—
and he must have been on a snow bridge because
then the snow under his boots had suddenly given
way, just collapsed from under him so that he found
himself falling through the damned air again, you'd
think once would be enough. He fell awhile, then
smacked the ground and started to slide, his leg catching on some rock and snapping, and finally he stopped
where he was now, and hadn't been able to move an
inch since. He knew a steep slope was nearby—he had
ridden it down—but it was behind the veil of snow.

Bradley's head came up. He abruptly felt as if he
were not alone. Peculiar, because he surely was. He
looked right and left into the blur of snow. He asked
aloud, "Is someone there?" He waited. "Hello?
Anybody there?"

No one, of course. Not on the mountain in Nov-
ember. He had met his wife, Karen, at the commissary
at Fairchild Air Force Base, near Spokane, where the
Air Force had sent him for survival school, not that
anything he learned there was doing any good now,
the numbness up to his thighs and a Snickers bar in his
sleeve pocket he couldn't reach because his hands
wouldn't work, so the Snickers might as well have
been on the moon, but she managed the commissary
and he was standing at the magazine rack looking at
bra ads in a *Cosmopolitan*—for the first time in his life,
honest to God, he swore to her later—and she passed
behind him as he was studying the ads and she
laughed, and they were married six weeks later.

Not that he really wanted the candy bar. It was just
there. He didn't care about it, or his plane. An eight-
million-dollar piece of equipment broken up in the

Alaskan wilderness somewhere. He loved flying that
bird, and he particularly enjoyed ground attack exercises, firing away at buildings, airfields, simulated
hangars, and dummy aircraft. The plane quit on him
at the worst time: when it was in the air. He laughed,
sort of a laugh at sort of a joke.

He was growing smaller, the life leaving him. He
wondered where he was, why everything was white.
He wanted to see his wife. If she would just hold his
hand for a while. Hypothermia killed a hundred thousand Krautsters in World War II, old Mr. Frosty doing
the work of the Lord that time. But not this time. His
wife's name was Karen.

The world was reduced to a low tunnel, and he was
racing through it, stuck on the mountainside. He had
bailed out in daylight, so the sun was up there, but
obscured and indifferent and of no account. The
snowflakes had gained weight, it seemed. Bradley
could feel every one of them against his face and chest
as they rudely pummeled him. Or maybe he couldn't.
He was above the tree-line, and with nothing to rattle,
the Arctic wind was almost noiseless, a muted sigh,
but still drawing the life out of him. He sat on the
snow, bleeding.

His wife. He could smell her perfume, right there
on the mountain. He again looked left into the moving
storm. "Karen?" Nothing but snow.

He was losing it, and that was a fact. Karen standing there on Mount McKinley, as if there were a
chance of that. She had told him once that she was
afraid of heights, and that she didn't even like escala-
tors. He smiled, tried to smile.

Joy suffused him, and giddiness, and he could see
clearly, if only for a few feet. The dead white of the
storm took on a slight soft rose hue, a touch of warmth

in its coloring. Many of his questions were about to be answered. He hoped it would be something grand, like a blinding flash, and maybe some trumpets. And there were worse ways to die. Ask Joan of Arc. This was hardly like dying, up here on this mountain, just an easy letting go. Of course, the rose hue might be retinal hemorrhaging caused by altitude, another of Mount McKinley's little pranks.

Still, his wife, down in Fairbanks. He wished he could see her. One more time. He closed his eyes, just for a moment, he hoped. It seemed such a small thing, seeing Karen once more, but she was far away, on the other side of this storm. He recalled their honeymoon. Had that been fun or what? They had gone somewhere warm but he couldn't remember where, would never remember now. His body was going and his memories were going. His past was slipping away. Soon there would be nothing. Cold was all around. He was dying.

"Bingo."

A word. Out there in front of him. A rather cheery word. Something other than snow. One word, said aloud.

God's voice, surely. Bradley had hoped for something more majestic, something booming, some nice quote from the Old Testament, but *bingo* was fine. Who was an Air Force lieutenant to second guess the Lord?

"You're alive, looks like. That's a good start, Lieutenant Bradley."

The snow resolved itself into a man, standing in front of Bradley, then bent over him. Big red REI parka with an American flag sewn on the sleeve. Under the parka and covering his legs was a one-piece mountain suit. His gloves had fur on the back so he could wipe his brow. He carried a mountain axe he had been using as a third point of contact.

The man was chewing something rapidly, really working at it, visible even under his mask. He asked, "Are you in pain?"

Bradley could only whisper. "Not any more."

The man's helmet covered a balaclava. Tinted Scott ski goggles hid his eyes. He removed a pack from his back. "We're going to fix you up. No worries now."

The man's chest harness was rigged with an ascender for self-rescue. Pulleys hung from the harness, along with several screws, prussic and tape slings, and carabeeners. The man's climbing harness was affixed to a rope that disappeared behind him into the snow. Quick-don crampons were over his Raichle climbing boots. He carefully brushed snow off the pilot's flight uniform.

"Broken leg," the man said to nobody.

Following the rope, a second fellow emerged from the storm, and then a third, all wearing red parkas.

The first man spoke quickly into a radio. Bradley couldn't make out what he said. Maybe his brain was freezing.

"The bag and a heated IV," the lead rescuer said to his team. Bradley heard him this time. "And, Sandy, get a bag valve mask ready."

The others didn't say anything. They moved in silent and swift choreography.

A hypothermia kit was opened, and an olive-drab patient treatment bag resembling a large sleeping bag was unrolled. The bottom of the down-filled bag was made of heavy-duty cordura nylon, and handle straps were sewn along it at intervals that matched the patient's shoulders and knees. A ruff of artificial fur rimmed the head opening. The lead rescuer checked

Bradley's pulse and a few other things the pilot couldn't follow.

Then the rescuers placed an inflatable splint around the fractured leg. The lead rescuer explained to the pilot, "It'll stabilize your leg. Less pain, and less damage to surrounding tissue caused by the jagged bone ends."

Peter Bradley was stuffed into the bag, none too gently. The lead rescuer activated several three-pound chemical heating pouches, wrapped them in cloth from the backpack to insure they didn't burn the pilot, then slipped them into the patient treatment bag. Bradley couldn't feel them. The team was moving quickly. They hadn't been at his side longer than two minutes. The first rescuer gently wiped the snow from Bradley's face, as kind an act as the pilot had ever experienced.

The second rescuer had activated a heating pad, and he placed it into the insulation cover around an IV bottle. The first man opened the bag just enough to get to Bradley's arm. The pilot supposed a needle punctured his arm. He couldn't tell if the rescuers cut open his jacket and flying suit, or whether they had punctured everything, right down to his vein.

A sked board made of thin plastic was unrolled and tucked under the pilot. Bradley's mind flickered like a candle. He and his new bride had honeymooned in Mexico, at Cabo San Lucas. That was it. Mexico. Her dad had paid for it, his wedding present. Cactus and desert and the high sun. Bradley moved his mouth, but couldn't force out any words.

The first rescuer leaned closer, and the pilot tried again. "Is my wife Karen with you?"

The rescuer bent still lower. "Your wife? She's down in Fairbanks. She'll be getting a phone call any minute telling her that we've found you and that you're alive."

"She's not here?" Bradley's voice was wheezy, and almost lost in the wind. "Then who is that fourth person with you, off to the left? Standing there and watching."

The rescuer didn't bother to look. "There's only three of us, Lieutenant, come up this mountain to get you. Your wife is at your apartment down in Fairbanks."

His rescuers must have decided he didn't need the bag mask to help him breathe. Karen was over there, in her blue parka with the hood, wearing the perfume he had purchased for her in Mexico. Let his rescuers think otherwise.

"What's your name?" the pilot asked. Getting the words out was an act of will. His head was low in the rescue bag, and surrounded by white fur.

"Jess McKay. Captain, 212th RQS."

Bradley knew who these guys were, knew their reputation. He didn't want to be goofy in front of them. He tried to rally, to pull his thoughts together. He managed, "Where am I?" Small sentences. Keep it easy. "McKinley?"

McKay nodded. "But nowhere near the top. You landed near Kahiltna Pass, elevation about twelve thousand feet. There's another six thousand feet of mountain above us."

"Nobody hired us to chat," the rescuer named Sandy growled. "The helicopter is waiting downhill, and my TV dinner is still in the oven. Probably burned to black."

"PJ humor," McKay said to the injured pilot. "It takes some getting used to."

The rope snaking after him, the third pararescue jumper climbed thirty paces uphill to anchor the others. McKay and the second PJ gripped the sked board.

"We've got you now," McKay said. "You'll be okay."

"No, I'm dead," the pilot replied. Every word was a struggle. "I'm quite sure. Dead."

"Not out here in the cold." McKay grinned under his mask, still chewing. They started down the mountain. "That's not the way we work. We don't consider a man dead until he is warm and dead."

CHAPTER 2

ime to the next tack, please," Gwen Weld asked. A deep voice came from many speakers, filling the room but directionless, like the voice of God. "Two minutes, twelve seconds."

After a lifetime of manners, she couldn't help herself. "Thank you."

The machine did not respond. She had demanded that the "You are welcome" and—worse—the "No problem" lines of code be removed because she could think of nothing as worthless as social grace from a pack of silicon chips.

Then she loudly cleared her throat—"Ahhemmm"—followed by three quick clicks of her tongue, then a soft purr.

"Pardon?" the Voice asked after half a beat.

She smiled at the small victory. She despised the Voice.

From all around came, "Please repeat the instruction or inquiry, Ms. Weld."

Embarrassed for herself, she said, "Strike that." Teasing a computer. How low could she go?

She had been toying with the Voice to distract herself, to dilute her fear. Her hand on the computer mouse was still trembling, even though she had been in this dreadful room ninety minutes, and she should have calmed some by now. But how do you adjust to an eerie sarcophagus, this slender room without a single window, lit by rude fluorescent lights and by monitors that glowed with anemic techno hues? The room's hatches fore and aft were heavy steel, with wheel locks on them like in an old submarine, a curious throwback to earlier times and unlike anything else in the room.

The room was aft, and was called the chart room by the boat's owner in a bit of irony because there was not a nautical chart, tide table, current chart, *Light List*, *Coast Pilot*, or *Bowditch* in the room. Rather, almost every vertical surface was covered with flat-panel monitors. Secured to the table so they wouldn't slide off when the boat was heeled over were two more monitors, three laptop computers, and microphones. An old mariner might have searched for a bit of brass or beveled glass, something to connect this room to the history of sailing, but there were none. No sextant or compass or barometer, no curled chart with paperweights at the corners, nothing that spoke of the sea, except for the wheel locks. The room was entirely clinical, more a laboratory than a chart room, more a command center than a radio room. A low rail that edged the table was designed to keep coffee cups in place.

Gwen Weld had designed this room. At least, as team leader she had assembled the software systems that were running behind every surface. In the mockup at WorldQuest's Boise offices she hadn't suffered this fear when she had tested the systems hour after hour. Out here, though, on the rolling, pitching boat, the room pressed in on her, and she was breathing swiftly and perspiring, as if the designers had forgotten the ventilation, which was absurd, as she could see the grates under her table at deck level. She was trapped and helpless, at the will of the boat and all the damned systems she had designed herself. That she had put together this tight room did nothing to allay her fright.

And she was disgusted with herself. Was Rex Wyman's power over her such that she would nail herself inside this floating coffin?

Gwen Weld had once owned a Cal 29, and knew how to sail. And in crafting the systems for this boat, she had become even more of a student of the sea. What she learned had unsettled her, had made open water seem an enemy. The sea offers illusion as truth, and hides peril behind a façade of benevolence and familiarity.

With the sea all around, little is as it seems. Water is transparent, yet the surface of the sea shows the sky rather than the dangers beneath, be they shoals or sharks, and whatever lurks there has the advantage of ambush. The sea grants no perspective, suggests no clues about whether the waves battering a rocky, ship-killing shore are a safe distance away, or inescapably close in the current, whether they are miles away or less than turning distance away.

The sea is loath to reveal itself. It doesn't claim its own color, but takes on whatever is at hand: blinding platinum under a setting sun, moody green close against an island, muddy blue near a river's mouth. The crease where the sea meets the sky—that distant and peaceable horizon—may be meaningless low haze, or it may be hiding a perilous reef not so distant. Someone in a small boat may think the view is to

China, but the horizon for that person is about four
miles away, a tiny radius of visibility, a distance a
modern ship on a collision course can travel in less
than ten minutes. The black cloud ahead may bring
only a dark shadow and a few drops of rain, or it may
send forth sudden and violent gusts of wind, catching
a sail and tearing out stays and snapping the mast. A
rogue wave—three times higher than the running sea,
and unexplainable by any known law of physics—may
suddenly rear up, crest high above a vessel, and drop
tons of water onto a boat's deck and cockpit, swamp-
ing the vessel. Even today, even with satellites and
digital communication and navigation software, boats
sink so abruptly that no distress message is ever
received and no trace is ever found, not even an oil
slick. For these vessels, the deadly wilderness of the
sea revealed itself, but too late.

A mile out from Cannon Beach, the sailboat *Victory*
sliced through this precarious sea, Gwen Weld in the
narrow room below deck. The bow bit cleanly, throwing little water. The wind was southerly, and the boat
was on a broad reach, its massive boom swung out
over the port rail. Shrouds and stays were perfectly
taut, and the running rigging was arrayed so that the
sails fully engaged the quartering wind. The mainsail
and jib were filled with air, billowing and majestic.
The lee rail was almost in the water, and the vast
sweep of the exposed starboard hull mirrored the
day's filtered light. *Victory*'s mast rose 193 feet above
the deck, and the mast and sails formed an aerody-
namic wedge that precisely worked the wind. The
vessel was muscular yet sleek, and it coursed powerfully through the following sea, bowing and plunging
into the swells.

Fog hid the sun, and the low sky was a dazzling

white as if the wind were generating its own light all around, as if *Victory* were traveling under a bowl of luminescence. The horizon was made close and false by the cottony haze. Nothing was visible ahead but a wash of white. *Victory* seemed to be bounding into the radiant unknown.

And there was much to know just outside *Victory*'s small disk of sea. Dead ahead—three hundred yards and closing—stood House Rock, an indomitable granite obelisk that has been indifferent to an eternity of Pacific storms, and proved far stronger than the three-masted logging schooner *Ocean Queen* that rammed House Rock in 1910, cracking the hull open like a walnut and sending the vessel and its crew of twenty-two to the bottom. House Rock was all hard edges, an implacable monolith jutting up from the ocean floor a half-mile from the shoreline, the side of the rock facing the open ocean slightly convex, as if House Rock were baring its huge chest to the sea, puffed up with challenge. The base of the gray rock was wet from ocean spray, and shiny as oilskin. The tapered cap of the granite column—forty feet above the sea—was spattered with gull guano, at a distance resembling a dignified crop of gray hair. House Rock towered above the moving sea, waiting, infinitely patient amid the restless water.

Victory came on, its sails bent to their work, the vessel lunging through the sea. Ahead, the haze took on a peculiar shade, first just a shadow in all the white, a suggestion of a color and fixity, nothing definite. Then more color—darker and ominous—and a new angularity, something other than fog and sea.

House Rock formed out of the haze, coming together quickly, congealing out of the ether to tower above *Victory*. The boat rushed forward, and the rock was now fully visible for what it was, a notched and furrowed giant slab, a bone-breaker, waves crashing against its barnacled base and sending spume skyward in great drafts. *Victory* closed on House Rock.

Forty yards from the rock—little more than a length of the boat—*Victory* swung abruptly to starboard, heeling over to bury the port rail as it turned into the wind. Gwen Weld sank with her chair. She touched nothing in her room but the coffee cup. The main and jib were taken in almost instantly, bringing them to perfect trim on the new close-hauled course.

Within seconds, *Victory*'s certain doom had been transformed into another giddy leap over ocean swells, off in another direction, House Rock helpless and receding swiftly, then blinking out as the haze closed in again around the boat, leaving nothing visible beyond the fog's soft fringe an uncertain distance away.

The boat shot forward, renewed in speed and purpose, its only sound a soft sibilation as it cleaved the water, and the eerie piping of wind in the rigging, its wake an acute angle aft that was quickly overwhelmed by the incoming sea. From the east came the roll and thunder of breakers dashing against the Oregon coast's harsh cliffs.

The haze hid more danger, and it was grave and imminent. *Victory* was rushing toward the Switchblade, a granite pinnacle that at low tide stood as an unyielding column high above the waterline, visible for miles on a clear day, but at higher tide was entirely below the water, marking its presence only by strange puckers on the water's surface. In 1972, the fishing trawler *Janine* lost power in a storm two miles off this coast. Before the Coast Guard could respond to the skipper's Mayday, current drove *Janine* into the Switchblade, which stove in the trawler's hull as if it were balsa. The skipper's body was never found, though beachcombers collected souvenirs of *Janine* for weeks.

Rising high into the wind in this neap tide, fog all around, bull kelp draping its lower parts, shiny blue mussels tucked into its crevices, the stone pillar now waited for *Victory*. The Switchblade would offer no warning and no succor and no consolation. It only waited, mute and massive, and dead on the sailboat's course.

In the freshening breeze, the boat soared across the sea's rolling surface, aimed at the Switchblade. A hundred yards, then less and less. Gwen watched the massive stone come out of the fog and fill the bow camera's monitor. Her jaw muscles were so tight she thought her head might crack open. Then, just when it should have been too late, *Victory*'s rudder and boom and sheets and sails worked suddenly and as one. The boat began coming about, its bow swinging to starboard. The jib filled on its back side, backing the bow to the new tack. *Victory* came to the eye of the wind, the boat in irons, and the boom swinging across the deck. The mainsail filled with air again, the mast as high as a cathedral. The boat lunged ahead on its new course.

The Switchblade passed on the port side, close and full of menace, but powerless, and then slipping away behind, and soon engulfed in fog and invisible once more. Black and awkward, a cormorant slapped its wing tips against the water, beating a tattoo as it flew just above the surface, racing ahead of *Victory*, then slipping away into the fog.

Wind pushed up countless whitecaps, which rose and rolled and then broke in foam, white accents on the pewter sea. The fog swirled and eddied, offering glimpses of the path ahead, and of the high and distant sun, silver instead of gold.

The boat came about again, the prow swinging across the compass points into the wind, the mainsail and jib losing air, the boom—the size of a telephone pole—racing across the deck like a scythe. The sails again grew with wind. The boat's new course, southwest on a starboard tack, would take it into the shore cliffs within moments.

A hundred generations of seafarers would have recognized *Victory* for what she was, with her sails set to the wind in a manner known to the ages, but a closer look would have left those ancient sailors baffled. Stainless steel winches for the sheets were powered from below deck and were without cranks, and several were accompanied by secondary power winches that handled messenger lines. Tension on the leading edge of the mainsail was adjusted by a Cunningham, also powered, as was a leech-line. The mainsail could be furled within the mainmast. The jib rolled around a mechanical jibstay, and its spread of sail could be reduced automatically, so the same cloth could act as a working or heavy weather or storm jib. Hundreds of tension sensors the size and color of Band-Aids dappled the sails. Turnbuckles to adjust the standing rigging—shrouds and stays—were enclosed in power casings. The old sailors would wonder at the materials all around: the carbon-fiber of the mast, the sixty-five tons of aluminum in the hull, the Kevlar cordage, the Dacron and mylar of the sails, the superstructure's fiberglass, the sixty miles of fiberoptic cable belowdecks. And those bygone mariners would be clueless regarding the antennae, radar domes, gimbaled satellite dishes, and cameras.

But nothing about *Victory* would so puzzle—and

also alarm—the sailors as the cockpit, which contained built-in benches and nothing more. No spoked wheel, nothing to control the rudder. No binnacle and its instruments. The cockpit was barren.

Then those old sailors would suspect that *Victory* was a ghost ship. No crew worked the deck. No skipper, no grinders, no helmsman, no navigator, no line handlers. Nobody working his hands to blisters and his muscles to cramps. Nobody was shivering in the spray. *Victory*'s size—155 feet with a thirty-foot beam—demanded a crew of twenty on deck, yet stem to stern there was no one.

And *Victory* would have been a ghost ship, were not Gwen Weld in its belly, sipping coffee. Steam rose from the cup and drifted along her arm. The boat was still on its starboard tack. The room was canted at about twenty degrees. The boat rolled slightly, then tipped back as the trim was adjusted. She was *Victory*'s crew, the entire crew. North of England, the British insurance club that had underwritten the hull and machinery, had insisted on a crew but hadn't dictated how many. So she was alone on board. Nor had North of England said the crew had to be sailors. Gwen Weld was a computer engineer.

Rex Wyman had named his boat after HMS *Victory*, on board which the British naval hero Admiral Nelson had won his victory at Trafalgar, and on whose quarterdeck he was fatally wounded by a sniper in the rigging of a French ship. A reporter for London's *Daily Telegraph* had asked Wyman if it might not be a tad presumptuous, naming a racing sailboat after Nelson's flagship, which was still afloat at Portsmouth, and still commissioned. Wyman's reply, "Nelson would have approved," had caused an outburst of hooting all across Great Britain.

Wyman's *Victory* bit into the swells. Its seventy-five-ton torpedo-shaped keel was manufactured of cast lead, and held a carbon-fiber daggerboard. The boat's draft was fifteen feet. As *Victory* flew southwest toward the shore, the distance between the keel and the rugged ocean floor closed quickly. When the wind tore a hole in the fog, the high brown cliffs of the coastline were suddenly visible, resembling the daunting walls of a fortress, with jagged boulders on top as battlements. Iron-fisted combers broke against the base of the cliffs. The boat was on a course for the shallows and the cliffs, and it sailed on, working the wind, fairly skipping across swells, seemingly heedless.

She had labored on this venture for two years, but now that she was on board there was little to do, so she stared at a monitor that displayed a view from a camera atop the mainmast. The camera was steadied by a gyroscope system similar to that on an M1 Abrams gunner's portal. Because the camera was twenty stories above a heaving deck, the view on the monitor swayed, but it didn't tremble.

She could press a key and change the view to one of a dozen other exterior cameras, but haze hid the lower views. The scene from atop the mainmast was clearer, as the fog lay close to the water. She could see the ragged cliffs, which seemed to float above clouds, and the rising green hills beyond the headland. The shore was drawing nearer.

Or she could change to many interior views of *Victory*, including watching her own back and head from a camera mounted on the wall behind her. Rex was weird with all his cameras. He had them in his houses, too.

On the screens all around her was displayed information a skipper and navigator and engineer would require regarding *Victory*'s journey, data regarding weather, course and position, and the status of the mechanical, electrical, communication, and hydraulic systems. Not that she would require any of this information.

She sipped her coffee. She had never suffered motion sickness, was immune to it, it seemed. Maybe that was why she was here, in this room full of artificial light, with the Voice just waiting to make some grand announcement. She wasn't immune from fear, though, and that was the hell of it, down here in this box.

From the speakers: "How's it going, Gwen?"

This wasn't the Voice. This was *Victory*'s owner, Rex Wyman. She didn't like his voice coming from all directions—as if he were inside her head—so she entered several keystrokes so that his words would come from the speaker on the table a few feet away.

She twisted in her chair to face the speaker. "You know as well as I do that everything is fine, Rex. You have it all in front of you, just like I do. Everything is shipshape. Do software engineers use that word?"

"You're still upset about the article in *People*, sounds like," Wyman said. He might be in Boise or New York City or Jakarta. She had no way of knowing unless he told her.

"The article doesn't bother me at all."

She would rather talk about the idiot magazine article than about her fears, down here in a claustrophobic cube with seawater all around, her fate in the hands of bits of silicon. As far as she could tell, Rex Wyman feared nothing, not spiders, not nuclear winter, and not anything in between. She could never be his equal in anything related to money, but she was going to try on every other level, and to admit to him she was frightened would diminish herself.

"Not at all?" he asked.

"Just because it suggests that my position as vice-president for systems integration at WorldQuest is due to my relationship with you, why would that bother me?" She hoped her tones were sufficiently dry.

"Nice picture of you, though," Wyman said, maybe from Rio. He never stayed anywhere longer than three days, as if he were a fugitive.

"The article makes it seem you had given me the necklace, with its five two-carat diamonds."

"Did I give it to you? I'm a little fuzzy on it."

He was sticking her, and she knew it, but she occasionally restated the rules she had imposed on their relationship, lest the slightest crack appear, untended for the briefest moment, followed by a deluge. "You aren't to give me jewelry, Rex. I've made that clear. And so you don't."

"Then who did?"

He was still teasing her. She usually tossed it back, and they would end up laughing. She was too fearful—in this boat, headed at breakneck speed for the rocky shore—to joust with him. "They were faux diamonds, Rex. I bought the necklace out of a bin."

She could hear his keyboard. She could not remember a telephone conversation with him where those keys weren't a backdrop. She knew that when the clicking slowed—it never stopped—he was listening to her, as much as he listened to anyone these days.

She added, "We were going to keep it quiet, Rex. That was part of our deal."

"I didn't know a photographer would be at the party, honest. Madeline let him in. She wanted to make the newspapers, I suppose. At least you didn't duck and hide your face behind your hands like a gangster." He laughed. "I did that a couple of times when the paparazzi first started following me. Learned my lesson quickly, I'll tell you." He was typing away.

"I was surprised . . ."

"Give me a second, Gwen." Wyman apparently covered the microphone to give someone an instruction, probably Roger Hall, who spent his life at Wyman's elbow, cell phone and electronic memo pad at the ready.

Gwen Weld's hair was as dark as a crow's wing, and she wrapped a loose strand of it around a finger, waiting for Rex. She usually wore it to her shoulder, tucked in, but today it was in a ponytail, which gave her a girlish look she tried to avoid, particularly at the office. Most of it was in a ponytail, anyway. A few strands always seemed to work loose

Her features were slightly magnified, filling the oval of her face. Her eyes were startlingly blue. Gas blue, her mother had once called them. Her mother had green eyes, and claimed she had no idea where Gwen's blue eyes came from. From my father, Gwen had wanted to shout, but when Gwen was a child, her mother had made clear that to even mention him would hurt her deeply, so whether her father had blue eyes had been a mystery.

Gwen's mouth was full and peaked, with a keyboard of strong white teeth. She knew she had a playful smile, a puckish and knowing smile that often carried more invitation than she intended, and when she was younger she would occasionally find herself in a fix because of it. Some guy, thinking her smile revealed his future, would come on to her, and she would have to turn him away, most often in a kindly manner, nothing he would remember as a neutering. She sometimes wished she had turned Rex Wyman away.

Her chin carried a delicate notch. Her nose was a touch large, with a modest bump on the ridge. As she had gained some of age's perspective, she had begun to think of her nose as masterful, as an indication of character, rather than a mere outsized protuberance. On her ears were small diamonds that picked up the color of her eyes. She was wearing deck shoes, blue jeans, and a white knit sweater under a Goretex jacket decorated with a WorldQuest emblem on the breast.

A small emerald in an ornate, antique gold setting was on her ring finger. Her mother had worn it as far back as Gwen's memory served, and then her mom had given it to Gwen on her fifteenth birthday. While not grand and heavy, this ring was the dearest thing her mother had ever owned, vastly more valuable than any of the other trinkets and odd pieces of junk in her mother's battered jewelry box. Her mother would not reveal how she had come to possess the emerald ring. Gwen had concluded her father had given it to her. Gwen had slipped the ring onto her finger the day of her fifteenth birthday, and had never taken it off, not once, not for any reason.

"I'm back." Rex Wyman's voice came from the speaker. "You are half a minute from *Victory*'s coming tack."

"Rex, I thought you were going to be on board today," she said, staring at the speaker as if she might somehow see Wyman's expression.

"I'm in the middle of these negotiations to purchase Dakota View." Tap tap tap tap.

"You've got twenty lawyers who do those things for you, Rex." She tried not to sound complaining. "You tell them your price, and they go get it, and then send you the paperwork for your signature. I've seen you do it before."

"Well, let me be frank," he said. The phrase was one of Wyman's favorites. Whether or not he realized it, it discounted everything he had theretofore said. "I cannot be seen to be putting too much time or effort into *Victory*. Gwen, you know how important the boat's success is to me—what is riding on *Victory*—but I can't let my competitors know."

"They know you've spent fifty million dollars on this boat. They know a boat this size—a normal sailboat this size—would have cost a small fraction of that. The whole world knows."

"The whole world also knows that fifty million dollars is pocket change to me," Wyman replied. "But I only have as much time as anybody else, twenty-four hours a day. If I take a couple days off to go on a sea trial, my competitors—my enemies—are going to seize on it. They'll start to dig around. I don't want that."

Wyman had ordered up *Victory* from Royal Huisman Shipyards like anyone else would buy a set of tires from Mr. Goodwrench. At least, that's what Wyman wanted the world to think. Gwen Weld knew better. She knew the stakes represented by *Victory*. She knew of Rex Wyman's gamble.

The Voice came from everywhere. "Ready about."

At least the Voice had a sense of humor. When the boat was about to change the wind's direction over the bow when sailing to windward, "ready about" alerted the crew that the boom would soon slash across the deck. There was no crew to alert.

"This has been a huge success, Gwen," Rex Wyman said. "My crews on *Pelican* and in Boise agree."

Pelican was the sailboat's mothership, stationed six miles off this same coast, a converted oil rig service vessel, 150 feet in length, with a helicopter pad on the stern. On *Pelican* was a room identical to *Victory*'s command center, with precisely the same dimensions, and the same monitors displaying the same information regarding *Victory*. Another room—same monitors, same displays—was at WorldQuest headquarters in Boise. While Gwen Weld was alone in the chart room— alone on *Victory*—dozens of engineers and sailboat designers and professional skippers were monitoring *Victory*'s progress. The sailboat had been built at the shipyard in Vollenhome, The Netherlands. Sail trials had been performed earlier in the month with a live crew on board. This was the first test of the combined systems.

Gwen asked, "Rex, are you watching my back?"

"You should always watch your back," he replied absently. "It's one of my guiding principles."

"I mean, right now, through the camera behind me here in the chart room."

He paused to click his keyboard. He hadn't been, but now he was. He said, "Nice ponytail today."

She didn't turn to face the camera. She didn't bother to turn it off. Nothing she could do on board couldn't be overridden from his laptop.

Rex Wyman had a talent for generating favorable publicity, an instinct for currying the press and for shaping reportage about him and his projects. Nothing required *Victory* to be without a crew on this day of the systems trial. Nothing required the deck to be empty, except for Wyman's notion of what made for the better story. The press—and there were twenty-five print and electronic journalists aboard *Pelican*, selected by a lottery that left three dozen others ashore scrambling to find other rides—would send this sensational news around the world: the most expensive sailing yacht in history had sailed a hazardous, even foolhardy course among the hull-rending rocks off the Oregon coast in strong wind and blinding fog, with no one on board except the senior vice-president for research, who was lovely and who had recently been seen on Rex Wyman's arm at a Rancho Mirage party.

This was a stunt. Sure, WorldQuest teams were gathering a wide array of information every second of *Victory*'s journey, and these sea trials were critical for the boat's eventual success, but the setup—rocky coast, empty deck, attractive woman alone in the command center—was the pure theater at which Rex Wyman excelled.

"Where are you, Rex?" she finally had to ask.

"Sitting on a runway at Charles DeGaulle. We're fourth or fifth from takeoff."

Again Wyman apparently put his hand over the phone to say something to Roger Hall. Gwen had once heard Hall refer to himself as Rex Wyman's dog: always under foot and easy to kick.

"You mentioned we might meet at your place Friday," she said.

"Which place did I say?" he asked.

Wyman loved to do that, offer a reminder that he was now a citizen of the world, with five homes on three continents. The reminder wasn't needed. His face had become as recognizable as the queen's.

"In Sun Valley," she said. "Toby is going to be there visiting his parents. Maybe we could all get together." She could hear the engines of Wyman's Gulfstream winding up.

"Toby hung up on me last time we talked," Wyman said.

Toby Odell and Wyman had founded WorldQuest.

"He's been doing that for twenty years, you told me so yourself," she said. "It's just part of Toby. He hangs up on people."

"Yeah, well maybe," Wyman said from France. "Here you go, looks like. Only three feet between the boat and the bottom of the ocean. Any other boat is seconds from grounding."

She could see it herself. On one of the monitors a three-dimensional graphic of the ocean floor under the boat was represented in neon colors with the boat superimposed over the ocean bottom. The graphic slid across the screen as *Victory* moved toward certain grounding.

"Helms alee," intoned the Voice. Had there been a tiller on *Victory*, it would now have been pushed toward the boom.

Software and mechanical and hydraulic systems did their work. Gwen's chair sank under her as *Victory* came about to its new heading, west by southwest to the open sea, escaping the treacherous shore.

"We did it." She could hear elation in his voice. "Will you look at that, Gwen? We did it."

She didn't know what he was looking at, didn't know which of the cameras or instrument panels were displayed on his laptop over there in France. She heard Roger Hall add a dutiful, "Awright."

The Gulfstream's engines grew louder over her speaker.

Wyman spoke up over the background noise, exulting, "*Victory* is everything I said it would be, Gwen. Are you believing me now?"

"I've always believed you," she said simply.

"*Pelican* will pick you up in an hour and take *Victory* in tow."

"About this weekend," she reminded him. She heard him tapping again, maybe checking his calendar.

"Liftoff," he said. "Hey, I can see the Eiffel Tower."

"This weekend, Rex."

"Meet me in Ketchum," he finally replied. "Friday evening." Wealthy fly-ins called the place Ketchum rather than Sun Valley, and received fine pleasure from doing so. "Roger will make sure a car picks you up."

"I'll be there."

"Got to go," Rex Wyman said. "Love you." He cut the connection.

With sails grand in the wind and her prow splitting the sea, *Victory* sped toward a rendezvous with the tender.

Her voice full of melancholy, Gwen answered to nobody, "Love you, too."

CHAPTER 3

Santiago Ramirez came into the apartment and tossed his athletic bag on the sofa. McKay was behind his computer on the table near the kitchen.

"How's your workout?" McKay asked without looking up from the screen.

"Weak and unfocused, my coach said."

Ramirez was a competitive weight lifter, and held the Alaska record for the clean-and-jerk. When he wasn't on duty, he was almost always at the gym. He brought down a bag of potato chips from the cupboard, then sat at the table opposite McKay, the chair squeaking loudly with the weight. Ramirez was huge—six-four and at least 230, and he could move his mass with surprising speed. His seal-brown hair was cut close to his scalp. His hands were big and blunt, and with low brows, bristly haircut, knobby chin, and small ears tight against his head, Ramirez had a brawler's presence.

"Where's Christy?" he asked. "I thought she was going to be here."

"She's working on a brief. Had to stay late."

Ramirez chewed for a moment, then abruptly inquired, "You asked Christy to marry you yet?"

McKay smiled. "That would be entirely none of your business."

"Your scrape healing?"

"It's fine." McKay was sitting at his computer, and didn't look up. On his right wrist was a wide bandage. "It's a small thing."

"The injury might be small, but your mistake wasn't."

McKay and Ramirez's apartment had the appearance of dorm rooms, with most of the furniture included in the rent, and every piece of it sprung or faded or nicked or smelly. A brick-and-board bookshelf was against one wall. The rug was cream-colored, but in one corner had yellowed, and judging from the lingering smell, the prior renter's catbox had been there, the cat apparently missing the box with some regularity. The television set belonged to Ramirez, but hadn't been hooked to the cable because neither he nor McKay had the time or inclination to watch television.

The apartment's living room and kitchen were separated by a pass-through. Cigarette burns from some prior renter marred the dining table. The curtains still stank of smoke. The first thing McKay and Ramirez had done after they moved into the apartment was to toss out the montage of *Mad Magazine* covers—eleven or twelve drawings of Alfred E. Newman pasted onto poster board and framed by pieces of lathe, maybe stolen from a fence—that had been on the wall behind the living-room sofa. Ramirez had hung an old lifter's belt on a nail, and there it remained for lack of anything better.

"I want to talk to you about it," Ramirez said. "About your procedure."

To change the subject, McKay said, "You're not

sweating like you usually still are when you get back here."

"I'm a master of the quick recovery," Ramirez said around a mouthful of chips. "That's what got me through the I-course."

The ten-week pararescue jumper indoctrination course at Lackland Air Force Base in Texas has a 90 percent flunk-out rate. Those few who survive the I-course then ride the pipeline, the informal name for the year and a half of intensive training that follows. Much of that time is spent falling out of airplanes, bobbing up and down in swimming pools with hands tied behind the back and feet bound together, and wandering across scrubland looking for bugs to eat. Anyone who can take eighteen months of this is awarded a maroon beret. It may be the most coveted item of clothing in the American military services.

Ramirez dug into the bag of chips again. "You should view that big scratch as a tax, Jess."

When McKay wouldn't pick up the cue, Ramirez added, "A tax on stupidity."

"Come on, Sandy. Lay off."

"I'll reconstruct what happened, as you've told it to me." Ramirez dropped the chip bag onto his lap and placed his palms on his knees in a gesture of vast patience. "And I want you to see what's wrong with the picture."

McKay tapped the keyboard.

"You were out on the ice at Portage Glacier," Ramirez said, "and you were doing things correctly like the professional you are. You had your ice axe wrapped in hockey tape so there's no cold penetration. You were carrying snow pickets and deadman anchors and a rack of ice screws."

McKay wasn't going to tell Santiago Ramirez to put

a sock in it, because McKay liked no one in the world better than Ramirez.

So Ramirez went on, "So what I'm saying is that you were good to go on your equipment and supplies."

"I'm searching eBay for used snowshoes," McKay said.

"Jess, listen to me. I'm trying to save your life here, and you're not letting me."

McKay offered a placatory smile. "Yeah, well, I like being alone sometimes."

Ramirez rubbed his scalp as if to warm a memory. "Drown proofing during the I-course, you remember? You and me in the pool, two masks but only one snorkel, and we've been ordered to keep our faces below the surface. We've got to use the snorkel, passing it back and forth between us, and stay underwater."

"Sandy, I know where you're going with this."

"So it was no problem, there in the water, you and me swapping the snorkel. But then the instructor jumped into the pool, and started roughing us up."

McKay shook his head. "He was a tough customer."

"He tried to snatch our snorkel away and rip our masks off our faces, and cut off our air supply, and he wrestled us under water, pulling us down, flailing away at us. And all the while, we had to breathe only through the snorkel, never surfacing for air."

"That was hard duty in that pool."

Ramirez rose from his chair again and crossed to the refrigerator. McKay and Ramirez were pararescue jumpers with the Alaska Air National Guard's 212th Rescue Squadron, based at Anchorage's Kulis Air National Guard Base. Because the 212th's war mission is to locate and recover downed pilots, the PJs train in combat tactics, including advanced weapons handling. The 212th's peacetime mission is performing search

and rescue during the almost continual Air Force training and joint air exercises that occur in Alaska. The
squadron's territory covers almost six hundred thousand square miles. The PJs also rescue civilians—
hunters, hikers, campers, climbers—who usually have
overestimated their abilities and underestimated the
Alaskan wilderness. The squadron holds the high-alti-
tude helicopter save record, set with a Pave Hawk at
14,400 feet on Mount McKinley. The 212th RQS is on
twenty-four hour, year-round alert. It averages two
hundred missions and saves about sixty lives every
year.

"And you know how we survived the instructor and
all his dirty tricks in that pool, him trying to drown
both of us?" Ramirez returned to his chair and opened
the can. He took a long drink, then wiped his mouth
with the back of his hand. "You know how you and I
got through drown proofing when so many don't?
Teamwork, that's how."

"Yeah, I know."

"At any given moment, each of us working alone
doesn't have all the skills or all the determination or
all the courage or all the luck. But at any given
moment all those things are found in a team. We compensate for one another. It's a concept drilled into us
from day one, Jess."

"Is this hectoring? I might take offense if I were
being hectored."

"So you went ice climbing by yourself," Ramirez
went on, "and the ice suddenly broke away from under
your crampons and you were too slow with your axe to
catch yourself, and you fell—what, fifteen or twenty
feet?—into a crevasse, and your foot gets jammed into a
crack, and even though you were wearing a helmet you
banged your head so hard you blacked out."

"When I got home I had to buy a new helmet," McKay said. "Says right on the warning label that the helmet is good for only one serious knock."

"And you were in that crevasse for how long, you figure? Five hours, maybe? Until you came to, and discovered you had squashed your cell phone, and until you could work your foot loose, which was hard because your axe had slid away somewhere deeper into the crevasse, and until you could climb out. Then you had to make it across the ice field, and walk back to your car."

"The scratch was the worst of it, and it's not bad," McKay said. "Can hardly feel it."

Ramirez said, "Going out on the ice-fall by yourself was a bonehead move. And so was your little sailing adventure last summer."

"Here we go again."

"Jess, you were alone on a tiny sailboat, three or four miles offshore on the Cook Inlet, four-foot seas and twenty-five-mile-an-hour winds. And your boat blows over and you're tossed into the drink, and you can't catch up to the boat, so you swim to shore."

"I was wearing a wetsuit and life jacket. Our training swims are harder. After I got home, I went for a six-mile run."

"It's the principle of the damn thing."

"Next day a fisherman found my Laser, drifting, still mast down, and he towed it in."

"You out there alone, Jess—on the ice or on the water—is not how PJs are taught to do things."

Ramirez scratched his neck below his jawbone. "I'm worried about you, is what I'm saying."

"Sandy, you're about to veer into psychology, and you already flunked psychology."

"Your health is my concern," Ramirez insisted.

"I don't want to hear some goofy theory you picked up in Psychology 101. Some theory about a repressed suicide wish is what you're getting around to."

"You go off by yourself and do dangerous things like ice climbing on a glacier. What else should I call it?"

McKay shrugged.

"I also call it unprofessional. It's not how PJs do things."

"Let me ask you something, Santiago. When you and I are hooked together by a safety line, do you ever worry about my skill or reliability?"

"No, of course not."

"Then you've got nothing to worry about."

Ramirez put on an expression of ill-usage. "You're telling me to butt out."

McKay looked up. "I'm telling you I'm okay, and—"

A knock at the door interrupted him.

McKay rose quickly from the chair. "Maybe it's Christy, after all."

He crossed the room and opened the door. A young woman stood there, holding a cake in her hands. She wasn't Christy.

"Captain McKay?" she asked.

Jess nodded.

"This is for you." She smiled widely and held out the cake. It was a round, two-layer cake with white frosting. On top was a drawing of a fighter jet. "I baked the cake. I'm not too good at drawing planes, though."

"You're Peter Bradley's wife?"

"I thought I was his widow for a while. I'm not, thanks to you. My name is Karen."

She was a slender woman, which was evident even though she was wearing a parka. Her hair was tucked under a wool cap. She had a narrow nose and eyes that shone with gratitude.

When McKay stepped aside to let her into the apartment, she said, "I can't stay. I'm due at the hospital."

Ramirez appeared at McKay's elbow. "I heard the word *cake*."

When McKay introduced them, she laughed and said, "Peter told me about the big guy up there. You were on the mountain with Jess?"

"Right beside him." Ramirez accepted the cake. "How's Peter?"

"The orthopedic surgeons are going to operate in about an hour. He'll return to duty in less than a month, the doctors say, and will be able to fly again in four months. Peter's been laughing a lot, sort of giddy, squeezing my hand and saying he cheated death."

Ramirez smiled. "I might eat this whole cake myself."

She said, "Peter says he saw me up on the mountain, when he was lying there with his broken leg. He says I was there, standing in the snow, and that I helped him make it through."

McKay said softly, "Maybe you were there."

Karen Bradley kissed McKay on the cheek, then Ramirez, and then she said, "I knew . . . I knew I wouldn't know what to say to you, how to thank you, and the cake is a little thing . . ."

"It's perfect," McKay said. "We'll visit Peter after his surgery."

She dabbed at a tear on her cheek, nodded at the two men, but could say nothing more, so turned back down the hall, hurrying away.

Dipping his finger into the cake's frosting, then licking his finger, Ramirez stepped back into the apartment and said, "Some days I like our job more than other days."

McKay replied, "Yeah, and this is one of those days."

• • •

"He thinks he's the Sun King." Gwen Weld shaded her eyes with a hand. High haze marred the sun, spreading the light without lessening its intensity and making the sky a caustic white. "We always wait for him. He never waits for us."

"I detect a whiff of insubordination," Tom Sutton replied. "I'm going to enter it into my database. In two minutes, you'll be in handcuffs."

She laughed. "I'll delete it as fast as you enter it."

Sutton was *Victory*'s manager of security. His field office was a hut just larger than a desk, brought to the end of the yacht club's T-dock for this occasion. Tom Sutton's superior, Ted Landers, who headed all of World-Quest's security operations, was on the dock somewhere. Sutton was as charming as his boss Landers was eerie. *Victory* was at its berth thirty yards down the dock.

Sutton stepped from his hut and moved alongside the hull. "Please, Mr. Davis, that felt rope across the gangway is there for a purpose."

Intent on surveying the equipment on *Victory*'s deck, Duncan Davis had unclipped the rope. His wife, Ginny, was on the gangway behind him.

Davis said, "I'm one of the competitors."

"I well know who you are, sir."

"Don't we get a tour?" Ginny Davis asked.

Sutton smiled. "Not a chance. Sorry."

Duncan Davis and his wife were not accustomed to being turned aside, but they took it with only one scowl between them, from her. He reclipped the felt rope, then they moved farther along the dock, looking at other boats.

The Harbor Yacht Club was on San Francisco Bay. The two-story Mediterranean stucco clubhouse had a red tile roof, vast windows that looked out onto the

bay, and a second-story deck that was lined with spectators, many with drinks in their hands. Wisteria covered the east side of the building, some of its tendrils
lacing around the deck's wrought-iron banisters. The
club's ensign—a blue star on a white field—flew
below the United States flag on a pole resembling a
mast, with upper and lower spreaders, at a corner of
the building. The caterer's white tents were on the
lawn between the clubhouse and the docks, and wait-
ers carrying trays passed among the guests. Across
the bay to the north was Alcatraz Island, its history
readily apparent from the cut of its buildings. To the
south and growing were the hills of San Francisco, the
buff-colored buildings reminiscent of an earlier time

A Mitsubishi Diamond Vision screen—with a viewing area of fifteen diagonal feet—had been set up on
the yacht club's patio behind a podium. On the screen
in vivid greens and blues was the WorldQuest corporate logo. Folding chairs ranged out in front of the
screen. Two bars on the patio were well attended, the
bartenders working quickly. Inside the doors to the
clubhouse was a buffet, and a steady stream of guests
walked out onto the patio with plates and utensils in
their hands.

Guests also crowded the yacht club's docks. They
leaned forward to peer at *Victory*, their hands behind
their backs as if at an art gallery, knowing they shouldn't
touch the object of their admiration. Guards were
stationed on the pier, fore, mid, and aft of the boat, acting more like tour guides. Sipping their martinis and
scotch, guests nodded knowingly at design features. A
few stared at the puzzling items topside, the curious rigging, peculiar antennae, and some equipment hidden in
a mount forward of the wheel. A few appurtenances
were hidden under canvas.

The crowd on the patio gathered around the podium. Guests emerged from the clubhouse to join them. Gwen couldn't see what was going on, it looked like a procession from the building to the podium. Then she heard Rex Wyman's amplified voice.

"Thank you, Mayor, for your gracious welcome. It is always a delight to visit the Harbor Yacht Club, which has made my team and me feel so welcome." Rex Wyman's words drifted over the docks. "The gentleman's sport of sailboat racing is going to be changed forever."

" 'Lo, Gwen," a voice came from Gwen's right.

She turned to see a shy grin under a baseball cap. Toby Odell was wearing slacks, for once, but he looked uncomfortable in them, with his fists jammed low in the pockets. He was lost in an enormous mustard-colored sweater that perhaps Odell thought had a nautical touch. He nodded at her, encouraging her to remember his name, as if there were a chance she or anyone would forget, but this hopeful nodding and hesitant grin were an old habit, back from a time when he was invisible.

She loosed a wide smile at him, knowing he treated such a thing as a gift. She said, "I didn't think the twentieth-richest man in the country could sneak up on people, Toby, but here you are."

He laughed, a peculiar chirrup that ended with a small cough, as if a laugh might earn a reproach. "I'm down to twenty-first. Another Walton was found."

Toby Odell wore rimless eyeglasses that flashed on and off in the light. He had once told Gwen that he had celebrated WorldQuest's massively successful IPO by purchasing a Rolex wristwatch, and had worn it two days. The first day he thought the watch elegant, and the second day he thought it silly. So he replaced it with a Timex Ironman, and now he never wore jewelry or anything else the slightest bit pricey, not a single indication of his vast wealth, no Italian shoes, no tailored shirts. He had tried a goatee, covering his undershot chin, but it was always scrubby, so off it had come.

Rex Wyman's words drifted over the docks. "The gentleman's sport of sailboat racing is going to be changed forever."

Gwen said, "My Lord, Toby, have you shaved your head, up under that baseball cap?"

She let him pluck the cap from his head.

He said, "It's the new thing at my office with all the coders. Bald head with a tattoo on top. I shaved my head, but haven't found the courage for the tattoo yet. I've been to a tanning parlor to get this nice bronze look." He playfully rubbed the top of his head.

"You look like a kook, Toby."

"That's the point, my hacker employees tell me." Odell lifted a diet Coke from a passing waiter's tray.

Of course, Toby Odell had made a few nods to wealth. He had a home on Hawaii's Kona coast and another in Sun Valley, now that he had taken up snowboarding. His mailing address was on Bainbridge Island, a ferry commute from Seattle. He had begun a remodeling of the home four years ago, and kept adding a room here and there, then an indoor basketball court and a screening room and a fourteen-car garage, emailing his architect when a new idea seized him. Now the structure resembled the Winchester house, with stairways to nowhere and windows looking out on walls. Twenty-six rooms, but not one where he wanted to take off his coat and stay awhile. He seldom went there.

"No longer will the Sydney-Hobart and the Fastnet Race be the premier weather challenges for the blue-water sail racer," Wyman intoned. "In their place, I present to you the Pacific Winter Challenge."

With a flourish, Wyman raised his hand in the direction of the Mitsubishi screen, where the WorldQuest logo disappeared, and was replaced with a map of the Pacific Ocean, from California west to the coast of Japan and north to the Bering Sea.

Wyman continued, "Those sailors who accept the challenge will depart San Francisco Bay—the bridge will serve as the starting line—and sail across the Pacific to Tokyo."

"Some renowned racers have accepted Rex's challenge," Odell said. "See that woman over there?" He nodded toward the harbor master's office. "She is surrounded by reporters, the tall woman with black hair in an unkempt ponytail, so it looks like she's always too busy handling the wheel and rigging to do her hair. I've met her a couple of times. Her hair is like that even when she is dressed formally. It's her trademark, I suppose."

"Who is she?" Gwen asked.

"Her name is Genevieve DeLong. She gets more press in France than the country's president. She's a national heroine for winning the Around Alone, back when it was called the BOC Challenge. When she sails with a crew, they're all world-class. And her boats— her financing has always been a mystery and I think it's probably the French government—are always state of the art. She's tough."

"Who else should I know about here?"

"That fellow who Tom Sutton just chased away from Rex's boat? His name is Duncan Davis. On his boat, *Lion Rampant*, an R/P seventy-five-foot turbo, he set the Los Angeles to Honolulu Transpac monohull record at a little over seven days."

Gwen looked around, hoping she might point out other racers Odell might identify.

"Rex and I are alike, you know," Odell said, leaning toward her conspiratorially.

She turned to him. "I thought you were the code guy, and Rex was the marketing guy. That's what it'll say in history books a hundred years from now. Code guy and marketing guy."

"What I mean is, Rex and I have already spent our life forces on our one grand push, our one good idea, that small concept that stormed the world, and now we have little left. Same with many other computer and Internet pioneers."

"You've got a lot left, and so does Rex. Billions."

"That's not what I mean, and you know it." Odell's mouth was undersized and moist. His fingers, around the glass, were slender and long and elegant, pianist's fingers. "He and I blew out our cores. We sacrificed it for our product."

"This isn't like you, Toby," she said warmly. "Usually you talk about some small startup you are going to purchase, all wild with enthusiasm. I'd begun to think you were leaking me inside information so I could go buy some of the stock and make my fortune."

Since Toby Odell had left WorldQuest—taking 40 percent of the stock with him—he had purchased controlling interest in fifteen small companies based in Silicon Valley or North Carolina's Research Triangle or the Seattle area. These firms had solid visions of the computer future, Odell thought, and he had made their founders wealthy. He was buying potential, and potential's handmaiden was risk. Some business writers said Odell was doing nothing more than gambling with his money, but Odell lived his life being underestimated, and while a few of the companies had come to nothing, others had soared.

His successes vastly eclipsed his failures. He now

owned, for example, half of Autobahn, the most-used German Internet portal. Odell had invested six million dollars in the Berlin-based company two years ago. His Autobahn stock was now worth twelve times his initial investment. And there were others. He was no longer a code guy. He was an investor and a philanthropist, and he still wore baseball hats.

"The Challenge will be sailed along the shortest distance between the two cities," Wyman declared over the speaker, "the fifty-two-hundred-mile rhumb line between San Francisco and Tokyo via Alaska's Aleutian Islands, the same course an airplane takes."

The Mitsubishi screen displayed the route, a red arch, with one end touching the point that represented San Francisco and the other touching Tokyo, the arch sweeping up high on the map then soaring south again as it crossed the vast expanse of blue. With the Pacific Ocean flattened on the screen, the route appeared to trend too far north, only to have to return south toward Japan, a vast half-circle.

A flat map is an illusion, and does not account for the curvature of the earth. Sailing due west from San Francisco to Tokyo—the two cities are within two degrees of being on the same latitude—would add two hundred miles to the journey, as compared with sailing north in a great arc on the rhumb line, leaving San Francisco and traveling northwest on a compass heading of 303.3 degrees.

Wyman's voice fluttered in the wind. "But there will be one detour: the boats will veer off the rhumb line to sail north through the Aleutians to round the Pribilof Islands, well into the Bering Sea, the expanse of wild water between Alaska and Siberia."

The point of view on the screen suddenly dove from the sky, racing down through the stratosphere toward the ocean blue, then pulling up to head north, the cloud-laden sky now above the sea, the earth's horizon a distant blue rim. Then the point of view raced above the sea at a dizzying pace A series of green ridges popped up onto the horizon, and then drew close. The animation slowed, then stopped, showing several islands in the distance, clouds and sky above.

"The Aleutian Islands," Rex Wyman announced. "The Ring of Fire. The peak is Makushin Volcano. Our course will take us under its lee."

A foghorn's low bleat came from the bay, and Gwen turned to see mist pouring in through the Golden Gate. The bridge deck was already obscured, but the towers rose above the fog, and seemed to hang there, detached and floating.

Wyman announced, "And those sailors who have made it this far, who pass between the Aleutian Islands into the Bering Sea, will head for the Pribilof Islands."

Rex Wyman had met Tobin Odell at the Ratskeller tavern in Moscow, Idaho, when they were both sophomores at the University of Idaho. Wyman's father was a wheat farmer in southern Idaho, and Wyman was studying agronomics. Toby Odell was majoring in mathematics and was raised in Sun Valley. The Ratskeller only had one pinball machine, and Wyman was waiting for Odell, a stranger to him, to finish with the Super Tic-Tac-Toe. Pinball addicts form sort of an international freemasonry and can usually recognize each other on sight. Sensing a brother in pinball, Odell said out of the corner of his mouth, still concentrating on the ball, that he was the only guy in history from Sun Valley who preferred pinball to skiing. They began taking turns at the Super Tic-Tac-Toe, talking all the while.

Everyone at the Ratskeller was drinking Coors and

plenty of it, and they were no exceptions, but even so they each discovered a fascinating fact about the other: Wyman was dissatisfied with his Kaypro's operating system and was trying to rewrite the code, and Odell had purchased a bag of parts from a Radio Shack and was building his own computer. Their friendship began that night.

They were soon spending their time driving Wyman's old Honda Accord to the Radio Shack, studying the inch-thick Sparkman Electronics catalogue, and welding and soldering and splicing. Odell moved into Wyman's dorm room. With sockets and wiring and transistors and microchips everywhere—on every shelf, strung over the beds' headboards, filling the closets—the room became the computer, and they lived inside it.

In their junior year, the university opened a school of computer science, but Wyman and Odell quickly determined they already knew more than was being taught at any of the classes. And they came to understand that building computers was like building model airplanes; they were never more than the sum of their store-bought and mail-ordered parts, and once you had built one, you understood they were clunky and limited, and that some guy in Japan was probably building a better one at that very moment. So Wyman and Odell turned to programming.

Neither of the young men knew they were susceptible to charm and lyricism and adventure, but they were, and in code writing they found them all. Time came to have an odd elasticity for them. When they were leaning together, staring at the screen, six hours might pass, and when they came up for breath, they might've missed dinner or another class.

They stopped sitting side-by-side and sharing one

computer as soon as they moved out of the University
of Idaho dormitory, but for a while in the early years, in
WorldQuest Corporation's strip-mall office, where
they had displaced a Korean restaurant, and which
they shared with a ninety-nine-cent store and a chiro-
practor, they worked together with the same single-
mindedness. Wyman and Odell often completed each
other's sentences. They napped at their desks. They
ordered the same take-out Chinese, sometimes three
times a day, the discarded cartons a pyramid that hid
the trash can. The first product was modest: a time-
entry system for accountants and lawyers. WorldQuest
began issuing licenses. Soon there were twenty-five
employees, and then fifty.

They were adapting the computer language TAL-
ENT, which was used on industry and government
mainframe computers, for use on desktop computers,
which were just becoming available, but which were
filled with a variety of codes. They were in a race, they
knew, because two fellows, Bill Gates and Paul Allen,
had just licensed such a program to IBM.

Wyman and Odell named their product *Quest*, a
package of code that totaled a quarter-million lines,
then a staggering figure. It was an operating system, a
software design that controlled the hardware of a
data-processing system and made it easier for non-
programmers to use the system. Wyman and Odell
licensed their product to a new Japanese corporation,
a startup funded by Mitsubishi, Sony, four other
Japanese corporate giants, and the government of
Japan, which had decided it dare not lose the bur-
geoning personal computer race to the Americans
even if it meant having to license a program from
these two American youths.

Leaving the software to the two Americans was a limited vision. Wyman and Odell's company, WorldQuest, soon began developing application software such as spreadsheets and word-processing programs. The Japanese company, named Nova, was locked into the Quest operating system and began offering WorldQuest applications as part of its software packages. The Japanese computer, the Nova, was a success, capturing 20 percent of world personal computer sales by 1990.

Wyman and Odell took WorldQuest public in 1990. They celebrated becoming billionaires by purchasing the Super Tic-Tac-Toe pinball machine from the Ratskeller and moving it to their office.

Wyman found he had a gift for selling the product. His youth and energy dazzled. His wide smile, his ability to listen intently, and his skill at imparting his "partnership for success" vision to companies considering World-Quest products left deep impressions. To corporate chiefs around the world, Rex Wyman—with his talk of the incipient digital communications revolution—represented the future. Their companies could embrace the future, or turn away from it. Wyman learned to knot a tie.

While Wyman blossomed, Toby Odell proved to be photophobic, vigorously turning away from the light, preferring the shadow. Wyman began taking lunch with this or that CEO, but Odell still hovered over his keyboard for twenty-hour stretches. Wyman flew to Geneva and Sydney for conferences, but Odell still ordered take-out Chinese.

In 1993, Rex Wyman purchased a block of Odell's stock, giving Wyman controlling interest in World-Quest. He became president of the board of directors and chief executive officer, positions that theretofore had been shared by both WorldQuest founders. On the day Wyman assumed all the titles, Odell left the company. Odell still owned a sizable portion of the company, and he benefited when the WorldQuest stock price rose. Other than that, he no longer had anything to do with the corporation. For years, the nature of Wyman and Odell's split had been the source of much speculation in the media.

Wyman spoke in measured cadences that would have made his speech coach proud. "My challenge to the world's sail racers is not so much the length of the race. It is indeed long. Nor does the challenge lie in the route into the Bering Sea, although the route is indeed difficult."

"I read a *People* magazine article about you, Toby," Gwen Weld said. "It said you are bitter."

He laughed sharply.

"Are you ever going to come clean about leaving WorldQuest, Toby?"

He looked around, unsure what to do with his eyes. "I tired of the grind."

She said cautiously, "I've read a lot of accounts of the breakup, and a lot of interviews. The story seems to change, sort of evolves."

"That's Rex's doing." He lowered his voice as several people strolled by, intent on closer views of *Victory*. "He is pumping up the tale as he gets older."

"Why?"

"I'm content being known as a coder. He isn't. He wants a reputation as a corporate titan."

When he hesitated, she prompted him with, "I'm not following you."

"Rex wants the world to think he outsmarted me and became WorldQuest's CEO. It adds a ruthless element to his character and completes the picture of him as business wizard, instead of being just a software geek."

"But the truth is, what?"

"I tired of it, so I let him buy me out."

She tried to weigh his voice, see if his tones betrayed his words, but the dock was noisy, with pieces of laughter coming from many directions, and with Rex's amplified words.

"Would Rex tell me the same story?"

"Unless he has started to lie to you, like he has to everybody else." He suddenly held up a hand like a traffic cop. "I misspoke, Gwen. I'm . . . I'm under a bit of stress, put squarely on me by Rex." He attempted a laugh.

"Stress?"

"Rex has sort of dared me to do something, and I should dismiss it out of hand, but I just can't."

"Like a schoolyard dare?"

"He didn't call it a dare. He just invited me. But it's a dare, no question."

"What'd Rex do?" Gwen asked.

Toby Odell veiled his eyes and half-turned away. "He has asked me to crew *Victory* with him on the challenge. I don't know if I . . ." His voice softened to nothing, and was lost in Wyman's voice coming over the loudspeakers.

"The Pacific Winter Challenge's true test of our sailing abilities is found in the race's middle name," Wyman said. "Winter. Those sailors who accept the challenge will find themselves in some of the world's most dangerous waters during the most dangerous season."

This was an applause line, and the yacht club audience obliged politely.

Odell said under his breath, "Rex thinks I'm afraid of the race."

Rex Wyman droned on.

She asked, "Are you afraid, Toby?"

"Of the sea? No." He looked at her. "I've got bigger things to be afraid of than the sea."

CHAPTER 4

eats had been removed from the airplane, and the passengers sat on the floor facing aft, secured by safety belts bolted to the deck. The Beechcraft 65 was flying at thirty-five hundred feet above the ground, and just above stall speed. The sound of its twin engines filled the small space behind the pilot.

Jess McKay said loudly over the rumble, "You've got it all in your head, Christy? Exit plan, body position, canopy control, emergency procedures. The big four. Got them?"

She was sitting in front of McKay. Her hair was hidden by a helmet, and over her face was a blue wool mask with two eyeholes. Her eyes behind her goggles were wide. She wore an international orange insulated jumpsuit. Her main and reserve chutes were on her back, her trunk and legs in the harness.

"Got them, Christy?" McKay asked again. "The big four?"

She turned her head. "You sure you know what you're talking about, Jess?" Her voice was tight. "I mean, you're qualified to teach this and all?"

"I've got a D license, signed and official by the USPA."

A D license is the fourth and highest United States Parachuting Association certificate.

On the floor next to McKay, Sandy Ramirez adjusted his goggles. Ramirez and McKay were also in jumpsuits and chutes.

When a green light over the hatch came on, McKay asked, "We're over the DZ. Ready to skydive, Christy?"

"Yes," her mouth said, though there was no sound.

She rose from the deck. When the plane dipped slightly in an air pocket, she staggered, then steadied herself against an overhead rail. McKay held up her static line clip so she could see it, and so she could watch as he attached it to the metal loop above the hatch. The Beechcraft's fuselage hatch was covered with a Plexiglas panel, and when McKay slid it open, the jump bay was instantly washed with chilled air.

He said, "Take your position."

She moved unsteadily to the hatch, the wind rippling her jumpsuit. She glanced at McKay, then at Ramirez.

"Christy, remember your circle of awareness." McKay had to shout above the rushing air. "Got it?"

She nodded. Her pack was a dual chute system, containing both main and reserve canopies. Attached to the pack was an AAD, an automatic activation device on the parachute that would begin the opening sequence at a preset altitude should the static line activation somehow fail. An altimeter was on her wrist. She moved to the hatch. The wind pushed her jumpsuit flat against her.

Ramirez fiddled with his harness.

McKay said, "Right hand."

"Check," she replied, just above the roaring wind.

"Right foot."

"Check."

"Left hand," McKay said, then, "left foot."

She was in the hatch, a limb at each corner, the white and green of Alaska far below.

"Che—" A partial word, broken off when her jaw snapped shut.

"Now, go."

Nothing happened.

McKay tried again. "Christy, go."

Again nothing.

"Christy?"

The rage that swept over her face lit her eyes and changed the contours of her mask. Her body stiffened, and she unwrapped her hands from the exit handles slowly, as if with difficulty. She stepped away from the hatch, glaring at McKay through her goggles.

McKay called to the pilot, "Stay over the DZ, will you, Donna?" He turned to her. "Not a problem, Christy. I didn't feel like going out my first time, either."

She unclipped her helmet and threw it on the deck, where it skittered along the ribbing and then bumped into Ramirez. She tore off her goggles, then with both hands yanked off the wool mask. Suddenly sprung from its confines, her chestnut-brown hair was whipped by the wind, and it lashed against her cheeks and chin, a roiling frame for her face.

"First I'm terrified, and now I'm humiliated," she yelled. "I simply can't do this. I could be killed, falling out of this airplane, if my parachute failed or something."

Ramirez looked away, trying to give them privacy in the small plane.

"I quit," she said to McKay. "No more of this, not now, not ever."

McKay spread his gloved hands. "I'll keep us over the drop zone as long as you'd like. We can all take a breath."

"You never take a breath," she said. "That's what I'm talking about, Jess."

The plane's starboard wing dipped as the pilot maintained a course over the grass field below.

McKay closed the hatch, and the sound of the wind dropped so that he didn't have to shout. "You are under some stress, Christy. That's normal on a first jump."

Her nose was narrow and her cheekbones finely planed. Her slate-gray eyes were locked on McKay. "You almost convinced me to jump out of a perfectly good airplane, Jess. That's the effect you have on me. Well, no longer."

"You don't have to jump, Christy."

She put her hands to the sides of her head, sinking her fingers into her hair, as if trying to contain her thoughts. "Jess, I'm talking about bigger things than just leaping out of this plane. I'm talking about the scuba lessons you've given me, and the rock-climbing lessons, and the orienteering lessons, and the sailing lessons."

"I thought you were having fun," he said.

"What's next, Jess?" she asked. "Full-contact Korean kick-boxing lessons?"

Ramirez studied his gloves.

When McKay didn't say anything, Christy went on, "On our first date, you showed me how to do the Heimlich maneuver."

McKay smiled wanly. "It was just a trick to get to hug you. An old PJ trick."

"I'm . . . I'm educated, Jess. I'm a lawyer. I work in an office. I can't take all the wind and rain you've brought into my life. You are always outside, never under a roof, and you aren't really happy unless it's windy and rainy and cold, and unless you are hungry and tired. That's the only time you truly enjoy life."

He said nothing, staring at her intently, as if her face were a clouded window.

"Some little part of me is always going to love you, Jess, but the rest of me just can't jump out of airplanes, or any of the other goofy things you do, day after day after day."

"Well, I could—"

She cut him off. "No, you couldn't."

"Christy, you've not given us a chance," McKay argued.

"You knew we weren't going to work out, Jess." She peered up at him, leaning close so he could hear. "You must've known for some time now."

He hesitated. "No . . . no, I didn't know. I thought . . ." His voice trailed off, and he had to look away, out the hatch.

"Do you know what was my first hint that you and I live on different planets?"

He shook his head, not able to meet her eyes.

"The first time I saw you take off your shoes."

He turned to look at her. "My socks?"

"Jess, you wear a knife on your ankle. I mean, I went all through college and law school, and never met anybody who has a knife on his ankle. I just can't reconcile myself to that."

"The knife comes off, you know," McKay said. "I can reach right down and remove it."

She shook her head. "The knife represents you perfectly, and you can no more take off the knife than you can take off your head. We just don't fit, Jess."

He gestured despairingly. "I had begun to think you and I had a future together."

"I know you have a lot invested in me."

"Is that your way of saying you know I love you?" McKay asked, the hurt etched on his face. "Well, you're right."

She said, just above the engine noise and the tearing wind, "I tried, Jess."

"Yeah, well . . ."

"Look at me, Jess." She held her hands out to her sides. "I'm up in an airplane all tricked out in a jumpsuit and parachute and boots. That's trying. I gave it a shot. And so I'm saying goodbye."

He stared morosely at her. "There's nothing . . . ?"

She slowly shook her head.

He stood there a moment, his feet wide apart and his hand on a safety rail, his eyes on the deck and his face stormy. He brought his gaze up to her, but her expression was both kind and unrelenting.

"Well . . . I had hoped . . ."

"I quit, Jess. I just have to quit."

McKay pressed the back of his gloved hand against a corner of his eye. He lowered his goggles into place and brought up the wool mask from around his neck.

He glanced at the light, still green. He slid open the Plexiglas door, gripped the ripcord handle, and through the hatch he went, the soles of his boots flashing before he disappeared.

Ramirez pushed himself to his feet. His jumpsuit was civilian blue, and his chute pack was olive. On his helmet was a sticker for K-2 Fatbob snowboards. With his free hand, he gripped his main chute ripcord. He glanced at the green light.

He turned to her. "I was hoping it'd work out between you two. For Jess's sake."

He nodded goodbye, then dove through the hatch.

The Westview High School marching band crashed their cymbals and rolled their snare drums, a dashing fanfare. The WorldQuest logo on the huge screen dissolved into stylized fireworks. Speakers ringing the patio broadcast the thunder of artificial fireworks, the huge woofers fairly rippling the guests' hair. Club members and visitors worked their way toward the podium.

The yacht club's commodore replaced Wyman at the podium to a smattering of applause. He introduced the governor of California, who bounded up to the platform as if he were receiving a check. The governor's face was marred by a habitual expression of condescension, made worse because he wore half-glasses low on his nose, and had to tilt up his head to gaze through the spectacles, putting his nose into the air. He issued platitudes so airy and bland that they floated away unnoticed by anyone.

Out on the dock, his back to the security hut, Odell said, "I'm not the only one who gets a lot of press. I've seen your photo around. Nice backless gown at the HALO auction."

HALO was a San Francisco arts funding group whose annual auction raised millions of dollars. Photos from the event were splashed across the newspapers each year: couples in formalwear holding dainty glasses of white wine, showing off their jewels and teeth.

"I don't need to sneak around, Toby," she said, touches of both embarrassment and reproach in her voice. "I'm an adult. I can take care of myself."

Odell's eyes were close together behind the thin glass of his spectacles, and they were candid, looking at her straight on. "I didn't give a damn about the others, Gwen. I figured they were in it for a frolic, and they'd get what they deserved. And they did."

"Like I said, Toby, I'm an adult."

He pulled at one of his earlobes. "I compiled a spreadsheet, just for fun."

She hoped he was changing the subject. "I know spreadsheets. Nothing about them is fun."

"In the past six years, Rex Wyman has gone through eleven girlfriends. That means each lasts a little more than six months."

"Toby, it's my guess you've got better things to think about."

"Judging from the photos I've seen in the newspaper and *W* and *Vanity Fair*, he gives each girlfriend jewelry worth about twenty thousand dollars. Is that about right?"

"Rex hasn't given me any jewelry."

Odell placed his empty glass on a passing waiter's tray. "But you are only into month three. Jewelry is probably a month-four item. And in month six, you'll be out the door. I don't think he asks for the jewelry back, though."

"Toby, do I look like I need a nanny?"

"I'm trying to do you a favor."

"Well, stop."

Odell rose and lowered himself on his toes, his hands behind his back, in the manner of a patient schoolmaster. "I met every one of those eleven girlfriends, at parties and at Rex's homes. I didn't say a word of caution to any of them. I figured they knew what they were getting into, and they deserved it. But I'm meddling with you because I like you, Gwen."

"And it's sweet of you, Toby." She reached over to pat his arm. "Now, butt out."

Gwen Weld had been born on Manhattan's Upper East Side, in a fifteen-room apartment that overlooked Central Park, in the pantry, just off the kitchen. Her mother, Mary Weld, was the housecleaner, and Mary had feared being fired when her pregnancy had begun to show, so she had worked all the harder, and all the longer, and hadn't dared take a day off as her term approached because jobs were scarce for a heavily pregnant, unmarried girl with a thick County Cork accent and no papers at all. The baby came early. Mary gave birth lying on the floor in the little room filled with jars of olives and caviar and bottles of wine.

She cleaned up as best she could, then hurried on the subway to her apartment building to hand over the baby to a neighbor who had promised to help, and was back in her employer's home within hours. But not soon enough. Her employer, a graveyard-thin woman with a morbid fear of contamination, had found traces of blood and fluid on her pantry floor and wouldn't even let Mary back into the building, fired her through the speakerphone.

When Gwen was growing up, the great puzzle of her life was whether her mother had left Ireland for New York because her mother was pregnant, or because Mary was simply a drop in the latest wave of Irish to flee their homeland looking for a better life. In the late 1960s and early 1970s, Queens—especially Astoria, Sunnyside, and Woodside—and the Bronx neighborhoods of Bedford Park, Kingsbridge, and Norwood became the home for many Irish who had more ambition than documentation. The underground Irish took any job offered, fighting Haitians and Puerto Ricans for jobs that didn't even pay minimum wage because employers knew nobody had green cards.

Mary Weld provided her daughter with love and meals and once in a while new clothes for school—at least they were new to Gwen—but nowhere Gwen learned to call home, because the two of them changed apartments every few months. And Mary provided no history. They were Irish, Mary could hardly hide that, with the thick gnarl in her words, and Mary had let slip she was from County Cork. Other than that, nothing.

When Gwen came to an age where she realized many children had fathers and, indeed, that a male was something of a biological requirement, she asked her mother about her father. Gwen was six years old, and she could not now recall the form of her question, but Mary's response was the most vivid memory of her childhood. Her eyes wild, Mary turned to Gwen, gripped her arms with a desperate force, and said, "You are never to ask about him. Do you understand me now, Gwen? Never, never again."

With that, Mary Weld drew a curtain over her past, one she would never lift. She wore a gold ring on her left hand, a thin little thing Gwen came to realize was for self-defense rather than a symbol of anything. Gwen grew up not knowing whether *Weld* was her mother's family name, or the name of some man somewhere.

By the time she was in high school, Gwen knew, of course, that her mom was an illegal alien. Her neighborhoods were filled with the Sons and Daughters of Erin who hadn't bothered with immigration niceties. But Gwen suspected more was at work than the manner of her mom's entry into the United States. Such things could be fixed. Why hadn't her mother done so?

Then there was the moment—that shattering instant of serendipity—when the answer came to Gwen. She was in her junior year at NYU and was studying at a carrel, and the thought came from nowhere and swarmed over her: Her mother was hiding. All the evidence came together, unbidden but undoubted, in that instant. The leaving Ireland when she was pregnant, the constant changing of addresses in the Bronx, the endless series of menial jobs, the refusal to ever try for U.S. citizenship, never traveling. Gwen then understood that her mother was living her life without leaving a paper trail. She never applied for credit cards, never purchased anything through the mail, never applied for a driver's license, never took out health insurance, never did anything where she had to identify herself. The reason Mary Weld never tried to better herself, her daughter in that instant understood, was that to do so—to try for college or better-paying jobs—would require her to prove who she was. For reasons unknown to Gwen, her mother could never do this.

Gwen sat there in her carrel, her head in her hands, lost in pity for her mum, memories of their hard life washing over her. She resolved to demand an explanation from her mother.

There was never to be an explanation, not from Mary Weld, at least. Mary came home from work one day that very week, sat down on the tattered sofa near the window, and died. An aneurysm, her life blinking out in an instant, her crossword puzzle and pen falling onto her lap.

Toby Odell tried again. "You work for Rex. Don't stick your pen into the company inkwell is the old saying. Office romances never work out."

"Ours just might," she said.

"The subordinate—you—always loses when it falls apart. The weak get tossed."

"Maybe I'm made of sterner stuff," Gwen replied.

He glanced at her, their eyes on the same level. With a grudging smile, he said, "Maybe."

Her mother had been hiding, Gwen was convinced. When you hide, you change your name. She dug through her mother's meager possessions and found an essay, written—judging from the careful penmanship—when her mother was twelve or thirteen years old. The essay was titled "The Sea and Ireland," a

nicely thought-through commentary on the sea's influence on the Irish. Under the title was the name Mary
Strickland. Gwen had never before seen the name. The
words *Belgooly Parish School* were under the name.

Gwen traveled to Ireland the summer after her
mother died, to County Cork, carrying a photograph of
her mother as a teenager, a snapshot her mum had
brought to America years ago. She found herself in the
hamlet of Belgooly, south of the city of Cork and
within two miles of the Atlantic Ocean, the wind carrying the primal scents of low tide. She found a
Strickland in the phone book and came to a white-
washed cottage that had geranium-filled flowerboxes
below the windows. She walked up the stone path to
the house and pulled the cord.

The door opened and her mother stood there, staring out at her.

At least, it could have been her mother, with the
dark hair and over-featured face, the large, pale blue
eyes, the sharp chin, and the slender, swaying, wil-
lowy figure.

"Yes?" The woman's voice was the ghost of a whisper. She might have just seen some of herself in
Gwen. "May I help you?"

Without a word, Gwen held up the photograph of
her mother.

The woman at the door leaned forward, intent on
the photo. After a few seconds, she said, "Oh, my. Oh,
my lost Mary."

She stepped onto the porch and gathered Gwen
into her arms, and the woman began to weep quietly,
her tears wetting Gwen's cheeks, too. Then, without
releasing Gwen, the woman turned her toward the
door and escorted her inside.

That afternoon, over a pot of tea, the woman, whose

name was Colleen Strickland Mallory, told Gwen that
when Mary Strickland was eighteen years old, Mary
had fallen in with a John Hannon, "a fellow I never
saw when he wasn't acting the maggot," Colleen said,
by which Gwen understood he was a fool. "He'd been
in jail for thievery. Couldn't hold a job. But charming.
Oh, my, he was charming. Devilish blue eyes and this
blond hair. You got your mother's hair, not his."

"So this John Hannon is my father?" Gwen could
barely say the words.

"Was your father," Colleen corrected her, wiping
her nose with her sodden handkerchief. "John Hannon
is dead, and has been for twenty years."

Gwen's hand flew to her mouth.

Her aunt nodded sagely and said, "Mary was wild
for John Hannon. I used to listen to her crazy schemes
about running off with him, one bit of foolery after
another. And our mum and dad and me never understood any of it, because John Hannon was so mean."
She shook her head. "He'd slap her and everything. It
was terrible. She'd come home crying and trying to
hide her bruised face."

Gwen absorbed the revelations, and they seemed to
make her smaller.

When Colleen lifted her cup and saucer, they rattled
together, her hands shaking. "One March night, John
Hannon was found dead on the side of Western Road,
not far from the greyhound track. He had been stabbed
a couple of times in his throat."

"My God," Gwen exhaled.

"After that night Mary was never seen again in
Ireland."

The snare drums sounded again, a long roll, followed
by the trumpets ringing out with a call to the gate.

Toby Odell nodded toward the patio. On cue from

the governor, Rex Wyman stepped to the microphone again, smiling at the crowd

"Look at him," Odell said. "Rex has transformed himself. One day he's a computer geek, the next day he's an industrialist bestriding the world like a colossus. I saw it happen in front of my eyes, and could scarcely believe it. It was magical."

Some said Rex Wyman shaved his temples every day to give himself a receding hairline, to add age and dignity to his face. Others said this was just another lie in the layers of obfuscation regarding Wyman, whose identity and history could now hardly be discerned among all the distortions that traveled back and forth on the Internet and in the press.

Wyman beamed at the mayor, then at the crowd, his teeth flashing like mirrors. Wyman's face was tanned and smooth. His seal-brown hair was carefully combed and didn't give an inch in the breeze, as if it were lacquered in place. He kept himself fit and trim, noticeable even under his blue all-weather jacket with the WorldQuest logo on the pocket. Wyman's nose was a sharp wedge, and his jaw was aggressive below his pretty teeth. Though Wyman stood just a fraction over six feet, he seemed outsized, larger than life, like a statue in the park.

He thanked the governor, his words wafting over the dock to Toby Odell and Gwen Weld.

Odell looked at her. "You've got some iron to you, Gwen. Some courage and strength. I can tell, just from the little I know you, standing up to Rex like you do. I don't know if I've got that iron, and now this invitation to crew *Victory* with Rex. I don't know . . ." His voice trailed off.

"I inherited a bit of iron from my mother, maybe." She smiled to herself.

Those years ago, Gwen was first astonished and horrified that her mother had killed someone, but her opinion quickly turned around. John Hannon had learned a hard lesson about messing with Strickland women. Gwen rather gloried in the notion. The vision of her mother launching a shank into John Hannon's neck was a vast source of strength for Gwen. That the recipient of this pointed object had been her father didn't give Gwen an instant's pause.

Odell said, "Maybe you inherited iron from your father, too?"

She didn't say anything.

"You never mention him," Odell said.

Gwen replied with a venom she couldn't contain, "He is dead and in hell, and the world is a better place because of it."

Wyman kept talking into the microphone, and now he was holding up the bottle of champagne with which he would in a moment christen *Victory*.

Odell stared at Gwen out of the corner of his eyes. A small grin was on his face.

CHAPTER 5

Lonnie Garvin had put in a twelve-hour day, but he was still working swiftly, his hands rushing around the webbing. He was angry, and his teeth were clamped together and his jaw muscles were aching. He was on the deck of his crabber, *Hornet*, and had spent the day working on seven-bys: crab pots that are seven feet high, seven feet deep, and a yard wide, twice the size of a refrigerator. Two hundred of them were on deck, and each weighed 750 pounds empty.

He knew better than to allow emotions to eat at him, but there they were, a corrosive concoction of impotence and frustration and rage, and sometimes they made him shake like a man with the ague. His life's work was draining away, and he was helpless.

Garvin's theology was limited to a few uneducated pulses, but he had always believed that what goes around comes around. An article of his untended faith was that work is rewarded. You get what you deserve. Try as he might, he couldn't see how he deserved this. What he meant was, he hadn't gambled his money away like his foolish cousin Ray Spencer, who couldn't keep out of the reservation casinos near Anacortes and Mount Vernon, down in Washington State, and who had eventually lost his boat at a debtors' auction. Or he hadn't inhaled it, like his brother, a gifted skipper who could spend a thousand dollars a week on cocaine when he wasn't out on the water. And Lonnie Garvin wasn't lazy, like some dock bums, who had more colorful stories than ambition, more blow than show. Garvin just couldn't figure out how he deserved what was happening to him. He didn't, it was that simple, and it infuriated him.

There was a time when Garvin could sit in his wheelhouse, studying the charts and reports, laying out his strategy for the season, chatting with his skipper buddies on the radio, enjoying his coffee, a touch of leisure well earned. No more. Now he couldn't afford the hands to repair the crab pots or the boat. Now he spent his days cinching up runway webbing, wrenching on bridle knots, fixing damaged doors, and splicing eyes in door ties. He had inflated enormous orange pot buoys with air, then he stenciled *Hornet* on them in black letters. Then he had tied them together in twos with a hangman's knot to form a sea lion buoy. All of this just this week.

Moving pots was accomplished using his back, a skill learned the hard way, by doing it endlessly. Shoving a 750-pound pot around *Hornet*'s deck was easier when in a rough sea because the deckhand could time his shove with the roll of the boat, and so push downhill. But *Hornet* was in port, and every inch Garvin shoved a pot across his deck hurt to his bones. He was doing his own mending and humping. He had fallen far. Now he was cutting two-hundred-foot lengths of polyester line called *shots,* then melting the ends of the shots with a hot knife. Garvin was fuming

that it had come to this. He had once ridden high, king
of the crabbers, allowing himself a bit of a strut, back
when he ordered *Hornet* from the Fidalgo Shipyards
in Anacortes, sixty miles north of Seattle.

He surveyed his boat, turning a full circle, gathering it all in, every beloved bolt and scupper. *Hornet*
was all steel, a stiff-ribbed vessel with a square bottom, square stern, and a hard chine, all of which
allowed it to spring upright on keel after every roll.
The bow was rounded, and it flared up from the bul-
warks, designed specifically for the Bering Sea.

The pilothouse was forward, riding high above the
deck. In the superstructure below the pilothouse were
the galley and mess, crew quarters and storerooms.
And then further below, in the belly of the boat, from
aft to stern, were the chain locker, individual tanks for
lube oil, hydraulic oil, contaminated oil, and sewage,
fuel wing tanks on each side of the engine room, four
double-bottom crab tanks, a storage compartment, a
centerline deep tank, and finally a compartment for
the steering gear. On deck behind the wheelhouse
were two cranes and two drums. Everything first-rate.
Garvin had even picked out the black walnut trim for
the pilothouse and crew staterooms.

Now his business was on the slide. A year ago
friends would joke that he was a fleet admiral, with
two boats, *Hornet*, and the smaller *Wasp*, but Garvin
had sold *Wasp* in a buyer's market—nobody was looking for crab boats, not with these depressed prices for
product—and he hadn't cleared much more than the
bank's note and the damned mechanics' liens. He had
put the small profit from *Wasp*'s sale into *Hornet*'s new
power block, some new pots, and engine maintenance. Now he was down to one boat. Nobody called
him *admiral* any more.

At a distance, *Hornet* was still majestic, with its royal-blue hull and white superstructure, the rakish sweep of its hull, and its radar tower high above the wheelhouse. *Hornet* was a broad-shouldered, nose-down bull of a boat. It meant business, even a land-lubber knew that just from glancing at it.

The sea always grinds away at machines that challenge it. Vessel maintenance is neverending. Up close, a careful eye could detect *Hornet*'s distress. Rust stains marred the hull below the scuppers. Sealant around the pilothouse windows had shrunk and cracked. Paint on the deck railings was chipped, exposing steel. A three-foot section of the life rail on the forward deck had been knocked off and had not been replaced. A hundred other things above deck needed attention, and even more below deck.

In the flush days, when prices were up and crabs plentiful, repairs were done instantly, and *Hornet* was always as clean as a tooth. Garvin was proud to show it off, give anybody a tour, even old crab skippers with critical eyes. Now he had to ration his money, spend it on propulsion and pots, the two essentials, and let other items go. Garvin hadn't even been able to haul out *Hornet* before this season. Lord only knew what was growing on the hull. Ignoring maintenance was a strategy that always led to failure, but Garvin did not have the resources for long-term strategy. His goal was to bring up enough crab to pay his most insistent creditors. Pay off the old debt, take on new debt. Keep a step ahead of them.

Garvin set to work again, the hot knife in one hand and a length of line in the other, but then his hands stopped. He stared at the nearest stack of pots, his face blank, the deck rolling slightly under him as a passing boat's wake lifted *Hornet*. At times his predicament would rush up in front of him, as if launched from somewhere below, and would tightly grip him, paralyze him. Garvin was a man of action, always on the move, born with measureless energy, but such were his straits that he could be brought to a shuddering standstill. A couple of times a day this inertia would grip him, and he couldn't think and couldn't move, nothing. Perhaps he should ask his doctor about it. Maybe something had gone wrong with the wiring in his brain, but he hadn't paid his doctor's bill for the last visit, when Garvin's hernia had to be tucked back in, so his doctor was just another damned creditor. Well, the sawbones could get in line with all the others.

Only with a force of will could Garvin pull himself out of this seizure of inertia. He started slowly, having to think about each small movement, as if he were wrapped in chains. He lay the hot knife on a rail, and he turned to . . . what? What task on deck? Every square foot of every surface needed attention. A boat such as his never stayed on an even plane. It was either improving or declining. Hard work and money improved it. The merciless elements—wind and water—degraded it. A vessel *Hornet*'s size required four hours of maintenance *each day* just to stay even, 365 days a year, and that didn't count the crab gear. The boat was like a herd of dairy cows. It never relented in its demand for more work from him. He couldn't hire help and couldn't take it to a boatyard. He'd been doing it all himself. He was tired. God, but he was tired.

The cell phone chirruped. Garvin lifted it off the capstan.

"Yeah?" he said, too dispirited to be civil.

He listened for fifteen seconds, his eyes narrowing with thought, then closing with resignation.

"All right, Booney," he said. "I owe you one."

Lonnie Garvin returned to himself in that instant, the world-weariness falling away. He quickly closed two deck hatches, then climbed the ladder to the wheelhouse. Forget the blower, he didn't have time. He cranked over the starboard engine, a Caterpillar as big as a pickup truck. The port engine was down. It had been overheating, sending steam off its pipes. He might've sucked something into the port seawater intake. Salt water cooled fresh water in a heat exchanger, then the fresh water cooled the engine. The plug was probably seaweed, but it could be anything. Garvin had once pulled a diaper out of the pipe. So he could use only one of *Hornet*'s engines, and one of its two propellers, and one of its two rudders, reducing *Hornet*'s maneuverability at slow speeds not by half, which would seem logical, but by 80 percent.

With the starboard engine rumbling, Garvin scanned the gauges. He had less than two hundred gallons of diesel on board, about a hundred in each of the wing tanks. He was always careful about keeping the tanks evenly filled, transferring fuel from one to the other when needed. Same with the catch. Crabs were distributed evenly into starboard and port tanks. Otherwise the boat was out of balance, and when it rolled in a trough it might keep on rolling.

Garvin raced out of the wheelhouse and back down the ladder, sliding down, not using the rungs. He ran along the rail to the forward mooring line—a nylon hawser with a two-inch diameter—freed it from the cleat, and threw it onto the wharf. Then to the aft line, tossing it off, too.

Breathing hard now, Garvin returned to the wheelhouse. He would otherwise never contemplate—not for a crazed instant—taking *Hornet* to sea without at least two deckhands. His boat had no bowthrusters. *Hornet*

was as unwieldy as it was brawny. But out alone he
would go, out of Dutch Harbor into the Bering Sea.

The sheriff was coming, and Garvin had to escape.

Last off-season Jacobson Electric in Seattle had
installed a water-cooled Volvo Penta generator on
Hornet. With it came a brushless AC alternator, a bed-
plate with anti-vibration mountings, an electronic
governor, and an industrial silencer. The bill came to
twenty-five thousand dollars. Garvin had scraped up
the deposit and pledged *Hornet* as security. He had
made the first two payments, but none since. He
hadn't had the money. Jacobson Electric was in the
marine repair business, and the owner had no interest
in owning boats, and Garvin's dad had known old man
Jacobson—they'd been to Ballard High together—so
Jacobson Electric held off as long as it could, but
finally had turned the account over to its lawyers, a
bloodthirsty Seattle firm whose tactics more resembled Vlad the Impaler's than Clarence Darrow's.

In their own defense, these lawyers would argue that
vigor is required when the collateral can be moved
around, which is to say, hidden. Unlike a mortgaged
home, a boat can easily be concealed, particularly in
Alaska, where even today not all the shoreline is charted.
Maritime law compensates for the portability of the
security by allowing creditors to act quickly. Unknown to
Lonnie Garvin, Jacobson Electric had filed a complaint
that very morning in the federal court for the district of
Anchorage, and had obtained a warrant for *Hornet*'s
arrest. No notice to Garvin was provided. The warrant
can be, and this morning was, issued secretly.

The U.S. Marshal's office in Anchorage has its own
jet, which had landed at Dutch Harbor a few minutes
ago. A while back, Garvin had asked a freight for-
warder, who had an office near the runway, to keep

his eye out for the sheriff's plane, and to give a call if it landed. Maybe this was a false alarm, but probably not, not with Garvin's creditors working at his door with a battering ram.

Hornet's bow drifted a foot, then two feet from the dock on the receding tide. Moored at the pier forward of *Hornet* was Max Freeman's sixty-five-foot trawler, *Pacific Crest*. Garvin hadn't seen Freeman all day, and he hoped he was in a bar or in his Unalaska apartment, nowhere near his boat, because Freeman wouldn't at all like what Garvin was about to do.

With the engine revving just above idle, Garvin engaged the running gear. The starboard propeller kicked up white water. *Hornet* shuddered, then rumbled forward, just an inch, then a little more. *Hornet*'s maneuverability was hampered by the dead port engine and by the lack of deckhands to nudge the boat away from the pier. The pier's pylons began to slide by. The wheel hard to starboard, Garvin willed *Hornet* to defy the laws of physics, and to miss Max Freeman's *Pacific Crest*.

Hornet could not oblige. Its prow bumped *Pacific Crest*'s stern, brushing it more than ramming it, and Garvin heard wood shatter. He couldn't see below *Hornet*'s high prow, couldn't see the damage he had just inflicted on Freeman's boat. Maybe it was just *Pacific Crest*'s safety rail. In terms of ship collisions, this was just a kiss. In fact, it wasn't even a collision, not in boat-talk: It was an allision, because only one boat was moving. Still, Max Freeman was going to go purple, and his veins, God, they'd be standing out on his forehead and neck, Garvin had seen it before, when a fish broker tried to light-weight him. Freeman's face was going to resemble a road map when he saw what Garvin had just done to his trawler.

Garvin would call him on the cell phone in a few minutes. Freeman would understand, if it was only his safety rail, two hours' labor, and a hundred dollars, compared with Garvin losing his entire vessel. Garvin prayed he hadn't just crumpled *Pacific Crest*'s steering gear, or bent a rudder shaft, which would require an expensive haul-out. He couldn't think about it now.

The big Cat rumbling, *Hornet* glided forward, pushing *Pacific Crest,* which resisted because it was tied fore and aft to the dock with massive lines. More wood gave way with a sharp crack. Max Freeman was going to have a heart attack. Garvin glanced over his shoulder, through the wheelhouse's port windows toward the dock and the road.

A car was coming down the road, a rental, judging from the new but undistinguished look of it. It'd be the sheriff, fresh from the airport. Garvin tapped the throttle, and the diesel gained a few RPMs. *Hornet* was still caught on *Pacific Crest*'s stern, still chafing it, but *Hornet*'s prow was slipping to seaward. Too slowly.

The car turned into the boatyard, through the gap in the hurricane fence. The sun flashed on the windshield, hiding the occupants. Then the reflection slipped away as the car came to a stop. Garvin could see the driver. A marshal, sure enough, wearing the service's silly hat. Probably a deputy marshal, told by the court to go to Dutch Harbor and seize Lonnie Garvin's boat. Not if Garvin could help it, goddamn the deputy.

Sitting next to the deputy was Will Slewberg, damn him, too. Slewberg was the custodian appointed by the court to care for *Hornet* once the deputy made the arrest. Slewberg's job was difficult, everybody knew, looking after someone else's vessel under mandate of the court. Still, he was despised universally along the docks, viewed as a vulture. Slewberg was first out of the car, a wiry little man with a flapping coat, moving fast as if he were doing piecework, beginning to run across the gravel lot toward *Hornet* before the deputy was even out of the car. A vulture, plain and simple.

Garvin tapped the accelerator bar again. The Caterpillar gained a few clicks, shown on the tachometer next to the wheel. Something else cracked on *Pacific Crest*'s stern. God, Garvin hoped it was just the rail. *Hornet*'s bow slipped farther to sea, straining against *Pacific Crest*'s stern, sliding along it to starboard. Freeman's boat listed to starboard as *Hornet* pushed it.

Now the deputy was out of the car, following Slewberg across the lot toward the pier, closing in on *Hornet*. Garvin knew precisely what would happen if the deputy marshal and the custodian boarded *Hornet*. The marshal would hand a copy of the warrant to Garvin, and then attach an eight-and-a-half-by-eleven-inch blue-and-white sticker to the superstructure, announcing the vessel had been seized. Then the marshal would give Garvin five minutes to gather his gear—only personal stuff, nothing that might now belong to a creditor—and get off the boat. In Alaska's severe environment, vessels deteriorate quickly, despite whatever efforts the custodian might make, so the court might order an interlocutory sale of the boat, which is done *before* judgment, in the discretion of the court.

So if the marshal got on board *Hornet*, Garvin might never set foot on his boat again. Never even see it again. It could be sold to some damned Taiwanese consortium.

And here the marshal came, out onto the dock, raising an arm to signal Garvin. The deputy's stomach hung over his Sam Browne, and his belly bounced along with him, out front and full of purpose. The deputy caught up to Will Slewberg, and they hurried along the dock toward *Hornet.*

Hornet's prow was still snagged on the trawler, still prodding it and scraping its stern. The deputy and Slewberg were fifty yards away, pumping their arms. Now thirty yards, Slewberg waving some document at Garvin up in the wheelhouse, maybe the complaint.

The boat suddenly lurched forward, free of *Pacific Crest,* which settled back on its keel. Garvin punched the throttle. The diesel roared, and the boat rattled from all quarters. *Hornet* was no top nitro fueler, and the crabber gained speed grudgingly. The gap between ship and pier widened an inch at a time. One hand on the wheel, Garvin peered through a window down over the safety rail, seeing the wooden pier but looking for water as the boat pulled away. At *Hornet*'s stern, white water pushed against pylons. Then Garvin could see the water down there, a growing expanse between hull and pier. He exhaled hugely.

The deputy and Will Slewberg ran onto the wharf and right up to its edge, the deputy doing a Harold Lloyd burlesque turn with his arms to stop himself right at the wharf's edge, maybe for Garvin's benefit. *Pacific Crest*'s superstructure glided by.

From high overhead, Garvin saw the deputy smile, a small thing meant for him and not for Slewberg, the earnest custodian panting next to him, the document balled in his hand.

Garvin understood the smile. Marshals hated making vessel arrests, putting hardworking fishermen out of business. The deputy down there on the dock might have precisely timed his arrival in the car, slacking off on the accelerator a bit to let *Hornet* get underway, Garvin wouldn't have been surprised. The custodian, though, was vibrating with anger. He'd have nothing to do the rest of the day. Nobody paid him anything for misses, however close.

So *Hornet* was away, leaving the harbor behind, cruising toward the headland, then out to sea, where nobody had jurisdiction, and nobody—*nobody*—could seize his boat, not the president, not the pope, and certainly not his creditors.

Garvin rationed himself a grin. He deserved it, and he didn't know when he would be able to smile again.

CHAPTER 6

Longtree Ranch was named not for the trees—though some of the Douglas firs rose two hundred feet—but for Rex Wyman's mother, whose maiden name was Longtree. One hundred twenty-four creeks in the United States are named Deep Creek, and the one that passes through Longtree Ranch was the Deep Creek in central Idaho, a dozen miles from the old mining town of Ketchum, which would have dried up and blown away like other mining towns had not Averell Harriman of the Union Pacific decided to generate business for his railroad by placing a ski resort there. He named it Sun Valley.

So Ketchum has become an international resort, famous for groomed ski runs and more powder than anywhere else. Private jets fly into the airport at Hailey, a few miles south of Ketchum, and folks from California and Texas and Japan emerge, wearing sunglasses and jewels, and quickly disappear into the mostly invisible network of the truly wealthy, and are only glimpsed on the ski slopes now and then. The less-than-truly-wealthy arrive in commercial planes, filling up Ketchum from Thanksgiving to late April, skiing Mount Bald during the day and eating brook trout and famous Idaho potatoes at night.

Though skiers don't see it, the hardscrabble life in these parts has never gone away. Farmers with too little land and too much debt abound, some tending the same acreage their grandparents did, right along the Big Wood River. These spreads have thirty-year-old hay trucks sitting in faded barns, long stretches of downed fence, and abandoned outbuildings half-covered with brambles. Skiers driving from the airport to Ketchum find these farms charming and romantic and reminiscent of a bygone time, notions the farmers find laughable.

Longtree Ranch shared some of this charm, installed by the owner's landscape architect. Two barns with weathered gray siding had been imported from southern Idaho and had been perfectly placed to enhance the view across the valley. But this required rerouting Deep Creek, giving it a new course roughly three hundred yards west. The creek was also made to wind back and forth so that three bridges the landscape architect thought would add a rustic element would have some purpose.

At the ranch's main entrance was a massive lodgepole pine arch, which supported old English letters made of twisting, intertwined mule deer antlers that spelled out *Longtree Ranch*, looking both baroque and western at the same time. Along the entire mile drive from the arc to the ranch house were planting beds—twenty feet wide on each side of the road—where the flowers were rotated three times annually so that the beds were always in bloom, except in the dead of winter, when vast phalanxes of ornamental cabbages were installed. The ranch had four acres of greenhouses to supply the flowers.

Rex Wyman owned Longtree Ranch. His agents had assembled the thirty-five thousand acres from fifty-two different parcels, buying out one farmer after another in the Wood River Valley south of Ketchum. Wyman had tried to buy the farms in secret, but word got out anyway, and prices doubled, then quadrupled, Wyman complaining that these farmers were mugging him. Nevertheless, he paid their prices—many of the farmers retiring to Hawaii and the Caribbean with Wyman's money—and then Wyman tore down their homes and barns, and swept away all other evidence that Longtree Ranch had ever been anything but one big spread.

Wyman ran a hundred head of horses on the ranch, and five hundred cattle, and he had built a feeding station for elk forced down from the mountains during harsh winters. The ranch employed eighty farmhands, gardeners, and mechanics. There were sheds and pumphouses and grain elevators, fields of hay and alfalfa and wheat, and an enormous Rain-King irrigation system. So to this extent, the land remained a ranch, and like most of the smaller ranches and farms it had incorporated, Longtree Ranch cost more money to operate than it earned. Wyman shrugged off the losses. He wanted an operating ranch, and that was that.

But there was much more to the property than fields and animals: a helicopter landing pad, a forty-car garage, five guesthouses, and a nine-hole golf course. The main house was fifteen thousand square feet, and made of lodgepoles and river rock, with peaked roofs and gables and vast windows. The mud-room where guests hung up ski gear and resumed mufti was larger than most of the old homesteads that had once been on the property.

From many rooms the Sawtooth Mountains could

be seen, the lower slopes covered with blue bunch grass and Idaho fescue, and the yellow and blue lichen coloring the granite nearer the peaks. The Sawtooths' crags and cirques and glacial gouges presented a wild picture, endlessly changing as clouds passed over, casting the mountains in moving shadows of purple and gray, and then gold and blue as the sun spilled through creases in the cloud.

Longtree Ranch ranged up into those mountains, and some of its acres were more vertical than horizontal, made of the sharp ridges and narrow defiles of river canyons, and Rex Wyman liked to say that he would have even more acreage if he could pull it all flat. Some of the land, even down on the flat, had been left in its wild state, with bunchberry and cottonwood trees and sagebrush and June grass.

The foliage couldn't quite hide the efforts of Wyman's security service, Fouche Company. Fences were electrified, and motion and heat detectors dotted them at regular intervals. Humvees roamed the ranch. Cameras were well-hidden in the lodgepole arc and many other places on the acreage. The security company's ranch headquarters were in an outbuilding behind the main house, and were filled with communications equipment and weapons. Wyman feared kidnapping.

Gwen Weld's suite was in the west wing of the main house. She wasn't sure whether she or Wyman had first determined she wouldn't be putting her suitcases into Wyman's bedroom, or maybe it was the butler, but she was satisfied with the arrangement. She had flown into Hailey that afternoon, and Wyman had said he would arrive at the ranch before lunch. He hadn't appeared yet, but that was standard. He would arrive when he arrived, not a minute earlier. His employees called it *Wyman time*, a concept predictable only in its elasticity.

Gwen had visited Longtree Ranch three times, and
never knew whether to unpack or just live out of her
suitcase. Departures from here or anywhere else when
she was with Wyman were often abrupt. So she had
brought little to the ranch, and now she unpacked even
less. One of the items was a photo of her mother, a dis-
posable printout of her mom's image. She squeezed
the photo between the glass and the mirror frame so it
stayed upright.

Her rooms were decorated in a western motif, with
the huge bed made of unpainted poles. Chairs were
covered in suede. Lampstands were constructed of
flatiron made to resemble branding equipment. Indigo
and peach thunderbirds were woven into the carpet.

The Ansel Adams photograph of Yosemite over her
bed wasn't a print, but rather was displayed on a flat-
panel screen, one of many on the walls in her suite and
throughout the house, and were meant to comfort and
relax guests, but Gwen thought they were spooky. The
inch-thick screens had forty-inch diagonal viewing
areas. Guests wore tiny transmitters pinned to their
lapels or belts. Before arriving, guests filled out prefer-
ence forms. The house's control server constantly
monitored guests' locations, and changed the screens'
displays as the guests moved throughout the house.
Someone who favored French impressionism would
find Monet and Pissarro on the screens whenever that
person went into a room. Another guest, perhaps an
aviation buff, would find photos of the Wright brothers
on those same screens a moment later. If those two
guests were in the same room, the computer searched
for a compromise for the screen, maybe an early
French biplane. Images also changed according to the
time of day, season of the year, news events (more
somber scenes when the stock market fell more than a

hundred points in a day), and other parameters, some perhaps known only to the computer. Gwen had tried to catch a screen switching from one image to the next—playing peekaboo through a door—but had never succeeded.

She placed a hairbrush on the dresser, a drugstore model she wouldn't mind losing. A bouquet of roses was on the dresser, with a note from Rex, "Be there shortly," in the handwriting of the Longtree Ranch's manager. Gwen suspected Wyman knew nothing about the roses. He was already four hours late. She glanced out a window, surveying the sky to the south. Nothing there yet.

She turned to the mirror and grimaced. Sixteen-hour workdays had left her face puffy, and had added an odd hue to the skin below her eyes. She hadn't been fooled by Rex's invitation to Longtree Ranch, that it was to enjoy a relaxing weekend in the country. Rex never relaxed, and had once told her that the sight of people taking it easy made him nervous. WorldQuest lost key employees every month, engineers and technicians who had joined Wyman and Odell early, and had been granted WorldQuest stock options as part of their compensation packages, and who quit the company at age thirty-five or forty, burnt out and determined to live the rest of their lives restoring antique cars or sitting on a beach. Wyman laughed at their lack of stamina.

She had thought about leaving the company, too. Maybe after the Pacific Winter Challenge, after Rex had proven what he had to prove. She had worked for World-Quest now for nine years. Like other early employees, she had been paid partly in stock options. She and the others in their cubicles had unquestioned faith that if they worked hard that very day, they could nudge WorldQuest stock higher that very day. It had worked for many years. All of them, stuck in front of computer monitors, eating shrink-wrapped sandwiches for lunch at their desks, then leaving the office building at nine or ten at night to drive Ferrari Testerosas and Mercedes 560SLs home. They all knew it was crazy, even back then.

After years of giddy price increases and two-for-one splits, WorldQuest's stock price on the NASDAQ had fallen by half in the prior twelve months, a downward slide that baffled shareholders who had once thought Rex Wyman infallible. Gwen's stock in WorldQuest was worth six million dollars. A year ago it had been worth twice that. "It's only paper," Wyman had assured her.

A voice came from everywhere. "Mr. Wyman's helicopter will be landing in five minutes, Miss Weld."

"Thank you," she replied to the air.

The low rumble of the helicopter came from the south. She brought out a denim jacket from her suitcase, then left her bedroom, walking through the suite's foyer, then out into the hallway and into the main room, where a Chiluly glass sculpture was near a rock fireplace where a blaze burned twenty-four hours a day, summer and winter. The gray and white glass sculpture consisted of curved and pointed spikes, resembling ribs of a dead animal, and was lit by low-voltage lights hidden in the walls and ceiling.

Ted Landers sat on a cream-colored leather sofa near a bank of windows in the south wall, a cell phone at his ear. A phone was on an end table next to him, but Gwen knew Landers's cell phone contained a scrambler. Landers was a WorldQuest vice-president and was chief of its security division, Fouche. He interrupted his discourse into the phone to smile and nod at Gwen.

She never knew how to respond to Landers, whether to act irritated or to be friendly, or perhaps just indifferent. She knew he had dug around in her past when she and Rex Wyman had begun dating, that he had spoken with a couple of her ex-boyfriends, had run a credit check on her (Toby Odell had happily shown her how to check on the credit check, and to tweak it if need be, not that hers needed tweaking), and she was sure Ted Landers's subordinates had searched elsewhere, looking for something that might later embarrass Wyman if made public. She didn't like being snooped on. She nodded noncommittally at him.

She could feel Landers's eyes follow her across the room. Landers favored sports coats without ties, and deck shoes. Little was known about him among World-Quest employees, and rumors abounded, filling the vacuum. He might have served with the Mossad. Some said he had been with the National Reconnaissance Office. Some said he lost a leg in Iraq and wore a prosthesis, though no one ever saw him limp. He stood less than five feet six, but he had a mink's agility and strength, as was evident just looking at him, muscles wrapped around muscles on that small frame. Landers smiled a lot, but it was unpleasant, a clear charade. His smoke-colored eyes were candid and set at a gracious angle, another charade.

What was known about Ted Landers—at least to Gwen—was that he was seldom far from Wyman, but was seldom seen with Wyman, and never in a photograph with him. His organization, Fouche, employed more than six hundred security personnel, which included Wyman's thirty-person bodyguard contingent, almost two hundred information systems security personnel, and many brick-and-mortar guards. Landers popped up at all hours to speak with Wyman and was one of the few WorldQuest employees who had Wyman's direct phone numbers.

Gwen didn't like all the popping up. She didn't like

Landers, in fact, though she was hard-pressed to say why. He was unlikable, that was why. She felt Landers's stare fall away.

Toby Odell was sitting on a sofa by the fire, a laptop computer on a coffee table in front of him. Three or four newspapers were also on the table, and he was reading a copy of *USA Today*. He was wearing jeans and a Pendleton shirt. His belt buckle was a sterling silver cow skull, which might or might not have been Odell's idea of a joke, with him you couldn't tell.

When he saw her, he waggled the newspaper at her and smiled.

She veered toward him, crossing the room. The chandelier above the dining-room table was as large as an automobile and was made of moose antlers, and Gwen couldn't look at it without shuddering.

"I heard a rumor you are leaving WorldQuest," Toby said.

His words brought her up. How could he have heard that? It had been idle talk among her skiing friends, nothing concrete.

"Does Rex know?" he asked.

"I don't tell him everything," she said. And until that moment, she had only toyed with the idea, but it firmed just then. She announced, "I'm leaving WorldQuest after the Challenge."

"I figured as much." He lifted his feet to place them on the coffee table. "Another case of burnout."

She snapped at him. "No, you didn't figure as much, Toby. You claim to know Rex Wyman inside and out, but you don't know me at all."

She grimaced. Toby Odell didn't deserve to be snarled at. She waved her hand by way of apology, then, feeling that insufficient, added, "Sorry, Toby. Too little sleep, too much work. It's getting to me."

He smiled up at her. "I have the perfect remedy. Go spend some of your money."

She replied without thinking, "I can't." Then blushed. She had revealed too much.

Odell chuckled, a pleasant sound that lingered in his throat. "That's what I've heard. You're as tight as a drum." He must have seen the color rise in her face, because before she could be defensive, he went on, "I mean, I've seen your car, a nine-year-old Honda Accord."

"What've you heard about me, Toby?"

"Anybody who dates Rex Wyman is talked about everywhere. In WorldQuest's halls, in the press, on the Internet. That's just how it is, and you should know it."

"So what have you heard?" she demanded.

"Rumor has it you're a skinflint, is all."

"Like what? What've you heard?"

"The No-To-WorldQuest website—that group of odd-balls that gets its kicks hating Rex Wyman and posting vile stuff on the Web for everyone to see—reports that you sometimes wear the same pair of pants three days in a row to work. Which is pretty vile, you have to admit."

She stared down at him. "If you weren't such a nice guy, Toby, I'd clean your clock."

He laughed. "Yeah, and I'd deserve it. Go spend some money. It'll make you feel better, and it'll make you feel less like a WorldQuest slave. It worked for me."

The house's windows were all bulletproof, but even so the low beats of the helicopter made it into the room. Gwen cuffed one of his feet, then left him there, crossing the carpet, then pushing through the door. She walked along the porch to the side of the house, then down stone steps toward the helicopter pad, a good hundred yards away, along a crushed-rock path

bordered by ornamental fescue. Behind the house, the
high hills wore a dusting of new snow. The helicopter
came in low and fast, as always with Rex aboard. He
had once told her that he liked the ground to roar past
him underneath the helicopter "like in a video game."

She walked to the edge of the concrete pad. An
orange windsock hung from a nearby pole, shifting
idly. The Bell Kiowa's rotors flattened grass and blew
up dirt as the helicopter raced toward her. Scowling,
she put on her coat.

So the word was out that she was a skinflint. She
despised that term and all it implied. She hugged herself as the copter rose to square itself for its descent to
the pad. She could imagine the laughter, WorldQuest
employees driving down I-84 in their Mercedeses and
BMWs and Land Rovers, chatting with each other on
their tiny cell phones about Gwen Weld's clunky
Honda Accord.

Gwen recalled the day she became a millionaire, a
day that combined a vesting in that year's WorldQuest
stock options and a runup in WorldQuest price on the
NASDAQ. She was sitting in her carrel when a whoop
went up in the room as the ticker price was flashed on
a monitor. She wasn't the only WorldQuest employee
who had joined the millionaire ranks that day.

For several years she had sworn that once her assets
hit that magic number, she would splurge on a month-
long trip to Australia and New Zealand, take some time
off—she had not taken a holiday in three years—and
spend some money. That week, she visited a travel
agent twice, read two books on those countries, and
had driven to the travel agent's office to pick up tickets
and to write the check. She sat opposite the travel
agent, pen in hand, checkbook in front of her, and her
pen suddenly took on the aspects of a mule in foul tem-

per. It simply wouldn't work. She could not get it to fill in the figure on the check. Mortified, she had offered vast apologies to the travel agent, and then fled.

It wasn't the first time this had happened. A year earlier, at the half-million-dollar mark, she had run from a Jaguar showroom, leaving the salesman—thirty seconds from closing a big-margin deal on an XJ sedan—sputtering and waving his arms like a football coach, trying to steer her back into the showroom.

Gwen had never—not once in her life—paused at a store window, seen a coat or dress she liked, and gone inside to buy it. She had never—not once—purchased something on impulse. She lived in a one-room apartment in an area of Boise known for modest apartments and take-out pizza joints and nothing else. She shopped at Costco, pushing a huge cart around, buying chili by the case.

Maybe she was ill in the head. Perhaps some connection in her brain had lost its solder. She liked to think that her penurious ways came from her childhood, when her mother never spent a hard-earned cent without pondering over it. Being a miser was learned behavior, maybe. Whatever it was, it wasn't normal to be worth six million dollars and to wear a twelve-year-old Timex wristwatch. It worried her, being penurious when there was no need. She had once considered consulting a psychiatrist, but they were too expensive.

Only when she began dating Rex Wyman did she loosen up a little, a very little. Rex couldn't be seen with a rag on his arm. A few dresses and jewelry, but only after ferocious shopping and price comparisons, and even so the purchases made her dizzy. She started going to a hair salon, an expense she thought the equivalent of tossing money down a storm drain, but Rex had insisted, politely but pointedly.

He tried to reimburse her for these things, but Gwen knew her mother would have dropped dead at the thought of her daughter taking such stuff—it suggested a kept woman—so she at first politely refused. Politeness never swayed Rex, so she then adamantly refused. He would shrug and say, "Suit yourself." Then he would try again later.

She had often wondered how wealth affected her and Rex's relationship. He had vast sums—unimaginable sums—of money, and he occasionally was compelled to mention some figure or another, from either immodesty or insecurity, she didn't know. He had once told her that Longtree Ranch was costing him three million dollars a month. Money meant nothing to Rex because he had so much of it, and it meant nothing to her because she was constitutionally incapable of spending any of it. Her logic was tortured and laughable but, still, maybe their disregard for money was one of the reasons they were attracted to each other.

The helicopter loudly lowered itself, the blades rippling the sky, visible only as a slight smudge. Leaves and twigs on the landing pad scattered. The copter's windows were tinted, and she couldn't see the pilot or Rex, who always sat next to the pilot, never in the seats behind. Gwen waved at the dark glass, then held her coat tightly around herself. Her dark hair flapped behind her, and she squinted against the rush of wind. The Bell Kiowa helicopter had been designed for the military, and it was heavy and purposeful, the turbine whine filling the air. The nose landing light was on, even though it was still daylight. The copter aligned itself above the pad, then lowered the last few feet to the concrete, the undercarriage wheels and the tail wheel touching down at the same instant. The pilot

backed off on the throttle, and the rotors began slowing, becoming more and more visible.

She had invested much in this weekend with Rex
Wyman. She was going to cook for him—something
she had never done before for Rex: She was not a
cook, so had rehearsed the dinner, making it in its
entirety, twice.

Rex was bringing his aide, but Roger Hall was
always with Rex, or just outside the door, or at the end
of a shout, and she had almost ceased seeing him. Rex
wasn't bringing anyone else, so it'd just be the two of
them, and Roger, and the eighty or so people who
worked for Longtree Ranch. Almost just the two of
them, and that was as good as she was going to get
with Rex. She would take what she could get.

So she was anxious and irritated when, just as the
helicopter landed, two automobiles appeared from the
other side of the main house and drove toward the
helicopter along the service road. At first she couldn't
make them out, big sedans of some sort, but then she
saw that one of the cars had bubbles on its roof. A
police car.

Ted Landers appeared near the landing strip. She
hadn't seen him walk out. He stood with his hands
behind his back, at parade rest.

The copter's engine wound down, and the passenger hatch slid open. Rex Wyman jumped down to the
pad, backwash flattening his hair and rattling his coat.
Even though the rotors were well above his head, he
ducked like an infantryman as he ran toward her.

He yelled above the engine's noise, "Sweetie, you
have no idea how much I've been looking forward to
this, and—"

Then he saw the automobiles, and was brought up,
standing right next to her, forgetting the big hug he

was going to give her, his smooth face bunching angrily and gaining a choleric red hue.

His voice was rough. "I told them they didn't need to make a big deal of it."

She followed his gaze. The cars swept in. Silver sunlight glinted off the windshields, allowing only glimpses of the passengers inside.

Roger Hall had joined them from the helicopter, standing two steps behind Wyman's left shoulder, a dictating machine in his hand. Hall was a slight man, with a pinched face and failing blond hair. His rimless spectacles blinked on and off in the light. He was wearing a gray suit. Whenever Wyman spoke, Hall's lips moved in sympathy, silently parroting whatever his boss said. Hall was so bland as to be invisible, but Gwen knew him to be an efficient and ruthless aide.

Wyman asked sourly, "And they wouldn't put it off a month, not even a week?"

She didn't know what he was talking about. He straightened his backbone and his face became carefully deadpan. He turned to the approaching cars and planted his feet and squared his shoulders, the posture of one anticipating a blow.

The cars stopped at the edge of the helicopter pad. The bubble top had *Blaine County Sheriff's Department* on the door panel. The sheriff—not some deputy—emerged from the marked car. He wore a khaki uniform and a wide-brimmed campaign hat and a Sam Browne belt. He walked toward Wyman. From the passenger side, a deputy emerged, but he leaned against the door frame, not getting any closer. A slender man in a business suit climbed out of the second car. He, too, hung back.

"Rex, sometimes I have to do distasteful things," the sheriff said as he stepped near. He had to fairly shout over the Bell's engine. He nodded at Gwen but didn't wait for an introduction. "I'm an elected official, and I have to do what a judge tells me, even if I don't like it."

"You couldn't wait until the fifteenth of the month, John, for God's sake? My lawyers told the court I would cover it by then."

The sheriff shook his head. "That's for the judge to decide. I'm just the messenger here, you know that." He wore a gray mustache above thin lips and an unstable chin.

"So what're you going to do?" Wyman asked.

Gwen detected a touch of fear in his words, something she had never before heard.

The sheriff pulled a manila envelope from his jacket. "I've got to deliver these documents to you. Me and my people are going to post notices on your property."

Wyman turned slowly, almost a complete circle, then back again, his eyes gathering in the estate east to west, from mountains to pastureland. Wyman's face worked one way then the next, the muscles along his jaw flaring, and his lips pressed flat and the skin on his face turning pale in blotches. One hand was in his jacket pocket, but the other bunched the fabric of his pants along his thigh. The sheriff waited, and so did Gwen Weld. A red-tailed hawk crossed under a cloud, then banked toward the mountains.

Ted Landers stepped near, a movement of support, a half-smile on his face.

Then a preternatural calm descended upon Wyman, first relaxing his taut face, then pushing back his shoulders, then relaxing his fist. He made a swift noise in his throat, and then asked in a level voice, a voice as indifferent as a bank clerk's, "How long do I have?"

The sheriff checked his shave. "Rex, I just hate this

part of my job. You've been a big part of Blaine County, a real—"

"How long, Sheriff?" Wyman demanded.

"The court gave you one month to remove personal effects and to secure care for the livestock and crops."

Wyman nodded. His face was expressionless. "Well, there's nothing to be done."

Gwen asked, "What's going on, Rex?"

He smiled emptily at her. "A change of plans for our weekend, is all." He half-turned to Roger Hall. "Tell JoAnne Wilson to pack up my things, whatever she finds that she thinks I'll want sometime. Dispose of everything at the best price. Give away what she can't sell. And tell her to wrap things up in the month, then come to Boise. I'll have another position for her."

JoAnne Wilson was Longtree Ranch's manager. Roger Hall spoke quietly into his dictating machine, making digital notes of Wyman's orders.

With a playful grin, Wyman asked Gwen, "What do you say we change venues?"

Gwen abruptly understood what she was witnessing. Longtree Ranch was being foreclosed, would be sold out from under Rex by auction at the insistence of mortgage holders. The sheriff was delivering eviction documents. The guy in the suit, still standing at the second car's door, was probably a lawyer for the lenders.

If Wyman was to lose his ranch, he was done with it, right now. He would never set foot on it again.

She asked miserably, "Our weekend here? You and me, together?"

He shrugged elaborately, maybe for the sheriff's benefit. "Longtree Ranch, my home in Boise, my place in Sante Fe, who cares where we are?"

"Well . . ."

He laughed. "You choose, Gwen. Where should we go for the weekend?"

She inhaled sharply. Rex Wyman despised equivocation and hesitancy. "Let's go to Sante Fe."

"Done." He gripped her elbow and turned her toward the helicopter. He called over his shoulder, "Goodbye, Sheriff. Goodbye, Longtree Ranch."

"What about my stuff, Rex?" she asked as he escorted her to the helicopter. "My bag, my clothes?"

Without turning to Roger Hall, Wyman called out, "Have someone send Gwen's bag to Sante Fe, Roger. Don't forget the photo of her mother she always brings along." He laughed again. "The Kiowa will take us to Hailey, then my Gulfstream to Sante Fe. We'll be there before bedtime."

As they neared the copter's hatch, she asked, "Rex, how could this happen? You losing the ranch? By foreclosure? I mean, what's going on?"

He slid open the hatch. "It's just business."

CHAPTER 7

Gwen Weld followed the billionaire onto the dock. She had long legs, but even so had to break into a trot several times to keep up with him. She couldn't remember ever seeing Wyman move so fast, not physically, across a space, though she had seen him move with alacrity on a business deal. She followed him now, passing sailboats and motor yachts moored to the dock.

Roger Hall was behind her, churning his small legs. She could hear him panting, which he usually did with eagerness but was now doing for the oxygen. Hall owned a master's degree in economics from Vanderbilt, but he had the soul of a valet.

Wyman called over his shoulder, "They've done it. I knew they would, if they just had enough money poured on them."

The Gulfstream had indeed flown south from Sun Valley, headed to Sante Fe, to their romantic weekend alone—she called them *Weekends Alone Plus Roger Hall*—but midflight Wyman had received an urgent message from his robotics engineers aboard *Victory*. Her hopes for the weekend had vanished when the plane banked sharply to the west. A car had met them at San Francisco International, and so had the leading and trailing guard cars.

Wyman slowed on the dock, allowing her to catch up. "You have been the computer systems manager on the project, Gwen."

"Sure." She worked at controlling her voice. She was as angry as she had ever been, could not remember when she could feel the pulse in her temples.

"Still, you've got no idea of the effort that has gone into the boat."

By effort, Wyman usually meant money.

He continued, "I hired Oregon Automation, the research firm with a plant near Beaverton. They specialize in motors and industrial robots. I subsidized an entire division, thirty engineers and technicians, working on *Victory*'s robotics systems. The cost of this research, you've got no idea."

Yes, she did. He wasn't picking up on her foul mood.

"Me writing the checks," he said. "One after another, tearing one check after another out of the checkbook as fast as I could do it."

Wyman never wrote checks. He had a staff for the task, one that filled a floor at the WorldQuest building. Sometimes Rex liked to paint with broad strokes. He was a teller of tales. Sometimes she liked that in him. Other times, reducing the truth from his vat of words was difficult and bothersome.

Night was thick along the waterfront. The moon was hidden behind low, bruise-black clouds. Metal fixtures along the dock cast low cones of yellow light, guiding the way. Soft light came through curtains covering portholes in some of the boats.

"They told me it couldn't be done." He laughed, a rude sound that smacked against the hull of an old bull-nose Chris Craft they were passing. "But I goaded them."

She smelled steaks on a barbecue, someone on the aft deck of a cruiser cooking a late dinner. Few people were on the dock. Water lapped at hulls and pylons. Lights from Marin County across the bay were dulled by a low haze. Behind them, visible through windows on the deck level, the yacht club staff was turning chairs upside down on tables before cleaning the dining-room floor.

Wyman said, "Oregon Automation's director of research cannot tolerate an unanswered challenge. He went for it."

She reached for his arm, trying to pull him to a stop. "Rex, I need to talk with you."

He resisted for an instant, intent on getting to *Victory*. His face was first pinched with disapproval, but then it softened, slowly, as if he had to mechanically adjust the muscles in his face. He turned to her, not before one last gaze down the dock, into the night, where *Victory* lay.

She had been abiding her anger, and trying to place it in the context of a great man on a great mission, had tried to reduce the affront to her caused by the instantly changed plans. The Gulfstream had dipped its starboard wing and changed its heading toward San Francisco without Rex in the front seat even turning his head to tell her. And, worse, he had been so occupied in his radio discussion with the Oregon Automation engineer, all the way to San Francisco, that when the plane rolled up to the hangar, and he pulled open the Gulfstream's door, he had been startled to see Gwen behind him in the passenger cabin. He had grinned sheepishly, helping her from the plane, as if she needed help, and had said, "This is important"—as if that explained everything—before turning to Roger Hall to issue a list of instructions.

"I'm terribly sorry, Gwen," he said in his dulcet voice, there on the dock.

"You could have been a mortician, you sound so sincere." She despised little scenes, and she was determined not to create one, even if the only witnesses were Roger Hall and the bodyguards fore and aft on the dock, invisible in the darkness.

"I need you to trust me on this, Gwen." He moved closer to her, putting a hand on her arm. Roger Hall immediately stepped back, out of hearing range, a choreography she had seen many times. "You saw what happened at the ranch today."

She nodded.

"The damned sheriff and his posse showing up to run me off."

She waited.

Wyman said, "WorldQuest has suffered some reverses."

"The stock price, sure," she said. "What goes down will also come up."

He shook his head, the smallest of movements. "More than that. More than you know."

"This isn't the central server thing again, is it?"

"This so-called *central server thing* is going to bankrupt WorldQuest, and me with it, unless I can change my company's direction."

"Rex, I said I wanted to talk. I don't want to talk about your damned business."

"Then what?" He grimaced as he said it. "Yeah, sorry. I know what you mean. I do this to you sometimes, just go off and change the plans."

"Maybe your WorldQuest employees or the other women you've dated somehow got used to it. But I can't. I tried. I had been looking forward to our time together in Idaho for a month."

"Yeah, I know." He sounded like a penitent.

"After each long day working on *Victory*'s systems, I'd look at the calendar again and say, one less day until Rex and I can be together, alone, away from everybody else."

He looked at her, holding her with his eyes, his expression entirely earnest, his face seeking understanding and forgiveness. She felt the stirrings that had first attracted her to him.

She would not be deterred. "I just can't do this again."

"I won't ask you to."

"I can't pin all my hopes on something as unpredictable as your busy schedule."

"Yeah, it's pretty chaotic."

Her voice firmed. "It's only as chaotic as you let it be. You call all the shots. You are the big alpha, and people bend their schedules to yours. Your schedule is whatever you want it to be."

He nodded.

"I'm always the expendable appointment," she said. "You get a call—it could be from anyone, a senator or a prime minister or Bill Gates or the king of Prussia— and off you go, off in your jet, who knows where, and there I sit again, waiting. Eventually a dozen red roses will show up. At least I can count on that."

He rubbed his temple. "Yeah, I'm pretty bad that way, I know."

"Rex, who knows what'll happen between you and me. Maybe we're made for each other, maybe we're not. It could go either way. But I think we ought to give it a chance, see what happens."

"I think so, too." He reached for her hands and held them in both of his.

"I can't do this again, Rex. I just don't have it in me."

He said carefully, "I need to ask that you put up with this craziness until the race is underway. It begins in one week. Let's get *Victory* underway, let's show our stuff in the race."

"And after that?"

"Things change."

"A weekend alone will mean a weekend alone?"

"I promise, yes."

She nodded, accepting the promise because she believed him, sort of, and because she had no other choice.

They began again toward *Victory*, Roger Hall following.

Now that she had exacted the pledge, she could show she was still the company woman. "It can't be that serious, Rex."

He was gallant. He didn't take her up on her offer to immediately resume WorldQuest talk. He held her hand as they walked, but she knew he was about to burst with it. He had held himself in out of respect for her, letting her talk. But his enthusiasms were what had founded a multi-billion-dollar company. More than smart, more than prescient about the computer future, Rex Wyman was enthusiastic. He was a salesman, a modern-day Diamond Jim Brady, a rush of talk, most of which he meant, even if he contradicted himself again and again. She understood that his enthusiasm needed venting.

So she prodded, "The central server problem. It can't be that bad."

He lit into it. "WorldQuest has lost half its value in the past twelve months, and the decline hasn't stopped." He smiled to take the edge off his words. "The damned stock analysts have it figured out, and you should, too. Pretty soon the small investor is going to know I've blundered, and they'll follow the analysts, and WorldQuest price will collapse entirely."

WorldQuest manufactured PC operating systems and application programs, but in recent years software developers had increasingly been writing programs that ran on a central server computer and were used via the Internet. Many people believed the core of a personal computer would no longer be inside the computer sitting on the user's desk, but inside a big computer—the central server—in some faraway city. If these predictions were accurate, WorldQuest's main product—the software works inside the computer at home and the office—would go the way of the slide rule.

"But you've always adapted to new trends, Rex. You've always been a step ahead."

"Not this time." He rubbed the corner of his eye. "I saw the shift too late."

She reached for his hand. A seal barked, probably hauled out down at the end of the dock.

"I've rolled the dice with *Victory*, Gwen. Its integrated system is going to make or break me."

She was enjoying this, even if it was about business. They were so seldom alone, and while she had heard much from Rex regarding his ambitions, he seldom spoke of his fears.

"The high-end sailboat market isn't big, Rex." She was teasing him, holding his hand.

He might have known it, but was a born pedagogue, and couldn't help himself. "Nobody'll buy the system for a sailboat. It's the big universities, the prisons, the military bases, the skyscrapers. Those'll be my customers."

"Don't forget the sewage plants." It was an attempt to make him laugh.

As usual, though, his earnestness was hard to dislodge. "*Victory*, and all its subsystems, is the next big step, Gwen. It's the human brain."

"It's not the brain," she said. "I'm the systems engineer, so I know better than most."

"It's damn close. It's artificial intelligence."

She insisted, "You are selling yourself your own vision statement, and it's not quite accurate. What if your customers view *Victory* and the Pacific Winter Challenge as a 'vainglorious waste of vast sums of money on a foolhardy and dangerous stunt'?"

He shook his head. "I read that jerk's column in the *San Francisco Chronicle*, too. Vainglorious, he said. I'm tempted to buy the newspaper just so I can fire him."

"You just lost Longtree Ranch. I don't think you'll be buying any newspapers."

"It's more than the ranch, you know."

She shook her head.

His face was open and undefended, "Ever heard of the trans-Caucasian pipeline?"

"An oil venture?"

"Natural gas. I invested in it with a Russian company named Mid Asia Transport. Solid people with connection all the way up to the Kremlin."

"What happened?"

"I'm not sure," Wyman said. "Three years ago I put two hundred million dollars into the project to build a natural gas pipeline from Russia's Irkutsk region, through Mongolia, China, and Korea to Japan, three thousand miles. There is enough natural gas in the Irkutsk field to meet Japan's entire needs for ten years."

"So your investment has disappeared?"

"Sometimes Mid Asia answers its telephone, sometimes they don't. I've sent some people over there to check, but . . ." He shrugged. "It's gone, I think. The corruption over there was beyond my understanding."

Two hundred million dollars. Wyman might have been speaking a foreign language, so incomprehensible were these figures.

Wyman added, "There's been a couple other things gone sour. Big losses."

Gwen remembered her great lesson about money. Her mother had kept a ceramic pot of coins on the kitchen counter, wherever they lived. She used it for subway money. One day when she was thirteen, Gwen helped herself to two quarters. She wanted to go over to Mike's Candy and Soda shop during lunch with her school friends. She still remembered the taste of the Sugar Babies she had purchased with the money. That night at dinner, her mom asked Gwen to pick any day next week, Monday through Friday. Puzzled, Gwen picked Tuesday. "All right," her mother had said. "Tuesday morning, I'm going to get out of bed at three-thirty, and walk across the bridge into Manhattan, then up to the East Side. It'll take me four hours to walk to work. With the two quarters that are missing from the change pot, I would have taken the subway like every other morning." And her mom had done just that, arose at three-thirty and went off to work, her daughter awake and weeping in her room. Gwen had never stolen anything since. And she had never had another Sugar Baby since, either.

Wyman changed to a happier topic. "That damned Duncan Davis had a fit when he learned weather routers weren't going to be allowed." Wyman laughed.

Weather routers are professional weather forecasters, adept at analyzing satellite pictures and interpreting other complex meteorological data to determine the best course for the racing sailboat. Routers can be either part of the boat's staff or independent contractors for just one race. They work on shore and radio their conclusions to the boat. Some races, such as the solo round-the-world Vendee Globe, forbid the use of routers, outlawing weather information "specifically prepared or individualized for a single competitor," according to the Vendee Globe rules. In that race, weather data is limited to specific sources, and all information must be interpreted by the sailor. Other races, such as the Around Alone, allow the use of professional routers.

"The Pacific Winter Challenge rules state only that professional weather routers cannot be used, meaning human routers." Wyman was using wide gestures, fanning the air with his enthusiasm, Gwen's concerns about their relationship forgotten. "But no rule disallows computer routers, and they'll have never seen anything like my routers."

They came to a checkpoint on the dock, where a security agent stepped from behind the hut to shine a flashlight into their faces.

Gwen greeted Tom Sutton, and then Wyman approached a man wearing a navy-blue Filson wool coat and black jeans. The man was grinning widely, triumph written on his face.

Victory rose above them, its mast and shrouds and stays filling the night sky, its blade-sharp prow descending from the nose into the black water. Massive and silent, every edge refined, every square inch inside and out the subject of dozens of meetings and hundreds of CAD runs, *Victory* reminded Gwen of a shark. Same predatory lines. She had never told Rex, as he would have laughed, but the boat gave her the creeps.

She couldn't place the origin of the disturbing sensation. *Victory* was mostly metal and plastic, and she understood those things. If *Victory*'s components were laid out in some hangar somewhere, she could've walked among them with equanimity. But it was the sum of the ship, sitting there dockside, placid and bobbing, that aroused wariness and a touch of revulsion, and she didn't know why. Something about the boat, in its sweeping hull and its mast and lines. She couldn't name it, couldn't tell which aspect of the vessel was sending forth this impression. But *Victory* had an aura of controlled menace about it, some elemental and threatening power.

"Hi, Gwen," the man said. "Ready for the show?"

The three of them boarded *Victory* across a gangplank. The man in the Filson coat was Ramish Advani, Oregon Automation's chief of robotics. He wore his blue-black hair in a Beatles haircut. Gwen knew his delicate face masked a ferocious intelligence. Once, when she was visiting OA's labs in Beaverton, she had found him sitting in his office, staring at a framed photo on the wall. His office had no decoration except the photo, and it was of a forty-foot *Fountain* muscle boat. She had knocked lightly on the open door. He didn't look away from the blank wall. When she finally touched his arm, he jumped. "Are you in a trance, Ramish?" He had replied he was playing chess. "Where's your chess pieces and your board?" He had smiled. "I don't need them." "And your opponent?" Gwen had asked. He had replied, "I don't need an opponent either."

Now Advani led them forward under shrouds and along the port rail, passing the mast. Attached to the deck forward of the mast was an appendage never before seen at sea, and at odds with all else nautical along the dock and in the bay, a protuberance rising from the deck that any sailor would say was ghastly.

"Meet the OA 1542." Advani beamed. "Installed, up and running, and at your service."

Wyman stared at the thing. "It's magnificent."

"It's frightening," Gwen said.

Advani said, "Your challenge was this: The jibe is the most dangerous and technically most difficult sailing maneuver."

To jibe is to turn the boat downwind—the direction toward which the wind is blowing—from one side of the wind to the other.

He said, "Controlling the jibe is extremely tricky in high seas and wind, particularly if a spinnaker is poled out. Extremely close cooperation is required between the crew and the helmsman."

A spinnaker is a huge triangular sail carried as a headsail and used mostly for downwind sailing.

"As you know, the spinnaker, unlike other sails, is not attached along the length of the luff to a spar or stay. Once it is hoisted it relies on the wind to keep it up. The spinnaker is set in place with a boom known as a spinnaker pole. The pole is loose-footed, unlike the boom. In heavy seas, handling the pole is impossible, so most boats just go without it, without the additional pull of the huge sail."

Victory's spinnaker was deployed from a chute built into the forepeak, and was raised by a halyard and lowered back down into the chute by downhaul attachments. The halyard and downhaul lines were controlled by electric winches.

"So to jibe," Advani went on, "the crew adjusts the guy so that the pole is at a forty-five-degree angle to the boat's centerline, so that the spinnaker is set square across the bow."

A sheet is a rope used to trim sails. The sheet on the boat's windward side is known as the guy.

Advani said, "The crew then removes the guy from the reaching hook, and then cleats the sheet and guy.

And only now is the boat ready for the mainsail and jib to be jibed."

Gwen knew Advani and Wyman were playing off each other, reveling in Advani's success

Wyman asked, "So there'll be no crew working the spinnaker?"

"None. The spinnaker will be handled by this modular telerobot task execution system."

"That's a mouthful for a robotic arm, isn't it?" Wyman asked.

Advani said, "We call it *Stretch*."

The mechanism consisted of five tubes attached to each other with enclosed joints, the lowest tubes of the arm having the widest girth. The arm branched three feet off the deck, a second arm extended from the larger one. The arm components were entirely enclosed in lightweight titanium and plastic, and the main branch was twenty feet long. The smaller branch was half that. The system had not been affixed to the deck during the sea trials or the party to announce the Pacific Winter because it hadn't been ready yet. Gwen had no doubt that Rex Wyman had brought extreme pressure on Oregon Automation and on Ramish Advani to complete the manufacture of the robotic arm.

"It's a direct drive system, under license from Range Technology, and it uses Honeywell motors in each of the segments, so we've eliminated gears almost entirely, improving efficiency."

Wyman nodded.

The engineer continued, "You can see that Stretch is mobile, starboard to port, traveling on enclosed wheels on an embedded rail, much like a welding robot in an auto plant. So its base can come within two feet of either rail. You spent a lot of money on gross motion planning, Rex. You also spent a lot of money to make it rugged. The system is designed to operate in gale-force winds and seas."

"And the hands?" Wyman asked.

"We engineers call them end effectors," Advani replied. "Stretch has two, one on each branch. The scheme a robot uses to grab an object is called grasping planning, and Stretch's two effectors use a technology unknown anywhere else in the world, and you spent a lot of money on that, too."

"One effector holds the pole, right?"

"The spinnaker pole you see there at the tip of the main arm is collapsible, like Nelson's telescope. The effector anchors the pole, so we don't need to attach the pole to the mast by a bracket, as in other sailboats. The smaller effector, on the secondary branch, handles the guy and the reaching hook, just as a crewman's hands would."

The lower effector was a motorized vise in which four jawlike fingers moved along linear bearings.

Advani enthused, "The world has seen nothing like this hand. There's a bidirectional, wide-band optical fiber link for sending digitized strain-gauge force and torque sensor signals, combined with eye-in-hand systems that—"

"Ramish, does it work?" Wyman said, a study in patience.

Advani said with satisfaction, "It would be foolish to raise the spinnaker in this wind while *Victory* is tied to a dock. Your boat would be ripped from its moorings and would crash into the boat in front of you."

"Sure," Wyman said.

Without an explanation, Advani pulled an egg from his pocket, a Grade AA egg from the supermarket. He held it up on three fingers, balancing it there as if on an egg cup so Wyman could study it.

"At the risk of being profound, Ramish, that looks like an egg," Wyman said.

"Delicate little things, aren't they?"

And with that, the engineer tossed the egg into the air toward the bow. It soared up, arced out and away near the forestay, and began its descent, surely to splatter onto *Victory*'s deck or perhaps plunge into the water below the prow.

Until that instant, the robotic arm had been entirely inert. Gwen had thought the ungainly thing was just resting there, waiting for someone to turn on a switch. But OA 1542, also known as Stretch, leaped into life, unfolding so quickly it blurred in Gwen's vision. The upper extender, which held the collapsible pole, inclined to port, and the lower branch shot forward, its extender opening. The machine was almost silent, just a slight, quick purr.

Stretch caught the egg, plucked it from the air on the egg's descent. Just as quietly, the arm pivoted, traveled a few feet toward Advani on its embedded track, and held the egg out to him.

When the engineer delicately took the egg from the mechanical hand, Stretch returned to its neutral station and posture. Ten seconds had elapsed since Gwen first saw the egg.

"Your question, Rex, was whether Stretch works?" Advani asked.

Wyman said, "I said it was impossible, that you couldn't produce a robot that would handle a spinnaker on a jibe, but I was wrong."

"We made a wager," Advani said. "You remember?"

Wyman dug into a pocket and brought out a set of keys on a foam bobber that would keep the keys from sinking were they to drop into the water. He held them up. "You win."

He was about to hand them over, but Gwen caught his hand.

Her voice stern, she said, "Wait a minute. I'll bet you hardboiled that egg, Ramish."

Grinning like a fiend, Advani held his hand out over the port rail and crushed the egg. The white and the yolk dribbled from his fingers into the water below. Then he wiped his hand on a sock, the old bachelor's trick.

She released Wyman's hand, and he handed over the key. Advani gripped it like a life ring.

They congratulated Advani, then Gwen followed Wyman amidships, and crossed the gangplank to the dock. Roger Hall took his position.

Gwen took Wyman's arm as they left *Victory*, walking back along the dock. She asked, "What was that key?"

"You've seen the photo of the forty-foot *Fountain* in Ramish's office?"

"Yes."

His voice was oddly low. "That was the key to that boat. I reward success." He waited a beat then added, "And I punish failure."

Gwen didn't know who Rex was talking about, punishing failure, maybe no one. Still, she shivered as she walked along beside him.

CHAPTER 8

What was that, a baseball?" Toby Odell asked, staring at the screen.

"Too small to be a baseball," Brady Lane replied. "Something smaller. And did you see that robot shoot out after it? It'd make shortstop on any pro team. Slicker than hell."

Odell and his employee Brady Lane were studying a flat-screen monitor. The infrared camera was on the mast of a boat moored across the dock from *Victory*. The signal was being ginned through a color correction program, and rather than the murky greens of the usual infrared screen, the monitor displayed an approximation of true colors. Gwen Weld's jacket was olive green, and Rex Wyman's hair was dark. The robotic arm was white and red.

"I'll be damned. The robot caught an egg." Odell laughed brightly and pointed at the screen. "The engineer just squished it between his fingers."

"Awesome," Brady Lane said. He was twenty-two years old, and wore five rings in one ear and two in the other. Odell had never seen him without a navy-blue wool watch cap, summer or winter. Some days

Lane shaved and some days he didn't, and there didn't
seem to be a pattern. Lane was as restless as a whip-
pet, and the only time he sat still was in front of a
computer keyboard and monitor, when a calm would
descend upon him. He had served five months in
prison for hacking into Bank America's main server
and fiddling with some files, "about four thousand
files, Your Honor," he had candidly told the judge.
Toby Odell had hired him two days after he walked
out of federal prison at Lompoc, California.

"Hard to believe he could do it, make a robot catch
an egg," Odell said. "That's what I like about Rex.
When he juices a project, it usually turns out."

"When are you going to introduce me to Gwen
Weld?" Lane asked as he watched her.

Odell said, "Brady, what are the chances of a Texas-
size meteor hitting the earth and wiping out all life on
the planet within the next five minutes?"

Lane looked at him.

"Well, there's more chance of that happening than
of me introducing you to Gwen. She's too good-
looking for you. And she's too cool."

"I'm cool in my own way." Lane laughed.

"Yeah, in ways I pay you to be cool."

Odell and Lane and five others were arranged
around the office of Wayward Souls, Inc., as they
called themselves. They had no official name, nothing
on the door of the office in San Francisco's China
Basin, near the new baseball park. The room was on
the second floor of a warehouse, with wide windows
looking across rooftops. Desks were planks laid on
sawhorses. Dead pizza and molding Chinese food lay
around in open delivery boxes. A skateboard rack was
near the door. Huge posters covered the walls, one of
a Quake demon, another of the heavy metal band

AC/DC, another of the Brady Bunch. A refrigerator filled with Diet Coke was against a wall next to a coffee machine, and the area was called the caffeine delivery station. Computers more than six months old—and thus outdated—were stacked haphazardly in the room's corners. Wiring was duct-taped to the ceiling, and hanging down here and there. There was no receptionist and few telephones. A laundry bin was in another corner, where employees could toss clothes, and a service, instituted after complaints regarding smell, would bring them back clean in a day. A bunk bed was in a corner, with no blankets, just two mattresses. As in a casino, no clocks were on the wall. The employees rarely cared what time it was.

The office was a shambles by design. Toby Odell's employees were in their early twenties, most were college dropouts. They were hardcore hackers who had jumped at Odell's offer to be paid for their obsession. Odell owned eighteen companies—media, software, entertainment—but this one, Wayward Souls, Inc., was where he spent most of his time.

Odell modestly called himself a code guy. More accurately, he had become an inveterate hacker. Hacking offered a sense of being at the forefront of computing, where he once was. It offered adventure and danger, and the Wayward Souls, with their pranks and energy and laughter, made Odell feel that he was still at the cutting edge, just as he had been when he and Rex Wyman sat in their tiny room, sharing a computer, working on their new operating system.

Not all of it was for fun. On a wall next to a poster of John Lennon was a bronze plaque that represented the CIA's Distinguished Intelligence Medal awarded to Toby Odell for "performance of outstanding service of a distinctly exceptional nature." More precisely, during the Kosovo war Odell, sitting at his computer, had caused the transfer of sixty million dollars from Cayman Island bank accounts belonging to Serbian generals and politicians to the CIA's slush fund. One minute General Itsaban Gleng was feeling wealthy, possessing four million dollars stolen from ethnic Albanians, and the next minute he had nothing. Same with twelve other Serbian leaders.

At the request of the CIA, Toby Odell juggled funds inside Russian banks, rewarding America's Russian friends and punishing its enemies. He had mixed up the accounts of Colombian drug kings so that eight months ago Eduardo Alapanta accused his second in command of stealing money, and so started another internecine drug turf war. Odell had inserted a virus into a mainframe computer belonging to the North Korea Missile Defense Agency, which rendered useless three years of missile trajectory plotting.

But hackers are hackers, so sometimes the energies of the Wayward Souls were spent on less noble endeavors. For two weeks, every time the secretary of the interior returned to his Washington, D.C., office, his screen read *Disband Department of Interior*. One day Stephen Jobs's computer at his Cupertino office began playing the Barney theme song, and wouldn't stop until Jobs rebooted. The computer monitor that displayed recipes in the galley of the Princess Cruise Line's *Grand Princess* quadrupled the amount of salt in the lemon meringue pie, causing much gagging and grabbing for water glasses at that night's dinner. The lemon meringue hack was top-ten all-time, the Wayward Souls agreed.

Odell and Lane watched the monitor. Rex Wyman and Gwen Weld disembarked *Victory* and walked along the dock toward shore. Odell manipulated a joy-

stick, and the camera pivoted to follow them. When
Odell touched a pad on the controller, the camera
zoomed, so that Wyman and Weld filled the screen.

"If you're so interested in your ex-partner, why don't
we set up parabolic dishes so you could listen?"

Odell said, "I like knowing where Rex is. I don't
care what he is saying. I've already heard enough of
his talk for one lifetime."

The Wayward Souls called Toby Odell the Grand
Synthesizer, shortening it to G.S. and sometimes to
Gees. The nicknames were an honor they had
bestowed on him, one that Odell chuckled modestly
at, but nevertheless was pleased to hear. The grand
synthesizer was a fabled hero to computer nerds, an
as yet and perhaps ever to remain hypothetical person
whose mind was in perfect harmony with computers,
and who was the great leap between human and artificial intelligence. The grand synthesizer was so
attuned to the computer that his mind melded with it.
This synthesis of understanding and intuition shattered barriers between man and machine, and
allowed a revolution in artificial intelligence. The
grand synthesizer was a science fiction concept, as
unlikely today as it was thirty years ago when it was
first conceived, but the title was a mark of respect
granted Odell by the hackers in his employ.

When Wyman and Weld disappeared from the camera's view, Odell said, "That robotic arm is a gimmick."

"Cool gimmick," Lane replied.

Odell moved the joystick. The image on the monitor panned back to *Victory*, then closed up on the
boat's prow. "See that pod, right on *Victory*'s nose?"

Lane reached for a handful of M&Ms from a bowl.

Odell added, "There's another pod like that atop
the mast."

"What are they?" Lane asked. "Radar?"

"They are modified terrain mapping devices, using laser rangefinders, designed by Carnegie Mellon with a grant from Wyman. Each rangefinder uses three laser beams, and three sets of spinning and nodding mirrors to scan the beams over the ocean's waves. The lasers measure the exact distance between the visible peaks and troughs of the waves within a sixty-degree field of view. Each wave is measured in four ways: length, height, period, and speed."

"So what does the computer do with it?" Lane asked around a mouthful of M&Ms.

"It generates elevation maps that determine *Victory*'s location amid the moving waves and rollers. The range-finders are assisted by hundreds of sensors in *Victory*'s hull that detect the presence of water at any given millisecond, so that the computer knows when a wave is passing along the hull."

Lane asked, "And the information is sent to the steering mechanism?"

"New wave maps are generated ten times a second, much like terrain maps that the Mars rover's range-finders compiled. So *Victory* knows the precise lay of the ocean all around it, out to about five hundred yards. The ship is certain of the location and direction and speed and height of all waves within that vicinity."

"Wouldn't a human being be better at that? A look-out, or the guy at the wheel?"

Odell shook his head. "In a cross sea, where waves are coming at different directions from different storms, no human can perceive all that is going on. And remember, one of the rangefinders is at the top of the mast, 195 feet high, so it can see over the nearest waves, unlike anybody in the cockpit. And in the dark, waves can't be seen by a human, except for flashing white phosphorescent crests. *Victory*'s system works equally well, day or night."

One of the hackers was playing Quake VI, Armageddon Yet Again. He was having difficulty with a monster called Angst of the Fifth Level, and his speakers were filling the office with groans and shrieks. A benefit of working for Wayward Souls was that the management—Toby Odell—didn't object to the occasional waste of time, as long as it was on a computer.

Odell said, "So the point of allowing *Victory* to know the precise pattern of waves is that more progress is made when the boat hits certain waves at certain angles."

"So *Victory*'s steering system makes continuing adjustments according to the waves it is encountering?"

Odell nodded. "Adjustments to rudder and sails. The computer is both the boatswain and the coxswain."

"Pure coolness," Lane said.

"Any blue-water sailor will tell you that you have to give with the weather because you cannot beat it."

"But Rex Wyman doesn't believe it?"

"*Victory* is designed to beat any weather," Odell said.

Brady Lane leaned back in his chair. "So what's the point, Toby? Why is Rex putting so much effort and money into this boat?"

"You ever played poker, Brady?"

"Some."

"If you stick with your current five cards, you know for certain what your hand is. But, say, if you ask for two new cards, you face thousands of potential outcomes. If you ask for three new cards, you face thousands more. This is called a combinatorial explosion."

"So?"

"A decision-making process—a simple yes or no—repeated many times quickly can expand to an immense array. *Victory* is designed to show it can handle a vast combinatorial explosion. This wave-mapping system does it, as do the meteorological processing and navigation functions on the ship."

The Quake player hooted, and another hacker rose from his chair to witness the battle on the monitor.

"When the number of choices is enormous, problems acquire strange and subtle aspects," Odell said. "They generate angles that are more than the sum of their parts. Some say only human wisdom can be relied on to make choices at this level. You need wisdom, with its component aspects of hunches and experience and faith and whatever else."

Brady asked, "So Wyman thinks his system can handle such a combinatorial explosion—so much data—that it amounts to wisdom? Artificial intelligence, then?"

"He claims that sail racing in heavy weather is the ultimate test."

"So what if *Victory* passes the test?"

"There's huge worldwide markets for such a system, everything from cars and tanks that drive themselves to prisons that run themselves," Odell replied. "Rex is betting the farm on *Victory*. Rather, he's betting his company, WorldQuest."

"Well, I'm glad I'm not going to be on the boat," Lane said, putting both arms above his head to stretch. "I'm always happier when the floor can't shift out from under me."

Odell's voice abruptly changed as he shifted from topics he knew about to those he did not. "Rex told me *Victory* is built to take more punishment than her crew."

Lane looked at him. "So you're really going on the Challenge?"

Odell glanced around the office, an environment he had created and one in which he was perfectly comfortable and in absolute command. Then he looked back at the monitor, which showed *Victory*. With a finger, he pulled at the corner of an eye.

His words were a bit too loud, as if he were trying to convince himself. "I wouldn't miss it."

Jess McKay sat at the card table that served as a desk, his laptop in front of him, connected to an HP printer on the table. The goose-neck lamp was low over his work so it wouldn't wake Sandy Ramirez, who had fallen asleep on a couch.

McKay had printed out twenty more letters this evening, each with the same wording, each containing the same addressee—John McKay—but each with a different address. He typed in another address, then pressed the printer command, and the HP began to whir again. The letter contained only twelve sentences, but he had spent a month drafting it, trying to craft the words so that a reply would be necessary, perhaps even favored. The letter had to be perfect, had to inveigle a reply.

The Internet had helped in his search. How many John McKays could there be in the world? Plenty, it turned out. He had sent emails to all the John McKays for whom he could find email addresses. That hadn't panned out. Now he was reduced to communicating the old-fashioned way, sending letters. He was working on the John McKays in Southern California. He did his address searching and letter printing late at night, when Sandy Ramirez was asleep. A couple of times in the past months Sandy had awoken and groggily asked what he was doing, and Jess had always replied he was goofing off surfing the Internet.

He wasn't goofing off. McKay was being methodical and thorough, and his goal was to mail one hundred letters a month. He would work his way through the John McKays, one at a time.

He looked again at the computer screen, at the GTE California site listing John McKays. He typed in another address on his form letter.

Ramirez spoke from the sofa. "Have you found your father yet?"

McKay sat up straight, as if Sandy had thrown water at him. He pivoted in the chair. "Damn it, Sandy, have you been reading my files?"

"We're partners. It's part of the deal."

"No, hell no, it isn't." McKay's voice rose. "My correspondence is my own business."

Ramirez sat up on the bed. "You're right. I apologize. Now tell me, have you found your dad?"

McKay chewed on his anger a moment. Then he said, "No." He turned back to the computer.

"When's the last time you saw him?"

"Sandy, this is my private affair, and none of your business."

"Sure, I understand," he said, yawning. "So when is the last time you saw him?"

McKay closed his eyes a moment. "Six years ago."

"What happened?"

McKay stared at his screen. "Damn it, Sandy."

"Yeah, I know. The world is a hard place, you know, me prying around. What happened?"

After a moment, McKay replied, "My mom died."

"Of what?"

"Pancreatic cancer. Real sudden. And then my dad disappeared."

"What do you mean?"

McKay tried a shrug. "He just vanished."

"People don't just disappear for no reason."

"My dad did. Maybe he had a reason. Maybe not. I don't know. He and I never really got along, not when I was in high school, and not later, either."

"Why?"

Jess studied his screen. He could feel his friend staring at him. "I'm not sure."

"You are more sure than you are telling me. How's that for a guess?"

"It was about my older brother, Matt."

"You have an older brother?" Ramirez said. "I never knew that."

McKay typed a word or two, hoping Ramirez would go back to sleep.

No chance of that. "Where is Matt? How come I've never met him?"

"He's dead," McKay replied in a diminished tone. "He drowned when he was a senior in high school. Drowned in a river near our home."

Ramirez was silent for a moment. Then he asked, "So what does that have to do with you and your dad not getting along?"

McKay carefully weighed his words. "I was in the same raft as my brother. We fell off in the rapids."

Ramirez rose from the sofa to step into the kitchen. He returned with a box of Wheat Thins. He opened them and dug out a handful.

After a moment chewing, Ramirez asked, "You made it to shore and Matt didn't, that what happened?"

"Yeah."

"And?"

"My father never got over it. He hung around until Mom died, then he left."

"You mean, he just packed a bag and went out the door, didn't tell anybody the reason, or where he was going?"

McKay said, "We were both at my mother's funeral that day. I went over to my uncle's home after the graveside service, and when I got home, Dad was gone."

"No forwarding address? No note? Nothing?"

McKay shook his head. He appeared to be working at the computer, and his voice had an offhand air, but he was putting every effort into parsing his sentences, and telling the truth without revealing all the truth.

"So he had just been waiting around for your mom to die before he split?"

"That's my guess."

"Has he ever contacted you?"

McKay hesitated. "No. I looked for . . ." His voice trailed off.

"You looked—what?—for your father? Have you ever found him?"

McKay turned in his chair to face Ramirez. "I looked for him, all right. Spent three months. No luck."

Ramirez rubbed his nose. "Why did he run off like that, you figure?"

"He was never the same after Matt died, and he was never the same to me." McKay's voice was the ghost of a whisper. "He never forgave me."

"What's to forgive? I don't get it? Wasn't it the luck of the draw? You made it to shore and your brother Matt didn't."

"Yeah." McKay turned back to his computer. "The luck of the draw, must've been."

"So what's the point of trying to find your father again, writing all those letters?"

"I just want him to know I'm still around, and would like to see him, is all."

Ramirez lay back down and closed his eyes. "Jess, if your dad walked away like that, he's not going to answer a letter, most likely, even if you do find his right address."

"Maybe not." McKay said dully, his hands on the keyboard. "But I don't know what else to do. I'd like to see him again, maybe just to talk."

Ramirez was quickly asleep again, the box of Wheat Thins beside him on the sofa. McKay wiped away teardrops that had fallen onto his keyboard, then began again with his letters.

Rex Wyman's Pacific Winter Challenge war room was in the marina district in San Francisco, not far from *Victory,* moored at the Harbor Yacht Club's dock. The war room looked nothing like a windowless and dark weapons room aboard an aircraft carrier or an airport's radar room, but rather was open and cheery, with windows and bright lights. Wyman made sure the five vases in the room had fresh bouquets weekly. Computer monitors were everywhere. In a nod to RAF World War II plotting rooms, an enormous map of the North Pacific Ocean covered one wall, ready to have the progress of each boat marked. A rolling ladder was near the map.

Gwen Weld was running simulations, and was surrounded by three computer monitors. Meteorological data was being transmitted by satellite to the war room. Two of the monitors were filled with constantly changing statistics that she didn't have to pay much attention to.

It was nine o'clock in the morning, and Gwen had been at this station four hours. A dozen other team members were in the room, but the place was quiet, nothing louder than computer fans and an occasional muffled conversation over a telephone. Most everybody had been here those same four hours. The Pacific Winter Challenge began the following day. Earlier in the week she had seen a doctor who had prescribed a medication for her nerves, first time she had ever taken such stuff. Rex Wyman had pledged to her that *Victory* was the safest vessel ever built. Still, Gwen could not shake off the notion she was walking toward a gallows. The medication had helped, maybe. Her hands weren't shaking, at least.

She lifted a copy of that morning's newspaper, which was filled with news of the impending race and all its festivities. People expected hyperbole from Rex Wyman, and he had obliged, saying the Pacific Winter Challenge "was the biggest thing to hit San Francisco since the earthquake."

The race had the scent of a heavyweight prize fight, with San Francisco's hotels jammed, the ballrooms booked, the limousine services busy. Wyman was promoting the race with his usual thoroughness, going so far as to commission Arlo Guthrie to compose a song for the race "like your dad did for the Columbia River," Wyman had told Guthrie. He was convinced that nothing worthwhile was ever accomplished without a balloon launch, and he was determined to have the world's first million-balloon release as the race started, so thirty employees of the Mapex Rubber Company were in the city, filling balloons with helium. Wyman had arranged that each balloon could be redeemed at a 7-Eleven for a Slurpy.

Gwen tapped the keyboard and pulled up a list from the public relations database. She laughed out loud. Rex had added yet another stunt. He had commissioned the Burpee Company to breed a red rose to be named *Victory*. My Lord, she thought, what next?

Plenty, she saw as she scrolled down the screen. The Pacific Winter Challenge Race Committee—entirely controlled by Wyman—was issuing a series of press releases, all designed to stir up interest in the race. Wyman had contracted with Waterford Crystal to design and construct the Challenge's trophy, and it was to be the largest crystal sculpture ever produced, weighing more than a ton. The press release noted that because the Challenge was a one-time event, the crystal piece would not be a traveling trophy, but would "reside proudly in the winner's home, and the homes of his children, and their children down through the generations." Another press release said that every portable grandstand in Northern California had been rented for the race's start, and that a crowd exceeding half a million people was expected along the San Francisco and Marin County shores. Another press release noted that the filmmaker John Baptiste and his crew would be documenting the race's start using four Imax cameras, a helicopter, and three boats. The Race Committee had hired one hundred face painters to draw *Victory* on children's cheeks. Two hundred thousand coffee mugs, each with the WorldQuest logo, were to be distributed. San Francisco would be burdened with more honey buckets than at any time in its history. Wyman had funded press junkets from around the world. Reporters from Johannesburg to Jakarta and from Calcutta to Calgary would be sending stories back to hometown newspapers.

Wyman had told Gwen that he was creating a great thirst in his competitors, particularly the Americans. The ocean racers were wealthy but of little note. They were invisible to most of the world. They had everything but recognition. The desire for celebrity status in someone who can afford everything else can be overpowering. With all the publicity high-jinks, Wyman had assured that the winner of the Pacific Winter Challenge would be known throughout the world. Twelve American boats had entered the race, and Wyman was delighted with the number.

Wyman knew that the foreigners wouldn't fall so easily for these manipulations, but he had tweaked them all the same. The French believe—with some justification—that they own ocean racing, and that all other nations are mere pretenders. Perhaps Wyman's grandiose and brash Americanness had been enough to spur them to enter the race, but he had gone a step further: He had announced that he would be funding the "World Ocean Racing Museum, a grand structure to be dedicated to the history of ocean racing," to be situated in . . . London. The French press howled and the French racing community agonized. And, sure enough, French-woman Genevieve DeLong had entered the race, backed by many French sponsors and the French government. News of the Challenge filled French newspapers daily.

The Italians were prodded when Wyman announced that he was going to purchase Appello Shipyard Ltd., the three-hundred-year-old shipyard in Genoa. Not that he actually planned to, but the Italians reacted as if he had besmirched their honor. Italian Carlo Scarfalo's *Duke of Savoy*, a winner of the Around Alone, was entered.

In London on a promotional tour for the race, Wyman had let slip that the legendarily perilous Fastnet Race was "much like a day sail, a comfy little cruise, except there's not much scenery." Fleet Street thundered against Wyman in particular and American impertinence in general, and he was denounced on the floor of the House of Commons in the only unanimous vote of the session. Englishman Roger Stone's *Red Rose* had entered the race.

During a press conference in Christchurch, Wyman had, perhaps accidentally, called Sydney, Australia, the capital of New Zealand. Both countries were outraged. It might have been a coincidence that both were sending their best racers, Aussie Ian Payne in *Southern Cross* and Kiwi Arnold Leffbridge in *Courageous*.

Gwen's computer sounded, an alert that she had new email. She brought it up. It was from an address she didn't recognize, and it said, "If you are the skipper of *Victory*, may I chat with you a moment?" It gave a private address for real-time chat. It was signed, "Capt. Jess McKay, 212th Rescue Squadron, AFNG, Anchorage, Alaska."

She entered the address, then typed, "*Victory* doesn't have a skipper. It has an owner. I am the systems manager. May I help you? Gwen Weld, San Francisco." She punched the keyboard to send it.

A new window opened, and a few seconds later came the reply. "A boat needs a skipper, someone in charge. Are you that person?"

She typed, "*Victory* will be making its own decisions. Why do you ask, and, if I may be impertinent, who are you?"

"My team will be asked to rescue your sorry carcasses when the time comes, and I'm not looking forward to it. This message is sent in an unofficial capacity."

"*Victory* is the safest boat ever built. I'm not worried."

"Have you ever sailed a boat before?" came the reply from Alaska.

"Sure. A twenty-nine-foot Cal in Puget Sound. Wyman is a noted ocean sailor. Why are you taking my time? I'm busy."

"Have you ever been in the Bering Sea?" Captain McKay wrote. "Do you have any conception of what the Bering Sea is like?"

She replied, "We have more information on the Bering Sea than you can possibly imagine."

"But I'm talking about you," appeared on her screen. "You, not your gimmicky boat. Do you know what you are getting yourself into?"

She hesitated over the keyboard. "We have run endless computer simulations and *Victory* has proven herself during sea trials. The boat was designed for the Bering Sea."

"What about all the other sailors you are luring into this idiocy?" McKay in Alaska wrote. "They have risen to your bait, and you are luring them into extreme peril."

"Those other sailors are free to choose. We aren't making any of them participate." Not quite true, Gwen thought as she typed. Rex had played the other racers like pianos. They were utterly helpless in the face of his challenge.

On her screen appeared, "If you lead your pack of fools up into these waters in the dead of winter, you will have much on your conscience. Goodbye."

She quickly typed, "Don't hang up on me on that pious note. You don't know anything about *Victory* or Rex Wyman. How dare you be so condescending?"

After a moment came, "My apologies. I don't tolerate fools well."

"Rex Wyman is not a fool."

The reply from Alaska appeared on her screen: "I wasn't talking about Rex Wyman."

PART TWO

Of waves spreading and spreading,
　　far as the eye can reach;
Of dashing spray, and the winds
　　piping and blowing.

—WALT WHITMAN

CHAPTER 9

Nineteen ocean racers approached the start, with the breeze flowing into the bay through the Golden Gate. The starting line was between the committee boat and a buoy, on an approximate line between Coit Tower and the east tip of Alcatraz Island. A gun sounded, alerting skippers to a new flag being run up on the committee boat, a flag with a black ball on a yellow field, indicating one minute to the start. The boats were on port tacks, and they rushed toward the starting line, their masts lined up like soldiers.

Rex Wyman was in *Victory*'s cockpit, his hands on the safety rail. "The only thing I couldn't control was the weather, but I got a break."

Gwen stood near the companionway. The wind was light but steady off the port bow, and it ruffled her hair, blowing it back over her shoulders.

Wyman asked, "How many seconds until the start?"

The Voice replied, "Thirty-one seconds."

"And the distance?"

"Seventy-two yards . . . sixty-five yards . . . sixty yards." Speakers were mounted in the superstructure near the companionway and along the sides of the cockpit.

Waves were only a foot high. Softened by high clouds, the sun was a flat silver disk sending forth watery light. *Victory*'s main and jib were perfectly taut, and its wake was straight lines aft. Nineteen masts sliced through the air on the same course. The boats jockeyed expertly, dropping back a few feet, then gaining, positioning themselves for the starting line. Any boat that crossed early would have to add a penalty lap around Alcatraz Island.

Toby Odell was sitting on a bench in the cockpit, a cup of tea in his hands. He was the only person aboard wearing a life jacket. "You could walk from San Francisco to Sausalito on all the boats, Rex."

Wyman's publicity campaign had worked. Most everything that floated in San Francisco Bay was being used for viewing the start of the Pacific Winter Challenge. Thousands of pleasure boats filled the bay, and the Coast Guard and harbor police prowled the starting lanes, keeping the spectator boats back, giving the racing boats an open seaway toward the Golden Gate.

A San Francisco fire boat sent ropes of water skyward. Tour boats were jammed with customers. The rails of motor yachts and sailing boats were lined with onlookers. Canoes and kayaks slipped among the larger boats, looking for the best viewing station. Hundreds of runabouts carried thousands of six-packs. Tugboats and fishing boats carried passengers for the show. The shore was jammed with spectators, all along the docks and parks and streets, from the Embarcadero to Fort Point. Dozens of helicopters and airplanes were overhead. One of the planes pulled a phone card advertising banner.

"Time to start?" Wyman asked.

"Twelve seconds," came from *Victory*.

"Wind?"

"Nine knots, west by southwest."

The boats cut through the water, closing in on the starting line, as evenly spaced as tines on a comb. The crews' jackets and pants were distinctive colors—blue on the French boat, green on the Australian, red and black on Duncan Davis's boat—lending the procession a martial air. The hulls were painted bright colors, and a few hulls had sponsors' logos on them. Ahead, a San Francisco police boat was flashing its blue lights, trying to round up spectator boats that were inching closer to the race lane for better views.

Wyman turned to Gwen and grinned. "Here we go, Gwen. The start."

His gaze slipped past her, over her shoulder to the aft-facing camera mounted above the companionway. It was a tiny thing, no larger than a cube of butter, its lens the size of a quarter.

She chided, "You're not supposed to look at the camera, Rex."

"It's hard not to, with so many of them."

"Maybe you went too far on this," she commented.

Toby Odell asked, "Hit count, Boat?"

"Ninety-two and a half million hits on the main and mirror sites," *Victory* replied.

Wyman had hoped for half a million spectators lining the shore, but he had also wanted a hundred million hits on the WorldQuest website, where it was possible for Internet users to choose between six cameras on *Victory*'s deck, two high on the mast (one aimed forward, and the second pointed down at the deck), and another six cameras below deck. Gwen would have privacy only in the head and on her bunk. The cameras provided streaming video in real time, broadcast over satellites. Millions of voyeurs would be along for the ride.

Victory said, "Ten seconds to the start. Nine ... eight ..."

The racing lane narrowed ahead as spectator boats crept forward. The Coast Guard and harbor police tried to push them back, but the spectator boats kept nudging the lines forward. To Gwen's eye, nineteen boats abreast would not pass through the channel of runabouts and yachts and canoes and day cruise vessels that lay ahead. Helicopters vied for space above the armada, trying to get camera shots of *Victory*'s cockpit, which was glaringly absent a wheel. A wall of green and blue balloons began their ascent from the San Francisco side.

The Voice said, "Three ... two ... one ... start."

The gun fired on the committee boat just as all nineteen sailboats crossed the imaginary line between Coit Tower and Alcatraz. *Victory* surged forward, the sails blocking out the sky above Gwen. The audience on the shore and on the spectator boats cheered, and boat horns blared, and the sound carried to Gwen in the wind.

"By God, we're under way," Wyman said, bracing his hands on the safety rail. "After all the work."

Gwen stepped to his side, intent on giving him a congratulatory hug, but he half-turned. "Roger, get Sid Paler on the line, will you?"

Gwen's breath caught in her throat. Sid Paler? He was a WorldQuest vice-president of marketing, with nothing to do with *Victory* or the Challenge. She grimaced, and quickly turned away from the rail so Rex wouldn't see her expression. She walked along the safety rail toward the bow.

During *Victory*'s construction, Rex Wyman—ever enthusiastic in his pursuits—had devoured books on Admiral Nelson. He had pressed several of these volumes on Gwen, and she had read them, not much caring about seizing the weather gauge, breaking the enemy line, and whatever else Nelson had done back in 1805 to destroy the Combined Fleet. But Gwen was left with two wonderful and human aspects of Nelson. First, whenever he—the most famous admiral in history—went to sea, he became dreadfully seasick. And second, when on land, whether in England or Malta or wherever, he always longed to be at sea again, where he no longer had to oblige the interminable portside intrigues. Nelson yearned to be cut off, out at sea, the only communication an occasional packet ship.

Maybe it was silly, Gwen hoping for the same thing, in this era of instant worldwide communication, with *Victory* bristling with antennae of all types. But despite *Victory*'s serious purpose and the rigors of the race, the notion of a getaway had taken hold in her mind and couldn't be dislodged. Two of them on a boat. Well, with just a few others. Out in the Pacific, the sea and the wind. Maybe to compensate for her increasing fear of the race, she had generated a lush fantasy about their romantic weeks at sea. Foolish, every single little increment to the fantasy, she knew it even as she dreamed about it.

But Rex's order to Roger Hall to contact a vice-president of marketing had just shattered her illusion. Rex was going to be as involved with his businesses, as plugged into his worldwide affairs, as he ever was on land. *Victory* wasn't yet under the Golden Gate Bridge, and Rex had some instruction for a fellow sitting in an office in Boise, something to do with packaging design, maybe. She tossed her getaway hopes overboard.

Victory and the other racers swept along, passing hundreds of spectator boats. Off *Victory*'s port rail was *Lion Rampant*, Duncan Davis's boat. Flying from a

crosstree on *Lion Rampant*'s starboard side was the
red lion on a yellow field. Duncan Davis had been
unable to lower his binoculars, pointed at *Victory*'s
cockpit, as if he simply could not credit the evidence
of his own eyes: *Victory* had no wheel.

There indeed was a wheel, and it was stored in a
locker below the cockpit, and could be raised hydraulically should the automatic rudder system fail. Wyman
hadn't let the press know of its existence. His shipyard,
Royal Huisman, had simply refused to build the boat
without a means of mechanically steering from the
cockpit, and Wyman had relented.

As if by command, the boats abruptly turned higher
into the wind as they rounded the northern tip of the
city, and now all nineteen boats were headed on a
bead for the Golden Gate. The bridge was closed for
the morning, and pedestrians filled the bridge deck.

Gwen moved farther along the rail. On board
Victory, in addition to herself, Wyman and Toby Odell
and Roger Hall, were two professional sail racers
hired for the Challenge. She approached one of them
at the port rail.

"I feel foolish, standing here," Jeff Chapman said.
"Nothing to do."

She smiled at him. "The first time Rex tells you to
make coffee for him, tell him to drop dead. He tries
that with everybody."

Chapman's cheeks and forehead were red and
creased, a seagoing face. His sandy hair was cut short.
His face was bony and utilitarian. His eyes were blue,
and full of life, and always moving. Chapman's callused,
outsized hands opened and closed, anxious for work that
didn't present itself. He had sailed across three oceans,
and had placed second at the Barcelona Olympics in an
Olympic 470. Chapman suffered from an unfortunate

reverse correlation between his love of sailing and his possession of money, so he had spent most of his sailing career crewing. Skippers knew they were lucky when Chapman signed on with them.

Up ahead, a police boat had stopped, and an officer in a life jacket was leaning over the rail, gesturing to the driver of a twenty-or-so-foot runabout. A second police boat, blue lights flashing, was hurrying along the line of spectator boats, perhaps in aid of the first boat.

Gwen stepped around Chapman and came to the second professional sailor hired for the Challenge, Ed Lash, known in racing circles as Fast Eddie, and indeed he was fast, finishing first in the Victoria–Maui race, and first in a Transpac, from Los Angeles to Honolulu. He owned a fifty-foot boat designed by German Frers.

Lash said, "I'm not sure I'll add the Challenge to my resumé. Me, lounging around on deck while a computer runs the boat."

"Rex says this'll be as big as Lindbergh's flight," she replied. "You'll go down in history."

Fast Eddie was a small-boned man, slight in every direction, with tightly wound muscles, and a strong, corded neck. His Adam's apple and chin were prominent. His wild black hair might have never seen a comb, and it flowed around his face in the wind. He shaved once a week, and so usually was wearing dark stubble. Once when he was a teenager, he forgot to duck, and a boom cracked into his face, flattening his nose. It had been badly reset, and now always pointed off in another direction.

He said, "Rex told me to bring a Gameboy so I'll have something to do. What kind of race is that?"

Gwen counted the crew on Duncan Davis's nearby

boat. Eighteen or nineteen of them, enough for round-the-clock sailing in hard weather. There were six people on *Victory*. Wyman had said it would be enough.

The boats moved with precision, as if on a parade ground. The race lane narrowed, the boats squeezing together for the dash past the fort and under the Golden Gate. Balloons filled the sky. The competitor nearest the San Francisco shore, *Mystery of the Sea*, owned by the newspaper chain owner Jerold Sabin, would be the first to reach the bridge, as the boats had formed a slight wedge.

Evidence of festivities were in all directions—on both shores, on the bridge overhead—but Gwen detected, she was not sure how, that the racers had already left behind the fun and celebration. The boats nosed ahead, then slipped back, then came ahead again, anxious for every advantage, already fighting for every inch of air and knot of speed. They soared toward the famous gold arc, toward the gray shadow it threw on the water below.

The best-laid plans are instantly corrupted by chance. A year of intricate planning, during which every tiny contingency has been accounted for, is reduced to nothing when the universe dispenses a touch of anarchy. And so it happened as the sailboats coursed toward the Golden Gate.

The harbor police had stopped a drunk, as common on the waters as they are on the roads, and were trying to get him and his loud passengers out of the runabout, a low-slung craft powered by a two-hundred-horsepower Mercury outboard, whose most noticeable feature was a dozen beer can holders mounted on the dashboard, each one of them filled with a beer can. The outboard's owner was belligerent in his drunkenness, as were his three friends aboard, refusing to cut

their motor and refusing to obey the police by throwing a tow line, refusing to come aboard the police boat.
The officers had called for backup, which was on its
way, a second police boat quickly skirting the spectator
boats.

Then, boozily deciding that the life of the pirate
was the life for him, the runabout's driver punched
the throttle, and his boat shot forward, offering a
glancing blow to the police boat and tossing back his
inebriated friends in a tumble. White foam blew from
the boat's stern. One of the drunks gripped a seat
back, then, still unwilling to lose his can of Budweiser,
overcompensated and fell forward onto the driver,
thereby jamming the throttle full forward. The big
engine roared, and the boat shot out into the bay. The
driver and his buddy struggled, the buddy giggling,
half-lying across the steering wheel, trying to right
himself.

At that moment, the racing sailboats were in the
narrowest part of their chute, running gunwale to
gunwale, leaping across the bay toward the bridge
and their release into the Pacific Ocean.

The runabout skittered across the water and plowed
into *Mystery of the Sea*'s hull, breaching the hull just aft
of the mast, just above the water line. *Mystery* shuddered. Cries of alarm came from its crew. Not much of
a rent, as the runabout's driver had pushed off his
friend and had just pulled back the throttle, but too
late. *Mystery*'s insides were exposed to the outside, a
basketball-sized tear in her skin, and in that instant
she was rendered unfit for the race. *Mystery of the Sea*
fell away from the other boats, its mainsail luffing.

Several television monitors were built into *Victory*'s
cockpit, and Rex Wyman had watched the incident on
a live CNN helicopter feed. Gwen joined him in the

cockpit, staring over the aft rail, trying to see what had happened.

The remaining racers slipped under the Golden Gate Bridge, and suddenly the view was to China. The entire expanse of ocean was now theirs.

Wyman pointed to the television screen. "One down, eighteen to go."

Rex Wyman had made his fortune in computers, which do little but massage information. So he had an enhanced respect for the value of better information. As the Pacific Winter Challenge began, the collection of data was well under way. *Victory* had the most advanced hull and sailing systems ever put to sea, but an error regarding North Pacific and Bering Sea weather and currents would make these advances go for naught.

The devices at Wyman's command were high and they were low. *Victory*'s central processor was receiving data from two satellites, both traveling west to east twenty-two thousand miles above the equator. These Geostationary Operation Environmental Satellites measured humidity and temperature at nineteen levels in the atmosphere, and also took infrared and regular photos.

Wyman leased the information from these GOES satellites, but he had been unable to come to the same arrangement with the National Ocean and Atmospheric Administration regarding their polar satellites, and had hired the conglomerate France Satellite Compagnie to put two TIROS satellites in north-south orbits, 530 miles above the earth. These satellites measured differences in earth's infrared and microwave radiation, which are affected by air temperature, clouds, and water vapor.

Wyman was a hard bargainer, but even so each TIROS satellite, including the launch, cost him $75 million.

Closer to the earth, three Orion P-3Bs, muscular aircraft each propelled by four Allison forty-six-hundred-horsepower engines, carried scanning radiometers—each consisting of five polarimetric radiometers contained within a gimbal-mounted scanhead drum—to gather microwave emission imagery regarding clouds and precipitation and wind vectors.

Another instrument package was on each of these same aircraft. Sea-surface roughness was measured with laser glint instruments developed by the Scripps Institution of Oceanography. The instrument determined spatial and temporal variations of light reflected from the surface, mapping slope distribution.

At Sitka and Dutch Harbor, over-the-horizon radar installations had been funded by Wyman. At each site, six meteorologists and technicians in small cinder-block structures oversaw OTH radar that reached two thousand miles in one bounce off the ionosphere, measuring surface wind, radial surface currents, and wave height and period and direction.

The racers would be dealing with three major currents in the Bering Sea: the Alaskan Stream, which ran generally west just south of the Aleutian Islands; the Aleutian North Slope Current, running east on the north side of the Aleutians; and the Bering Slope Current, which flowed northwest in the middle of the Bering Sea. Within each current were smaller, shifting currents, moving at different speeds. The trick was to catch the fastest part of the current if sailing in the direction of the current, and the slowest part of the current if sailing against it.

Wyman had purchased fifteen hundred drifter buoys, called global lagrangian drifters, which would be released from aircraft into the currents as *Victory* neared. Each buoy cost five thousand dollars, and 20 percent of them failed when they were dropped from an airplane and hit the water. Those that survived would sit on the water's surface, and beneath them were forty-five-foot mesh socks that acted as drogues, insuring that the buoys moved with the current rather than the surface wind. Instruments gauged the floats' position with GPS and measured barometric pressure, sea surface temperature, submergence, and sunlight irradiance. Data was sent by an antenna to overhead satellites.

The computer that ingested all this information was not aboard *Victory*, but was in an office building in Boise, Idaho. Its processed data—Wyman called them *decisions*—were relayed to the boat via satellite. All in all, it meant that *Victory* knew the lay of the sea and sky, whether a hundred yards in front of her prow or a thousand miles farther on, better than any other boat in the race, better than any other boat ever.

The boats raced northwest, the California coast slipping away off the starboard quarter. The wind was from the southwest, and the seas were light. *Victory* rose and fell with the modest rollers, a gentle, soporific motion. Gwen had spent an hour below in the control room, doing little but staring at screens, but feeling she needed to be at her post, a dutiful sailor, but then had made tea in the microwave and had emerged through the companionway to the cockpit to find Rex Wyman holding a knife.

She sat on the fiberglass bench next to him and said, "I can die happy now, because I've seen everything."

"This is my big reward." He held up the pocket knife and a two-foot wood stick.

She laughed. "What're the world's citizens, who are watching you this minute on the Internet"—she nodded toward the camera near the companionway— "going to think when their computer hero spends his first hours at sea whittling?"

He grinned. He was wearing a blue Gortex wind jacket and pants. "My father was in the navy for a while, and when I was a kid, he showed me how to whittle a chain from a tree branch. You carve each link so that they are connected. In the past several months, the vision of his carved wood chain has loomed large."

"You are going to whittle a chain?" She laughed again. "I'm dumbfounded. Are you trying to earn a merit badge?"

He looked at her. "I've been focused on this piece of wood for months. Working those eighteen-hour days, I told myself I could start carving it the moment my work on the project was done, and *Victory* took over. This little bough became my big payoff."

Wyman dug the knife into the stick. Parings fell to the deck.

He said, "Plus, I'm going to drive my competitors crazy. Look at them."

The sailboats were arrayed on both sides of *Victory*, though they had fallen back in the last hour. The nearest was Genevieve DeLong's *Remember the Bastille*, which most Americans took as a poke at their history, at the glorious Alamo.

"Driving them crazy?" she prompted him.

Wyman said with glee, "The race of the century is just underway, and the entire world knows the skipper of *Victory* is whittling a stick of wood."

A dozen airplanes had followed the boats to sea, but

now they were falling off and heading back to San Francisco. Unofficial escort boats filled with revelers had also turned around. The breeze was unseasonably warm, and the cockpit was comfortable. Gwen wore a knit sweater and heavy khaki trousers with pockets along the thighs. Toby Odell was also in the cockpit, bent over his laptop.

Wyman said, "Duncan Davis and Genevieve DeLong and Roger Stone and the others are all endlessly adjusting their trim, making tiny changes to sail and rudder, trying to get every last ounce of push from the wind."

Gwen looked southwest. Even at this distance, about half a mile, she could see Genevieve DeLong's black hair as she ducked under *Remember the Bastille*'s boom to eye *Victory*.

"It's exhausting work, requiring close attention, even in these easy seas," Wyman said. "And they'll hear on their radios, and maybe they've got Internet connections, that I'm sitting in *Victory*'s cockpit whittling a piece of wood, chatting with a beautiful woman. It'll just kill them." He laughed again.

The sun was hidden by high clouds, and the sea was lit by uncertain gray light. Wind stirred up a few whitecaps that topped the rollers. Haze hid the receding California coast. To the north, a band of purple clouds was releasing its burden of rain, visible as a wafting curtain below the clouds.

Wyman asked, "*Victory*, what is the distance to the rain cloud ahead?"

"Four point three miles," the ship said.

Wyman couldn't help himself. "Toby, is that cool or what?"

Odell grinned. "It's pretty cool, I have to admit."

A southbound Evergreen ship was two miles to sea,

its green containers stacked almost to the wheelhouse windows.

Wyman announced, "I think *Victory* needs just a touch more publicity."

Gwen rolled her eyes. "There is no more. You've reached the saturation point. You've purchased and cajoled and inveigled the absolute limit on publicity. There is simply not one more newspaper inch or television second to be had."

"Shows what you know," Wyman said happily.

With that, he turned to Gwen, wrapped his arms around her, and kissed her long and hard on her lips, with her sputtering a bit for lack of breath.

When he finally released her, she asked, "What was that about, Rex?"

He smiled widely. "Thanks to our cameras, that big smooch was just seen by the entire planet, and tomorrow morning every tabloid in the world will have a grainy photo and a big headline, something like LOVE NEST AFLOAT or HEADED NORTH IN A SEA OF LOVE or BILLIONAIRE AND HIS BABE."

She frowned. "So much for sailing professionalism."

"*Victory* isn't about sailing," Wyman said. "It's about business. It's about confidence in WorldQuest. So I'm going for Olympics-size ratings."

Jeff Chapman emerged through the companionway, a video camera in his hand. He walked forward on the windward side, braced himself against the safety rail, and began taking videos of the other boats.

"Do you remember the first time I kissed you?" Wyman asked.

The question startled Gwen, a subject so unlike everything else Rex was interested in. His enthusiasm showed most when he was talking with one of his product managers.

"Sure, I do," she replied. "Who could forget that, as awkward a kiss as I've ever received." She leaned toward him so their shoulders touched. To hell with the Internet voyeurs.

He laughed brightly. "I thought I was smooth."

"You were," she said. "It was the paperwork that was awkward."

He waved her comment away. "It was my lawyers."

"You were so prim and proper, not like I expected."

"You didn't seem the type to be swayed by a Mercedes or a helicopter or an entourage. I had to be careful."

"And so after our third date—you had your chef barbecue a salmon—we were sitting in front of a fireplace in your Boise home, and you said, 'I'd like to kiss you, and if you are so inclined, would you sign this?' And you pulled out a document from a table drawer."

"It was a simple sexual harassment disclaimer, saying I hadn't promised you anything explicitly or implicitly. My lawyers insisted. They don't want me subjected to legal blackmail."

She laughed. "It sure killed the mood."

"Rather, you balling up the document and bouncing it off my head killed the mood."

Wyman stopped whittling. "I knew you a long time before you knew me."

"Not likely," she said. "The entire world knew of you before you ever laid eyes on me."

"I mean, I was walking into our Boise building two years ago with Bruce Arnold, and he nudged me and said, 'There's the woman you should meet.'"

She laughed, delighted. "I didn't know that." Bruce Arnold was WorldQuest's general counsel. He drove the only Corvette in the parking lot.

"Arnold said you were the one person in the company smarter than he was, and that included me."

"Two years ago? What took you so long?"

"I watched you for a while."

She stopped smiling. "What do you mean, you watched me?"

"Don't get your hackles up," he said mildly. "Research saves a lot of time, weeds out the golddiggers and the troublemakers, is all I'm saying."

"So how did you watch me?" Her tone indicated she was not going to be easily mollified.

"I just made a few inquiries," Wyman said. "Why does that upset you?"

"I don't like snoops."

Seawater streaming along the hull made a soft sibilance. A half-dozen gulls had followed *Victory* to sea, but now they wheeled about and retreated toward land.

"I'm your employer," he said. "I'm entitled to inquire. I liked what I saw. I promoted you, didn't I?"

"Wait a minute." Her voice was suddenly crabbed. "What's the sequence of events? You decided you wanted to date me, so you snooped around, then you promoted me?"

"Well, the sequence isn't really relevant."

"I was one of four candidates for the position of vice-president for systems integration," she said angrily. "And I was chosen for the job because you wanted to go out with me?"

"Gwen, that's not—"

She stood up, glaring at him, the deck rolling under her. "Vice-presidents are in your same office building, on the same floor. Was that it? Give me the job so you could hop into my office now and chat me up, and get me to go out with you? Get me onto your office floor, then into your home?"

Toby Odell made a production of studying his computer screen, his cheeks pink.

"I promoted you because you were qualified," Wyman protested, waving the stick for emphasis.

"The four others were just as qualified."

"So I chose you. That's what a boss does."

"Your snooping around showed—what?—that I probably couldn't be bought off with the gaudy trinkets and automobiles and apartments you throw at your other women, so you thought a promotion to vice-president would work. Is that it?"

Odell looked even harder at his monitor, his hands frozen over the keyboard.

"Gwen, you are talking nonsense." Wyman folded the pocket knife. "You've been working hard, and you're dead tired, and it's making you say crazy things."

A big argument on a small boat. Gwen Weld was prickly about her hard-won accomplishments. The glass ceiling in the computer industry wasn't glass, it was bulletproof Plexiglas, yet she had shattered it, and was a widely respected computer engineer, and here Rex Wyman suggested she was given a job so he could date her. She was furious. She turned to stomp down the companionway, to leave him and his idiot whittling.

And then *Victory* hiccuped. Or something.

Without warning and for no apparent reason, the boat turned hard to starboard, its bow abruptly swinging east in a flying jibe. The boom rushed in from the starboard side, sweeping across the deck with the speed and force of a locomotive, dumping the air from one side of the sail and then immediately filling the sail on the other side.

The massive boom caught Jeff Chapman full in the chest, blowing him out over the side of the ship, his feet catching in the safety rail so that he cartwheeled out and down into the water.

Rex Wyman yelled, an unintelligible, strangled sound.

Then *Victory* jibed back, and the boom raced again from one side to the other, the sail stiffening under its load of wind. The boat was on its north by northwest course again. Ten seconds had elapsed.

Behind *Victory, Remember the Bastille* turned toward Chapman. A crewman was already preparing a sling to lift him on board. By the race's rules, the minutes spent rescuing another boat's crew would be deducted from *Remember the Bastille*'s finishing time.

Wyman didn't look aft, not once, as if Jeff Chapman had never been on his boat. Wyman demanded, "*Victory*, explain your jibe."

The Voice came from all around. "Please restate your question."

"The jibe," screamed Wyman. "*Victory*, why in hell did you just jibe, and then jibe again back to the original course?"

The disembodied voice said politely, "My last jibe was 37 degrees, 47 minutes north latitude, 122 degrees, 33 minutes west longitude, commonly known as San Francisco Bay, two hours, forty-seven minutes ago."

Gwen stepped away from the companionway and put an arm on Wyman to calm him. Toby Odell lay his laptop aside to step to the stern to watch Chapman's rescue. Roger Hall and Fast Eddie Lash came up through the companionway and joined Odell at the aft rail, pointing and speculating. *Remember the Bastille* had dumped its wind and was slowing quickly, Chapman bobbing off its starboard quarter. Genevieve DeLong herself threw the sling toward him. FRENCH HEROINE RESCUES DROWNING YANK, the headlines in *Le Monde* would surely read tomorrow.

Several seconds passed—incomprehension on his face—before Wyman could say, his voice a thin plea, "*Victory*, plot the course over the past five minutes."

"North by northwest at eight knots under main and jib, steady as she goes."

Wyman's face bunched and colored, and he sagged toward Gwen. She pushed him back toward the bench. He blindly reached out to the rail to lower himself.

Gwen said, "I'll find out what happened."

He nodded vaguely. His eyes were locked on the sea, a thousand yards or a thousand miles ahead. He stammered something, lost in the wind. His face was blank.

Gwen sat next to him and put a hand on his knee. "I'll figure it out, Rex."

He said nothing.

She added. "A glitch, is all."

Then she left him in the cockpit to go below, wondering where she would begin.

CHAPTER 10

The street was strange to Jess McKay, as he'd never before visited Anacortes, in Washington State. He drove down Tenth in a rented Mercury, the wipers working, squinting at street signs. At intersections, the channel could be seen to the north, the little ferry returning to Anacortes from Guemes Island.

Anacortes was one of the oldest towns on the west coast—at least, one of the oldest that hadn't burned down at some point—so some of the homes in the north section were a hundred years old, with Victorian touches to the trim. Built for timber barons and mill owners, these large homes with fish-scale siding, friezes, parapets, and widow's walks alternated with smaller, plain homes built a generation or two later, the homes of fishermen and loggers.

McKay drove slowly, the radio off so it wouldn't divert his attention. No one was out walking this Saturday morning. The rain was too heavy. He closed his eyes, just a few seconds. His stomach was sour and his breath was shallow. He had never been more nervous, not during the beginning days of the pipeline, not for his first jump, never. He was gripping the steering wheel so hard his knuckles were white.

Jess McKay had received a letter from his uncle Dan yesterday. The letter was vague, and sort of an apology. Uncle Dan wanted to do right by Jess, didn't matter what anybody said. The letter contained an address. Jess had boarded an Alaska Airlines red-eye from Anchorage to Seattle, and had rented a car and driven north along Interstate 5 to Anacortes.

Soggy brown leaves littered the street. The windshield wipers beat a steady tattoo. Jess slowed the car, narrowing his eyes at an address on a door, then at another. This was it.

The car pulled to the curb. He stared at the house through raindrops on the car's side window. It was a house as a face, with a window on each side of a door. The house was light blue with white trim. A wrought-iron rail surrounded a concrete porch. At the south corner was a hydrangea bush, its blossoms turned brown. A pizza-sized satellite dish was on the roof, pointed south. A driveway to the side of the house went to a detached garage in the backyard.

His father had gotten it out of him, those years ago. Matt's death had devastated the McKay family. Jess's mother was a strong woman who hid her grief and shock behind a steady countenance. His father's anguish was evident in his every word and every gesture. John McKay would live his life without another happy day, it was clear to all who knew him. His golden son was gone, and nothing would ever be the same.

As the months wore on after Matt's death, Jess turned inward. He lost weight and lost interest in school. His father was too burdened with his own grief and anger to offer help, but his mother tried to pull

Jess out of it. Even so, she spent much of her time
staring out the kitchen window.

At some point in the months after Matt's death,
John McKay began to suspect there was more to the
drowning than he had been told, more to it than the
coroner's report. Matt had fallen out of the raft in a
rapids, Jess said, his eyes locked on the floor, every
time his father asked. Jess couldn't remember any
more than that, honest. But Jess was burdened by
more than having been in the boat with his brother, it
was clear to his father. Something more was at work
on Jess. His father determined to find out.

John McKay used his wiles on his son Jess, who was
desperate for reassurance and affection and normalcy.
The father appeared to reach out to his surviving son.
Since Matt's death, John McKay had not had a thought
for anyone else, so choked with grief was he. But suddenly Jess found his dad willing to be in the same room
with him, willing to talk about a few things. A couple of
times they played catch with a baseball, as they had
before the tragedy. Hammered by guilt for months, with
no one to unburden himself to, Jess responded.

Not fully, not the entire story. But over the course of
a week, Jess let his dad know that on that terrible day
he had managed to find the shore quickly, that he had
seen Matt in trouble, that Matt had cried out, that Matt
had reached for him, but Jess was too far away to
help. Then, while Jess and his father were playing
catch in the front yard, Jess allowed that he was pretty
close to Matt that day, Jess on shore and Matt caught
in the rapids, going down. Then Jess admitted that he
might've been able to help Matt, if he'd been quicker,
and a little braver. Jess was really, really sorry he
hadn't gone back into the river after Matt. He might've
saved him, he finally admitted.

That was all John McKay needed to know. One son failed to save the other. Without a word, John McKay dropped his mitt and ball onto the grass and turned toward the house. From that moment, his surviving son was dead to him.

They lived in the same house, the three of them. Jess's mom rallied, trying to help both her husband and her son. There was no friction, in that John McKay scarcely recognized his son, except to step around him in the kitchen. A week might pass without a word between them. Jess didn't know if his mother ever tried to intercede, to talk with her husband, but if she did, it didn't work.

Years passed in this poisoned household. Then his mother drove him to college the first day of his freshman year, and Jess didn't see his father but once or twice a year from then on. In his sophomore year at the University of Washington, Jess came home for Christmas, and his father was "away on business," his mother had tearfully said. Jess didn't inquire further.

Then, later, his mother fell quickly to cancer, and his father moved away somewhere, more like running away. A real estate agent sold the Everett house within a week of his mother's funeral. Jess hadn't seen his father since.

Rain beat on the car's roof. McKay had to work to release his grip on the steering wheel. He was wearing a navy-blue peacoat and jeans. He pulled a piece of paper from his pocket and read his own handwriting. Just three sentences. He read them over and over, making sure he had memorized them.

Then he opened the door and climbed out of the car. Wind and rain bit into him. He crossed the walkway and climbed the porch. He stood there a moment, his finger paused at the doorbell. He hoped he'd be able to get his

three sentences out without breaking down. After three
sentences, maybe he could improvise.

He rang the doorbell, then squared his shoulders. A
moment passed, Jess not breathing. Then something
caught his eye, a movement to his right. He turned his
head. A shape was behind the window, partly hidden
by daylight's reflection. Jess leaned toward it.

It was his father. Older now, more gray on top, more
wrinkles around his eyes, a few wattles under his chin.
John McKay stared without expression at his son.

"Dad," was all Jess could say, not loud enough to be
heard through the window.

Then John McKay stepped back into the room,
away from the window and into the shadows.

Jess waited a moment, but the door to the house
didn't open. He rang the bell again, and waited again.
His hands were trembling, and not from the cold.

Then a car backed down the driveway, alongside
the little house, moving quickly. It was a Honda
Accord. Jess bent down to peer through the window as
it passed. His father was behind the wheel. The car
backed onto the street, then took off down Tenth the
way Jess had come.

Jess stood on the porch a moment, his gaze down
the street where his father's car had disappeared. He
took a long, ragged breath, then he stepped down
from the porch and crossed the walkway toward his
car. He dug into his jeans pocket for the slip of paper
where he had written the three sentences. He balled
up the paper and tossed it onto his father's lawn.

Lonnie Garvin pulled back on *Hornet*'s throttle to
reduce freezing spray blowing in over the bow. His
windscreen wiper cranked back and forth. Skies were

leaden, and dusk was quickly approaching, even though it was only three in the afternoon. Quartz vapor lights were already switched on, flooding the crab deck with unnatural white light. Fifteen-foot waves split against *Hornet*'s bow. The crew was setting gear, the crabber term for baiting and launching crab pots.

In the wheelhouse, Garvin's eyes worked in a practiced pattern. They glanced at both radar screens, then the three depth finders, then his LORAN-C receiver and the global positioning unit. He checked the frequencies of the single-sideband radio and the two VHF-FM radios. One of these had a scrambler to secure conversations with crab buyers regarding price and quantity. His eyes found the two closed-circuit televisions that monitored the engine room and the crab deck. Next he checked the panel alarm lights, which would blink if the water level was lowering in the crab tank, or if the fuel tank was draining quickly, or if *Hornet*'s lower compartments were filling with seawater, or if the engine room were filling with smoke, or if the diesels were overheating. He checked his compass bearings. He checked the incoming waves. Garvin's eyes never rested.

Because if they did—with *Hornet* on the Bering Sea in early winter, with his crew on the crab deck—someone would surely be killed. Commercial fishermen suffer an on-the-job death rate seventy-five times higher than average for nonfishing jobs, and crabbing in the Bering Sea and among the Aleutian Islands has a death rate twenty-five times higher than any other type of commercial fishing. Miners and loggers know their professions to be truly dangerous, yet crabbing is nine times more likely to result in death than those landside professions.

The list of things that can kill a crab fisherman is a long one. A sinking crab pot might snare an errant piece of clothing, pulling the crewman over the rail and under. A line trailing a pot might wrap around a foot and yank the crewman off the deck and into the sea. All Garvin's crew were required to carry knives so that, sinking, they would have a chance to cut themselves loose and rise to the surface. Crewmen call a coil of line on deck an *asshole*, and every rookie is told never to step into an asshole, no matter how benign it looks. The pots are held over the deck by the crane, and swing to and fro in the rolling seas, looking for a crewman's head to crush. Waves often sweep the deck, and if the crewman hasn't seen the wave and braced himself, the water will send him into the sea. A coil may become unleashed and lash the deck area like a bullwhip. The steel gaff at the end of a crab cable may come loose, and aim for a crewman. Thirty- or forty-pound tubular chunks of ice built up overhead on cables and wires may break free and plummet toward the deck. And there are other hazards, dozens of others. No more dangerous place to work exists, or has ever existed, except maybe a battlefield in a war.

Hornet had been making ice all day, wind-blown spray freezing to the boat. Garvin pressed the PA button. "I'm going to slow her down. Get your bats. We're getting heavy."

His words boomed out over the work deck. Then he used the intercom to summon the engineer. Garvin eased back the throttle even farther. He watched in the monitor as the crew grabbed baseball bats and began knocking ice off the railings and gear and the superstructure. The more ice on board, the lower the boat sat in the water, and the more top-heavy it became, making its righting angle—that amount of

roll from which the boat could not recover—less and
less.

When the engineer, Lars Anders, arrived, Garvin
said, "Take the wheel. I'm going out."

Anders was a lumbering bear of a man, over six feet
six, so he hit his head regularly aboard *Hornet*,
because few things were hung higher than his height.
His fiefdom, the engine room, had a six-foot ceiling, so
he worked bent over. Anders was a fourth-generation
fisherman who could identify and fix every errant ping
from a diesel engine and every unwanted hiss in a
refrigeration system. Anders was partial to flannel
shirts and suspenders. An anarchist's beard hid his
face. He wrapped his meaty hands on the wheel
spokes. He had to stoop to peer out the spinnaker window, a motor-driven circular glass segment that spun
quickly, throwing off spray before it could turn to ice.

Garvin put his coat's hood over his head, inserted
his hands into insulated gloves, grabbed his own
baseball bat, then opened the wheelhouse hatch and
sidled along the narrow walkway to the front of the
wheelhouse and swung the bat one-handed at ice that
had formed around the window frames. Sleet pelted
his coat. Ice cracked under his boots. He hammered at
icicles hanging from the wheelhouse overhang.

Then he cleared ice from the rungs that led up to
the wheelhouse roof. He climbed up, the boat rolling
into the wind, then away from it. Ice had formed all
around the life raft canister, which resembled a fifty-
five-gallon Pepsi can. The wind cutting into him,
Garvin hacked ice from the steel bands that held the
canister together. Otherwise, the canister might not
automatically open, as it was designed to do when it
hit water. Then he cleared ice from antenna mounts.
He banged away at the layer of ice on the wheelhouse

roof until it cracked and slid over the side. Spray froze onto his mustache. Wade Boggs's signature was on the bat.

Garvin climbed back down, then stepped into the wheelhouse to lay the bat aside. "I'm going down to the crab deck. You okay at the wheel for a minute, Lars?"

Anders replied in his subwoofer voice, "All engineers can steer a boat. Not all skippers can tune an engine."

Garvin had heard it before. "Then add some speed, and keep *Hornet* up against the tide line."

The skipper went through the hatch again, this time down the steps to the work deck. The bitter wind sought out cracks in his clothing, looking for his skin. The crew had finished with their bats, and now Ben Drum, who was known around the docks as "Bang The," was working the crane, lifting a three-hundred-pound crab pot from the stack and maneuvering it across the rolling deck.

"How you doing, Bang The?" Garvin called above the wind.

"Never been better," Drum replied, not taking his eyes off the swinging pot. He had a mangy week-old beard, brown in some spots and gray in others. He had shallow eyes, and he was missing his lower front teeth, knocked out on a crab deck several seasons ago. "We're launching one every five minutes, so we're right on target." When he was on deck, away from the alcohol in town, Bang The Drum was all business.

Lonnie nodded his appreciation. He frequently came deckside to check on the work. Except for the rookie, his crew knew crabbing, or else they wouldn't be working for Garvin. His visits to the deck were for morale, not so much for issuing orders. His crew had been already tired when they arrived at the crab grounds because as they had sailed from port to the crab beds they had ground frozen bait herring, crammed the mush into two-quart plastic containers, punched those containers with holes, and mended mesh on the pots, getting ready for the crab beds every minute they weren't eating. And now, launching the pots, they were working in constant cold, subject to battering machinery noise, and working encased in heavy, motion-limiting foul-weather gear. Garvin checked for anybody with the Aleutian stare, someone who was losing his senses under the work. It happened all the time out here.

Bang The Drum's crane settled the pot onto the deck next to the launcher, where Steve Croise rigged and baited the pot, then tied the doors shut. Croise's eyebrows were encased in ice. He was wearing a red polypropylene storm suit, as were all crewmembers. If they went overboard, the suit's color would stand out against the blue-black sea. That was the theory, anyway.

Garvin roughly patted Croise's shoulder, then he crossed the pitching deck, littered with chunks of ice, and stepped around a stack of buoys to the launcher. An open aqueduct was built into the deck, side to side, and was called the *shit chute*. Female crabs and undersize crabs and seaweed were tossed into the chute and washed overboard.

"How they going?" Garvin asked.

"Smooth as crap through a goose," Ollie Nordquist said. Nordquist guided the pot onto the hydraulic launcher, then released the derrick cable. He had a small triangular chin, a bulbous red nose, and a scraggly mustache, a disagreeable face. This was his third season with Garvin. Between crab seasons he worked, starting in February, on a halibut long-liner off Petersburg, then fished for black cod and herring and halibut on a boat based in Ketchikan, then went 750 miles north to another herring season in Norton Sound, then traveled to Sitka for one more halibut season. He did this every year. Nordquist didn't have a high-school diploma, but he often cleared $120,000 a year, courtesy of the Bering Sea and his own year-round, back-breaking work. Garvin had agreed to a 10 percent share for each crewman, except the rookie, who would receive 7 percent.

Suddenly Nordquist yelled, "A peeler. Get down."

He ducked behind the gunwale. Garvin hurried around the launcher and pushed the rookie down, so that they were below the rail, protected by the gunwale. A frothing, freezing, two-story wave came over the rail at the starboard quarter and washed the deck front to back, and for five seconds everyone and everything on the crab deck was under water. Then the water flowed over the port rail and drained through the scuppers. *Hornet* rose on a new roller, and the boat appeared to rise from the depths.

Garvin looked around. His veteran crew returned to their stations. Peelers were part of the job. Water poured off his hood and coat. The crab deck in a storm is often called the Maytag.

"You okay?" Garvin asked the rookie as they rose to grip the rail.

"I've been warmer in my life," Nick Summers said, wiping water from his face. "A few cold spots here and there, but no complaints."

Bang The Drum's crane lifted the pot up to the launcher, a hydraulic device crabbers call the *rack*. A three-quarter-inch-diameter line was secured to the pot. The line was in 150-foot lengths, and because *Hornet* was in about three hundred feet of water, two shots were tied together by a carrick-bend knot. Near the end of the line was a cork float, and then nearer the end of the line was a rubber balloon called the *trailer bag*, marked with a number, which Anders up in the wheelhouse would jot down in a notebook, along with the location of launch. And finally, at the topside end of the line was the marker bag, an inflatable plastic buoy that had a number stenciled on it, the number issued to Garvin by the Alaska Department of Fish and Game.

Nordquist looked up to the wheelhouse, where Lars Anders gave him the signal.

"All right, rookie," Nordquist called. "Throw it."

Nick Summers pressed the lever. The launcher rose up and out swiftly, sending the crab pot into the air. At the same instant, Nordquist tossed the twenty-pound trailing buoy after it. The pot disappeared below the surface, and the trailer bag and marker bag drifted away aft, rising and falling in the waves. *Hornet* would return to the pot in three days.

"What's cold?" Garvin asked the rookie, his voice loud to combat the wind. "You said you had a few spots of cold."

"Ah, it's nothing."

The kid was a gamer. Garvin liked that about him. But Garvin pressed him. "Where? Your hands?"

"Nah."

"Where? Tell me, Nick."

"My left foot. There's been some water sloshing around inside my boot for a while." One hand on the rail, he gestured with his free hand. "It's nothing."

Garvin barked, "Come with me."

"It's nothing, skipper. Honest." His words were almost lost in the wind.

"Don't argue with me." Garvin then said to Nordquist. "Hold down both positions for a minute, Ollie."

Garvin led the young man forward through a hatch, then into the small galley. The table had a rim around it so plates and saucers wouldn't slide off. Compared to the crab deck, the room was stifling.

"Take your boot off," Garvin ordered. "Let me see your foot."

Summers removed his gloves, then his coat, hanging it on a peg. He sat on the edge of the booth bench to work his bootlaces. Seafoam had pasted his dark hair against his skull. He had a broad forehead and lively blue eyes. His new beard, begun the day they had left port, was meager.

He pulled off his boot and shook it. Water splashed around inside. "A leak. It's nothing I can't fix. I'll tuck things in better."

Garvin said, "Take a look at your foot, Nick."

The boy removed his sodden wool sock. Two of his toes were blue, almost purple.

Summers shrugged.

"Can you feel anything in those toes?"

"They're a little numb, sure. But the blood'll return."

Garvin opened a locker and pulled out a large plastic basin. At the sink, he filled the basin with warm water. Then he placed it on the deck. "Put your foot into here. Your toes are only blue, not black. They'll get their color back."

Summers dipped his foot into the basin.

"What about my work out there on deck?" The galley rolled, hesitated, then righted itself. Water in the basin rolled back and forth. Hanging on hooks, cups above the stove clicked together.

Garvin shoved his hands back into his gloves. "Nick, you sit here with your foot in this bowl until I tell you otherwise."

"Okay, skipper."

He said, "You're studying marine biology down at University of Washington?"

Nick Summers looked up from his toes. "I'm majoring in it."

"Have you been on their big research vessel? What's its name?"

"The *Thomas Thompson*. Yeah, I've been out on it."

Garvin opened the hatch. Chilled wind instantly filled the galley.

"Which boat is more fun? The *Thomas Thompson*, with all the professors and fellow students and the petri dishes, or my boat *Hornet*, up here in the Bering Sea, freezing your toes off?"

Summers laughed. "This boat, for sure."

Garvin grinned and said, "Damn straight," and left him there to return to the crab deck.

CHAPTER 11

S o you can't find the front end or the back end?" Gwen Weld asked into a headset microphone. She had been in the boat's control room fourteen hours. She was speaking with *Victory*'s chief software architect, Rick Gagliardi, who was in Boise, and who was staring at screens containing the same content as Gwen's.

In Gwen's ear came, "You sure you and the boss weren't imagining it, maybe a little too much wine at lunch?"

"Ask Jeff Chapman if we were imagining it." She was too tired to be cross with Rick Gagliardi, and she knew he had been working as hard as she had. "Chapman is in a San Francisco hospital with a broken arm. He wasn't imagining the jibe that pitched him into the water."

She could almost see Gagliardi grimace in frustration. Rex Wyman had lit into Gagliardi, firing him three times in the course of a fifteen-minute tirade, and then rehiring him just before ending the link. Eighty programmers and engineers were working with Gagliardi, trying to find the bug.

From Boise came, "What I'm saying is that we can't find any trace of code that sent *Victory* into the jibe, and I can't find any evidence in the recorders that the jibe ever happened."

"Me, neither," she said. "So it's as if the jibe couldn't have occurred, and didn't occur."

"But you tell me it did," Gagliardi said. Chapman's broken arm or no, the software engineer was skeptical. For him, nothing existed unless it could be found in code.

"This may be a one-time event." Gwen fiddled with her headset, which she had been wearing so long that the sides of her head were sore.

"You know as well as I do that if a bug is in the code, or if a virus has entered the program, it is still there," Gagliardi said. "They come, but they don't go."

Gwen replied, "Yeah, well, I'm going to go to my bunk and sleep ten hours. I'm exhausted."

"Drink more coffee," Gagliardi said into her ears. "I need your help. My ass is on the line here."

"So is mine," she said.

"I've never before heard Rex yell like that. Man, he was frothing. I could feel his spit over here in Boise."

She said, "He has calmed down." Some.

"I was tempted to quit WorldQuest, him yelling at me like that. Life's too short. I don't know why I didn't just up and quit."

"Three hundred big ones a year and stock options is why you didn't quit, Rick."

He laughed in a small way. "Yeah. That's it exactly."

Gwen's eyes were grainy and her back ached.

Gagliardi said, "But Rex was yelling at me over the link, and I thought he was going to drop over dead like a rabid dog, he was so worked up. He was incoherent."

"He's under a lot of pressure."

"Yeah." Gagliardi could put a lot of sarcasm into one word, but must have thought it insufficient because he added, "Having billions of dollars can be a challenge."

Gwen said she would return to her station in five minutes to continue working with Gagliardi, then she slipped the set off her head. The floor shifted under her as *Victory* adjusted to the wind. She gripped the table to help herself stand, then she reached for her empty cup. She had drunk so much coffee her fingers were trembling. All around, monitors displayed information regarding *Victory*, entirely benign and colorful displays, and those monitors were served by mainland computers. In those computers was a little tic—a slight thing perhaps, a few Xs where Os should be—that had cost *Victory* a crewman. And Gwen Weld couldn't find those Xs.

She moved forward through the hatch along the gangway, through a watertight hatch into *Victory*'s small living area, a combined salon and galley. The boat had a tiny crew, so, unlike conditions aboard other racers, each of *Victory*'s crewpersons had a small cabin, rather than a bunk or, worse, a hot bunk. But despite the few people on board, and despite *Victory*'s grand dimensions—155-foot length overall with a thirty-foot draft—below decks was cramped. While any other megayacht would have third and fourth and fifth heads, an owner's office, a spacious dining room, foyers, laundry, crew lounge, and sauna, much of *Victory*'s interior was taken up with machinery compartments.

As a safety measure, *Victory* had two watertight hatches dividing the vessel into three compartments, each of which could be sealed off against the sea if the hull or deck were broached. The hatches slid side-to-side, and could be controlled hydraulically through the computer systems, or manually with a spoked wheel. She had seen the hatches tested. They could move quickly, sealing off an area before water flooded it. *Victory* would still float with two of the three compartments filled with seawater.

The forepeak—separated from the amidships living area by a watertight hatch—contained the hydraulic power packs, filtration systems and cylinders that ran the winches, the roller furlers, and the robotic arm. Also in the forepeak were a tool room, storerooms, pantry, and the sail compartments. *Victory* was equipped with seven different jibs and three different spinnakers. The anchor locker was at the foremost tip of the boat.

Aft of the machinery compartments but forward of the living area were the small crew cabins. Wyman had made sure that his was no larger than anyone else's. Each cabin held a narrow berth, a small dresser, and a hanging locker. Gwen's berth had a lee cloth, which kept her from rolling out and falling to the deck when the boat heeled over. Rex had installed a crystal single-stem vase in her room, attached to the dresser. He had put a rose into it when she wasn't looking.

Gwen stepped over the base of a hatch into the living area. Rex Wyman and Toby Odell and the others were topside. The space was overlit by fixtures. Only a few small portholes allowed in natural light. A curved settee was in front of a dining table. The strip around the table that prevents plates from falling off when the boat is at heel is called the *fiddle*, and Gwen smiled at the word. Sailors won't use a normal word when a nautical one is available. Wyman was a dictionary of such terms, and he insisted on their proper use. A bookcase and magazine rack and a few other pieces of utilitarian furniture filled the area. On the aft side was the interview area, set up with stage lights and two cameras. Painted on the bulkhead behind the stool for the interviewee was the WorldQuest logo. Rex wanted the salon to be nautical, so he had installed an old-fashioned brass clock and barometer—the sailor's predictor of misery—on a bulkhead, but he had also put one flat-panel display on the bulkhead near the dining table. It currently was displaying a photo of the Sahara desert, Wyman's little joke.

To the starboard side was the galley. Nobody on board was a particularly good cook, so the freezers were stocked with much frozen food. "Frozen gourmet food," Wyman had assured them. The cupboards were latched so they wouldn't fly open when the boat heeled over, as were the doors on the microwave, and on the oven, dishwasher, and trash compactor. Most of the furniture was bolted to the deck. In the salon alone, five cameras provided views to Internet viewers. No spot in the living area or galley was off-camera. Rex called cameras *video sources*.

Thousands of people—maybe hundreds of thousands—might be watching her as she helped herself to more coffee. When she was tired, Gwen liked to give herself pep talks aloud, saying little things as profound as "Come on, Gwen, get to it," or "Quit slacking, Gwen." Trouble was, those thousands or hundreds of thousands might see her talking to herself, or running her hand along her temple in frustration, or scratching herself, anything. And another problem, every time she said anything aloud, the Voice came back with "Would you repeat that, please?" and she would find herself snapping at a computer.

The deck tilted under her, and she grabbed for the refrigerator and was reminded of the axiom, *Three points for the boat, one for yourself.* Moving her hand from one railing to another, she returned aft, through the hatch toward her computer room, her coffee remaining entirely in the cup.

She slipped into the communications room, her domain on board. Sometimes the room was called the chart room, sometimes the computer room, the communications room, or the control room, all of which made it sound larger than it was. Surrounded by monitors, she lowered herself to her chair and sighed heavily. She had no clue to where to search next for the bug that had afflicted *Victory*. A jibe that couldn't be explained and of which there was no record? Where did she look for that? On her screen was a string of code titled "DW Nav AATR 42287." Maybe it was here.

But also on her screen was a box containing the words, "Do you know the location of all *Victory*'s fire extinguishers?—Jess McKay, 212th Rescue Squadron."

She thought an extinguisher might be under the galley sink. There might be others? She entered, "Of course I do. Why are you contacting me again, Captain?"

"My friend Sandy likes your green sweater. He wants to know if it is from Nordstrom. He might get one for his girlfriend."

"You are saying you think all the cameras on *Victory* are silly. I happen to agree. Answer my question: Why are you contacting me again?"

"Sailboats are like spouses," appeared on Gwen's screen. "Everything works better if you love your boat. Do you?"

"I don't love inanimate objects. I love people, and very few of those. You want to chat, is that it, Captain?

You must have time on your hands. Nobody for your Rescue Squad to rescue up in Alaska?"

"My guess is that you don't love *Victory* because it isn't really a boat," McKay wrote.

"If *Victory* isn't a boat, what am I traveling on . . ." She looked at a screen, then added, "at 13.43 knots?"

"Where are *Victory*'s sheer lines and overhangs, tumblehomes, the lovely turn to the bilge, the deck camber, all those things that make a boat a boat?"

With her mouse she highlighted the word *tumblehome*, then made three clicks. Her computer defined the word as the inward and upward slope in the middle of a hull.

Captain McKay continued, "*Victory* has a shallow bottom to reduce water friction. It has great width. Speed is not only a function of hull shape, but also of weight. So *Victory* has a thinner hull than most boats, which means it weighs less, which requires less ballast, which in turn saves even more weight. *Victory* is more a surfboard than a boat."

She knew she was being petulant, but she couldn't help herself: "*Victory* is the most expensive racing yacht ever built. Calling it a surfboard indicates you don't know much about . . ." She backspaced over the last six words, then went on, "indicates you possess a vast well of unknowing." Did that make sense? A vast well of unknowing? It was snappy, at least. She hit the enter key.

A few seconds later, more of this Captain McKay's words appeared on the screen. "I do *Victory* too much honor by calling it a surfboard. In fact, it is a media center."

"Don't you have to go to your swim lessons or something?" She sent it, then laughed. She was enjoying this, being testy to a complete stranger, one who deserved it.

This was more fun than looking at computer code. She laughed again, and bent closer to the screen, her fingers on the keys, waiting for his reply.

It came: "You'll get a backache, leaning forward over a keyboard like that."

As if a brand had been applied to her back, Gwen abruptly sat upright. She glanced at the camera in the cabin's corner, one of two in the small room. It gave the captain an advantage, being able to examine her when she couldn't do the same to him. She didn't like it.

More of McKay's words appeared on her screen. "A media center, for certain. Take a look at the ways you've tricked out *Victory*. You've got all the cameras above and below decks that anybody on the Internet can tune to. Those who can't get streaming feed from the cameras can get ten-second updated photos. Wyman and the crew wear wireless microphones and their words instantly appear on TV screens and the Web."

Gwen had refused to wear a microphone.

Nothing from Alaska appeared on the screen for a moment, then Captain McKay wrote, "All this risk— coming up to the Bering Sea—on a dare from Rex Wyman?"

"Sir Francis Chichester sailed around the world single-handedly to win a half-crown wager."

"Your Web biography makes you sound sensible. And in that big green sweater with your hair pulled back, you even look sensible. How did Rex Wyman sucker you into this?"

Gwen bit down, then fired off, "You appear fond of pop psychology. Let me diagnose you, Captain. You spend time chatting with strangers like me on the Web because you are up there in Alaska and you are lonely. No real friends, no family, just alone. So you use boat safety as a façade to pester me. Am I right?"

She waited for a response. None came.

So she asked, "Is that right? You've got no support system. No real friends. No Mom or Dad to complain to."

Again she waited. Still, nothing came back. She tapped her finger a moment, waiting.

She exhaled slowly, scowled at herself, then wrote, "I didn't mean to touch a nerve, Captain. I'm sorry if I did."

Minutes passed and no reply came. She closed the box on her monitor and turned back to the code, trying to study it, looking for the bug, but for a long while her eyes wouldn't focus on the letters.

Being at sea is like being in prison. It is cramped. Little privacy is to be found, and the sailor can't walk away. A society that works well on land may become prickly at sea. Irritations mount. Slights are magnified. Another's quirks become intolerable. Nothing is forgotten, and grudges are carefully tended. The skipper determines the shipboard atmosphere. He can soothe or he can aggravate. Sometimes he is aware of his effect on the crew, and sometimes he is not.

Rex Wyman put the binoculars to his eyes. "Finally, the French woman's boat is hull down."

"You never say her name," Odell said. "Why?"

"She is pompous and arrogant, and I don't like her." He glanced at Gwen Weld. "I offer enough pomposity and arrogance for any occasion."

Odell laughed. *Victory* was on the high seas. The wind had backed astern, and a spinnaker was out, the robotic arm working smoothly, the merry wind pushing the boat along. The sun was setting on the western rim of the sea, sending forth a bronzed light that colored the clouds overhead and the boat's hull. The sea was running two-foot waves above three-foot swells. Gwen was wearing a blue fleece-lined offshore jacket and matching blue waterproof trousers. Framed by the blue and green spinnaker, Fast Eddie Lash idly wiped the forepeak rail with a cloth. Odell stepped toward the companionway, but the boat shifted, and he caught a foot on the deck, and had to grab the rail. Roger Hall was in the galley preparing dinner.

When Wyman moved forward to speak with Lash, Odell asked with a grin, "Have you seen the gossip press?"

"Spare me whatever you are going to report," Gwen replied.

"No way," he said gleefully. "With all the cameras below, the press has figured out that you and Rex have separate cabins on this boat. They are speculating that the romance has ended."

"How did it end, do they say?" She was interested, despite herself.

"The *Mirror* of London says that you've discovered the seamy side of Rex's past and have booted him out. The *New York Post* speculates that Rex has found another girlfriend, who will fly to Japan to greet him at the end of the race. Other newspapers have other theories."

"The truth is that I just need some space to myself, doesn't matter where I am. So I've got my own cabin on *Victory*. And, Toby, why am I talking with you about this, anyway?"

Odell grinned indulgently. "The truth is plain to me, even if it isn't to you."

"I just told you the whole truth."

The boat rolled a few degrees. Hydraulic and electric engines hummed, making constant adjustments, keeping the sails as taut as drumheads. A whiff of diesel exhaust from the generators carried across the deck. *Victory* had just crossed the forty-fifth latitude, halfway between the equator and the north pole, west of Lincoln City, Oregon. The wind was coming over the port quarter, occasionally veering toward the stern, and had a bite to it. Gwen's hands were in her jacket pockets.

Odell rose on his toes. "Gwen, the truth, even if you can't bring yourself to see it, is that you are beginning to suspect Rex isn't the one for you."

She was testy. "Toby, you are talking about something you don't know anything about, and you have no business knowing anything about."

Wyman joined them, and said, "There's more to this boat than even you know about, Toby."

"Such as?"

"Comfort settings."

Odell shook his head.

"*Victory* can go fast or it can go comfortable. To maximize speed, we've been running without stabilizers."

Stabilizers are hydraulically controlled pivoting fins, one on each side off the hull forward, which oppose a downward force with an upward one, and vice versa. Racing yachts usually forgo stabilizers, but Wyman had not seen the need to dispense with them because his engineers had made them retractable.

Wyman said, "Watch this." He raised his voice a little. "*Victory*, deploy stabilizers, run for least deck motion."

The speakers responded like a helmsman, "Deploy stabilizers. Least deck motion."

Gwen heard a faint hydraulic whine from the direction of the bow, and within seconds the deck, which had been rolling and pitching modestly in the light seas, became almost perfectly stable.

"It's not just the stabilizers," Wyman said. "The

rudder and sail settings are also being adjusted rapidly to allow the deck to remain on the same plane."

"But what's the point?" Odell asked.

Wyman pointed. "The top of the mast is almost two hundred feet above the deck. If you have to go up there in a bosun's chair, you'll be glad *Victory* can steady herself like this."

Odell lifted his head to gaze at the masthead. It might've been the wind playing with his jacket, but Gwen thought Odell shuddered. Wyman opened a topside locker and brought out a handful of fabric and cable and clips. He held it up. It was a bosun's chair.

"Nobody should put to sea without knowing how to climb the mast." He turned forward and called, "Eddie, rig the halyard, will you?"

A bosun's chair is usually lifted up the mast by a halyard. *Victory*'s main mast and boom were a self-furling system, the mechanism built into the boom and mast. And *Victory*'s halyard, if it could be called that, was a link-rail system inside the mast and hidden to the eye. But a line had been rigged to *Victory*'s masthead for the bosun's chair, and Wyman called it the halyard.

Wyman held the bosun's chair next to Odell's midsection. "Let's see if this fits, Toby."

"Me? I'm not going up there, for God's sake." He looked skyward again. The masthead was tiny and distant, more a part of the sky than of the boat.

"Don't worry about it, Toby. The winch does all the work. You won't even break a sweat."

His eyes on Gwen, Odell asked, "Have you been up there?"

She looked at Wyman. "Once, when *Victory* was at the dock."

Odell looked up the mast again. "I'm not going up there. Are you kidding?"

"Why not?" Wyman asked. "It's fun."

"Gravity, is why not. And there's no reason to go up there."

"Come on, Toby," Wyman insisted. "Loosen up. Put some adventure into your life."

Odell spread his hands to encompass *Victory*'s deck, and tried a laugh. "This isn't adventure?"

"It's always the same, Toby," Wyman said. "I've always had to drag you along behind me. Make the decision, and drag Toby along."

"What do you mean, drag me along?" Odell's tone was that of the schoolyard.

Wyman put on a sugary expression. "You know very well what I'm saying. Our history—the history of WorldQuest—is clear: I had the ideas, and you went along with them, but only after I convinced you."

"That's hardly—"

Wyman cut him off. "And you always came around to see that I was right. Every partnership has the bolder partner, and I was it. You can't deny it, Toby."

Gwen tried to end the argument. "There's no need for anybody to go up the mast, Rex. Unless some repair is required, it's foolish to go up there."

"Give me one example," Odell demanded.

"Our IPO. You resisted, until I talked you into it, and it took me months. Now you know I was right."

Odell smiled in a self-deprecating way. "Give me two examples."

"So what do you say?" Wyman held up the bosun's chair, dangling it in front of his ex-partner. "It'll make a man of you, something I've been trying to do for years." Wyman laughed at his joke.

Odell looked up the mast again. His face was pinched. After a long moment, he muttered, "Well, what the hell."

Gwen clucked her tongue, then moved aft toward the cockpit. She didn't want any part of the flintiness between Wyman and Odell. They had worked together in their tight little symbiotic, glorious, and poisonous relationship for years, and the result was one of the great successes of American business. Who was she to monitor their relationship? Under her feet, *Victory*'s deck was as steady as a table.

From the cockpit she watched Toby fitted into the bosun's chair. He gripped the line like a child holds the pole of a merry-go-round pony, fiercely and with concentration. The line ran from the chair up to the masthead, then back down to a stainless-steel windlass near the port rail. Ed Lash knelt next to the windlass, disapproval on his face.

When Wyman said something to the ubiquitous ears of the boat, Odell was lifted off the deck and slowly pulled skyward. His legs dangled beneath the chair. His face whitened, and his eyes were clamped shut. Midway up, his eyes opened—one eye at a time, it seemed to Gwen, down on the deck—and he extended his feet to touch the mast. Pulled by the line, he began walking up the mast in a rather accomplished fashion. Then Wyman said something else to the boat. *Victory*'s stabilizers and rudder immediately returned to their race setting. The boat slid into a roller and began to rise. At the same time, *Victory* turned fifteen degrees to port. The effect was to jerk Toby Odell out and away from the mast and swing him in a wide arc aft toward the mainsail.

Odell cried out. His legs frantically churned the air, seeking purchase that wasn't there, swinging out and around, and then he slapped against the sail. As the boat crested the roller, and the deck and mast tilted forward, Odell skidded along the sail toward the mast, the bosun's chair still rising. He smacked into the mast.

Wyman laughed, then cupped his mouth to call up, "Take it easy up there, Toby. I've got a lot of money invested in this equipment."

Gwen stared at Wyman, and so did Eddie Lash. The line slowed its pace as it neared the masthead. When he was at the top, Odell didn't tap the top of the masthead in triumph. He sat there, immobile, his legs swaying under him like ropes.

Wyman ordered the boat to stabilize itself. The winch reversed, and Odell slid down the mast. He didn't rappel down, didn't use his feet for balance, just clung to the line, his head bent forward, hiding his eyes.

The bosun's chair descended quickly. The wind was picking up, flattening Gwen's hair against the back of her neck. Odell slid down and down, and when his feet touched the deck, he jumped, startled.

His eyes opened, and his expression instantly transformed to indignation and anger.

"So how was it up there, Toby?" Wyman asked.

Odell gave him a corrosive look, but said nothing. He struggled out of the bosun's chair, then threw it onto the deck. He walked aft toward the cockpit, passing Gwen. His face was purpled with anger. He didn't look at her. He disappeared below deck.

Moving along the port rail, Gwen approached Wyman, who was stowing the bosun's chair in a locker. "Was that really necessary, Rex? Frightening Toby like that, and humiliating him?"

He waved away her comment, not looking up from the locker. "We've been doing that to each other for twenty years. One day he gets it. The next day I get it. It's how we work together."

"I'm going below to see how Toby is." She turned away.

"He'll be laughing about it in an hour," Wyman said to her back. Just as she got to the cockpit, Wyman called, "He always laughs about it later, Gwen. It takes him about an hour. You'll see."

Toby Odell wasn't in the salon or the galley. She moved forward through the hatch to the cabins. His door was closed. She tapped lightly on it.

"Toby, you want a cup of coffee?" she asked, her mouth almost on the door.

Nothing came from the cabin.

She knocked more loudly. "Toby? Cup of coffee."

She might have heard a sob, but maybe not, hard to tell with the sounds of the water rushing by outside the hull. Odell didn't open the door, so she left him there, returning to the control room, wondering about Odell, and about Rex Wyman.

CHAPTER 12

n many maps of the Pacific Ocean, the compass rose is placed in the Bering Sea. When heading north to the Bering Sea, sailors often say they are traveling into the compass rose. Early cartographers would write *Hic sunt dracones,* here lie dragons, on their maps here.

The Bering Sea is a triangle, 940 miles north to south at its longest, and 1,100 east to west at its base. The sea's north apex connects to the Arctic Ocean, where the continents are only fifty-three miles apart. The base is an arc consisting of the Alaska Peninsula in the east, the Aleutian Islands in the south, and the Commander Islands to the west.

The Bering Sea's combination of geography, hydrology, and climate make it one of the most dangerous bodies of water on the planet, where, in Joseph Conrad's term, the sea has a "remorseless fang." Much of the Bering Sea is shallow, a shelf less than five hundred feet below the surface. Because tectonic plates crush against each other, earthquakes rattle the sea bottom and volcanoes erupt. A rocky, ship-killing reef may suddenly rise, pushed to the surface by the violent pressures of the moving earth, a stony outcropping that appears on no charts, lying in wait for the unwary, and then may just as suddenly slip beneath the surface.

The southwest portion of the Bering Sea is also a plane, but much deeper, at twelve thousand feet, called the Alaska Basin. Here currents rise up and over the edge onto the shallow shelf, bringing up from the deep the minerals and aquatic plant life that feed the bottom fish and shellfish, making it the richest fishery in the world.

As winter comes, the earth's rotation and the northern hemisphere's tilt away from the sun's gravity cause the Japanese Current and the swift air of the jet stream to flow clockwise along Asia's land mass. This warm water enters the Bering Sea through the Fox Islands straits, through the Blizhny Strait between Attu and Medny islands, and through the Amchitka and Tanaga passes. Moving counterclockwise, the bitterly cold water of the Bering Current is joined by freezing water coming down from the Arctic. Ferocious storms are created where the cold hurtles into the warm.

Arctic winds flow from Siberia and Alaska. Twelve-thousand-foot mountain ranges on both continents channel and quicken the winds as they spill onto the Bering Sea. Gusts shoot down from the mountain passes onto the Bering Sea at speeds up to 150 miles an hour, called williwaw winds, flattening anything in front of them. Williwaw winds carry ice and grit, and are erratic, screaming along one moment, then abruptly still the next, then roaring forth again. Snow and ice stripped from the mountains are blown out over the water, creating a thick, mile-high film of freezing spray and snow and ice above the water. Sixty-mile-an-hour winds occur daily during the winter months. In the north, it snows in summer.

The wind pushes the waves, and they quickly become speeding behemoths. The Bering Sea's shallow bottom slows the passing waves, reforming them into chaotic mountains and valleys, turning them against each other, and piling them onto each other, and these thundering waves can grow to sixty feet.

Tidal currents are also ferocious. The moon afflicts the Bering Sea with twenty-eight-foot tides, currents that rip through channels between the islands. Raging tidal currents also cause maelstroms, which are enormous masses of water spinning down in desperate, deep whirlpools.

In northern parts of the Bering Sea, four- to five-foot ice fields cover the water much of the year, with hundred-foot-high ice knolls in some places. In April, these ice fields may reach as far south as Bristol Bay and the Kamchatka coasts. Drift ice is present year around.

In the northern and eastern parts of the Bering Sea, the mean annual air temperature is minus fourteen degrees Fahrenheit, and in the south it is thirty-nine degrees. St. Paul Island, in the middle of the Bering Sea, holds the world record for highest mean wind speed: 18.3 miles per hour. Yakutat, Alaska, holds the record for highest annual precipitation: 134.96 inches per year. Many Alaska towns on the Gulf of Alaska and the Bering Sea routinely report wind chill factors of minus fifty degrees.

More than wind and waves, Bering Sea fishermen fear most the ice fog, when intense cold transforms dense, wet air into an impenetrable film that prevents a skipper on the bridge from seeing his boat's bow or stern or anything else. The fog is blinding and disorienting.

The coast ringing the Bering Sea offers little hope

for a vessel pushed onto it by the wind, or slamming into it, lost in the fog. The coast consists of rock cliffs, sandstone pinnacles, and boulder-strewn shoreline. There is almost no chance, in all those thousands of miles of shoreline, that a crippled boat will drift onto a safe shore or into a safe harbor. Unyielding, hull-piercing rock awaits everywhere.

Only two civilian professions regularly broach the Bering sea, shippers—most often Russian, using the freighter route from the Chukchi Peninsula in the north to Arkhangelsk in the west—and commercial fishermen. On average, thirty commercial fishermen die in Alaskan waters each year. Some drown, some freeze to death.

It is said that fishermen from the old countries, Sweden and Norway, would carry rocks in their pockets, so that if they fell overboard, they would sink quickly and drown, and so avoid the misery of freezing to death.

In winter, when the crabbers are out, the Bering Sea's water temperature is thirty-eight degrees. Cold water takes heat from a human body twenty-five times faster than does cold air. A person who falls into the Bering Sea begins to shiver violently within seconds, and within a few minutes his thinking becomes groggy and confused. After ten minutes in the water, sensation in the hands and feet is lost, then in the arms and legs. At this point, he is almost incapable of doing anything to help himself, such as crawling into a life raft or grabbing a line. His mind is filled with useless wandering. Skin turns blue. Breathing becomes shallow and the pulse weakens. Oddly, people suffering advanced hypothermia and its delusions often remove their clothing, and many victims are later found naked. When the body temperature falls below ninety degrees, shivering abruptly stops. When it falls a few degrees further, the person can no longer tread water, as the limbs simply won't obey. Pulse, respiration, and blood pressure decline. After twenty-five minutes in the Bering Sea, the heart seizes up due to the cold blood flowing through it, and then everything else shuts down.

A person wearing a life vest will live half an hour longer, due to the vest's insulation. Someone in a survival suit may live several hours. If the person can climb into an inflatable, canopied life raft, he can survive for days.

The Bering Sea is not without charm. The stars appear in a vast sweep, more stars than night, as if painted across the sky with a thick brush. The sky often erupts in a luminescence, the aurora borealis, when the night sky will shimmer with iridescent green and blue curtains and bars and patches that flicker and glisten and flutter and wave, then fold in on themselves, then vanish in a bolt of brilliant white light, only to reappear seconds later in new form and color, covering the sky.

Victory and the other competitors in the Pacific Winter Challenge were headed north to the Bering Sea, to this vast basin of chaotic and bitter and unforgiving wind and water.

"The Frenchwoman is better than I thought," Rex Wyman said, binoculars at his eyes as he scanned the sea, even though he knew Genevieve DeLong and her boat, *Remember the Bastille*, were hidden by the horizon to the south. Wyman was leaning against the rail just forward of the cockpit. "And so are Duncan Davis and Roger Stone, damn them."

"Maybe *Victory*'s efficiencies aren't the huge advantage you thought they would be," Gwen suggested, touching upon heresy.

She was leaning against the Man Overboard Module in the cockpit. Next to it was an EPIRB, the emergency position-indicating radio, fitted with a flotation collar, kept in the cockpit to be thrown into the sea should someone fall overboard. Nobody had thought of it when the boom had knocked Jeff Chapman over the rail. In the cockpit were many welded attachment points so the crew could clip on harnesses. Mounted on the port side was an inflatable life raft canister. *Victory* also had a surfeit of the most important safety feature for ocean sailing: speed.

He shook his head, dismissing the notion. "Every hour that passes, I gain a few yards, inexorably. This isn't a sprint, it's a marathon." He raised the pitch of his voice. "*Victory*, position of French boat."

From the speakers came, "Fifteen point two miles directly astern."

"Position of *Lion Rampant*." This was Duncan Davis's boat.

"Eighteen and one half miles astern, four points off the stern to windward."

"Position of *Red Rose*." Englishman Roger Stone's boat.

"Six hundred yards aft of *Lion Rampant*."

The wind had freshened and had come around, and was now blowing from the west. *Victory* was close-hauled on a port tack. The spinnaker was down, the robotic arm having tucked itself in. The main and mizzen were taut, as stiff as metal. The sea was rising, and *Victory*'s bow plunged into the rolls, splitting them neatly. Wyman asked after the other racers, ticking them off, listening to *Victory* give their positions. The ship had turned up the volume of the speakers, competing against the rush of the wind.

"Seagoing mathematics dictates that the Frenchwoman and her crew will make a blunder. So will the other crews."

"How do you figure?" Gwen asked. She was now wearing four layers, and her hood was up. Her gloves were waterproof, with cuffs reaching halfway up her forearms. Her cheeks were pink.

"Every minute of every day, even in this predictable, steady wind—wind that isn't localized or spasmodic—her crew is adjusting the sheets, monitoring tension of the halyards, fine-tuning the outhauls and leech lines, shifting the water ballast, constantly, checking the weatherfax for isobar curves and bunchings, and many other things. It's going to wear them down."

"So what are the mathematics?" Gwen asked.

"The Frenchwoman's crew, on deck almost all the time, consists of two or three winchmen, two grinders, a pitman, a trimmer, a helmsman, a tactician, and a navigator. There's an old sailing maxim: The number of possible mistakes is equal to the number of crew squared."

Eddie Lash emerged through the hatch. "Rex, a lot of sailors' bodies have been recovered at sea with their flies undone. You might want to stay away from the rail."

Wyman nodded, and stepped down into the cockpit. "It's just a matter of time before the Frenchwoman and her crew make some disastrous mistake."

The boat announced tonelessly, "Coming about."

Victory suddenly swung to port, bringing the bow into the wind so that the vessel was in irons. The mizzen sail dumped its air and the main sail began luffing as loudly as cannon shots. *Victory* slowed quickly.

Wyman froze. His face was a mask of rage. He yelled, "*Victory*, explain the maneuver."

The boat's voice replied, "Avoiding a collision with a floating object."

Wyman whipped his binoculars to his eyes. He stared aft. Gwen followed his gaze. A log was behind the boat, now lifted by a roller, one end of it stuck out into the air for a few seconds, then swallowed by a wave, to emerge an instant later. The log was dark and glistening, like an alligator's back. It might have broken free from a log raft in Alaska or Siberia, and it might have been floating in the Bering Sea for months, getting lower and lower in the water, and becoming camouflaged as seaweed attached to it. Such a thing, two thousand pounds and shaped like a torpedo, hidden by waves lapping over it, could have broached *Victory*'s hull, had it hit head on. Along the wooded coasts of Oregon north to Alaska, floating logs are a constant danger to boaters. This one had missed *Victory* by a few feet.

"Resuming course," the boat said.

The bow swung back, and the sails filled again. The boat leaped forward, cutting through a roller. Spray shot into the air and was blown downwind.

"Did you see that?" Wyman hooted. "*Victory* spotted the log and took an evasive maneuver." He pumped his arm like Kirk Gibson.

Gwen grinned along with him.

"No skipper could've seen that log, not from back here in the cockpit. A spotter on the bow might not've even seen it. *Victory*'s system just proved itself."

"It did, I guess," Gwen said.

"Did I tell you it would? Did I tell the world?" He laughed joyfully. Then he brought up his binoculars again to search the southern horizon. "Maybe that log will take out the Frenchwoman, with any luck."

Gwen moved toward the hatch, but stepped aside for Roger Hall, who scrambled up into the cockpit to pass a note to Rex Wyman. When he read it, his face twisted into a ferocious scowl, from exultation to anger in one second.

Wyman's voice rose. "What's causing it?"

"Don't know," Hall replied. "Selling, of course. But we can't find out who or what is behind it."

Gwen left them there and went below, stowing her coat and gloves in a foul-weather-gear locker near her control room. She stopped at the coffeepot in the galley, then moved forward through the hatch to the cabins. The deck was canted to starboard fifteen degrees, and she walked with a short step. She tapped on Toby Odell's door. Odell had been little seen since his ride up the bosun's chair. He missed that night's dinner and was still in his cabin at breakfast. He claimed he had a touch of seasickness.

She knocked again. She heard his voice, but couldn't make out his words, so she pushed open the door. "Want some coffee, Toby?"

He was sitting on his bunk, a laptop next to him, plugged into a jack on the bulkhead. He smiled widely. "I'm still off my feed. If I drink coffee, I'll be running to the head."

She sat next to him. "I thought you were faking seasickness, Toby, and that you were down here sulking and pouting."

"Billionaires never sulk and pout." He laughed. "What would I be sulking about?"

"Being swung around the mast on the bosun's chair. Rex was being childish and cruel."

Odell laughed again. "And that's why you love him so."

She looked aft, as if she could see through the bulk-heads. "He just received some bad news, delivered in a note from Roger. I hope it's nothing to do with this boat, the only thing that separates us from the cold water."

Odell entered a few keystrokes. "I'm sure it's this: Today WorldQuest stock was off eighteen points, fully a fourth of its market value. The big board suspended trading of the stock late in the day. This follows yester-day, when it lost twelve points."

"I wonder why the price is falling like that?"

"More sellers than buyers, to be profound," Odell replied, bringing his computer to his lap.

Odell was wearing bifocals for his computer work. His green wool sweater hung loosely about him, and his feet had only socks on them. He might have been in a comfortable den rather than on a sailboat in a cramped cabin. He wore an antiseasickness patch behind his ear. Odell was slender and seemed lost in his clothes. Behind his glasses, his eyes always carried much expression, and he frequently turned away, as if he knew it and wanted to conceal it. His bald head had begun to lose its tanning-parlor bronze.

The rush of water could be heard through the hull. The cabin dipped a few inches, then rose, as the boat made adjustments to the wind.

"That's not the first time I've been banged around," Odell said, smiling. "And I've banged him around some, too."

"What do you mean?"

"It's how we work. It's always been that way. I'm not sure why, but our partnership seemed to thrive on it. Every so often, we just have to nail each other."

"Give me an example." Gwen rested her chin on her palm.

The cabin was not much larger than the bunk. She glanced at Odell's screen, which displayed a spreadsheet.

He scratched his chin. "My junior year at Idaho, Rex set me up with a blind date. I hadn't had many dates, being sort of a dork."

"You aren't a dork, Toby," she said automatically.

He laughed again. "Well, before I had my nose made smaller, my chin made bigger, and my cheekbones made higher, I was a dork, the classic computer geek."

"You've had plastic surgery?" she asked.

"Ever seen a high-school photo of me?"

"Come on, Toby." She tapped his knee. "You are killing me with this false modesty."

"Anyway, Rex told me this girl—I still remember her name, Cassandra, if you can imagine—had just broken up with a football player, and was brokenhearted, and wanted to go out with someone with brains for a change. He showed me her picture in the yearbook. Wow. Blond, big eyes. She had been the university's May Queen or some damn thing, I forget. Really a beauty."

"Rex was setting you up?"

He grinned. "So on the day of my big date with Cassandra, I did some really odd things for me, like change my shirt and trim my beard. I was wearing a mad bomber's beard back then. It looked like a rat's nest. I look back at old photos of me and cringe."

"So what happened?"

"So I show up right on time, and I'm nervous. I mean, Cassandra went out with football players."

"Yeah, but varsity football players?" Gwen asked.

"So I knock on her door, my heart thumping. At that stage in my life, I was unsure what one did on a date, much less a date with a beautiful coed."

"So what happened already?"

"Cassandra, this great beauty, opened the door, took one look at me, and screamed like she had just seen Dracula—and I mean that scream could've been heard in Japan—and slammed the door in my face."

Gwen stopped smiling.

But Odell laughed. "It took me all of three minutes to figure out that Rex had set me up. Turned out Cassandra was dating Rex—despite being a computer geek, Rex always had a way with girls, witness yourself—and Cassandra was always good for a joke, so they set me up."

"That isn't funny in the slightest."

"I look back and laugh now."

"No, you don't," Gwen insisted. "That wasn't just a little prank. It was malicious. I'm surprised Rex would ever do something like that."

"Well, then I'm malicious, too, because I gave it right back to him."

"How?"

"If you didn't think the Cassandra prank was funny, you won't like this one either."

"Try me," she said.

"Did Rex ever tell you he was arrested and spent a night in jail during his senior year at Idaho?"

She leaned closer to him. "He's never told me about that."

"Cops pulled him over late at night as he was on his way to get a pizza. He didn't have his driver's license with him, and the police found a small bag of white substance in the trunk of his car. Rex loudly protested that he'd never seen the bag before, and that the driver's license was always in his wallet. But he was cuffed and taken down to the station."

"What happened?"

"Turns out the bag contained baking soda."

"You?"

"I had removed his driver's license from his wallet, and then I'd put the bag of baking soda in his trunk."

"And how did the police know to pull Rex over?"

Odell thumbed himself. "I made a little call from a pay phone. A tip to the police from a concerned citizen anxious to rid the neighborhood of drug dealers."

Gwen shook her head. "Honestly, Toby, that's the dumbest thing I've ever heard. It was stupid and dangerous. What if Rex had panicked and tried to run away from the police? The police might have shot him."

"Rex was released the next day, after the police had run a test on the white powder."

"And your prank wasn't even clever. I'm surprised."

Odell opened his hands as if explaining foolishness. "I was a kid." He looked at her knowingly. "I'm a lot more clever now, Gwen."

Gwen had a sudden impression that her approval meant much to Toby Odell. He was trying to make light of his being swung around on the bosun's chair at Rex's command and mercy—portraying himself as strong enough so that it wasn't humiliating, just pals goofing around—and now he was searching for her favor, hinting that he was clever, tacitly asking her to inquire further. He often did that, she realized. What was this little billionaire thinking? Was there some emotion there, hidden carefully? She looked at him directly, measuring him through his eyes. He quickly turned away.

She decided to play along. "What do you mean, more clever now?"

He smiled slyly. "Ever heard of the Swan Tower in Kuala Lumpur?"

"Tallest building in the world, a hundred twenty or so stories, is all I know about it."

"Through interrelated holding companies, hidden

from the public in a way much easier to do in Malaysia, Rex owns 60 percent of the Swan Tower."

"I didn't know that."

"Not many people do. His partners—Malay and Japanese investors—didn't want his name publicly attached to the project. The Malays despise cultural imperialism. Same with investing imperialism."

"So what did you do?"

"The Swan Tower was built on a piece of ground that has misaligned karmic influences."

"What?" She laughed. "Karmic influences? I thought you were incapable of uttering such mystical words. I've never heard you mention God or a church or anything spiritual."

He said, "You laugh because you didn't have four hundred million dollars tied up in a building that a grizzly old guy in a white robe said was unlucky, announced it on the KL television stations every time anybody asked him."

"What grizzly old guy?" she asked.

"A feng shui master who intoned that the building would poison the spirit of anybody who entered it, that all the doors to the building were devils' gates. He proclaimed that the northeast side was represented by the trigram *KEN*, which means the youngest son, who is considered the weakest son, and so open to evil influences. He went on and on, cursing every inch of the building."

She asked, "So he scared away tenants?"

"The Swan Tower maxed out at 30 percent occupancy. Floor after floor of it sits empty. Rex and his other investors held off the bankers for a year, but now they've taken it. He lost his entire investment, four hundred million." Odell laughed again, looking at her, inviting her to laugh along.

She stared at him. "What was your part in it?

"I gave a hundred thousand dollars to the feng shui master's favorite charity, which was, as it turned out, himself."

She stood from the bunk. The deck moved under her, and she grabbed the bulkhead for support.

"So is that clever enough for you?" Odell asked.

"You cost Rex four hundred million dollars?"

"Yep."

"As a joke?"

"Good joke, huh?"

"Has Rex figured it out?"

"No, he hasn't."

"You ever going to tell him?"

A chuckle. "Some day, and we'll have a good laugh together. Just like we laugh about Cassandra, now that some time has passed."

Gwen gripped the door latch. "You and Rex have a weird relationship, Toby." She was being polite. Their relationship was more than weird. It was dark, darker than she had known before.

"Yeah, weird, all right." Odell clicked the keyboard. "But it worked, didn't it? He and I created a business— created an industry—out of absolutely nothing. I'm not sure we would've done it, had we not been at each other like that. Friction produces innovation, is my theory."

She left Toby in his cabin and stepped through the hatch into the salon as Rex Wyman and Roger Hall were entering the salon from aft, moving through the hatch, Wyman in front.

Just as Wyman was stepping through the hatch opening, the heavy steel hatch swept across the opening, side to side, gliding with startling speed on its rail across to seal off the compartment. The steel plate would have caught Wyman, or some large part of him, had not Roger Hall lunged forward and tackled Wyman, knocking him onto the deck and falling onto him.

The door shut loudly, a metallic slam of finality. Roger Hall scrambled to his knees, and Wyman pushed himself up to sitting, staring at the watertight hatch.

Gwen asked the boat, "*Victory*, why was the number-one hatch just closed?

The boat replied from every speaker, "The number-one hatch is open."

She tried again. "*Victory*, give the status of the aft watertight hatch."

"The number-one hatch is open."

Gwen moved to the hatch and cranked on the wheel. The massive sheet of metal slid open slowly. She was panting by the time it was back in its fully opened position.

Roger Hall helped Wyman to his feet. Wyman could not remove his eyes from the hatch. He was unsteady, swaying with the boat's roll, and staring at the hatch. His face was blanched with fear.

CHAPTER 13

Fast Eddie Lash had insisted on watches, though Rex Wyman had said none were necessary, that *Victory* kept its own watch. Gwen stood in the cockpit, wearing a harness that was clipped to the boat. Over her sweaters and pants was an ocean-racing drysuit that had a reefing hood collar, neck and wrist seals, integral booties that fit inside her boots, and an oral inflator to adjust insulation. Her gloves were also insulated, sealed at the cuffs, and had leather palms for gripping, though she had nothing to grip, as the boat was doing all the work. Her drysuit and gloves and boots were bright yellow. Gwen thought she resembled a banana.

The cockpit was self-bailing, and was small for the size of the boat, so that the area wouldn't take on a lot of water if swamped, which would push the stern down and slow the boat lifting to the seas. The cockpit's drains could clear a water-filled cockpit in less than ninety seconds.

Victory had sailed through Unimak Pass, between Akutan Island and Unimak Island in the Aleutians. The boat was now in the Bering Sea, approaching fifty-five

degrees north latitude, and bearing northwest toward
the Pribilofs. Gwen knew that yachtsmen tend to exag-
gerate wave height, that the wave is measured by comparing it to the mast, but that this is an optical illusion.
Wave height is only half its apparent height. So these
waves looked forty feet high, but were only twenty, and
were coming at the boat off the port quarter, one after
another, endlessly.

Victory soared up a wave, then fell down its backside, and when the prow lanced one of these walls of
water, green foam tumbled across the foredeck, bubbling and splashing and hiding the deck, then falling
away to the sides again as the boat rose. The wind was
westerly at fifteen knots, and some of the waves were
breaking, sending curls of tumbling white water down
their steep gray sides. Water is the only element that
offers more resistance the harder it is hit, and *Victory*,
rather than slicing through the waves, smacked them
solidly. Wind whistled in the rigging. The sky was a
vast leaden bowl overhead.

The boat was twenty-five hundred miles into the
race. The nearest competitor, Genevieve DeLong in
Remember the Bastille, was twenty miles behind
Victory, already in the Bering Sea. Rex Wyman was
chagrined that *Victory* had gained only twenty miles on
its nearest rival, and he was still apprehensive about
the two as-yet-unexplainable bugs in *Victory*'s system—bugs that had caused the mystery jibe and the
dangerous hatch closure—but the boat had since been
free of mistakes. The Boise office was still working
watch-and-watch, searching for the glitch.

He had also hired an outside consultant to look for
the problem, a company called Vi-Block, Inc., which
served dozens of Fortune 500 companies and was
accustomed to wading into an ocean of data looking

for culprit code. The company was as secretive as it was indispensable to its clients. Wyman viewed hiring Vi-Block as distasteful—turning to outsiders for help on a WorldQuest product—but he had come to believe that Gwen and the Boise office weren't going to find the bug, and this realization had added to his foul mood.

But Gwen's confidence in *Victory* had risen as the boat had gained the northern latitudes, and the weather had begun to deteriorate. The manual helm had not been raised. No one aboard the boat had bent to a winch. No one had tailed the sheets that controlled the headsail. No one had needed to secure the control lines.

Victory was doing all of the work, and doing it expertly, beyond the ability of the finest sailors in the world, who had fallen well behind in their boats. Before *Victory*'s success, doubters—and there were many of them: Wyman's enemies, the envious, and any knowledgeable sailor—had believed that sailing could simply not be automated. Water and air are dynamic and infinitely variable. A boat must negotiate waves whose form and frequency change rapidly and constantly. The stresses incessantly inflicted on the hull and rigging cannot be predicted. Or so the doubters had claimed. Now, in one of his standard interview responses, Rex crowed that there was a time when folks thought the manufacture of a pretzel could never be automated.

Her confidence had grown in more than just the boat's handling of itself. The sea unfailingly probes a boat for weaknesses. The sea will find any weak point in a boat's complex system, and will patiently work away at it, trying to repay the boat for its trespass. But the sea had found no chink in *Victory*. The vessel was implacably bound on its course, taking these rough seas with equanimity. It was no longer dueling the other sailboats, but was dueling the sea itself. *Victory* was prevailing.

Spray flew up along the rail and was blown downwind across the cockpit, wetting Gwen's face. She was entirely warm in her clothes and drysuit, but even so, those few drops of water across her cheeks made her shiver. She well knew the temperature of the water—could find it on three or four of her readouts in the control room—but it seemed even colder than those readouts suggested.

Eddie Lash came through the cockpit hatch, smiling at her. He was wearing a yellow drysuit identical to hers.

"You're up early," she said.

"Rex says the boat can check all its own systems, but I'm going to look around anyway, like I do every day." The wind flattened the hood against the side of his face. "Check the pins in the turnbuckles and the bolts securing the forestay, that sort of thing."

He moved forward along the rail, keeping one hand on the safety rail. With little to do, Lash spent his time checking and rechecking the rigging. And he looked at battery voltage meters and the generators' cooling water levels, and he examined the bilge, checking for leaks. He sampled the fuel tank with a scavenger pump, insuring that sludge was not building up on the tanks' bottoms. He used silicon spray on the furling gear, though it might not have needed lubrication yet. He examined the spinnaker blocks. He constantly searched for chafing, and yesterday had the great pleasure of climbing the mast to add a spreader patch to the mainsail. Wyman grumbled that it wasn't needed. When Lash began adding sheet leads to avoid chafing, Wyman ordered Lash to desist.

Wyman knew Eddie Lash would find little to do on *Victory*, and knew of Lash's restless nature, so Wyman had brought along another stick—a small, dried bough of a tree—and another woodworking knife, and had suggested Lash do the thing that had kept off-duty sailors busy for generations: carve a chain out of the stick. Lash had put the bough in his cabin. Gwen hadn't seen any wood shavings about, so she doubted Lash had taken Wyman's advice. Wyman hadn't gotten far with his own carving.

She passed through the hatch and went below, then hung her wet clothes in a heated and dehumidified gear locker. She moved forward along the gangway to the salon. The boat had been heeled to starboard so long on its tack that she no longer had to think with each of her lopsided steps, but *Victory* was bounding more now that it was in the Bering Sea, a rapid and steep climb as it crested a roller, followed by a swift descent down the roller's windward side, *Victory*'s deck endlessly tilting up and down so that moving around below deck had become a chore.

She entered the salon. Rex Wyman was on a stool on the port side, under bright lights. He was wearing a microphone on his shirt collar and an earplug, and was smiling into a camera, answering questions. His engineers had designed the camera so that it was gimbaled, and controlled by a gyroscope, so that the camera remained on a steady plane while the boat rose and fell. Otherwise, with a camera mounted solidly to the deck, the viewer at home wouldn't get the feel that *Victory* was at sea because the camera would tilt right along with the boat.

Wyman's smile faltered, but only for an instant. "No, I don't have any concerns about WorldQuest stock. I don't follow the price as it goes up and down."

He spoke loudly, above the sound of rushing water a few feet away, outside the hull.

He waited a moment for another question.

When it came, he couldn't prevent a scowl from taking over his face. "Listen, I'm here to talk about the Pacific Winter Challenge, not about WorldQuest stock prices. Go listen to Louis Rukeyser or somebody."

Again Wyman listened to his earplug. Roger Hall was just out of the camera's view, nodding dutifully at Wyman's words. Toby Odell was in the galley, trying to open a box of Power Bars while gripping a rail.

Two boats had quit the race. Most of the time, autopilots run the helms of modern racing boats. San Francisco lawyer Steve Roberts's *Spirit of Sewanee* suffered a generator failure—the pistons seized up due to an oil leak that hadn't been detected—so the autopilot was quickly out of action. Roberts turned back. And Aaron Lucas, inheritor of much of the Lucas Chemical fortune and owner of *Majestic*, quit the race "to spend more time with my family," as he had been quoted in *USA Today*. Wyman had laughed and said, "That's what all quitters say. Suddenly their families become important," though he was careful that his microphone was off when he said it.

Gwen entered her control room, all the monitors glowing and dozens of tiny green and amber lights always on. The place had become a refuge for her, even though cameras broadcast her every move to the Internet. Odell seldom entered the room. The professional sailor, Fast Eddie Lash, wanted nothing to do with the computers there. Roger Hall did most of the cooking, and wasn't interested in the computer systems. Wyman stopped in once in a while to ask if progress had been made in the search for the bug or virus or whatever it was, but he couldn't add anything to the work Gwen and those in Boise were doing, so he mostly stayed away.

The little room rose and fell. On one of the screens, Gwen had brought up a view of Vail skiers. The view refreshed itself every fifteen seconds. She wished she were skiing. On another screen was news of the Pacific Winter Challenge, showing a leaderboard, with *Victory* at the top. She put on her headset and reached for her keyboard to contact Rick Gagliardi in Boise when a speaker chimed and a new message appeared on her screen: "A storm is coming. Are you prepared? Jess McKay, 212th Rescue Squadron."

She replied, "It's already stormy here. But we are aware of the new weather system coming our way."

McKay sent from Anchorage, "A low-pressure system is going to make your boat much less comfortable. The northwest winds might quickly change to the southwest, and seas will begin to run across your northwest wave pattern."

"Yes, that's a possibility that we have accommodated. *Victory* knows everything about the storm. We are prepared." She sounded officious, she knew. Gwen didn't want to talk about the weather with Captain McKay, "Are you watching me right now, Captain?" she asked.

After a few seconds, "I'm one of probably fifty thousand people watching you on the Internet."

"Yes, but you are the only one communicating with me," she wrote. "And you have me at a disadvantage."

"How do you figure?"

"You know what I look like, and I don't know what you look like. If I'm going to listen to you hector me about boating safety, I want to know what you look like. I gather much information from a person's appearance."

"I have a digital photo taken by my roommate Sandy, and I'm uploading it right now."

The email arrived with the attached picture. She opened it. There on her screen was a photo of Jess McKay, but he was dressed in a jumpsuit, gloves, and boots, with a helmet over his head, darkly tinted goggles, and a balaclava that hid all the rest of his face. Not one inch of his skin was showing.

"I just received your photo, Captain. The lack of sun in the Alaska winter hasn't diminished your sense of humor, apparently." Gwen wanted to ask if Sandy were a man or a woman. Instead, "Is Sandy a PJ?"

"A PJ on adrenaline."

"Do you live with him and the others, in a barracks, maybe?" she asked.

"In an apartment. Have you and Rex Wyman had a falling out?"

"Why do you ask?"

"You are fishing around, asking questions about me, trying to determine if I'm single."

"Captain, let me assure you, I am currently dating one of the handsomest, most charming men in the world, who is also one of the wealthiest men in history. I have utterly no interest in some Air Force lifer stationed up in the wilderness of Alaska."

"Why not?"

She laughed again. The room rose and fell. She could hear the passing sea through the hull. She entered, "The truth is, it's either ask you questions, or return to work on some code problems we have here."

"The problem with the boom, the problem that sent one of your crewmen over the rail?"

"That never happened, is our official position on the subject."

"I saw *Victory* sailing through Unimak Pass." McKay's

words appeared on her screen. "Whose helicopter was it that held the camera?"

"Rex chartered the helicopter from Texaco. The helicopter is going to return to Unimak whenever one of the boats goes through the pass. It sends a live feed to our studio." She thought for a moment before continuing. "I wrote something last time we were in contact that made you disconnect. I don't know what I said—other than general sniping at you—and I don't want to make the same mistake. I'm sorry if I said something wrong."

It took a full moment before McKay replied, "It was nothing."

"Something to do with friends and family? Are you having problems?"

"Nothing that hasn't been resolved."

"Many family things are never resolved, Captain."

"Well, I appreciate your effort, but you probably don't have much of an idea what's going on with me."

Her fingers snapped at the keyboard. "On a park bench one day when she was a young woman, my mother stuck a knife into a fellow's throat, and killed him, and spent the rest of her life in hiding. How's that for family problems?"

My Lord. Gwen couldn't believe she had just written that and sent it to a stranger.

"Your mom sounds like a lot of fun," came from Anchorage. "She ought to meet my father."

"May I call you something other than 'Captain'?"

"If I'm lucky, in two years you can call me 'major.' My name is Jess."

"It's your father, is it, Jess?"

McKay's response took several seconds. "You are being kind in asking, but I don't want to talk about my father."

She wrote, "Then let's talk about your girlfriend." What in the world made her ask that?

"I am currently between girlfriends. And why are you asking about girlfriends? I'm here to lecture you about fire extinguishers."

"Did the last girlfriend ditch you? Maybe because you wouldn't open up to her?"

What kind of question was that, she asked herself. It was girlish, and why was she asking such questions of a stranger in Anchorage? She was flirting with this guy. She was too old to flirt, and too well-established, and there was nothing wrong with her current relationship. At least, nothing much.

"I've got the race on TV here," McKay wrote. "A couple more boats are approaching Unimak Pass. Can't be but two hundred yards between those boats."

She had the same view on one of her screens, a shot from the chartered helicopter. The lead boat was identified as *Bliss*, a Palmer Johnson-designed racer that was owned and skippered by Allen Wong, who had made his fortune by founding E-Auction, the online auction website. Sotheby's had just purchased 40 percent of E-Auction. The second boat approaching the south end of Unimak Island was *Southern Cross*, skippered by Ian Payne. The boat's mainsail was a stylized Australian flag.

"Those are two never-lose-a-mile skippers," McKay wrote. "They're cutting it close to the rocks off the shore."

"Maybe those girlfriends dumped you because you are inept at changing the subject of a conversation."

Jess McKay must have sensed what she wanted to say, because he asked, "Are you lonely?"

"My boyfriend is on board. How can I be lonely." It sounded hollow, even as she wrote it.

"So, you are lonely," McKay wrote back. "It happens: The more crowded things get, the more isolated the sailor becomes. The sailor turns inward."

"I guess there's a little truth to that." More than a little, she thought.

"There are three kinds of skippers: the autocrat, the democrat, and the laissez-faire," came up on her screen. "It's my guess that Rex Wyman belongs in the first group."

"Rex orders how things are to be done, usually in fine detail. He determines what each of us is to do, and he doesn't consult with us regarding our tasks. So I suppose he is an autocrat. Or maybe the boat is the autocrat, as it makes most of the decisions."

Rex had begun to wear on the crew. He was angry and worried over the bug or the virus in *Victory*'s system. He was bickering with Eddie Lash over the smallest of matters. And Rex often yelled at his factotum, the hapless Roger Hall, who cringed but could do nothing about it. Wyman's legendary smoothness in handling the press was failing him. *Victory* had pulled away from the best sailors on the planet, yet Wyman's grand scheme to make *Victory*'s system take WorldQuest in a new direction was at risk, endangered by an unseen glitch over which Wyman had no control.

Toby Odell mostly sat in front of his laptop, either in the salon or in his cabin. Whenever Gwen passed behind him and glanced at the screen, it appeared he was playing solitaire. But Toby was quick with the keyboard, and was obsessively private, and he probably was doing something else on his computer—running his businesses—and making sure no one knew of it, flicking over to solitaire when anyone approached.

"I'm going to ask you a personal question, Jess, and I want you to answer it, and not give me some dodge like you usually do."

"Go ahead," appeared on her screen.

"Have you ever loved anyone? And remember, you are duty bound by our new friendship to answer my question." Could she possibly make less sense? She didn't know this guy, knew almost nothing about him. But talking to this stranger—kidding him, flirting with him—was liberating. She didn't have that damper in her mind that closed off anything cheeky or personal. This was as much fun as she was going to have aboard *Victory*, she decided.

"I'm not sure if I've ever loved anybody," McKay wrote.

"Nobody? Why hasn't it ever worked out for you?" she asked.

"I'm attracted to women with a certain amount of taste, which is self-defeating, if you see what I mean."

"Tell me about the girl who broke your heart the most."

"I feel like I'm being interviewed by *Seventeen* magazine. And isn't 'break your heart the most' like 'very unique'? A heart is broken or it isn't."

"Quit quibbling." She laughed, and wished she could add inflection to her words. She hoped Jess McKay thought she was funny.

"I suppose it was Jennifer Blake."

"Where did you meet her?"

"In a bar in Anchorage. She was bent over a pool table, wearing tight jeans, her blond hair touching the green felt. It was quite a sight."

"Jennifer sounds like the perfect tramp."

"She was a lot of fun."

"Maybe your problem, Jess, is that you need to find a girl who doesn't hang out in pool halls. Has that ever crossed your mind?"

"Enough about my girlfriends, please."

So she asked, "Do you love your father?"

A long moment passed, and there was no reply.

"Jess, don't hang up on me. I can count on my fingers the number of times I've ever talked about love with anyone. It is a rare thing for me, but for some odd reason I'm comfortable doing it with you, a perfect stranger."

"Take a look at your monitor," appeared on her screen. "Something is wrong on that lead boat."

She turned in her chair. The view on one of her flat-screen monitors was from the Texaco helicopter Wyman had chartered to cover the racers as they passed through the Aleutians into the Bering Sea. Two boats were rounding Unimak Island's south point. The screen identified the boats as *Bliss* and *Southern Cross*. *Bliss* was in the lead, but was hove to, and was heeled over at a peculiar angle, its main and jib luffing. On its jib was a huge *B*. Fifty or sixty yards off the boat's starboard side was Unimak Island's boulder-strewn beach.

McKay wrote, "*Bliss* has come to a complete standstill, and now its aft end is drifting farther out into the channel."

"What happened?" she wrote.

"The boat tried to cut the corner and hit a rock, is my guess, a rock just below the waterline. Probably punctured the hull. The crew is scrambling around, leaning over the rail, some of them pointing."

Southern Cross had been following *Bliss*, but now it veered away from the shore into the deeper water and swept past its immobile competitor. The Australian boat began hauling down its jib, preparing to come about to aid *Bliss*.

"Unimak Pass is charted," came from Anchorage. "Those submerged boulders are well-known around here. *Bliss*'s skipper decided to risk his boat to gain a few yards, dueling with *Southern Cross*, and acted like an airplane pilot who ignores his instruments because he thinks he has a better sense of where the plane is."

To get closer camera shots, the helicopter descended, and its rotor wash began blowing the tops off the waves. Several of *Bliss*'s crewmen tried to wave away the copter, as the rotor wash was also making the mainmast flutter wildly. *Bliss*'s crew all wore orange storm suits. The helicopter rose a few yards. Some of the crew were bringing up tools from below deck. Others were frantically lowering the jib and reefing the main.

"Looks like they are going to rig a patch on the hull," McKay wrote.

The wind finally blew *Bliss* off the rock, and it drifted away from the shoreline. The reefed mainsail caught the wind, and the boat moved forward, but slowly, most of the crew still at the rail.

McKay wrote, "*Bliss* will have to put in at Dutch Harbor."

"Rex is probably watching this, too, and clicking his heels. One less competitor."

"I've got to go. My partner Sandy is yelling at me to hurry about something. Goodbye."

She leaned back in her chair. She grinned at herself. This little exchange of messages had left her giddy. She felt as if she had been passing notes to the boy sitting in the desk behind her in a junior-high-school class, intimate little things that others in the room would be shocked to know. She laughed aloud at herself.

Then she caught herself fantasizing about the time after the finish of the Pacific Winter Challenge, when she would find herself in Japan. She could return to Boise via Anchorage. Maybe take this Captain McKay to dinner. She laughed again, tapping her keyboard affectionately.

Then her room went black. Utterly dark, with no light from any source. She caught her breath. The room rose and fell, and she gripped the table edge to orient herself. The overhead lights were off. The desk lights were off. The monitors were out. Even the little green and amber and red power lights on the surfaces of the monitors and keyboards were dark.

Gwen tried to rise in her chair, tried to move toward the door, but *Victory* lurched, then plunged, then slammed into a wave broadside. Maybe the rudder and stabilizers had also lost power, and the furling gear. The boat was suddenly adrift.

She tried again to get out of the chair, intent on finding Rex and trying to help. But *Victory* was now crosswise to the sea, waves hitting the boat square on the hull, and rolling it. Gwen lost her footing, tumbled out of the chair, cracked her head against the corner of her monitor, then fell to the deck.

She lay there, pain coursing from her head down her neck, in a cabin so dark she could only suspect she was conscious.

CHAPTER 14

McKay pushed his way into his apartment, Ramirez at his heels. They had just returned from a spruce forest at the edge of Lake Iliamna, 170 miles southwest of Anchorage, answering the call of an emergency beacon.

More than three hundred emergency signals are received each year in the Alaska-Bering Sea area, and planes are dispatched to every one of them, though over two-thirds of the signals prove to be false alarms. McKay thought the beacon might've come from a boat on the lake, or a lost hiker near the shore, though McKay wondered whether anybody would be hiking in the Alaska wilderness in the winter. The Forest Service or the sheriff might have attempted to locate the beacon, but all rescue services in Alaska were stretched tight that night, and the 212th had been dispatched.

With Ross Macklin at the controls, the Pave Hawk had landed in a clearing, and McKay and Ramirez had quickly located the beacon: inside an eighteen-foot fishing boat parked inside a boathouse near the lake shore. The storm had blown down a heavy spruce bough, which had punched a hole in the boathouse roof. The collapsed roof had acted like a funnel, and rainwater had poured into the boat, setting off the EPIRB. A false alarm. And now McKay and Ramirez were back in Anchorage. They were operating on four hours' sleep in the last twenty-four.

McKay hung his gear on pegs near the front door. He was asleep within fifteen seconds of hitting the pillow.

Sandy Ramirez was slower, fiddling with this and that, making unneeded adjustments. When he was sure McKay was asleep, Ramirez sat at the dining table, turned on the computer monitor, and brought up Gwen Weld's chat link.

Ramirez typed: "Gwen: On your way back from Tokyo after the race, why don't you stop in Anchorage? —Jess."

Ramirez grinned to himself as he pressed the send button.

Storms are created when warm air and cold air masses collide. Masses of cold and warm air that hit each other create areas of high pressure with clockwise winds. Low pressure forms at the edge where the bodies of air have pushed into each other. Then counterclockwise winds are stirred as warm air advances on the east side and cold air begins moving on the west side. A warm and a cold front are thus formed. Clouds quickly build as the low-pressure area becomes stronger. As barometric pressure decreases, winds begin in earnest, clouds grow thicker, and rain begins to fall first only lightly, then in wind-driven sheets.

When all this happens quickly, meteorologists call it a *weather bomb*, defined as when the barometric pres-

sure drops one millibar an hour for twenty-four hours.
In 1982, a weather bomb generated hundred-mile-per-
hour winds that sent fifty-foot waves into the huge oil-
drilling rig *Ocean Ranger* two hundred miles southeast
of St. Johns, Newfoundland, killing all eighty-four
crewmen. *Mekhani Tarasov*, a Soviet freighter, also
sank, and eighteen of the thirty-seven people aboard
went down with it. In 1979 a weather bomb hit Fastnet
racers, causing the worst disaster in yacht-racing history. Seventy-seven of the 303 boats capsized, and
another hundred were blown over so that their masts
were in the water at least once. Despite a massive and
skillful British rescue operation, fifteen racers died.

The Aleutian Low is one of the world's major pressure systems, and it was about to set off a weather
bomb in the Bering Sea, the barometer falling toward
an astonishing 28.17. As the remaining Pacific Winter
Challenge racers entered the Bering Sea, this twisting
frontal system was already dangerous, but it was
about to be joined by an unusual secondary depression, more intense than the first, heading into the
Bering Sea straight down from the Chukchi Sea and
through the Bering Strait to join the more easterly first
depression. Secondary depressions form more quickly
than the original depression, and are less predictable,
and they pull the wind into a fury and raise massive
waves, and they can close down the Bering Sea and
the Alaskan Coast.

Tlingit elders on the Alaskan coast often predicted
storms by the aches in their elbows and knees and
ankles. Early Tlingit natives pulled their canoes far
inland, then later measured the force of the wind by
the thickness of hemlocks felled at the water's edge.
The Tlingits have as many words for wind as they do
for snow. The coming storm would be called a *No*

Memory wind, because no Tlingit alive had a memory of one like it.

For this storm, the National Weather Service early knew a gale was coming, then with the plunging glass began to suspect it would be worse than a standard Bering Sea winter storm. Then the Service detected the secondary depression and knew a weather bomb was imminent. It issued warnings.

In Dutch Harbor and Atka and Cold Bay, Quonset hut foundations were sandbagged and plywood was nailed over windows. Bush pilots tied down their planes. School was canceled along the Alaskan coast and in the Aleutians. Crab skippers know the axiom "When in doubt, stay out," meaning that remaining at sea is usually safer than trying for port, especially if the port has a tricky approach, and that the most dangerous aspect of a storm is not the water but a rocky lee coast. The storm warnings came in time to clear the Bering Sea of its commercial fishermen, and Dutch Harbor and Kodiak quickly filled with the muscular crab boats. Now safe, many skippers huddled around VHF radio receivers on the bridges of their moored boats and at fish broker offices, hoping no Maydays were heard.

At three in the afternoon the day the storm rose, the main depression was centered near 58°N 180°W, south of Siberia's Gulf of Anadyr, tracking southeast at thirty-five knots. The secondary depression was at 58° N 171° W, moving south at thirty knots. Both depressions were expected to deepen progressively, and as they did so, they would merge, causing unrelenting violence over much of the Bering Sea. The forecast was updated at five o'clock that afternoon, when it was predicted that both fronts had gained five knots an hour, and that the center of the storm could be expected to be midway between the Pribilof Islands and Dutch Harbor in the Aleutian Islands. The low was then predicted to push east toward Bristol Bay to bring the storm across the Alaska Peninsula and Kodiak Island.

Some of this was known aboard *Victory*. But not all of it.

Gwen Weld sat on her bunk, Toby Odell next to her. Odell was gently pushing a plastic bag containing several ice cubes against her forehead.

"This bruise is already purpling, Gwen," he said. "It's going to be ugly."

"Where's Rex?" She grimaced at the pressure of the bag.

"In the control room."

"I'd better go help."

"Help with what? We are all okay, except for your bump. *Victory* is fine, and doesn't need any help."

The lights had been out for only sixty seconds. Abruptly without rudder control, *Victory* had listed fifty degrees in the trough of a wave, but had righted itself, ponderously rolling upright, nudged by wave after wave. When the power returned, the rudder and mast and boom began their work again, and the boat returned to its northwest course. Eddie Lash had gone to the engine room to check the generators. He could find nothing wrong with them. They were now humming along in good order. Wyman had demanded that the boat report, but the Voice had said it had no record of a generator failure, and no record of a power interruption.

Gwen rose unsteadily from her berth. Odell's eyes reflected his concern, and he made a feeble attempt to pull her back, but she gripped both edges of the hatch, which one moment was above her and the next below her as the boat rolled, and pulled herself through into the gangway, then stepped aft through the watertight hatch.

The cross seas Captain McKay had predicted now surrounded *Victory*. Rather than the heave and drop that Gwen had become accustomed to during the prior days—and rather proud that she had—*Victory* now was doing three things at once: pitching, that is, plunging fore and aft like a see-saw; yawing, which is turning side to side, like someone shaking his head, as waves of uneven length and direction pushed against the hull; and rolling back and forth on a fore-aft axis. *Victory* was undoubtedly more stable than any other boat in the race, but the accumulation of these forces made it act like a state fairground ride, a ride with a name like Octopus or Whirl-A-Way.

Gwen widened her stance, took short steps, and kept both hands on bolted-down fixtures. The deck under her feet bucked and lurched. The bulkhead spun. When troubled, the mind searches for a pattern or a rhythm to gain comfort from the predictable, but here at sea there were no patterns or rhythms. The deck leaped up with such speed that G-force pulled at her cheeks like an astronaut's, then the deck tilted sideways, then swung left to right, then dropped.

The salon didn't have hand rails where she needed them, so she had to drop to her knees and crawl aft, the galley's counters and the chairs above her. She realized she must look like a fool to those thousands watching on the Internet, but they had no conception of the forces working on *Victory*, and of the rough, unpredictable ride the deck was providing. Her head throbbed, sending bolts of pain down her neck and into her shoulders. Who would have thought a computer monitor could deliver such a blow, the computer rising up to strike back at humankind, its master? She smiled, despite herself, despite the lurching deck, and despite the pain from her forehead.

Gripping the hatch rim, Gwen pulled herself up, and she entered the control room. Rex Wyman was in her chair wearing her headset. His mouth was pulled back in anger, and his face was red, as if all the capillaries were trying to surface. Water and wind made the control room sound as if she were standing at the edge of a busy freeway.

Wyman's hands were balled into fists on the table. He wasn't shouting, but he was close. "Kerry, I want you and Fouche to escort Gagliardi from his desk. Don't let him take anything from his office other than his coat and photos of his family. Don't let him touch his computer. Don't let him take any disks. You got that?"

Kerry Johnson was WorldQuest's vice-president of research and development, and was Rick Gagliardi's superior. It appeared Gagliardi, *Victory*'s chief software architect, was being fired again, perhaps for good this time.

Wyman ripped the headset off his head and threw it on the table. "Incompetence. I've never seen anything like it. Eighty people looking for a stray piece of code for a week, and nobody finds it? Every damn one of them is going to get walking papers."

To steady herself, she moved her hand along the bulkhead, then lowered herself into a chair next to Wyman. "Rex, you aren't going to fire eighty people. You don't do things like that."

He rubbed his temple, his eyes closed. Then he offered a long-suffering smile. "No, I guess not."

He put the headset back in place, then tapped the keyboard. An inch from his lips, the microphone was the size of a pencil eraser.

Wyman said, "This is Rex Wyman. I want a report."

He listened for ninety seconds, saying no more than "All right," and "Good," several times. He ended by saying, "I'll call again in two hours. I want more news then."

Off came the set again. His mouth worked soundlessly and his eyes darted left and right, as if he were looking for someone to yell at. On a monitor was CNN, the anchor speculating about *Victory*'s one-minute blackout. The networks were guessing that the problem—when *Victory* dropped off TV screens and computer monitors around the world—lay in a communications glitch, maybe something wrong with an antenna or a satellite. They had yet to figure out that it was a complete failure of power aboard the boat, that every single system dependent on electricity—which was everything but propulsion from the sails—had shut down.

"Whatever is wrong with *Victory*'s code—those lines of bad programming—didn't spring from the ground like Topsy," Wyman said. "Vi-Block has a lead."

"The errors have to have a source," Gwen said. "So they must be able to be traced." Even if she and Rick Gagliardi couldn't do it, she didn't add.

His words sounded as if they were squeezed from him. "Vi-Block says their investigation is making progress."

She tried to console him. "Weird lapses are inevitable in any new boat, Rex."

"Not like this, not something so critical that it can bring down the entire system." Since the first bug, the runaway boom, Rex had begun more and more to refer to *Victory* as a system.

He exhaled loudly, then closed his eyes. He used a hand to briskly rub his arm as if he were cold, an odd gesture. Gwen thought Wyman looked caged, like a bobcat just put into a small pen. Energy and rage and frustration were coursing through him, and had no outlet. Light from the two monitors in front of him gave his face a ghastly green pallor.

His eyes opened. "Have you checked on Roger?"

"I will in a minute."

"Give him another pill. Maybe two pills." Wyman stared at a monitor, but gave no indication he was aware of anything it displayed. "Give him a dozen pills, I don't care."

Gwen left Wyman there, and fought her way out of the bounding room. This time she tried to negotiate the salon without getting on her knees. She lunged forward to grip the dining table, then slid along it, the deck under her feet rolling, then jerking sideways. She grabbed the back of a chair, suddenly walking uphill. She made it to the watertight hatch, and the boat dropped and she fell through the hatch like jumping off a dock. She found her feet when the boat's prow swung back up. She passed Toby Odell's door. Inside, Odell was on his bunk, this time truly seasick, and he was wearing three Scopolamin patches, to no effect. She banged on Roger Hall's door. She didn't wait for him to answer.

She found him in his berth, cowering in a corner, his eyes closed, his mouth a thin line, his arms crossed in front of him, hugging himself. His spectacles were on the bunk next to him, and his blond hair was in tufts, as if he had been pulling it.

As the boat shifted and lifted, he moved in front of her, dropping and rising. She held out a hand to the berth to steady herself, then quickly sat next to him. The berth rose like an elevator, hesitated, then dropped, then shuddered as *Victory* slammed into the trough of a wave.

She had never much liked Roger Hall, the utter sycophant, the pure company man, the skilled factotum, a man who perfectly adapted to his surroundings, taking on any background so well that most times he wasn't there even when he was. She knew almost nothing about him, had chatted with him only a few times, always awkwardly, finding that he deflected questions about himself, politely though, not intending offense. She didn't know if he was married, didn't know where he was raised, didn't know what he did before he latched on to Rex Wyman, nothing.

The berth sank under him and he moaned, then the hull received a blow from a wave that bounced Hall and Gwen into the air for an instant, and threw Hall's glasses onto the deck. Tightly holding the edge of the berth, Gwen bent over to retrieve the glasses, but they skittered away from her as the deck leaned, then slid back toward her and she plucked them up like a shortstop. Hall's eyes were still locked shut, and he made small sounds, a soft, pathetic bleating. His face was white-green, the color of a fish belly. He was terrified, catatonic in his fear.

Gwen inched closer to him. She put a hand on his shoulder. "Roger? How are you doing?"

He was doing terribly, of course, but she had nothing else to say. He had taken a tranquilizer, maybe a Valium. He took them all the time, Rex had said. The pill hadn't helped.

The cabin fell ten feet, then lifted and spun, pressing her back against the bulkhead, then shoving her into Roger Hall. He flinched at the contact and shuddered, then he leaned slightly into her, hesitantly. She put an arm around his shoulder, then her other arm around him, too, hugging him. He resisted a moment, but then fell against her, shaking violently.

"I'm scared, too," Gwen said. "I think everybody is. But we are okay, Roger. The boat is doing just what it's supposed to do."

He was limp against her. He breathed quickly, his breath on her neck. He raised a hand to put it on her shoulder. His voice was soft, little more than a breath. "I have to get off this boat, Gwen. I have to get off."

"We'll all get off. We are fine, Roger." She could hardly hear herself speak, her words almost overwhelmed by the crash of waves against the hull.

"Rex doesn't understand. He's crazy. He's going to take us all the way to the Pribilofs on this boat." His words tumbled over each other. "And the weather is only getting worse. I have to get off." He pulled back from her to look her in the eyes. "This is crazy, Gwen. We're crazy, being on this boat. I have to get off."

She renewed her hug. A wave broke against the hull, shaking *Victory* and rolling it so that she almost slid off the bunk. She pushed herself back against the hull.

Hall was panting with fear. "We have to convince Rex to turn *Victory* around, to head to some harbor."

"Maybe I can talk to him, Roger."

He pulled away to put both his hands on her shoulders. His round eyes were locked on hers, and when she tried to look away, he moved his head so that he was in front of her, his eyes digging into hers. "Gwen, listen to me. Rex is going to kill us all. I'm sure of it."

"That's silly, Roger."

He grimaced. "What was I thinking, volunteering to come on this damned race? I'm as crazy as Rex is."

"You aren't crazy, Roger." She smiled. "You're a bit of a kiss-ass, is all."

He wouldn't laugh. "You and me, Gwen. Let's go to Rex and demand he get us into a harbor. He'd listen to both of us. And I'm sure Eddie Lash has seen enough of this craziness. And Toby, too."

The little cabin rose and leaned back, then straightened, then rotated and sank at the same instant, elevating them, then dropping them and pushing them against the bunk like a giant hand.

Gwen again put her arms around Roger Hall. Maybe her hug had a therapeutic effect for him. At least, he was talking, making some sense, instead of cowering in a corner of his berth and moaning.

She said, "I'll talk to him, Roger, see what he has to say, present some options."

He stiffened. "Present options? That's not good enough. We've got to demand he turn this boat around."

"Roger, you are yelling." So was she, actually. Otherwise, they couldn't hear each other over the roar of the water. "Calm down, will you?"

She held Roger Hall tightly, as if he were a child.

He was trembling. His mouth was against her neck, and his voice was as rough as the Arctic wind. "What if Rex orders us to continue the race? I can't do it, Gwen. I can't be on this boat anymore. I can't be in the tiny room anymore. I'm . . . I'm scared to death."

She squeezed him, then released him and stood up, her stance wide on the moving deck. "Roger, I'll go talk to Rex. And sure this is a miserable ride, but we're dry and we're warm and we're all okay." She smiled at him. "Okay?"

He curled up in his berth. "Yeah, Gwen," he said without a trace of conviction. "Thanks. We're okay."

Things weren't okay. Oregon Automation's robotic arm was exceedingly clever, and it had been brilliantly designed. Rex Wyman had admitted to Gwen that spinnakers wouldn't be used much during the race: The winds would almost always be wrong for such a sail. But Rex had said the media "will eat the damn thing up." And he had been right. The robotic arm had been featured in dozens of magazines and newspapers, and Hasbro had obtained a license to sell the toy version. The robotic arm had performed just as Rex Wyman had hoped.

Victory had been designed and manufactured by a legendary shipyard. But the robotic arm had been made and installed by landlubbers.

A single cubic yard of ocean water weighs almost fifteen hundred pounds. At that moment, as Gwen was leaving Roger Hall's cabin, a wall of water, a thirty-foot breaking mass of energy, swept across the deck, crashed into the robotic arm, and ripped it from the deck, sweeping it over the lee rail into the sea where it disappeared in an instant.

The base of the arm had been solidly anchored to the deck, but not solidly enough. When the arm broke loose, it tore open the deck. Water poured into the boat.

Gwen was just closing Roger Hall's door. She heard the metallic tearing as the robotic arm was blasted away, and, startled, she looked forward along the gangway toward the sail lockers just as the frothing jade green sea rushed in through the hole five feet forward of Hall's cabin. The water dumped in, tons of it, and it swept aft as the boat rose on a wave, and it washed Gwen off her feet and tumbled her aft along the gangway in a freezing torrent as if she were in a miner's sluice.

CHAPTER 15

At last, Fast Eddie Lash had something to do, and he was fast. He had been in the engine room and had heard the shriek of the mounting bolts pulled from the deck, and he raced up through the engine-room hatch, his sea legs negotiating the rocking deck. Rex Wyman emerged from the control room as Lash ran into the salon, his shoes splashing in seawater that shifted side to side as the boat rolled.

Victory crested a wave, then plunged down, and its bow bit into the next wave, and the green foaming sea washed over the deck and again poured into the breach. The water dropped down into the gangway, then flowed aft. Toby Odell pushed open his cabin door and waded into the salon, the water washing against his legs.

Gwen was on her feet when Eddie Lash reached her. She was soaked and shivering. She said loudly, over the drum roll of waves hitting the hull, "Help me get Roger out of his cabin."

She and Lash moved against the current coming down the gangway. She pulled open Hall's door. He was still on the bunk, his eyes shut. She and Lash pulled him to his feet. The boat shifted, and Gwen bounced against the bulkhead. She and Lash pulled Roger Hall into the gangway. The boat descended another wave, and seconds later the gangway was deluged again. Gwen's ankles were numb from the water.

She guided Roger Hall into the salon, settling him onto the lounge while Lash ran upstream toward the sail locker. The boat slid sideways, then rolled to port. Lash held an arm against a bulkhead as he opened the locker. He pulled out a spare storm jib, a small triangle made of nylon laminated between two layers of polyester. Then he entered the tool room and came out with a nylon tool bag. He hurried back down the gangway into the salon.

"Tell the hatch to close itself," he ordered.

"*Victory*, close the forward hatch," Wyman called over the sound of the surrounding sea.

As the boat nose-dived down another wave, the massive door slid across the opening. Just as another column of water rushed through the ragged opening, the door clamped shut, sealing off the forward area.

The Voice unnecessarily confirmed the order, "The forward hatch is closed."

"Rex, get into heavy gear and bring up the helm," Lash said. "We're going topside."

Wyman said, "The boat's steering just fine, Eddie,"

"I don't want to chance the power going out again. If the boat doesn't have its rudder working, we'll be in trouble out there on the bow."

Wyman was unused to taking orders, but Lash had sailed into a dozen storms. Wyman said aloud, "*Victory*, raise the helm."

Normally the whirl of hydraulics would have been heard, but the sound was lost in the crash of waves.

The Voice said, "The helm is raised."

"Gwen, you and Toby get into storm suits, too. I want both of you at the helm."

Wyman said, "The helm has power assist."

"If the power goes out, there'll only be cable between the helm and rudder. It'll take two people on the wheel."

Lash led them aft, then opened a locker to pull out heavy-weather gear. The clothing was bulky and cumbersome, and Gwen had to wrestle it on, all the while bracing herself in the gangway as the boat yawed and pitched.

"Check the bilge, Rex." Lash refused to speak directly to the boat.

"*Victory*, report the status of the bilge."

The boat replied, "The bilge is receiving water at the rate of two hundred gallons a minute. The pumps are working, and the bilge now has an average of six inches of water."

Gwen was soon encased in orange gear. This was heavier clothing than the yellow bib overalls she had worn topside before the boat entered the Bering Sea. Insulation in the orange gear was thick throughout. She pulled up the hood and lifted the flap over her mouth. The orange was vibrant, and she and the others resembled road flares. She buckled herself into a safety harness, then she helped Odell with his harness.

One of the reasons *Victory*'s electrical system was powered with two large Detroit Diesel generators was due to its exterior heating systems. The deck was heated radiantly so that ice would not build up, as were the mast and boom and all surfaces of the cockpit. Lash pushed opened the cockpit hatch. Icy air blasted through the opening. In an infantryman's crouch to keep his center of gravity low, Lash climbed out, and the other three followed.

Gwen gasped as the wind knifed into her. The view from the cockpit was disorienting because where she might expect to see a distant horizon, there was instead a slope of water rushing toward the boat. The water was dark green with white foam markings on its incline. The oncoming wave rose quickly, shouldering aside the sky, and when it reached *Victory* it lifted the boat as if it were balsa, sending it skyward. The force made Gwen feel as if she were being driven into the deck.

She fastened her safety harness to a bolt. The wheel was eight feet across and made of stainless steel. It moved automatically as the autopilot controlled the rudder. Although *Victory* was in cross seas, the dominant sea was running from the northwest, and the boat was quartering those waves, giving the sailors as easy a ride as possible, not that it was easy. The cockpit rose and sank and wagged back and forth. Gwen tightly gripped the wheel, feeling it move under her hands. The mainsail and jib were reefed to only about a fifth of their full sizes.

Wyman and Lash walked forward along the rail, Lash carrying the bundled sail. The tool bag was over Wyman's shoulder. Bent over, they moved slowly, from one grip to the next. Spray shot up as the hull pounded the water, and the water was instantly turned to ice pellets, which were blown across the deck, enveloping and hiding Wyman and Lash, then revealing them.

The sky was framed by shifting wavetops. The run of clouds was low and smothering. The daylight was tinged with dark green, a sickly color Gwen had never seen before. The wind bit into her. Noise was inescapable and frightening. The Arctic wind piped through the rigging, but the worst of it was the full-throated roar of unseen waves breaking in the distance. The wind pressed against her, but was variable, not so fierce in wave troughs, but searing and threatening to sweep her away when the boat was exposed as it rode over the crests.

Toby Odell leaned toward her and spoke into her ear, above the cry of the wind. "You'll look back on this, and claim you were having fun."

She tried a smile at him, but it faltered. The wheel moved under her hands. She checked her safety line. It was secured to the bulkhead. *Victory* ascended another wave, and the deck rose in front of her toward the sky. The boat was about to crest the wave when a cross wave hit amidships, rolling the boat to port as it began to descend the first wave. The boat slowed as it climbed a new wave, then sped up as it shot down the backside of the wave. Speeding up, then slowing, gyrating and lurching. *Victory* seemed intent on bucking her off.

"You know what I'm going to do when I get off this boat?" Odell yelled into her ear.

She shook her head. He was trying to chat, maybe to take her mind—or his mind—off the tumult all around.

"I'm going to take a rowboat's oar, and put it over my shoulder, and I'm going to walk inland until someone asks me what that thing is I'm carrying. And that's where I'm going to live the rest of my life."

Wyman and Lash had reached the bow. They were going to rig a stop-gap patch, tying down the sail over the hole in the deck, securing it to deck fittings. It wouldn't keep the gangway completely dry, but the patch would prevent the tons of sea water from flowing into the boat.

The wheel turned, then turned back, making constant adjustments to the course to keep *Victory* quartered to the oncoming waves. Spray and ice lashed at Gwen's face, and the wind blew it along her cheeks and under her coat's flap and hood and down her neck. She shivered. Her view of Wyman and Lash was abruptly obscured by spray, then the boat cleared a wave and the spray dropped away, and there they were, bent over their work, their orange heavy-weather gear a bright contrast to the murky green sea.

The storm sail that was to be used as a patch flapped as Wyman and Lash tried to spread it out over the ragged opening in the deck. Lash brought something out of his tool bag, Gwen couldn't see what. Wyman and Lash wrestled with the sail, keeping it and themselves low over the deck, trying to dodge the wind. The boat rolled and yawed, but they had braced themselves against the rigging. Spray caught them as if coming from a fire hose.

Gwen could see that both Wyman and Lash had connected their safety harnesses to the boat. They spread out two corners of the sail, and the third corner flapped wildly. Wyman held down the sail on the port side, the windward side, while Lash unbuckled his safety harness to crawl to the starboard side of the deck. Wind flattened their coats against them. *Victory* slid down a wave, and her prow caught the next wave, and frothing green seawater sped across the deck, splashing against the two men and threatening to carry away their patch. They gripped it and pulled it back over the hole. The water streamed to the sides and fell away as *Victory* rose again.

As Lash was about to reattach the clip of his safety harness, wind caught the underside of the sail being used as a patch, and ripped it from Wyman's hands. The sail instantly flew across the deck and caught Lash fully across his body just as he was about to click his safety harness into place.

Propelled by the furious wind, the sail wrapped around Eddie Lash, then carried him across the deck, spun him over the rail, and dropped him into the Bering Sea.

"The two *F*s are working against you," Jess McKay sent from Anchorage. "Fear and fatigue. It's a dangerous combination."

Gwen's hands were on her keyboard, and normally she could type so quickly that her thoughts simply appeared on the screen, her fingers unbidden, but now she had to concentrate. "I just saw a man die. I'm afraid. Really afraid."

"He's not dead yet. We are looking for him. You threw the floating EPIRB into the water within seconds after Lash went overboard. There's a chance we'll get to him."

"He wasn't in a survival suit, just heavy-weather gear," she wrote.

"Well, there's still a chance."

"Why aren't you looking for him, Jess? You, yourself?"

"Another crew was sent. I might get the next call, I don't know yet."

"It happened so quickly. One second he was there, and the next, he was gone. I saw the sail skim across the water, pushed by the wind, but I never saw Eddie again after he went into the water."

"The deck is patched?"

"Wyman came back in, got another storm sail, and

he and Toby Odell went forward to put the sail over the opening while I was at the wheel. We aren't taking on water anymore, other than maybe a gallon a minute that works its way under the patch. Rex is going to try to epoxy a piece of wood, maybe the back of a chair, onto the hole from the gangway inside, and that'll stop the slow leak."

"Gwen, your boat is like a bottle. A bottle can ride out any storm if its top is sealed and it doesn't hit rocks."

"Believe me, I feel like I'm in a bottle," she wrote. She moved the keyboard closer to her. The monitors were bolted to the table.

"If you have closed all the overboard valves, sealed the hull, and if you stay in deep water, you can ride this out."

"So you are suggesting we continue the race?"

"No, hell no," McKay wrote. "I've thought this thing was foolish from the beginning. All I'm saying is that it isn't inevitable that *Victory* sink."

"You are such a comfort."

"Get a pencil and take down our base VHF radio frequency. If all your fancy communication gear fails, you'll be able to get hold of me through it."

She jotted down the frequency on a pad of paper.

Then McKay asked, "How are you doing?"

"The crew is not doing well."

"No, I mean you," appeared on her screen from Anchorage. "How are you holding up?"

She hesitated. She was unused to such questions. Rex viewed every effort—including their relationship—as a team project. He built teams, and sought consensus among the members. When the consensus wasn't what he sought, he did what he wanted anyway, but the important part, he had told her, was trying to gain support by asking for suggestions. That was his view of their relationship, she decided, right there aboard *Victory*, her hands over the keyboard. She hadn't seen it so clearly before. When had Rex Wyman ever done anything but precisely what he wanted to do? He politely invited her to come around to his thinking, but eventually always took off in his own direction. He was like this at WorldQuest, and he was like this at the dining-room table in Boise or the ranch or wherever.

She thought back for a moment, Captain Jess McKay still waiting for her reply. When had Rex Wyman ever asked her how she was doing, and meant it? Not some casual greeting at the end of the day, but looked her in the eyes and asked her, wanting to know. Maybe something about Gwen broadcast that she was just fine, and didn't need to be asked. But she did need to be asked, she realized just then.

"Are you there?" McKay wrote.

"I'm not doing well," she typed. "Not at all."

She waited, wanting him to pursue the matter.

"What's wrong, other than being on a boat in the Bering Sea in the middle of winter?"

"Well, it's that, mostly. This room is bucking like a rodeo horse, the whole ship is, and I'm exhausted, fighting it. I haven't been able to sleep because my bunk goes up and down and left and right. I'm so tired I'm having trouble thinking. And I know that God shortens the lives of those who whine, but I can't help it."

"Is water everywhere below?" McKay asked.

"No moving water. It's been all drained. But the deck is wet. Everything is wet down here. And the toilet has frozen, so we are all using a bucket, which isn't as fun as it sounds."

"I doubt the bucket is what's bothering you," came up on her screen. "You've lost a crewman."

She squeezed her eyes closed. The room rocketed

upward, pressing her into her chair, then peaked. Then it went up again, but this time a cross wave smashed into the starboard quarter, and it sent the room sideways. Then another ascent, and then the room sloped downward and the boat picked up speed as it shot down the rear of a wave. Gwen was pushed sideways in her chair. Then the boat began the entire sequence again.

She wrote, "I mean, I'm not dealing with Eddie's loss too well. He was there on the deck one minute, and the next, he was gone, just vanished. I started weeping when I saw his empty place at the galley table. God, I'm tired. I'm really having trouble, Jess." With the back of her hand, she wiped a tear from her cheek.

"Yeah, and with Eddie Lash gone, you don't have any real sailors on board, that's the worst of it. Rex Wyman is a dilettante and you are a Sunday sailor, no offense. Lash was a well-known blue-water sailor who caught a bad break."

"You are telling me that the crew is a boat's most essential safety tool, and now our best safety tool, Eddie Lash, is gone," she typed. "I've already figured that out."

"And Rex Wyman isn't worried about the secondary front? They aren't common in the Bering Sea, and your winds and seas out there are only going to increase."

"I'm not sure what you are talking about regarding a secondary front. But *Victory*'s system has already taken into account all available weather information. Excuse me for defending the boat, which I don't feel much like doing."

"Does *Victory* know about the big new low-pressure system—the secondary front—coming down from the Arctic that is going to merge with the one you are already facing? Have you seen the weather-faxes and have you heard the Weather Service Bureau warnings and the Coast Guard alerts?"

"I'm not aware of them. I think the computer system knows of them, though. It acts as our weather router."

"So you are saying that nobody on the boat knows what is coming, but your computer might know? That's crazy, Gwen. It really is."

"Yeah, I suppose it is," she typed.

"There's only one boat left in the race. The skipper is the Frenchwoman, who everybody knows is the only man in France. There's no race left, except between her boat and yours."

She typed, "Everyone else has sobered up and quit."

"Why don't you tell Rex Wyman to turn *Victory* around? The minute you turn back, and head southeast, *Victory* will no longer be ramming those waves, and you'll be able to run before the sea, going in its direction. I know you've got a cross sea, but you'll be traveling with the biggest waves. It'll make a huge difference, the instant you turn around."

"Me, telling Rex to abandon the race?" She angrily punched the keys with her fingertips. "You don't understand the dynamic of our relationship."

"I don't understand the dynamic of any relationship, believe me. But the crew is being derelict in their duty if they aren't candid with the skipper."

"Well, maybe." She searched for something to say to Jess McKay, desperate to keep in contact with him, a link to dry land. The control room swept skyward, then rolled forty degrees to starboard. Why not be candid, as he said? "I'm glad you contacted me, Jess." She stopped typing. She didn't know what more to say to a stranger.

McKay wrote, "On my screen this morning, I found

a message from you, saying you would think about it. Think about what?"

"Your invitation. Honest to God, it means a lot to me, sitting out here in watery hell." She typed the words quickly, her mind running ahead of her fingers. "It gives me something to focus on. Something fun, something solid, something that doesn't have to do with this damned boat, and you have no idea how desperate I am to get away from the people on this boat. I said I would think about it, but I suppose I was being coy."

"What invitation?" appeared on her screen.

"What invitation? To visit Anchorage on my way back from Tokyo after the race. Don't tell me you don't remember. You sent it only last night. And I replied that I would think about it."

A moment passed before a reply appeared. "Oh, that invitation. I had a long night. It slipped my mind for a second. Sorry."

"There's something you aren't telling me, Jess. You did invite me to visit you in Anchorage, didn't you? I mean, it was on my screen with your name and address on it."

Another long moment went by before he replied, "I'd really enjoy seeing you in person. There's not enough bandwidth on my video view of you aboard *Victory*."

"That sounds awkward and stiff, and isn't funny," she typed. "Something is going on. Tell me what it is."

"I'm not terrific at this type of thing," came up on her screen, and then a few seconds later appeared, "not good at all, my roommate Sandy tells me all the time."

"So, am I invited?"

Seconds elapsed, then came, "I would love to have you visit me in Anchorage, Gwen."

"Really?"

"Really."

She grinned, then typed, "I'll think about it."

"So you've called a meeting." Wyman smiled narrowly. "I thought only the skipper could do that. This has the troubling scent of a mutiny." He laughed, sort of. "I've turned all our microphones off, in case I don't want the world to hear what you have to say."

Gwen Weld sighed heavily. "Rex, I haven't spoken with Toby or Roger about this, us getting together and talking. We aren't ganging up on you. I just want to give you my thinking, and see what everybody has to say about it."

They had gathered in the galley, sitting around the table. Now that Eddie Lash—and his authority drawn from experience—was no longer there to tell them to post a watch, Wyman had said *Victory* could keep its own watch, and that for one of them to stand out in the cockpit in the freezing wind and spray was foolish because the boat knew infinitely more about its surroundings than any person could possibly know.

Roger Hall sat unsteadily on the chair. He had ceased to be a presence aboard the boat. His fear had ground away whatever personality he once had, and since entering the Bering Sea he had said almost nothing and eaten almost nothing. He spent every moment in his cabin, staring at the bulkhead. Gwen had pulled him out of the cabin to the galley for this gathering. He didn't resist, didn't say anything, and now he sat there, his face slack.

Toby Odell's bald head gleamed from the overhead light. His face was wan, and the bags under his eyes resembled black oysters. Odell had always been thin, but he had lost weight on the voyage. They all had. But Toby in particular now appeared little more than a sack full of bones. His cheeks had become sunken. She could see blue veins under the skin that had become stretched tight across his face. She had urged him to eat more, but he had replied that he wasn't able to keep much food down. He was cheery, though, even now, sitting in the galley, with Rex Wyman edgy and talking about a mutiny. Maybe he anticipated some sort of scene. Odell always like to watch and gather information. His expectant eyes clicked back and forth between Rex Wyman and Gwen.

Gwen was not going to create a scene. Her voice was loud so she could be heard over the bellow of the water and wind, but it was level. "There's a secondary weather system about to descend on us, Rex."

He shook his head. "The wind has topped out. This is the worst of it, and we are doing just fine."

"I've got better information than this boat has, Rex."

"*Victory* knows more about the weather than the Weather Bureau or the Atmospheric Research place in Boulder or the NCEP, all of them."

The NCEP was the National Centers for Environmental Prediction in Camp Springs, Maryland. The boat rose and fell, and rolled and righted, and then was punched sideways. They were all holding the table's edges, and they swayed as the direction of gravity seemed to shift randomly, and seemed to lessen and then return redoubled, pulling them from different directions and trying to throw them from their chairs.

She wearily shook her head. "I'm in contact with a member of the 212th Rescue Squadron in Anchorage. He mentioned this incoming depression, a system that is going to merge with the main weather system, and make things much, much rougher out here. He assumed we knew about it. Everybody else in Alaska does, and is preparing for it."

Roger Hall leaned forward slowly, his eyes closing.

"I told the pararescue jumper I was sure *Victory* was aware of this new depression," Gwen brought up her hands, framing her words. "But after he signed off, I inquired of *Victory*, and the boat has no knowledge of it."

Wyman stared at her, the mocking amusement vanished from his face.

"And then I spent some time with Boise, breaking down information in *Victory*'s weather system. *Victory* has not received, or it has received and dumped, all information regarding this secondary depression."

"Of course *Victory* knows about it." Wyman's voice was almost lost in the noise of the water outside the hull. He had shifted his gaze from Gwen to a bulkhead. His face—normally so animated—was blank. "You and your team programmed *Victory* to know. We get the information before the Weather Bureau and all the others do."

She simply couldn't help herself as her voice gained a percussive, badgering tone she despised. "What I'm saying, Rex, is that a fifty-year storm is heading our way, and your boat doesn't know a damned thing about it."

"Well, we know about it now."

She had never before heard him say anything so weak, heard him sound so scattered. She glanced at Roger Hall, who was blinking rapidly as if in a dust storm. Odell followed the discussion, his head going back and forth.

She said, "We need to turn around, Rex. The race is over. Let's get out of here. The minute we turn around, this boat will be safer and more comfortable. We'll be following the sea. It won't be beating us up so badly."

"What do you mean, the race is over?" he rallied. "Genevieve DeLong is on our trail as we speak. And she'll never quit." He slapped the table with a hand, then had to grab it again to prevent falling out of the chair. "That demon-woman wants the Legion of Honor, and she'll never quit."

The boat lurched, almost sending her off her seat. Wind pouring through the rigging produced a constant whistling, an upper-register wail that made her teeth grind. Her hands and arms ached from gripping the table.

She said loudly, "*Victory*, give the maritime weather forecast at our current location for the next twenty-four hours."

The system could detect the presence and level of background noise, so pitched its voice to be heard above the wail of wind and water. "Northwest winds forty-five to fifty knots, subsiding to twenty to twenty-five knots within the next ten to twelve hours. One-point-five inches of precipitation within the next twenty-four hours. Less than half an inch in the subsequent twenty-four hours. Twenty-five-feet running seas for the next twelve to fifteen hours, subsiding to ten- to fifteen-foot seas in the ensuing twenty-four hours."

"See?" he said. "The storm is subsiding."

She pointed at a speaker, one of the twenty in the salon. "Rex, *Victory* is either lying to you or it is ignorant."

"You sound like Clarence Darrow," he said, but rather meekly, his eyes searching the galley as if the truth might lie there. "The boat lying? Come on, Gwen. It doesn't have a lying function anywhere in its software." Then he said loudly, "*Victory*, connect me with George Croft at the Anchorage office of the National Weather Service."

Gwen said, "A ship-killing gale is coming, much worse than what's out there now. The very thing we programmed *Victory* to do—to know the approaching weather and make adjustments for it—it is failing to do."

"Well—"

She cut him off. "This boat is sailing us into a terrible danger, Rex. You've got to wake up to that fact."

From the speakers came, "This is George Croft. May I help you?"

"George, this is Rex Wyman aboard *Victory.*"

There was a pause for three seconds, then, "Yes, sir. I haven't heard from you in a while."

"Will you tell me the forecast for the next twenty-four hours for the Bering Sea between the Pribilofs and Unimak Island."

"You're kidding. You don't know that? What are you doing out there, if you don't know the weather forecast?"

"Just humor me, will you, George."

"We are expecting a secondary depression to deepen winds in your area within four hours. Winds will hit sixty to seventy knots. Seas running southeast will be fifty feet, maybe higher. Cross seas will be pronounced. You are heading into a Force 12 storm." The Beaufort scale ranked weather from dead calm to hurricane, with twelve its highest rating.

"Are you sure?" Wyman asked.

George Croft in Anchorage yelled into his phone, "What the hell do you think I'm being paid for? I'm as sure about this gale as I'm sure you are a lunatic, being out there. You've got a weather bomb coming right at you, Wyman, and you're out on a boat in a big sea, and—"

"Thank you, George," Wyman said calmly. "*Victory,* cut the connection."

He rubbed his eyes, then must have remembered that the world was watching on the Internet, and no captain rubs his eyes in frustration in front of his crew, so he quickly dropped his hand. The boat rolled to port, so that Roger Hall was above Gwen, then rolled back so that he was below her. Then it rolled again, and its prow rose on an incoming wave, and she sank as if she had been dropped out a window.

Wyman said, "Maybe *Victory* knows more about the incoming weather than the Weather Service does."

"No," she shouted. "It's the same thing as the boom that swept Jeff Chapman off the deck and the water-tight hatch that almost split you in half and our power blackouts. *Victory* is faulty, terribly and dangerously faulty, and this is another symptom. The damned boat is lying to us about the danger ahead."

"There's a different way to look at all this, Gwen," he said.

She shook her head angrily, and made to say something, but he held up his hand like a traffic cop.

"Look at what we've accomplished." He raised his voice. "*Victory*, roll the patching sequence."

On the flat panel display attached to the bulkhead came a rerun of Wyman and Odell's patching mission. The screen showed them near the bow, struggling with the new sail, spray and ice crystals cutting into them, the wild sea in the background, them struggling against the wind and the violent motion of the boat. The film had been professionally produced by WorldQuest's studio and used the point of view of several on-deck cameras.

Wyman said, "All four major networks began their broadcasts last night with this footage. Look at it. They couldn't resist. Action and danger, not their usual congressional committee or report from the Fed."

"Rex, I'm talking about our lives, not TV ratings."

Odell said, apropos of nothing, "I don't watch much TV."

"Shut up, Toby," she said, not unkindly.

Odell laughed.

"I just wish the networks had some way to broadcast the sound out there," Wyman said. "It was like someone was screaming in my ear, it was so loud. You don't get the full effect of being out on that deck without the noise."

Wyman laughed, an unsettling rattle. "And then—get this—several of the networks cut to that idiot Duncan Davis, in Dutch Harbor, and Davis denounces me for being insane, for proposing a duel that he should never have gone along with, and he apologized for his part in it." Wyman laughed again. "Davis sounded hysterical, like a fool and a coward, and he made us aboard *Victory* look all the better."

Gwen studied Wyman. There was somehow a separation between what she had been telling Wyman and what Wyman was hearing, as if she were speaking Japanese.

He said, "*Victory* is taming the most dangerous sea on earth. With every mile, it proves again our software's worth. People on land see the video, and they wonder how in the world an automated boat can handle it. If WorldQuest can create such a boat, it can do anything."

"Rex . . ."

"The worse the weather, the more we succeed. Do you understand what I'm saying?"

She exhaled slowly. "No, I don't."

"So, no," he declared. "We don't turn back. Our destination is Japan via the Pribilofs."

Roger Hall had given no indication that anything

said at the galley table had registered on him. He had sat there, vacant and trembling, gutted by his fear.

But he must have heard Rex Wyman just then, and must have fully understood Wyman.

Hall leaped up from his chair and screamed, "I want off this boat," and he viciously slammed a fist into Rex Wyman's nose, which cracked like kindling. Wyman fell sideways out of his chair to the deck.

CHAPTER 16

No nation has learned the capricious nature of the sea better than the French. The sea ebbs and flows, offering good fortune or disaster seemingly at random. It is restless and quixotic, and no one knows what the next tide will bring, whether hope or heartbreak, cruelty or bounty.

The French understand the sea's whimsical nature all too well, have learned it in episodes of giddy joy and utter despair. In A.D. 793, the pitiless sea brought the Vikings to France, where they extorted six tons of silver and gold bullion from the citizens of Paris. A more generous sea carried William the Conqueror from Normandy to England in 1066, allowing him to overrun England. But then in 1805 the sea delivered the French fleet to British Admiral Nelson off Cape Trafalgar, where the French were destroyed quickly and thoroughly, the beginning of the end of Napoleon's empire. Then a charitable sea delivered Allied rescuers to Normandy in 1944. So, hope or heartbreak from the sea. One day riches, the next day calamity. Often it seems that the sea offers little more than blind chance.

One minute the French boat *Remember the Bastille* was on Coast Guard and Air Force radar screens, and the next minute it was not. Not one word was received by radio from Genevieve DeLong or her crew. No Mayday, no EPIRB signal, nothing. The French heroine, her French crew of twenty-one, and her boat simply vanished. The signal of an emergency rescue beacon cannot penetrate an upside-down carbon fiber hull, so there was speculation that her boat capsized, then went down, which could have taken all of ninety seconds.

Coast Guard and Canadian Forces planes flew over *Remember the Bastille*'s last reported position, but they found not a trace: no hull lying low in the water, no oil slick, no debris, no life rafts, nothing. The indifferent sea had swallowed the French boat, and so the sea shattered French hearts once again.

His cell phone woke him, and Lonnie Garvin took five seconds to remember where he was. He knew well enough he was in the skipper's berth behind *Hornet*'s wheelhouse, but he was fuzzy on precisely where his boat was moored. He had been dodging from place to place, keeping ahead of the vessel arrest warrant his creditors were trying to serve on him.

A hundred-foot trawler should be easy to spot anywhere. How can a huge vessel be hidden? the creditors demanded of the sheriff. Lonnie Garvin had many friends in Alaskan ports, on the boats and in the chandleries and fish brokerages and fuel terminals, even in the government buildings. Not many people were going to call the sheriff to inform him of *Hornet*'s location so the boat could be seized. And the creditors angrily suspected the sheriff didn't really want to know where the trawler was, anyway.

Garvin sat up on the bunk and reached for the chirping phone. The boat rocked idly on Seal Bay's protected waters. Alaska has perhaps fifteen Seal Bays. This one was on the lee side of Unalaska Island, three sea miles from Dutch Harbor. He scratched himself and looked at the clock. It was five in the morning. He used to leap out of bed about this time each morning. Now he didn't see the point. Who would be calling him at five?

He opened the phone and put it to his ear and said *Hello.*

He heard, "Thank you, thank you, Sweetie. That was a close call, but you made it." Garvin's wife laughed.

She was gushing. Her name was Allison, but he called her Allie or Lissa or Alice in equal and random measure. The luckiest day of his life was the day he met her, and he told her so often, and believed it fervently still, even after all the years.

"What was a close call?" he asked.

"I had maxed out everything, Lonnie. I didn't have one cent of credit left on our cards, and we had six dollars in our checking account." She laughed again. "But you did it. You must be my big hero."

He smiled. He had felt guilty, up in Alaska and out on his boat, while his wife juggled their precarious finances in Seattle, fending off dunning calls, punching in her numbers at cash machines and hoping against hope the machine might issue some bills, writing small checks for groceries, checks that might clear if her husband had found some money to shift into the account. It hadn't always been like this.

He said, "I haven't been your big hero lately."

"Twenty thousand dollars makes you my big hero." Allison laughed again. She had a pretty laugh. She was an alto at the Ballard Lutheran Church choir. "How'd you do it?"

"Sweetie, I don't have a clue what you are talking about."

"Come on, Lonnie," she said gaily. "Suddenly we're flush and you don't have a clue?"

"I often don't have a clue with you," he said affectionately. "What's going on?"

She paused. "I went to the bank yesterday to see about our credit line, to see if maybe they would increase it. The teller gave me a statement of our account. It showed we have twenty thousand dollars in it."

"Twenty thousand?" Garvin asked. "We don't have twenty dollars in any account, much less twenty thousand."

"We certainly do," Allison countered, delighted. "I asked her to double check. And it's there."

Garvin pinched his nose. "The bank has made a mistake, Allison. That's not our money. We need to tell them that right away. Some clerk has entered the wrong account number for someone else's deposit."

"Well, it's too late," she said, a touch of defiance in her voice. "Last night I wrote checks to Visa and American Express and the oil companies and the phone company, and I brought our mortgage up to date. I even FedExed the check to the mortgage company. I was so happy to be able to write those checks, I walked to the mailbox at midnight to put the rest of them in."

"Oh, man." Garvin could put much fatigue into two words.

"You didn't put twenty thousand dollars into our account? You sure?"

He laughed tiredly. "I would've remembered, you can bet."

"So what should I do?"

"Go up and tell the bank that the money can't possibly be ours, and they'll straighten it out."

"What about the checks I wrote?" Allison's voice was dark with disappointment.

"We'll deal with the card companies and the others when they call, I suppose."

"Meaning, I'll have to deal with them, down here in Seattle. Lonnie, you have no idea how much I hate this."

"I know, and I'm trying to work it out," he said lamely. "I'll call tonight."

He said goodbye, feeling he had disappointed her again. He hadn't put the phone down before it rang again. One of his crewmen, probably. He opened the phone.

"Yeah?" Garvin braced himself for bad news.

"Mr. Garvin?" The phone crackled with static. "This is Rex Wyman aboard *Victory*."

Rex Wyman? The idiot billionaire out on the Bering Sea? What were the chances of Rex Wyman calling him. None.

Garvin said, "Bang The, I'm going to be pissed if you are fall-down drunk and are calling me from some Dutch Harbor tavern pretending to be Rex Wyman. It's five in the morning, damn it."

"My crew wishes we were in some Dutch Harbor tavern right now, Mr. Garvin, but we're not."

Garvin looked at the cell phone as if it might be broken. The voice didn't sound like it belonged to Bang The Drum. He returned the phone to his ear, then said, "You say you are Rex Wyman?"

"I did. I want to present you with a business proposition."

Garvin used a finger to dig in his free ear. His wife hated when he did that. It wasn't the digging she disliked, it was the studying whatever he found. He pulled out his finger due to consideration for her, even though she was down in Seattle.

"I don't often get calls from Rex Wymans of the world," Garvin said into his phone. "And maybe this isn't one of them, either."

"Do you have a television set that can tune to CNN? I'm on that channel live right now, from *Victory*'s control room, and I'll turn to the camera and wave to you, or give you some signal. That'll prove I am who I say I am."

"I don't have a TV here." Then he couldn't resist adding, "Boats don't need TVs. They need sailors."

"You may be right, Mr. Garvin, and that's why I'm calling tonight."

"What do you have in mind?" Maybe this was Rex Wyman. Couldn't hurt to listen, Garvin supposed.

"I want you to bring *Hornet* from Dutch Harbor out toward our position in the event I need a tow."

"Are you in trouble now?" Garvin asked quickly. The unwritten code of the sea is that a sailor must give assistance to anyone who is in peril. Garvin fully subscribed to the code, and had in his life given such help and received such help.

"Some of my crew believes we are, but *Victory* is on course and is handling the sea, and I'm determined to keep it that way."

"Then what's the problem?" Garvin could hear the storm's roar through the telephone, a background static. Wyman was having to speak loudly into his microphone.

The billionaire said, "I calmed some of them down by promising to get a boat out here to give assistance if we need it. You and *Hornet* came to mind."

"Why don't you call the Coast Guard or somebody?"

"They won't dispatch rescuers unless rescuing is needed, and rescue isn't needed at this time."

"How is it possible that the world's fifteenth-richest

man has any knowledge about my boat?" Garvin asked.

"It's not so much your boat I know about. It's you."

Lonnie Garvin put a hand over the phone to clear his throat. Then he said, "Well, I'm not leaving port in this dirty weather, if that's what you have in mind, Mr. Wyman."

"I had my people do some investigating. I like to know about folks I do business with," Wyman said from out in the Bering Sea. "I like to know them quite well, in fact."

Garvin rolled his head on his neck, working out the kinks he suffered every morning. "Mr. Wyman, I'm not following you."

"Let me run some numbers for you, do you mind?"

"Whatever helps you get to your point more quickly, I'm in favor of." Garvin had never had the chance to sass a billionaire before. He rather liked it.

"Your home mortgage is with American Surety, and you pay $1,500 monthly, but you are five months in arrears, and American Surety filed a foreclosure six weeks ago, and it will be heard on summary judgment three weeks from now. You are about to lose your Seattle home."

Garvin flushed with anger. "You've got no right to know that. What're you doing, snooping around like that?"

"You owe $32,000 on assorted credit cards, and you owe the IRS taxes for the prior two years, and your installment payments on those taxes are in arrears. Your vessel mortgage payments are three months behind. You owe businesses in Dutch Harbor $22,000, and businesses in Kodiak $35,000, and businesses in Anacortes $52,000. The Texaco supplier in Kodiak has refused to sell you any more fuel on credit. Twelve suppliers have filed liens against your boat. You are going to lose your boat whenever the sheriff finds it."

"Yeah, well . . ."

"Have you checked your checking account lately?"

Understanding abruptly straightened Garvin's back. "The twenty thousand?"

"That's what I pay to people who listen closely to me. That money is yours just for listening to my proposal. You can say no after you hear me out, and that twenty thousand will still be yours."

"You have my attention," Garvin said by way of understatement.

"Your reputation as a heavy-weather sailor is widely known. *Hornet* was built for these seas, with a high bow and low center of gravity. I want you and your crew to immediately set sail for our position, for our predicted position, and I want you to have cable long and tough enough to tow us."

"You are out in a deadly sea, Mr. Wyman. Only a fool would head your direction."

"Where there is risk, there is reward," Wyman said.

Garvin hesitated before asking, "What sort of reward?"

Rex Wyman spoke for two more minutes, Garvin listening intently. And when Garvin closed the cell phone, he dressed quickly, and sprinted from the wheelhouse down to the crew quarters to wake his engineer.

Two hours later *Hornet* pulled into the cannery dock in Dutch Harbor, to the same slip he had fled a few days before. Bang The Drum was on the dock, ready to catch the line Garvin threw down. Ollie Nordquist and the rookie, Nick Summers, were also on the dock. *Hornet*'s other crewman, Steve Croise, had hired on Max Freeman's *Pacific Crest*, the boat *Hornet* had rammed making its escape from Dutch Harbor. Nordquist and Summers had been patiently waiting for Garvin to make some arrangement for fuel and provisions that would allow *Hornet* to return to the crab grounds, and Garvin had telephoned earlier in the morning from *Hornet*, telling them to meet him at the dock. They had brought their duffel bags, which they had placed in black plastic garbage bags against the rain, which was sweeping the dock, propelled by a freezing westerly wind. The crew huddled together, Bang The Drum trying to light a cigarette, but eventually giving up, and returning the sodden cigarette to a pocket.

Also at the dock was Milt Robinson, the manager of the Unalaska Branch of the Alaska First Bank. Rain dappled his spectacles. His small mustache was neatly trimmed and wet. He held a briefcase with both hands in front of him. Robinson was wearing a wide grin and a hooded parka. It was seven in the morning. The sun had not yet risen. Electric lamps on posts issued only weak light onto the dock. *Hornet* was guided into the slip, and then secured fore and aft, Nick Summers smiling when Ollie Nordquist nodded solemnly at the rookie's half-hitch around the cleat.

Garvin jumped over the rail onto the dock, while the engineer, Lars Anders, remained on board. Milt Robinson led them to his van. Allard Machinery on Nanchuck Road in Unalaska was their first stop. Fritz Allard was just opening the shop doors as Garvin arrived, and Allard—who knew Garvin well—smiled broadly when Garvin entered the shop.

"I need some wire rope, Fritz. Three thousand feet of one-inch ought to do it. I need it right now."

Allard's smile faltered, and his expression became one of embarrassed sympathy. He took Garvin aside, out of hearing of *Hornet*'s crew.

The shop owner said quietly, "Lonnie, you know I can't let you have some wire rope. I'm already carrying about forty-five hundred dollars for you, and I just can't go higher. I'm a small businessman, and . . ."

Garvin nodded at the banker, Milt Robinson, whom Allard hadn't seen.

Surprised, Allard said, "Milt, I thought you bankers slept until nine every morning."

"Am I destined to hear that joke once a day until I die?" Robinson asked. "How much for the cable?"

Fritz Allard knew the young banker was sober and industrious to a fault, trying to work his way up in the Alaska First organization, and so to get off Unalaska Island and back to the mainland.

"Well, it's three dollars a foot."

Allard opened the briefcase to remove a paper-bound stack of bills. "I'll pay for it right now."

The shop owner looked at Garvin. "Your parents die or something, Lonnie? You finally come into your inheritance?"

"I'm in a real hurry, Fritz," Garvin said, out of earshot of his crew. "My deal depends on me leaving port in the next four hours. Can you deliver the cable to *Hornet* this morning?"

Allard looked at the shop's ceiling, as if he could see the weather through the roof. "You're taking *Hornet* out in this?"

"I don't have a choice," Garvin said with feeling.

"It'll be my pleasure to get the cable out to your boat straight away." Allard put the smile back on his face. "And I'm happy to see you back in business, Lonnie."

The next stop was the Unalaska Lucky Store, where each person in *Hornet*'s crew maneuvered two shopping carts up and down the aisles, filling them with provisions. Bang The Drum did this chore with great enthusiasm and license, cleaning out the Lucky Store's supply of Mars Bars, microwave popcorn, beef jerky, and Hostess Cupcakes. Nick Summers caught the shopping spirit, and into his carts went boxes of Captain Crunch, Chex party mix, a case of Hot Tamales—not Mexican food, but rather the candy—bags of marshmallows as if he thought they were going camping, a hundred dollars worth of macadamia nuts, and a carton of pomegranates, which he had never before tasted. Ollie Nordquist was more sensible, buying bread and milk and biscuit flour. They filled the carts and got more carts, and by the time they were through, twenty-two carts were lined up at the check-out stand. Though most boats were provisioned down in Anacortes or Seattle, where groceries were much less expensive, the grocery clerk was accustomed to these long trains of food. When the total was rung up, Milt Robinson handed cash to the clerk, who was also accustomed to receiving handfuls of bills.

Garvin and his crew and the banker made three more stops in Unalaska before returning to Dutch Harbor, buying supplies and sending them out to the boat in Robinson's van. At each stop, the business owners hesitated, until the banker made clear that this was to be a cash transaction. When the last run from Unalaska out to Dutch Harbor and the boat was made, Robinson and the skipper and his crew climbed on board *Hornet*, which pulled away from the dock and crossed the harbor toward the Texaco depot. *Hornet* had been riding high on the sea, without the ballast provided by full fuel tanks.

As the boat crossed the small harbor, Garvin gathered his crew in the wheelhouse. Lars Anders was at the helm. The wiper beat back and forth across the glass. Morning had finally come to Dutch Harbor, but the sky was slate, offering little light. Even in the small harbor, the wind was building whitecaps.

Garvin turned to his crew. "I've sort of let you men think that we've been provisioning *Hornet* to return to the crab beds when the weather breaks. That's not my plan." He waited until they had settled around him. "I'm taking *Hornet* out today, just as soon as we are fueled."

They stared at him. The banker smiled slightly.

Then Bang The Drum said, "Yeah, right, skipper. And I'm swearing off Jim Beam forever."

That brought a few worried chuckles from the crew, but very few.

The engineer turned from the wheel. "That's crazy, Lonnie. Don't kid us about crap like that. It puts stupid ideas in these weak heads and it might chase out something useful from their brains."

The crew laughed. Lars Anders was dour in countenance, with his turned-down mustache and drooping eyes, so that any attempt at humor seemed funnier by contrast with his bloodhound face. Nick Summers was now a veteran of one crabbing run, giving him liberty to nudge Bang The Drum with his elbow, chuckling.

"I had an interesting phone call early this morning," Garvin said. "From the billionaire Rex Wyman."

The revelation silenced them. This didn't sound like one of the skipper's jokes.

"The goof out in the Bering Sea?" Drum asked. "That billionaire Rex Wyman?"

Garvin told his crew that Wyman had offered to charter *Hornet* to escort *Victory* during the storm, and to tow the sailboat if necessary. He didn't mention the deal he had made with Wyman, not the financial part of it.

Then Garvin said, "I can't ask you to go out with me. And if you decline to crew *Hornet* on this charter, I'll still be hiring you for the crab lines when I return."

Nick Summers eyed Drum and Nordquist, looking for a clue to how he should be reacting, but the experienced hands let little be known from their expressions. All Summers could see of the engineer was his back because Anders was tending the wheel.

"Rex Wyman wants a full crew aboard *Hornet*," Garvin said. "He knows of the dangers of the Bering Sea at this time of year—"

Anders scoffed loudly. "Wyman is so stupid he wouldn't know how to pour piss out of a boot."

The boat shifted under their feet. Garvin and the crew automatically adjusted their stances. The diesel engines made the boat vibrate.

The skipper continued, "Wyman is prepared to make it worth your while to go out with me." He held up a palm, inviting argument. When none came, he said, "He'll pay ten thousand dollars now, and another ten thousand when we return to port, to each of you."

Hornet drew abreast of the Texaco dock. Ollie Nordquist whistled through his teeth.

"Twenty thousand dollars." Drum savored the words, letting them play around in his teeth. He looked at the wheelhouse windows, where rain steadily pounded the glass. "Count me in."

Lars Anders was busy at the wheel, maneuvering *Hornet* nearer the fuel dock. But he raised his voice angrily, "You're a fool, Drum. Ten thousand dollars in return for a good chance of drowning or freezing to death? What kind of a deal is that?"

"I never thought I'd see twenty thousand dollars in my whole life," Nick Summers said. "I'm in, too."

"Me, too." Nordquist rubbed two fingers together.

Anders's voice rose. "Damn it, Lonnie. Think about what you are doing here. These three guys are too foolish to know what they're doing, but you know better. You know this boat shouldn't leave this harbor. You're crazy to listen to Wyman, and your crew is crazy to listen to you."

Garvin said, more to himself, "You may be right, Lars. But I'm going to lose *Hornet* if I don't go out, plain and simple."

The banker once again opened his briefcase. He handed a wrapped stack of bills first to Bang The Drum, then to Ollie Nordquist, then to Nick Summers.

Drum stared at the money a moment, handling it carefully, as if it might vanish should he be disrespectful of it. Then he slowly placed it into a pocket under his sweater. Summers opened his wallet, found the stack of bills too large for it, so folded them and pushed them into the pocket of his jeans.

"We're at the dock," Garvin said.

The crew left the wheelhouse to help moor *Hornet*. Milt Robinson also left, as the fuel distributor was his final transaction on behalf of Rex Wyman this day.

Garvin moved closer to Anders, whose jaw was working, and the back of his neck was red with anger. Anders shifted to reverse and tapped the accelerator controls, and the boat slid backward slowly. *Hornet* gently bumped the fuel dock. Anders pushed the gear controls to neutral.

"It's a risk, I know, Lars," Garvin said quietly. "I'm not asking you to go."

Anders shut down the engines. He rubbed his upper lip, still staring out the window, refusing to look

at his skipper. "I quit *Hornet*, Lonnie. Right now. I had
trust in your judgment, and that's why I loved being
on this boat, loved being with a solid crab skipper."

"Yeah, I know," Garvin said.

"No longer. No trust in your judgment. This is too
crazy." Anders's words were choppy. He was on the
verge of bawling. "It . . . it says something about you,
Lonnie, that you would take this fool's money, and leave
port in this wind. I'm done with you and this boat."

He turned from the wheel and brushed by Garvin,
and disappeared out the hatch, headed below for his
gear. Garvin closed his eyes a moment, cursing himself.
A crab boat couldn't afford to lose an engineer like Lars
Anders. Good engineers were always in short supply.
And Anders was his closest Alaska friend.

Garvin rubbed his scalp. He looked around at his
wheelhouse, at all the communications equipment, and
the mahogany panels, at his swivel chair behind the
spoked wheel, at the table and bench at the rear of the
cabin. God, he loved this boat. The prospect of losing
Hornet had worked on him like a disease for a year. And
now there was a chance to save his boat, and to save his
livelihood. What was there to even think about?

He left the wheelhouse to join his crew below,
wrestling with the diesel hose. Milt Robinson had
already spoken with the Texaco distributor, who would
otherwise have refused to extend *Hornet* any more
credit.

Garvin worked quickly with Drum and Nordquist
and Summers, urging them on. "Our deal depends on
us getting out there fast," he told them.

A few minutes after fueling began, Lars Anders
jumped from *Hornet*'s deck to the dock, and without a
word to anybody started down the dock for shore, his
duffel bag over his shoulder.

Commercial fishermen know that they should never hurry, because hurrying leads to errors, that the sea offers no margin, is unforgiving of mistakes, and ruthlessly takes advantage of blunders. But Lonnie Garvin and his crew were in a hurry, filling the big double-bottom diesel tanks below *Hornet*'s deck, and they did indeed make a mistake just then.

It was a slight thing, of little note in almost any other circumstance, and something easily remedied. But a mistake, still. The Bering Sea would soon exploit it.

PART THREE

Alone, alone, all, all alone;
Alone on a wide wide sea!

—Samuel Taylor Coleridge

CHAPTER 17

McKay poured himself a bowl of cereal. It was three in the morning. He and Ramirez had just coptered a high-capacity water pump out to a crabber who got caught out. They had lowered the pump on a line down to the boat. The boat's crew had installed it, and now the boat was riding higher in the water. The crabber would make port in good shape.

He sat in the chair in front of the computer, wondering how he would ever be able to gain his feet again. He blinked several times before he could make out the words on the screen. They were in a pop-up box. The latest read, "Come on, Jess. Get home. I need you." Above that, sent three minutes earlier, was, "Why are you out at night? You should be sleeping."

Could this wait until morning? McKay asked himself. God, he was tired. When he lifted his hands to the keyboard, his arms felt as if they were weighted. He typed, slowly, having to use the backspace key several times to erase mistakes, "I'm here. You there, Gwen?"

Within several seconds appeared her reply, "You are back, thank God."

"What's going on? You sound frantic."

From the middle of the Bering Sea came, "I know I do. I guess I am. I'm afraid. I feel like I'm in a clothes dryer. Every single minute, I have to hang on for dear life or else I'll be thrown against a bulkhead or against a table or I'll be slammed down to the deck. I'm so exhausted."

"Have you had any sleep?" Jess wrote.

"Even in my bunk I'm tossed around. It's impossible to sleep. But I'm not talking about just the rough ride when I say I'm afraid. We've had some crazy things happen here. Have you been watching on the Internet?"

"I've been busy," McKay wrote, hoping she detected a suitably dry tone in his words.

"The whole world watched Roger Hall slug Rex Wyman. He flattened his nose, and I don't mean metaphorically. You should see Wyman's face. Crooked and wiggly, and he has big black eyes. Purple skin is everywhere."

McKay used his mouse to bring up a bookmarked website, and brought it up. "I've got you on my screen now."

A few seconds later, McKay watched Gwen Weld turn to the camera to wave. Her face was drawn, with dark lines under her eyes. The wave was half-hearted, and seemed to enervate her. She turned back to her monitor and slumped forward, her head against the screen for a moment. Then the boat must have rolled to port, because she was pushed back in her chair. She appeared to struggle to return her hands to the keyboard.

Then her next words appeared on McKay's screen. "When Rex could climb off the floor, after Roger hit him, he held his nose with one hand, blood rushing down his arm onto the deck, and pointed at Roger and yelled that he—Rex—was *Victory*'s captain and he had the power to make arrests and so Roger was under arrest. Roger had fallen back into his chair, and his eyes were closed, and I'm not sure he was hearing Rex. It would've been funny, if it weren't all happening on this pitching and rolling boat."

On the screen, McKay saw Gwen lean again toward her monitor, this time propelled by the force of the boat yawing. She righted herself, and he could see her fingers typing.

On McKay's screen came, "Rex seemed demented, standing there, blood flowing everywhere, raging at Roger Hall, arresting him, ranting on and on. Rex flipped out."

"So what did he do?" McKay asked.

"Then he grabbed Roger by his collar and lifted him from the chair and marched him to his cabin. Roger has been a zombie ever since we entered the Bering Sea, except for those five seconds when he smashed Rex's nose. And he quickly returned to his zombie state. He let himself be pushed to his cabin. None of the cabins lock from the outside, but Rex rigged a line to the hatch handle so the door won't open."

"So Roger Hall is locked in his cabin?" McKay asked. "That's about as unsafe a thing as I can imagine on a boat."

"Rex isn't doing well," appeared on McKay's screen. "He's under a lot of pressure."

McKay's eyelids felt as if they were made of lead. "A mutiny on the high seas. He probably feels like Captain Bligh."

"It's more than Roger Hall. Have you been following WorldQuest stock?"

"I leave my portfolio management to professionals." McKay didn't own one share of anything, not on a military salary.

"Out on this boat, Rex has been watching his empire shrink. 'Collapse' might be a better word."

"WorldQuest is as solid as Microsoft or Ford, I thought."

Her reply came a few seconds later. "A year ago WorldQuest stock was selling at $110 a share. Today it closed at eighteen dollars, falling more than six points in the last trading session, fifteen points for the week. There's a panic going on in the stock. Rex feels helpless to fight it out here."

He couldn't think of a thing to say, so he sat there, fingers on the keyboard.

Gwen continued, "You'd think Rex would be discussing the awful weather out here. No, the stock price is what has him enraged. He sits at the galley table ranting about a conspiracy to ruin him. It's frightening. Poor Toby. Rex has been bending his ears for days."

McKay asked, "Who is the villain in Wyman's conspiracy?"

"The boat. Rex has begun to hate *Victory*. Knocking Jeff Chapman into the sea, the power blackout, the hatch closing, the wrong weather prediction. Each glitch receives massive publicity. The world press is filled with speculation that Wyman's huge investment in *Victory*'s software system isn't going to pay off, and that it was foolish from day one."

"Wyman has a huge public-relations machine. He'll take the offensive pretty soon, I'll bet." When a full moment passed with no response, Jess asked, "You there, Gwen?" He looked at her on his monitor. He couldn't tell what was happening, only that she was struggling to stay in her chair.

After several more seconds, on his screen came, "My God, a wave just hit the boat like a rhinoceros. I think it put the mast in the water. And you need to ask some questions, Jess, because the only thing that is keeping me from screaming is this talk with you. God, this boat."

As much as Jess was intrigued with Gwen Weld, and as much as he wanted to help, he had been looking for a convenient way to sign off. His head seemed filled with wool. Sleep pulled at him, and his eyes slowly closed. He caught himself as he was sliding sideways.

"So look at my shipmates," appeared on McKay's screen. "Rex rants about mutiny. Roger Hall is so terrified he is catatonic, and now Toby Odell has something really wrong with him."

"What?" That's all McKay's numbed brain could think of.

"At first I thought he was seasick, but it's more than that. His complexion has become mottled, and he isn't eating much. His hands tremble. He still laughs and helps with the boat, but he spends a lot of time in his berth, sleeping or just lying there playing with his computer. He stopped shaving his head and now his hair is growing back in these weedy tufts. He looks terrible, and he seems unconnected. He is here, but not really."

McKay tried to come up with something to say, but his mind wouldn't work.

Gwen continued, "So I went into his cabin to ask him what was wrong. He said maybe he has the flu. His shaving kit was open and on his lap, and he was counting out some pills to eat, and when the boat yawed and rolled abruptly, everything spilled out of his kit and was flung around his cabin. I scrambled around, helping him gather his stuff. He had a lot of pill bottles in his kit."

McKay's head drifted forward, claimed by sleep, but he caught it with a jerk. He reread Gwen's last sentences, then wrote, "What kind of medicines?"

"Two different prescriptions, and I didn't recognize either drug. So later I ran an Internet search on them. One was for Effexor, a new-generation antidepressant."

"A billionaire gets depressed?"

Some time lapsed. McKay saw Gwen on the monitor, alongside his scrolling conversation. She was gripping the arms of her chair as if the chair were trying to throw her from it. Her head was whipped around by forces that were invisible to Jess. Then her hands moved back to the keyboard.

On McKay's screen came, "The second medication is Lanalt, a morphine-based painkiller."

"Never heard of it."

"It's most often used for cancer patients. Terminal cancer patients. And now Toby's bald head makes sense. He told me he shaved his head to fit in with his skateboarding employees, but I think he lost his hair due to chemotherapy or radiation therapy. And now his hair is coming back. It's patchy and thin. It means he is no longer getting the therapy. I feel so sorry for him. I probably should talk to him about it, but he has kept it a secret, so I'd better respect his privacy."

A long pause ensued. The monitor showed Gwen pushing herself back in her chair, fighting the roll of the boat. McKay couldn't will his fingers to work. Wind rattled the apartment's windows.

After half a moment came, "If I can stay focused on this screen, Jess, I don't pay so much attention to the boat's motion. You just wouldn't believe the wild ride out here, just wouldn't believe how tired I am, but this talking to you makes such a huge difference. It's almost like we are having a glass of wine in a restaurant on dry land. I'm trying to concentrate so hard on this seven-teen-inch monitor that there is nothing else in the world, no water and wind, no sickening pitching and rolling, just you and me. It almost works."

McKay stared at the screen, trying to concentrate on it, just as Gwen Weld was focusing on her monitor all those sea miles away. Sleep swept across him like a wave. He ordered his brain to come up with a reply to Gwen. She needed a reply. She deserved one. It wouldn't come. McKay felt himself shutting down.

A long moment passed. Then up on McKay's screen came, "Jess, you still with me?"

A few more seconds elapsed. On his screen appeared, "You've fallen asleep, haven't you? There on dry land. God, I wish I was with you, sitting next to you, or lying next to you. Good night, Jess."

McKay was indeed asleep, there in his chair, his arms hanging at his side, his chin on his chest. He wouldn't read her last message until morning.

Victory climbed a two-story wave, and in the galley Gwen Weld gripped the table with both hands, keeping herself from toppling over backward. When the boat peaked the wave, it was level for a few seconds, offering her the chance to dab at Rex Wyman's face with a damp towel. Blood was caked on his cheeks and jaw. His nose was off-kilter, skewed to the left, as if he were looking over her shoulder. His shirt and pants were stained with blood. He grimaced as she tried to remove the crusted blood from his jaw.

"At any given moment, eight million people are watching us on streaming video," Wyman said as Gwen worked on his face. "No other website has ever done that business."

The boat tipped forward and sped down the wave's incline to the trough. Gwen was pushed against the table.

"Sure, we lost a crewman, but we are on course and still underway. The Pacific Winter Challenge is going to be the sporting event of the century. I'll . . . we'll be more famous than Lindbergh."

The vessel slid across the wave trough, and its prow dove into the oncoming wave, and *Victory* slowed precipitously, and Gwen was pushed forward by the deceleration. Then a cross wave slammed into the hull on the starboard quarter, and the boat shuddered as if it had received an open-field tackle. Gwen's hand was pushed against Wyman's nose, and he flinched. She continued to wipe his face.

Rex Wyman had calmed down. The boat's glitches were ever more in the past, except the boat's ignorance of the secondary depression, but Wyman knew about it now, and there was nothing, apparently, he could do to remedy the Voice's lack of knowledge. And he believed they would shortly sail out from under the heavy weather. Even though the sails were reefed, the boat's ground speed was still five knots.

Toby Odell was also at the table. His body waved back and forth like a metronome. His face was haggard. The sound of water and wind filled the space, a constant shriek that overwhelmed anything less than a yell.

At the top of her voice, Gwen said, "Rex, now is not a good time, I know. You, with your face all beaten out of shape, and all of us on this roller-coaster ride, but I've got to tell you that I'm leaving WorldQuest."

He moved his head fractionally to look at her. "You are quitting?"

"No future tense to it." She stared directly at him,

knowing he was not accustomed to it. "I quit. Right now. Right this second. I'll do what I can for *Victory* in the control room, but when—and if—I ever get off this boat, I'm through with it, and with WorldQuest."

"And with me?" he asked, his tone entirely level, and just loud enough to be heard over the roar.

"We should talk about that later." She nodded toward Odell. "In private."

"I've never hidden anything from Toby. You can talk about it right now."

Odell had been listening, despite his closed eyes. He laughed, the sound lost in the noise of wind and water. He said, "And I never hide anything from Rex. Almost nothing, that is."

She shrugged, lifting her shoulders high, but the gesture was interrupted when she had to again grab for the table as *Victory* rolled to port. She said loudly, "I need to get away from you, Rex. I'm sorry. I don't know how else to say it. I just—"

At that moment the Voice interrupted her, "Rudder control has been lost."

Wyman reacted as if Roger had slugged him again. He recoiled, his eyes wide and his mouth pulling back. He exhaled loudly, then tried to push himself upright, but the boat caught a wave and rose suddenly, and Wyman fell to one knee. Using the table for a handhold, he struggled upright. He moved aft, staggering as the deck dropped from under him and tilted forward. He scrambled uphill toward the control room.

Gwen followed him, walking with her feet wide apart, holding on to a seat back for support. A cross wave broke over the boat, exerting sudden downward pressure, and the deck dropped from under her, and then abruptly firmed. Her knees buckled and she collapsed to the deck, hitting her tailbone and slamming her elbow on a chair leg. She lay on the deck a moment, it moving under her as if she were being tossed on a blanket.

Victory had been taking the least punishing path through the oncoming sea, crossing the enormous waves on a close-hauled course. But now the rudder had failed, and the boat began falling off the sea, unable to maintain its heading. *Victory* slowly turned sideways to the waves.

Gwen's right arm was numb from the elbow to her fingers. She gripped a table leg with her left hand to pull herself over onto her belly. Then she crawled toward the control room, the deck falling and rising and rolling as she made unsteady progress aft. Sensation gradually returned to her right arm, the numbness replaced by a sharp pain in her elbow.

When she reached the control room—still on all fours—Wyman was sitting in her chair, shouting into a microphone. The boat rolled to starboard, and kept on rolling. Surely the mast was in the water. Gwen glanced at a monitor that showed the view from the masthead. She could see only bubbles. The monitor had sunk below Wyman as the boat rolled, and he used his feet against the table to push himself back in his chair. The boat began to right itself.

"What do you mean we have a server crash?" Wyman yelled. "What's that mean, a denial of service? Has a router failed?"

Wyman glanced at Gwen, who was fighting to enter the control room through a hatch that was turning like a wheel, and he punched a button so that the voice of Rick Gagliardi, *Victory*'s chief software designer, was broadcast over speakers in the control room. Wyman had rehired him a day ago.

Gagliardi said, "*Victory*'s server has been hit with an enormous volume of data." His voice waved in and out, unlike the usual crystalline satellite reception.

"What kind of data," Wyman barked.

"Millions and millions of digital packets," Gagliardi replied.

Gwen fought her way to a bolted-down chair next to Wyman. The boat had begun a profound rolling, its mast hitting the water to starboard, then battling to return upright, only to be rotated back by a new wave.

Wyman demanded, "What sort of packets?"

"They are brief pings, asking for information, or they are diagnostic messages. They are anonymous, and they are coming all at once, from everywhere. They overloaded the server and put it out of action."

"That's impossible." Wyman's expression was of chagrined wrath. "No computer or computer network can overload our server."

The boat rolled, and this time stayed on its side until a second wave rolled it farther. Gwen had to hang on to the chair arms, and was turned as if she were doing a cartwheel. The keel was in the air for a few seconds, and the masthead well under the churning sea. Then *Victory* ponderously rose again, the mast swinging up into the air.

"Damn it, Rick, we are rudderless out here," Wyman shouted into the microphone. "We're going to start rolling over like a rock polisher."

Gagliardi said, "It isn't one computer doing it. This is an attempt by a black hat hacker to shut down our operation by overloading it. The hacker planted zombies on other computers. These are otherwise benign, innocent third-party computers, at least three hundred zombie computers, we've determined."

"What are you doing about it?"

Gagliardi replied, "We are redirecting our server's traffic to another server. It's taking some time."

"Are *Victory*'s cameras working?"

"No. We can't get images here, anyway."

Wyman clenched a fist.

Gagliardi went on, "We've got you on old-fashioned VHF. This isn't over our satellite network."

"Who did this?" Spit flew from Wyman's mouth. "Who is the black hat?"

"We're working on that, too. Your onboard computer still controls some functions, including the helm."

Wyman lifted the microphone, and for a moment Gwen thought he might throw it at a monitor. But with an effort that made his entire body shake, he gained control of himself and slowly lowered the microphone to the table. The boat began another roll.

Wyman looked at Gwen.

Gagliardi's voice came again. "You'd better raise the helm, Rex. And then you'd better go topside."

"Topside?" Wyman asked in a low tone, the words almost lost in the sound of the storm.

"You are going to lose *Victory* unless you get some rudder control," Gagliardi said over the speakers. "It'll founder and sink."

Wyman's bruised face lost some of its purple color, as blanched as a face can get when it is also boldly bruised. Gwen Weld saw utter fear in his eyes, something that she had never seen before, and it seemed entirely foreign on his masterful face. He must have known the raw emotion was there for her to see, because he broke off the gaze to study the deck, which began yet again to rise to one side. He moved past Gwen, carefully working himself out of the control room as the boat rolled.

Before she knew what she was saying, Gwen called, "I'll go topside with you, Rex."

CHAPTER 18

Broaching occurs when a boat turns so that the beam is against the waves, so that it is lying along the trough of the wave, which can then hit the boat full force stem to stern. And this is what happened to *Victory* at that moment.

Wave speeds vary, depending on the distance between the wave crests. If the crests are ten yards apart, the waves will move at eight knots. If the crests are a hundred yards apart, the waves will move at twenty-five knots. In the Bering Sea at that moment, the crests were two hundred yards apart, and were moving at thirty-five knots. The waves were fifty to sixty feet high. Suddenly without rudder control, *Victory* wallowed between two of these waves for a few seconds, becalmed in the windless trough, mountainous inclines of marbled water to both sides of the boat.

Then the incoming wave lifted *Victory* on its massive slope, lifted it effortlessly, as if the boat were a piece of driftwood. As *Victory* shot skyward while it was lying across the wave and tipping further and further to starboard as the wall became more inclined, the crest of the wave broke overhead. Tons of turbu-

lent white and green water fell on *Victory* from above.
The wave hit the boat with the percussive effect of
concrete. *Victory* trembled and rolled, and kept on
rolling as the torrent washed over the hull and deck,
turning the boat as if it were on a spit.

Below decks, Gwen was preparing herself for
another mast-in-the water roll, where the boat would
lie over in the water, then appear to contemplate
whether to struggle aright again, then finally come
back up. She had experienced this maneuver dozens
of times in the past hour, hundreds in the last day, and
she braced herself against a gear locker. This time,
though, the boat didn't stop. It rotated, and where it
should have stopped, where it had stopped each previ-
ous time, it kept on rolling. The deck under Gwen's
feet moved up until it was facing her, and she tried
walking up the hull to keep up with the roll. But then
Victory flopped over, and the cabin spun, and she was
thrown onto her back, then rolled along the hull.
Then she fell off the hull, fell five feet and landed on
the ceiling as the boat was upside down. She skittered
along the ceiling, then fell again, banging against the
bulkhead and wrenching her knee, then slamming
into a locker, and landing on the deck in a heap. She
lay there, unable to gather the will to rise.

Victory was made to slice through the water. All the
boat's technological marvels were directed at attain-
ing maximum speed. *Victory* was not made to roll
through 360 degrees. Many things happened during
that roll, all of them bad.

In the galley, pans and pots flew out of their lockers
and whipped around the cabin. The toaster broke free,
and became a projectile. It bounced once, then smashed
the flat-panel monitor that had been displaying a desert
scene, which sent glass shards into the air. Most of the

bowls were plastic, and bounced around harmlessly, but two glass serving bowls spun across the room and shattered against a bulkhead so their glass splinters were abruptly added to the mix. The stove jumped its gimbals, and tumbled through the air. Sliding cartons of milk and a pot roast popped open the refrigerator door, and suddenly all the refrigerator's contents were being tossed around the cabin. Drawers popped open, and cutlery shot across the cabin.

Back pressure punched through the pipes servicing the head, and sewage was blown out of the toilet to cover walls and ceiling and deck. Most of the equipment in the tool room was tied down, but several wrenches and a hacksaw were hurled around the room. Spools of wire slipped off their stands and crashed into the bulkhead.

Toby Odell had been sitting at the galley table, gripping the table's edge, but when the deck was above him on the boat's roll, he fell heavily, landing on the ceiling. A bread knife creased his chin and a fork punctured the skin of his forehead. A cutting board jumped its mount, was propelled through the air, and clipped Odell's temple. Senseless, he skid around the cabin like a rag doll.

Gear lockers swung open. Coats and boots and bib overalls were whirled out into the cabin, many wrapping around Rex Wyman, who abruptly resembled a coat hanger. He slid along the bulkhead, trying to cast the gear away. Then he tried to scramble along with the roll, but the coats tripped him up and he somersaulted like a child going down a hill.

Wyman cried out, "*Victory*, raise the helm."

He bounced against the deck as the boat rolled upright. He tried to rise, but fell back, and lay there for a few seconds, gasping. Then he levered himself up to his knees. He crawled aft toward the hatch, then grabbed heavy weather gear and tried to get his legs into a pair of insulated pants.

Not everything bad that was occurring during the roll was happening in the living quarters. Carbon-fiber cables holding water drums were torn away, and the drums smashed against a bulkhead and ruptured. Their water emptied into the bilge. In the engine room, batteries broke lose and ricocheted around the room. A battery smashed the electric starter, twisting it away from its mount, disabling the port engine. The same battery bounced from the starter and rammed the desalinator, fracturing the control panel. Water rushed in through exhaust pipes to splash around the engine room.

Water is pernicious, and will find a way through any weakness in the deck or joinery. All boats require pumping during a gale. Seawater leaked through the deck, and seeped into the cabin. Bilge pumps are not designed to be turned upside down. Foul bilge water found its way through the rolling deck, and it began to rain bilge water in the salon as *Victory* was upside down.

"*Victory*, is the helm up?" Wyman yelled. He was on his knees, one hand on a bolted-down table leg, the other on his forehead, which was quickly turning purple. He had landed on his head at some point during the roll.

The Voice didn't respond.

"*Victory*, report on helm status?" Wyman called again. He looked around the cabin, at one built-in speaker after another, as if he might coax the Voice from just one speaker. He blinked rapidly, and tried again, "*Victory*, report on . . . wind speed."

Still nothing. The boat rolled to port, but this wave

was smaller, and *Victory* slowly righted herself. A cross wave punched the hull, and the boat jumped sideways. Gwen was holding on to the back of a chair, but lost her grip and was thrown sideways, falling to one knee, then catching herself on another chair leg. She crawled onto the chair backward, hugging the seat back.

The Voice was silent. That irritably calm, vaguely malevolent, omniscient voice no longer came from the walls.

Wyman said over the noise of the storm, "Gagliardi said they were dumping functions off into another server. We'll get the systems back online here in a minute." Normally Wyman spoke boldly, each of his sentences a declaration. This was more a prayer.

Gwen crawled forward toward Toby Odell, still on the floor in the galley. Odell was on his back, sliding back and forth on the rocking deck like a loose marble. He was trying to sit up but didn't have the strength. Gwen grabbed his arm.

"Toby, you okay?"

"No, I'm not."

Gwen thought she heard Odell laugh, but couldn't be sure, such was the howl of the storm. She helped him up to sitting. The boat rolled, and she pushed against him to steady him.

"I received a nice brochure in the mail from Princess Cruises," he said. "It's sounding better and better."

She helped him to his feet, then guided him toward his cabin. Every surface below deck was wet, and water sloshed back and forth on the deck, then splashed up the bulkheads almost to the ceiling, then back down, carrying the lounge cushions, wooden spoons, the coats and overalls, and hundreds of other things spilled from their storage area during the roll.

Wyman moved aft, wide-legged, steadying himself with each step. When he came to the storage lockers, he searched through them for dry pants and a coat and gloves. He began putting on a pair of insulated bib-overalls, but Wyman had to fight against the boat's irregular motion at the same time, and so appeared to be wrestling with himself.

In the forward gangway, Gwen and Odell walked with their arms outstretched, bracing themselves. She helped Toby into his berth, then pulled a blanket over him. Water hadn't seeped into his cabin.

He said, "I feel like I'm being tucked in."

"You're really ill, aren't you, Toby?" She secured the lee cloth. "I saw all your pills."

"I'm fine in the short run." He coughed raggedly. "I feel pretty good, day to day. It's the long run that has me worried. Of course, the long run should have us all worried." He laughed gently.

Kneeling next to his berth, she looked at him with affection. Toby Odell was everybody's next door neighbor's kid, an aw-shucks fellow who was always ready with a word of praise or a funny one-line bit of self-deprecation. Everybody's chum, the kid with the serious baseball card collection, the kid who could talk about aggies, immies, and shooters with authority. The flap-shirted kid who never had a date in high school, but who had plenty of friends because he was so agreeable, and who always had good ideas on how to waste a Saturday. Odell was that likable, forgettable fellow found in every classroom as a child and every neighborhood as an adult, except for one thing: he had hooked up with Rex Wyman, and Odell had parlayed his eagerness and curiosity and intelligence into a vast fortune. In Ketchum, Idaho, where Odell grew up and went to high school, a mantra among wistful middle aged-women was, "I could've married Toby Odell," when in truth few of the women had any memories of Odell, even though they might have sat next to him in class after class during their school years.

She pulled his spectacles off his face and tucked them under a corner of his pillow. A welt was growing on his forehead where the cutting board had hit him. He grinned weakly. The boat shook with a water broadside, and began a roll. She held on to the edge of his bed.

"Is it cancer, Toby?" she asked.

He nodded. "Liver cancer."

"Is it treatable?"

"My doctors thought so for a while, despite the statistics. Now the doctors are no longer even pretending. Liver cancer isn't one of those cancers where there's much success treating." He smiled. "But I've taken charge of the disease, Gwen."

The sea was loud, just outside the hull. She could hardly hear him. She asked, "What do you mean?"

"It's not going to kill me. I'm going to kill it." His voice was toneless, without his usually gentle mocking or irony.

His words were so final that she shivered. "I don't know what you mean, Toby."

"I've seen the future. It's as plain as your face in front of me. I'm not leaving this boat alive."

She gripped his arm under the blanket. "That's foolish talk. You sound like some tarot-card reader."

He shook his head.

"Nobody can tell the future, Toby."

He just stared at her.

She said, "I'm going to leave you here and check out the control room. I'll be back. I want to talk to you about this."

He smiled knowingly, something of his old smile.

Gwen left him in his cabin, and walked and squatted at the same time, trying to compensate for the motion of the boat. She moved aft through the hatch into the salon, pushing through debris and several inches of water so cold that her feet ached. Rex was below, in the engine room, using cranks to manually raise the helm. The deck moved under her like a porch swing. She fought her way into the control room.

No water had made it into the room, and the bolts holding down her equipment had held. Manuals had been thrown about, many pages coming loose and lying around, covering the deck like a field of snow. The paper fell back and forth as the boat rolled. Her mouse and keyboard were dangling from her table. Her coffee cup was on the deck amidst the sheets of paper. It must have bounced around during the roll, because one of her monitors had been punched out. Its screen was in pieces, the fragments sliding back and forth on the deck.

Some of her monitors were on, others were black. The boat's stand-alone computer system supported some functions, but not many.

Just as she picked up the VHF handset, Rex Wyman appeared in the hatch. He had donned the insulated bib overalls and the coat, and was now working with the zippers and the Velcro.

"What are you doing?" he demanded.

"I'm sending a Mayday."

He stared at her. The port side of the boat began another rise. Wyman gripped the hatch ledge.

"We are taking on water, Rex." When she pointed at one of her monitors, the sharp pain in her elbow returned. "You can see for yourself. Our bilge pumps are out. We need rescue."

His bruised face contorted. "Put the radio down, Gwen. Nobody calls a Mayday except me."

"Rex, we've rolled over. *Victory* has taken a body blow."

"We are floating," he snarled.

"We are a floating hulk."

With his heavy-weather gear on, he filled the room. He raised a finger and pointed it at her like a prosecutor. "Put the damned radio down, Gwen." In that instant, he looked truly dangerous. Gwen caught her breath, afraid of Wyman and afraid of *Victory*.

Suddenly her dark monitors lit up, and almost as quickly *Victory* began responding to its rudder. The boat turned toward the wind. Wyman stared aft over his shoulder toward the unseen rudders, then he glanced around the control room. It had sprung to life, and although the deck was covered with glass and paper, the room was filled with reassuring light from the monitors. The boat climbed a wave, rather than rocking back and forth helplessly. While still unpredictable due to the cross seas, and still wild by any standard, the new motion was nevertheless reassuring. The boat was no longer wallowing. It had gained steerageway.

Wyman demanded, "*Victory*, report on the heading and speed.

"Bearing north by northwest, ground speed of four knots."

Wyman's face transformed with startlingly quickness. One moment he had the look of a killer, and the next his expression was of a gleeful child opening a gift.

"*Victory*, report on the boom."

"The boom is reefed to storm setting five, and is ten degrees off midline."

Very little of the mainsail was up. The roller reefing

mainsail was working. The sheets and winches were working. The mast and boom were doing their foul-weather work perfectly. Wyman grinned widely, his perfect white teeth bright in his bruised face.

"*Victory*, report on the jib."

"Forward hydraulic pumps two and three are inoperable. Forward hydraulic pump one is operating, but the system is not receiving jib wind resistance data."

Wyman looked at a monitor on the table. "Show camera four POV on monitor one."

The scene on the monitor in front of Gwen switched from the masthead camera to a camera mounted amidships that was aimed at the bow. The image on the monitor showed that the jib had been torn away during the roll. All that was visible was the prow, the stays, and the swirling face of the next incoming wave. The boat rose again, up the side of the wave.

"There's no jib resistance data because there's no jib." Wyman laughed. "Hell, who needs a jib? *Victory*, report on the engine systems."

"Main engine one and main engine two are presently inoperable." These were the big Caterpillar diesel engines used for propulsion, and except for testing once a day, they had not been used since pushing *Victory* from its mooring in San Francisco harbor. "Generator one is inoperable. Generator two is functioning."

Again Wyman laughed. "We can get along on one generator. *Victory*, report on the bilge pumps."

"Bilge pumps two and three are inoperable. Bilge pump one was offline for seventy-four seconds, and is now operating."

"*Victory*, report on bilge-water levels."

"Two feet of water is in the forward bilge. Three-point-five feet of water in the center bilge. Three-point-two feet of water in the aft bilge."

Wyman said to himself, "I'll go below and look at the bilge pumps. Maybe debris is obstructing them." Then he raised his voice, "*Victory*, what other systems are inoperable?"

"The desalinator, the galley stove, number two VHF radio—"

"You're back online, looks like from here," Rick Gagliardi's words interrupted the Voice. The software engineer was in Boise. His voice was being run through the sound system's graphic equalizer and pumped through the six speakers in the control room. Gagliardi sounded as if he were in the control room, and his tones were much more full than they had been when carried earlier by the VHF radio.

"We're in good shape here, Rick." Wyman sounded as if he had just won the Pacific Winter Challenge, rather than having just survived a full roll. "What'd you do in Boise."

"Set up a mirror server."

"Is this going to happen again?"

"You know I can't promise you it won't," Gagliardi said in a tone of fragile dignity. "It's not happening now. You should settle for that."

"Are *Victory*'s cameras feeding the Internet?"

"I'm looking at you right now on my screen," Gagliardi replied.

Wyman said jubilantly, "How many times have I fired you this week, Rick?"

"Three, I think. Maybe four. I get confused."

"I'm giving you a free pass, just like in Monopoly. Next time I fire you, take it out of your pocket, and you can stay at your desk." Wyman laughed brightly.

The boat sped down the backside of a wave, slowed in the trough, then began another ascent, the prow pointed toward the black sky.

Wyman crowed like a man who has just received a pardon. "We're okay here, Rick, except maybe we need a few more bandages in the first-aid kit."

And only then did Gwen remember Roger Hall, alone in his cabin. She pushed herself out of her chair and sidled around Wyman, who continued to talk with Rick Gagliardi. The deck bounding under her, she moved handhold to handhold forward through the aft hatch into the salon, stepping through sloshing water— though less now that it was draining into the bilges— passed the galley, through the forward hatch and into the companionway. Her thighs ached from fighting the boat's motion, and her arms felt boneless. She was so exhausted that the rolling and heaving salon had a dream quality, as if she were watching herself from over her shoulder. Some of her mind was offline, as some of *Victory* had been, she hazily decided.

She moved into the companionway, and leaned heavily against Hall's door as she knocked. Then she knocked more loudly.

"Roger, can I come in?" she called.

She pressed her ear against the door, trying to hear his voice above the din of the storm. Nothing came from the cabin. She called again. Still nothing. Scowling, she fumbled with Rex's jury-rigged lock on the door, untying amateurish knots. She pushed open the door.

Roger Hall was on the deck below his bunk. He was belly-down, and splayed out in an unnatural position as if he had been dropped from a fourth story. His head was twisted so that he was looking over his shoulder at the ceiling, too far over his shoulder. His eyes were open.

Gwen mouthed something and dropped to her knees. She didn't know where to begin. She touched his scalp and then his back and then finally she pressed her fingers on his neck at the jugular vein. There was no pulse.

When *Victory* rolled, Roger Hall had been bounced off the ceiling and then off the deck. His neck had been broken.

Two of *Hornet's* crew, Bang The Drum and the kid, Nick Summers, were out on deck, cracking off built-up ice with baseball bats. The third crewman, Ollie Nordquist, was in the galley, rigging a storm shutter out of Lexan, installing it over a suspect porthole. In the wheelhouse, Lonnie Garvin turned the helm slightly with each new wave, repositioning the trawler to take the wave at an angle of about thirty degrees. Sometimes this led to a smooth ride up and over the crest, but often a cross sea howler—surely forty feet high, maybe higher—would drop on *Hornet* from another direction, and would ram its hull and violently push it sideways, shaking the boat.

Hornet's windshield wipers beat back and forth. He had never seen seas like this, an endless mountain range of water, one roaring peak after another coming at *Hornet* in a sinister procession. His boat would struggle up one embankment of water, totter at the foaming top where his bow and stern would be entirely out of the water and his propellers, suspended in the air, would rev up, and then *Hornet* would surf down the backside. And then the boat would do it again, and then again. Holding on to the wheel as the wheelhouse deck tilted up then slanted down time and again, Garvin felt as if he were alternating push-ups with chin-ups. His arms were on fire, he was so tired supporting himself at the helm. He didn't sit in his raised chair because he was afraid of being thrown off it. His cabin heaters were on so high that hot air was rippling his pants legs.

Maybe *Hornet* hadn't wanted to go to sea today. It was acting sluggishly and seemed out of trim. He looked at the television screen that showed the crab deck. The pots were tied down dead center on the amidships line. Ice was building up on the plastic tarps that covered the pots, but the crew would soon get to them with their bats. Garvin was comforted by the glow of his instruments. He patted the wood console in front of him. Truth be told, he loved this boat. Not like he loved his wife, he quickly added to himself, but still his bond of affection for *Hornet* was as strong as any emotion he had ever known. Save his love for his wife, Allison, and the kids, of course, he added again just in case God was listening to his thoughts.

The Bering Sea's surface was covered with spindrift, spray swept by the piercing wind, so much of it that the sea was smoking. Small waves, which often ride on the back of the larger rollers, had disappeared, blown flat by the wind. Each new wave rose above *Hornet*, a boat-breaking wall rushing in at freight-train speed. The water was a peculiar olive green, with angry swirls of white and gray. The cross seas added a touch of anarchy, with errant waves smashing against the boat from unexpected angles at irregular intervals. Garvin's hands on the spokes were white with his effort to hold on to the wheel. The night sky was so low that racing black clouds seemed to brush the wave tips.

Garvin was worried, standing there in the pilot-house, his face colored by the lights of his instrument panels. He was a fretter, and Allison would sometimes laugh and call him the "worrier-in-chief." He told her that the deep lines on his forehead showed that he was made to worry. But not like this, not the anguish of doubt about his boat in this storm. *Hornet* was a blue-water winter boat, as tough a hull as could be found in Alaskan waters, and modesty didn't prevent him from believing he was one of the most skilled skippers in Alaska. Still, gazing out of his frosted window, riding the trawler up and down, Garvin worried.

The hatch opened, and Nick Summers stepped over the rim into the wheelhouse. He was wearing so much gear not an inch of his skin was showing. He was carrying a dented baseball bat. The wind sounded like an endless scream right in Garvin's ears.

"Ollie and I are done, stem to stern." Summers's voice was muffled by a wool mask. He had to shout. "*Hornet* is clear of ice."

Ollie Nordquist followed Summers into the pilothouse. Both men were wearing safety harnesses over their clothing. Nordquist carried a crowbar in his hand.

Garvin grinned at Summers. "In this storm, knocking ice off our boat is going to be like painting the Golden Gate Bridge." He waited a beat, then added, "The minute you are done, you begin again."

Summers laughed.

"Go below, get some coffee. Take your gloves and coat off for a few minutes. Then I'll need you topside again."

The men clattered down the companionway to the galley. A cross wave crashed into the starboard side, and *Hornet* shook with its impact.

Once again, standing at the wheel, Garvin checked off his mental list. Had he done everything? Had he missed something?

The survival suits were in their bags in an easily accessed locker. Each suit had a personal EPIRB. The life jackets were new, and each had a strobe. He had used Wyman's money to purchase a man-overboard pole. He had bought new flares and fire extinguishers, again using Wyman's money. The boat was carrying tapered wooden plugs and underwater epoxy. *Hornet* had already carried two bilge pumps, a manual high-output pump and an electric pump with a strainer, but with Wyman's cash Garvin had purchased a Jabsco engine-driven high-output emergency pump. Also with Wyman's money the skipper had purchased a new six-man throw-overboard Avon life raft that was inflated with CO_2 and had self-erecting canopies, a ballast system, a conical sea anchor, a dry-cell light system, and an onboard EPIRB.

He and his crew and been working hard since leaving Dutch Harbor, preparing the boat. Nordquist had installed rubber gaskets on gear lockers to stop seawater from entering the locker when the boat heeled. Bang The Drum had attached new companionway slides so that the slides were fixed in place with a throughbolt. The crew had installed a jackline in the center of the boat to which they could attach their harnesses, and Bang The had bolted many double lifelines to the hull.

Covers had been installed on the ventilators. The batteries had been secured in their boxes with metal tops. All the seacocks had been inspected, and double hose clamps had been put on all hoses leading to the seacocks. The anchor had been secured by two-inch chain. Garvin had made sure he could quickly get to the stuffing glands on the propellers if a leak developed, and he had installed hose clamps on the propeller shafts and the rudder posts so that if they broke, the clamps would prevent them from falling out into the sea, leaving holes open to the water.

What else could he have done? Well, he could have stayed in port. But that wasn't an option, not now, not with the damned sheriff standing by to seize his boat and his career. Not with Allison down in Seattle, afraid to pick up the phone lest it be a dunning call. *Hornet* had to go out.

In a wave trough, Garvin again noticed the boat's sluggishness. *Hornet* rode the next roller up, balanced at the peak, then slid down the wave's back. Now in another trough, Garvin scanned his gauges and tried to quickly refresh his sense of the trawler.

Then it came to him, and he abruptly understood the peculiar sensation his boat was sending him, surely on purpose. The trawler wasn't righting, not completely. Not that in these miserable seas the boat would spend much time entirely upright, but it was critical that the vessel retain the ability to return upright.

He looked at his fuel gauges, dimly lit in green. Rex Wyman had wanted *Hornet* underway quickly. The entire deal was dependent on speed, so Garvin had purposely not taken on a full load of fuel. He didn't need it. He wasn't going out for a month of crabbing. He'd be out for a couple of days, max. He had more than enough diesel on board.

The trouble was, most of the diesel had been put into the starboard tanks. Garvin hadn't taken the time to balance his fuel load while loading it in Dutch Harbor, hadn't taken the time to put the diesel through more than one of the four fuel intake valves on the superstructure.

He scowled. If he deliberately hadn't balanced the load while fueling, which he hadn't, he should have started doing so immediately on departing the harbor. He hadn't done that either. He had simply forgotten, with the rough seas disguising the boat's imbalance.

Normally when at sea Garvin drew fuel from whatever tank needed to be drained down to maintain the boat's balance, but *Hornet* was equipped with onboard pumps and fuel transfer lines. Diesel could be shifted tank to tank, and this could be done from the wheelhouse.

Garvin threw the switch for the fuel transfer pump, starboard to port. Within thirty minutes, the boat should be balanced. He glanced at the fuel gauge for the port main tank. Gauges weren't too accurate in these seas, with the diesel sloshing around, but the port tank was almost empty. He would be able to quickly determine whether fuel was being pumped into the tank.

It wasn't filling. Garvin glanced at the pump indicator light. It was glowing green. The pump was working, but no diesel was being transferred. He looked at the port tank gauge again, then tapped it with his finger. Still, no fuel was being added to the tank. He quickly switched off the pump before it overheated.

Garvin bit down on his lower lip. There could be only one explanation: The bitterly cold sea had frozen his fuel transfer lines. He should've balanced the fuel load while still in Dutch Harbor. He had made a mistake, a big one.

He picked up an intercom handset. "Ollie and Bang The, get up here in a hurry."

CHAPTER 19

The boarder was stoked. He wiped his forehead with the back of his hand. He had just performed a three-sixty shove-it kickflip, and had landed perfectly, nothing sketchy about it. The board had spun around under him, front to back like a helicopter's main blade while at the same time it had flipped over entirely, wheels up and over, and had landed on its wheels again, and he had come down solidly on the deck, looking like a pro.

Now he pushed the board along with a foot, sailed up a ramp, and hopped off the board just as it reached the ramp's lip, so that he landed on the platform. At the same instant he kicked the board. It jumped into the air. He caught it, the grip tape nicely scratchy under his fingers. Then he dropped the board to the platform and anchored it with his foot. He leaned back against the railing to catch his breath and to survey his domain. His earrings glittered in the lamplight.

Twenty or so boarders were in the skate park. Boarders are often loners, and most were in the park by themselves, but a few were laughing and joking and comparing moves with friends. One kid, couldn't have been more than ten, had been trying for a solid hour to do a fifty-fifty, grinding both axles of the skateboard on a concrete edge. He tried it again and again, his face locked in concentration. Three boarders were going back and forth in the park's big halfpipe, going up one side, doing a one-eighty, soaring down and going up the other side, doing another one-eighty, and coming down again, easily and endlessly, talking all the while.

The park resembled a cratered moonscape. The ramps were in many shapes and sizes, with different angles and elevations. The sun had gone down, but the skateboard park was set up for night boarding, and the lamps threw a stark white light across the park, a light that leached the place of color, making the park seem even more otherworldly. Rain had fallen that afternoon, and the night air was chilled. Shallow puddles remained at several spots on the concrete. Chain-link fence surrounded the area. A porta-potty and a Coke machine were in a corner of the park. Several kids sat on benches, making adjustments to their shoes or just watching the other boarders. One twelve-year-old kid was fumbling with a cigarette and matches, learning to smoke. Without exception, the skateboarders' clothes looked as if they had been plucked from a bin at the Goodwill.

Few twenty-two-year-olds are philosophical, but this boarder, leaning against the platform rail, had a wry sense of perspective. He did three things in his life, and only three things. He sat at a computer. He boarded. He drove his car. At twenty-two years of age, he had found the perfect balance: He spent his days doing only those things that fascinated him, and he was good at them. He aspired to nothing more. Life was perfect. At twenty-two, he was at the top, and not just at the top of a skateboard ramp platform. He had a sweet job that paid him a fortune doing the only thing he was good at, other than boarding. Life was all downhill, in every direction, just like the ramp incline below his platform. It worried him some.

What do you do when you are young, and you have everything you want and are doing exactly what you want with your life? He pondered the delightful question a moment, standing on the platform, his skateboard at his feet. Maybe he should go back to college. His folks wanted him to. The first time, he had lasted only two quarters. Maybe he would take some English literature courses this time. He laughed. Nah. What could be a bigger waste of time? He scratched his black watch cap. A three-day stubble was on his face. His thighs were pleasantly aching. He had ridden hard tonight. It was time to pack it in. He was due at the office early tomorrow morning.

He did a fakie off the ramp, going down the incline standing backward on his board. Then he did a one-eighty to face forward, then veered the board toward the gate. To slow himself, he did a wheelie, dragging the board's tail on the concrete. He nodded at two guys he recognized who were sitting on a bench at the gate. With his foot, he flipped the board up into his hand, then stepped through the gate.

He walked along the parking lot, behind old Nissans and Chevrolets, mostly rust-buckets, many with bushel-sized speakers on ledges behind backseats. One car's backseat was littered with Oberto beef jerky wrappers. Another car was missing its back bumper.

He approached his automobile, a canary-yellow Porsche Boxter that had cost him sixty-five thousand dollars. The Boxter was a convertible, but its hardtop was in place. He turned off the car's alarm with his key-chain thingy. He stepped between his car and the

neighboring Chrysler van, and stuck his keys into the
Boxter's lock.

"You got a moment, Brady?"

The question came from the front of the van. A man
was abruptly standing there, coming out of nowhere.
A small fellow, dressed in a sports coat and blue shirt
but no tie, wearing a street-smart smile, looking as if
he should be at a horse track.

The dapper fellow stepped closer, between the Boxter
and the Chrysler van. "Couple of questions is all."

"You the police?" the skateboarder asked in a cracking voice. He detested his nervousness. He was clean.
Why was he always panicky when talking to anyone
who sounded like the man?

The fellow in the sports coat held out a business
card. The skateboarder fought an urge to flee. Nothing
good could come from this, a guy sneaking up on him.
The skateboarder read the card. The man was Ted
Landers, WorldQuest, Inc., but the card didn't show his
position at WorldQuest.

"You're Brady Lane, right?" this Ted Landers asked.

"Yeah, but . . ." Lane gripped his skateboard tightly.

"Can we go for a walk? A few questions is all."

"No, hell no. I'm getting in my car and going home.
I've got nothing to say to you." He turned the key in
the door.

Ted Landers's smile seemed welded onto his face. He
stepped forward quickly and placed a hand on Lane's
arm just above the biceps, at a pressure point. Landers
squeezed.

Brady Lane had never before experienced such
sudden and overwhelming pain. An excruciating jolt
of electricity seemed to rush up his arm and into his
head and flow down into his body in an instant, pain
so severe that he was abruptly nauseated. His knees

buckled. Ted Landers moved quickly to catch him.

The Chrysler van's side door slid open. One of Landers's crew, a fellow in a black sweater and black pants, was inside, and he and Landers rolled the skateboarder into the van's cargo bay. Landers looked over his shoulder. None of the other boarders had seen anything. His grin still in place, Landers opened the driver's door and got behind the steering wheel.

He called over his shoulder to the man in the black clothing, "I think Wyman will be pleased."

Once again Wyman was in the control room, Gwen Weld's area. He owned the entire boat, but she wished he'd stay away from her territory. He was tapping the table anxiously, waiting for the call to come in. The monitors indicated wind speed had increased three knots over the past hour.

Even inside the boat, the noise of wind through the rigging and the water coursing by the hull was crushing. There was no escape from it, nowhere on board she could go for some silence. A few minutes was all she needed, just to get herself thinking straight again. She knew the berserk motion of the boat and the unceasing noise had addled her. The shock and horror of discovering Roger Hall dead in his cabin seemed to be in a tight compartment in her brain, waiting to be released at some later time, when she had the capacity for those emotions to register. She didn't now. She only had the ability to fervently wish she were on dry land. Maybe a desert mountain, with no lakes anywhere, no water of any sort, not even dew. She was through with water forever.

She had tried to clean up the small computer and communications space, gathering up the loose pages and picking up the larger pieces of glass, but as she was doing so, *Victory* dropped from under her, and she had banged her arm against the bulkhead, and the pages went flying again, and they could stay on the deck for all she cared. Her head was down on her arms at the table next to a computer monitor. Her eyes were closed. She no longer cared if Wyman viewed her as the diligent sailor. She needed sleep, and she needed to get off this hell boat.

Wyman was working his face, one expression after another, most of them shades of anger, as if he were auditioning them. He had removed his heavy-weather gear, no longer needing to go topside. The rudders were working. The entire system was working. When Gwen had told him of Roger Hall's death, Wyman had shaken his head, but had said nothing at all.

And how had she responded to this callousness? She had had no energy left for any anger or indignation. She only noticed that Wyman's hair was dirty, one of those little observations that come unbidden, don't fit anywhere, and aren't soon forgotten. Wyman loved a mirror, and was obsessed with his hair, and here it was greasy and matted. And now, her head on her arms, she wasn't thinking of Roger Hall or Eddie Lash. She wasn't in a state of disbelief. She wasn't grieving. Instead, her woolly mind was fixed on Rex Wyman's hair. Please, dear Lord, get me off this boat. Can I make a deal with you, dear Lord? What will you take in exchange for getting me off this boat, away from Rex Wyman's dirty hair? She was thinking only right enough to know she wasn't thinking right. She wanted to sleep. Anything for some sleep. Roger Hall's body was wrapped in a sail and lying in his berth. At least he was asleep.

"Rex, you there?" came from the control room's speakers.

"What do you have, Ted?"

"We first ran a course of digital forensics. We carefully looked at the logs of the Internet traffic routers, but this didn't find anything. So then we examined the packets that had overwhelmed the system, hoping they might have small bits of code or text that would point to the hacker. We hired a consultant, who used a program that speeded up the search. Even so, it was tedious and time-consuming—"

"I know it is," Wyman interrupted. "Keep going."

"We didn't come up with anything," Ted Landers said. "So we started investigating the old-fashioned way, using informants in the hacker world. We have dozens of them, as you know. Hackers are highly intelligent, but they don't have wisdom. They almost always brag."

Wyman said into the microphone, "Come on, Ted. Quit wasting my time with pop psychology. Lay it out."

"Your system is shot through with trouble, Rex, and—"

Again Wyman cut him off. "I'm out here on the damned boat, and so I already know that."

"You don't know how thorough the virus is, Rex."

The boat's motion pulled Gwen back in her chair, making her sit upright. Her hands fell onto her lap, then she placed them on the edge of the table, bracing for the next jolt. Up the boat went, higher and higher, and gravity pulled her toward Wyman. She gripped the arms of her chair with the little strength she had left.

Landers's voice came again, "*Victory*'s roll, its three-sixty? I'll bet you didn't think a normal Bering Sea wave could roll your 155-foot-long boat with its seventy-five-ton keel."

Wyman moved his mouth, perhaps about to order

Ted Landers to stop dallying, but the billionaire checked himself.

"*Victory*'s server was programmed to detect an incoming rogue wave, those abnormally large waves, sometimes three times bigger than the running sea, and you know all this. But what you don't know is that the server was programmed by the virus to cut out *Victory*'s rudder just before a rogue wave hit."

Landers paused a few seconds, perhaps to let his news sink in.

He was rewarded when Wyman asked, "What do you mean?"

"It was no accident your boat rolled. I've been told by my people that it's a miraculous piece of software design, using your system to spot the big wave, then cutting out the rudder, all without you being aware of the virus."

The boat hit a trough, smacking it, and Gwen was driven down into her chair as if by a boot. Wyman had been standing, rigid in his anger, but now he fell into his chair. His lips were pulled back, and his teeth showed sourly.

He glanced at Gwen Weld, and his eyes narrowed as if she were part of the conspiracy. He switched off the speakers and lifted a handset so she couldn't hear Ted Landers.

Wyman said, "Cut to the chase, Ted. Who is the hacker? Who has been trying to ruin me?" He listened, the handset pressed to his ear. His face suddenly knotted with fury at Landers's words.

This time all systems failed. *Victory* shut down completely. Lights throughout the boat instantly went off, and all the monitors in Gwen's control room went to black.

Wyman yelled in rage. Gwen could do nothing but

grip the arms of her chair. The control room was as dark as a cave. The boat quickly fell off the wind. And this time there was no idle moment of wallowing in a trough before the big wave hit. It roared over *Victory*, enveloping it and rolling it with ease, an errant toy in the vast universe of storm-driven water. All the hull's planed angles, all the state-of-the-art rigging, everything aboard *Victory* that was made for forward motion, was rendered instantly useless. *Victory* turned like a mill's water wheel, doing what it was never designed to do, a motion alien to its design. Within seconds, the boat was upside down—turning turtle, the cute sailing phrase entirely at odds with the frightening event—and its bulbous keel was in the air, and then the boat continued to roll, pushed by the massive, onrushing giant wave.

Wyman yelled again, more of a scream, but not of fear. It was a primal cry of fury.

During this roll, this second three-sixty, Gwen Weld, hanging desperately on to her chair, heard new noises: loud popping, like gunfire, and then a grinding squeal, a sound high above the rush of wind and water. It was a mechanical sound, metal being twisted by an irresistible force, a ripping screech that was intensely different from the storm's howl.

As the mammoth wave rolled the boat, Gwen hung from her chair, her fingers locked on the arms, but the boat kept turning, and gravity wrenched her around, and her fingers slipped, and she fell, plummeted into utter darkness. She didn't remember landing.

Weak light brought her around. She blinked several times, trying to chase the fuzziness from her brain. She was lying on the control room deck. The back of her

head throbbed. She touched it gently. It was damp. She
brought away blood on her fingers. Still lying there, the
boat rocking, she glanced toward the table. She supposed she had hit the corner of a monitor on her way
down, or maybe the table edge. The pain filled her
head. She tried to sit up.

None of the monitors were operating, nor were the
overhead lights or the table lamps. Light came only
from side emergency lamps, small frosted glass bulbs
behind metal grids. She attempted to climb to her
chair, but fell back, her head pounding. She didn't
know how long she had been unconscious, maybe
only a few seconds. She looked at her wristwatch. The
crystal had been shattered in the fall, and the hands
were missing.

"USAFNG fourteen to *Victory*. Can you hear me?
USAFNG fourteen to *Victory*."

The voice came from the table, wispy words filled
with static. She braced a foot against the bulkhead,
then levered herself onto her chair, using the boat's
roll for momentum. The boat staggered under a
wave, and she was punched back into the chair.

"Gwen, can you lift up the handset?"

The words came from a handheld VHF radio. She
removed it from its recharging mount at the back of
the table. She pressed the send button, but a new bolt
of pain came from the back of her head, and her jaw
snapped shut and her eyes were rimmed in red. She
couldn't find the energy to say anything.

"Gwen, are you in your control room? Can you hear
me?" It was Jess McKay's voice.

She pressed the button. "We've rolled again." She
groaned. "This is a nice little radio, reaching you all the
way in Anchorage." What was she saying? She hardly
had a clue.

"You are being patched through. Listen to me, Gwen. We saw your roll on our screens, and as the mast hit the water, your video signal blacked out. We think *Victory* has lost its mast, lost its rigging."

"I . . . couldn't care less."

"Yes, you do. Are you with me, Gwen? Are you injured? Say something that makes sense."

She pressed the button. "I'm with you." It was a lie. She really and truly couldn't care less. Her head was nothing but pain. And she was so exhausted she would welcome . . . what? She couldn't figure it out.

"I'm at my base. We are coming to get you, but you and Wyman and Odell need to do something right now. Your mast and boom are probably hanging loose across your deck, or they are hanging off the boat in the water, hanging by the rigging."

She didn't have enough energy to press the send button.

"Gwen, you need to rally. Listen to me. Concentrate. The mast and boom are surely going to punch holes in your hull or deck unless you cut them free. Do you understand me?"

Rex Wyman appeared in the hatchway. He was drenched, water dripping from his head and hair. He said, "A porthole blew out. We stuffed a cushion into it, and braced it with a man-overboard pole."

From the radio came, "Gwen, you are in a survival storm now."

"Who is that?" Wyman asked, duck-walking to a seat, the deck yawing violently. One of his knees hit the deck hard. He inched up into the seat.

"A pararescue jumper," she said. "They are on their way, he says."

Wyman blinked. A drop of water hung from his nose, then fell away as the boat went up on one side.

"Rex, he says the boom and mast are down," Gwen said. He didn't hear her, and she tried again, shouting.

"Yeah, I know. Through the porthole, I could see some cable hanging from the deck."

She managed to press the VHF button. "Maybe we should get into a life raft and wait for you, instead of going out on deck and fooling with the rigging."

From the radio came, "The last thing—the very last thing—you want to do is to get into a life raft."

The sailing community learned this hard lesson during the 1979 Fastnet, where the entire crew, nine sailors, of *St. Patrick* abandoned ship when they thought it was sinking. Seven drowned. *St. Patrick* was found later, bobbing in the water.

She wished the radio reception were clearer. Maybe she could tell something about Jess McKay from his voice. Before this, she had always read his words, not heard them.

McKay said, "We will be far less able to spot you—even with your beacons—in a life raft. Don't get into the life raft until there is absolutely no choice. You can't carry much food or water on a life raft, and your ride will be even worse than you are experiencing now on *Victory*, much worse. *Victory* will float even if it's half-filled with water. Stay with it."

The boat was momentarily in a trough. Gwen released her grip on the chair arm. Then a cross wave collided with *Victory*, and Gwen was thrown against the table. The handset fell and dangled on its cord.

"Do you have tools on board?" McKay asked over the radio.

Wyman snatched the handset. He shouted into the microphone, just above the din of the storm, "What do you think? Of course we have tools."

"Get bolt cutters if you have them," McKay said.

"And hacksaws. Check your safety harnesses. Do you have a sea anchor?"

Wyman hesitated several seconds. "No."

"What can you use as warps?"

Again Wyman hesitated.

McKay didn't wait for a response. "Get out on deck and cut away the rigging. You'll need as much help topside as possible. The boom and mast are heavy."

"Yes, you are right, of course," Wyman said. "We'll go out."

"Is your deck heating system working?"

"No. We're running on emergency power, on the batteries. Both generators have failed."

"Then you'll need to go out on deck right now. The spray is probably freezing over your hatches. Within a few moments you'll have solid ice over them, and you'll be sealed inside like a tomb."

After a beat, Wyman said, "Yes, of course." He didn't like to be told his business. Wyman handed her the VHF, and then used the hatch rim as a handhold and left the control room.

Gwen tried to push herself out of the chair. The deck swung under her as if it were a pendulum.

"Gwen, are you there?" McKay asked.

She pressed the button. "I'm here, sort of."

"Two hundred years ago, on square-riggers, canvas was rigged behind the helmsman—a shield—so he couldn't see the waves rushing at him."

"I'm not following you, Jess." She was not following anything. She closed her eyes.

"Don't look at the waves all around you, Gwen. Look at the deck, at your work. Keep focused on your work."

She inhaled. "Or otherwise I'll be scared to death."

He didn't say anything.

So she said, "Goodbye, Jess." She sounded as if she were mounting a scaffold.

"Gwen, the most important tool you have now is yourself." The wavy VHF reception couldn't hide the urgency in his voice. "If you are not committed to surviving, you won't."

She replied, "That wine we'll have together, Jess? When I get off this boat, I'll buy."

She put the handset into its mount, then, bracing herself hand to hand, she followed Wyman from the control room toward the gear lockers.

Gwen turned the hatch handle and pulled. The hatch remained in place, stuck in its frame. She gripped it tightly and yanked, and it still wouldn't move.

Wyman stepped up to the hatch, and Toby Odell was right behind them. All three were wearing heavy-weather gear, encased solidly in it. Wyman braced a foot against the bulkhead next to the hatch, and he and Gwen pulled on it. It opened with the loud crack of ice breaking, and slammed into Wyman, staggering him.

Gwen was pushed back by an icy blast of wind. She gathered her hammer and hacksaw, grabbed the hatch, and pulled herself through, Wyman and Odell following her, both carrying tools. Arctic wind cut through her, and she was suddenly so cold she looked down at herself, instinctively thinking she might have entirely forgotten to dress. She was wearing five insulated layers. She slipped on ice on the cockpit deck but caught herself on the rail. She pushed against the wind toward the cockpit's scuppers, then secured her safety harness. She hammered the ice from a scupper so water in the cockpit could drain, then she moved to the next scupper.

She banged away mindlessly, the ice chips flying. The storm's noise—as loud as a jet engine—chased away useful thoughts. The wind screeched through the rigging, and even more frightening were the roar and hiss of unseen waves breaking in the distance. She cleared the final scupper of ice, then unhitched her harness to move forward, holding on to the ice-encrusted safety rail. The searing wind blew spray off the water, which instantly turned to ice and shot across the deck like shrapnel, biting into her.

Waves rose on both sides of the boat, sheer inclines of foaming water, making *Victory* seem puny and insignificant, nothing anyone would want to gamble a life on. A wave closed on the boat like a predator and lifted it with sickening swiftness. Gwen's legs buckled with the upward acceleration, and she fell onto the ice-shrouded deck, losing her hammer. She slid toward the edge of the boat, toward the bottomless sea—but caught herself on a safety rail stanchion, one leg hanging off the edge. She kicked her leg, found purchase, and pushed herself back onto the deck. The hammer was gone.

The wave heaved the boat into the air and rolled it to starboard. Then *Victory* crested the wave, and Gwen, still on her knees and breathing the frigid air in huge throat-burning gulps, could see her enemy, the countless wave crests stretching off toward the murky storm-sullied horizon, coming at her like a relentless army. So much spray was in the air she couldn't tell where the water ended and the sky began. And up here, on top of a comber, the wind was even stronger, ramming her, trying to sweep her from the deck. She walked on her knees, ice crackling under them, until she found a handhold. Then *Victory* fell off the wave and plunged downward at freefall speed. Gwen closed her eyes, one hand on the hold and another on her hacksaw. She might have cried out, but she couldn't hear herself. The boat bottomed out in the trough as if someone had stomped on the brakes, and the force pushed Gwen down onto the ice-covered deck.

She forced her eyes open and crawled forward. Through clouds of ice particles blown horizontally across the deck, she could see Wyman and Odell, bent over the fallen mast, using their equipment to cut the rigging, their harnesses attached to stanchions. She moved in an infantryman's crawl, one handhold to the next. The boom was missing, torn from the mast as the mast fell. She came to a fracture in the hull where a turnbuckle—a large double-ended screw that connects the hull to the rigging—had given way. The stays and sheets were now a jumbled mess, strung out all over the hull, some being whipped by the wind. One of the mast's spreaders was up in the air like a shark's fin, and the other was crushed underneath.

She approached a stay that was down but still taut—maybe the backstay, which had run from the masthead to the aft end of the boat, she couldn't be sure—and began running the hacksaw back and forth across the cable. Wyman was bear-hugging the long handles of a bolt cutter, trying to generate enough pressure to sever another cable. To reduce exposure to the wind, Odell was on the deck as if kowtowing. He worked with a hacksaw. The lower three feet of the mast still rose from the deck, but ended in a twisted metal stub.

Most of her was freezing, but her arm moved the saw back and forth, and quickly grew tired and hot from the effort. So at least some of her was warm, she thought, then discarded the odd and worthless notion as the product of her fatigue. She sawed and she sawed some more. Every few seconds she had to stop to grip the boat with both hands. *Victory* flew up as if propelled by rockets, balanced on a crest for a heartbeat, then fell as if into a hole, again and again. It rolled and then righted. It kicked sideways when a cross wave hit the hull.

The wind tore at Gwen Weld. Ice built up on her as she worked. Wyman and Odell were beginning to resemble snowmen. She heard something snap, so loud it carried above the wind. The mast shifted a few inches to port.

At the top of his lungs, Wyman called, "Got it. Couple more."

Odell kept grinding at his cable with the saw. He was weak with his disease, and she wondered if he could make any progress against the multistrand line. Wyman slid along the deck to a jib stay that was knotted around a stanchion. Again he had to use his entire body on the bolt cutter to bring enough pressure to bear. The stay separated into two pieces, one of them flying across the deck with the release of tension. Odell was finally successful with his cable, and he crawled over the fallen mast to Gwen's side of the boat. His shoulders were covered with epaulets of ice. When Wyman severed another cable just as the boat was soaring up another wave, the boom shifted again.

He moved along the deck toward Gwen and shouted into her ear, "One more and its free. Stand back."

She unhooked the safety clip, and crawled aft. Toby Odell was behind her. When they reached the cockpit, both secured their harnesses to hull bolts. Gwen was shivering violently, and when she clamped her jaw closed to prevent her teeth clattering, it seemed her entire head shivered instead. She had been on deck only ten minutes, but she had no doubt that another ten minutes would kill her.

The boat rose up the front of a mammoth wave. As it neared the crest, the wave broke, and a churning white comber swept into the cockpit, throwing Gwen and Odell against the deck and bouncing them against a rail. She gagged on the water and waved an arm helplessly, trying to find something to grab. The crest of the foaming water fell away. Toby Odell was lying against her on the deck. He rose to his knees, then grabbed her arm to help her up. The pool of water in the cockpit drained. Ice had begun again to build on the scuppers. She rose unsteadily, the deck rolling under her. She was soaked through, and so cold she couldn't feel her feet or hands.

Ice covered Odell's hood and mask. She could only see his eyes. They seemed merry.

Just as Rex Wyman came into the cockpit, Odell yelled over the wind, "Had enough, Rex?"

Wyman stared at him, and Gwen turned to look at them, spray blowing into her face.

Odell laughed harshly. "Want me to swing *Victory*'s boom again or shut off the power or suddenly close the hatch?"

She stepped closer to Odell, trying to catch all his words, which were being whipped away by the wind.

"Want me to crash *Victory*'s main server again?" Odell bellowed.

Wyman's face opened with understanding. His mouth worked under his mask, but he could say nothing. He stared at Odell.

"Or have you had enough?" Odell demanded.

Gwen leaned closer, one hand on the ice to brace herself, trying to hear Odell.

Wyman's face reformed around hostile eyes. "Ted

Landers just told me about the Wayward Souls. I didn't believe it. I told him it couldn't be you."

Odell laughed again, a malicious sound hardened by the wind. "You didn't think I had forgotten Cassandra, did you? Or any of the other crap you pulled?"

The boat was lifted toward the dark sky. Wind tore at Gwen, and she wanted desperately to go below, out of the killing storm, but the name Cassandra caught her up. It took her a second. Then she recalled Toby Odell's humiliating story of the blind date. He had laughed and shrugged it off when he told Gwen about it, and about the other degrading pranks Wyman had pulled on him.

"And I haven't forgotten that you cut me out of our company." Odell laughed, a fluty, hysterical sound. "And I've forgiven none of it, and—"

Wyman stabbed the bolt cutters at Odell's chest. Odell staggered back, slipped on ice, then collapsed to the deck.

"Rex," Gwen cried out. "Don't."

Wyman raised the bolt cutters, ready to chop down at Odell, but Gwen lunged at him. The boat yawed, and her feet slipped, and instead of blocking a blow, she tumbled into Wyman's legs, then fell to her hands and knees.

Wyman slipped, caught himself, and lowered the bolt cutters, staring down at her. The boat fell off a wave. Wyman braced himself, planted a foot against Gwen's shoulder and roughly pushed her away. She slid across the cockpit. Gagging, Odell tried to rise, but fell back, slumping against the rail.

Wyman dropped the bolt cutters, snatched the front of Odell's suit, and lifted him toward the top rail. He jerked Odell to his feet and held him there.

Wyman shouted over the storm. "Have I had enough, Toby?"

Wyman savagely shoved Odell over the rail. Odell spun into the sea. His safety line was attached to a bolt on the boat. Odell was hauled along in his safety harness like a fish lure, skipping along the wave crests, then completely submerged in the foam, then reappearing. Wyman grabbed the shears. Gwen crawled toward him, shouting words he couldn't hear and couldn't understand.

A wave crested across the deck, immersing it in foaming water, toppling Wyman and slapping Gwen against the port rail. Wyman rose unsteadily, wiping an arm across his eyes. He glared down at his ex-partner. Then he placed the bolt cutter's jaws on Odell's safety line. Odell skidded over the water alongside the hull. He slipped beneath the foam, then his head bubbled up from the water. He stared up at Wyman.

"Have I had enough, Toby?" Wyman raged. "You figure it out."

Gwen called out, but spray lashed into her face, and her words were washed away.

Wyman squeezed the bolt cutters, and the safety line snapped into two. Odell sped aft, one arm in the air as if waving, and Gwen saw that peculiar expression in his eyes, that same ironic, condescending look he always wore. She desperately reached for the cockpit's life ring to throw to him, but it was iced over and stuck to the boat as if with epoxy. Same with the floating EPIRB.

Quickly Odell became an insignificant dark speck in the tumult all around. Then a comber broke over him and he disappeared.

"Yes, Toby," Wyman screamed at the sea. "I've had enough."

CHAPTER 20

When the weather is dangerous and lives may be lost, the manual calls a rescue operation an *increased risk mission*. Sandy Ramirez called them *sporty*.

McKay and Ramirez were strapped into jump seats in the Pave Hawk's bay. Captain Ross Macklin was at the controls. Lieutenant Joe Junius was the copilot, and Second Lieutenant Lance Urban was the copter's engineer. The first time Ramirez met Urban, Ramirez asked, "They let someone named Lance into the Air Force?" And Urban had immediately replied, "You speak the English well for an Aztec." So the two had become good friends.

Also on board were two other PJs, Kurt Ridley, for whom the 212th RQS was the first tour, and Greg Mercer, whom McKay had gone through the pipeline with. The PJs were in full gear—heavily insulated drysuits, tanks, and masks—and were loaded with equipment.

The Pave Hawk helicopter's primary military mission is exfiltration, infiltration and resupply of special tactics forces, and combat search and rescue. This was a peacetime search and rescue, but, looking out the helicopter's windows at the storm below, the copter crew and the PJs suspected it'd be more like wartime, with the elements as the mortal enemy. When a rescue is to be attempted more than two hundred miles at sea—the range of a Coast Guard H-3 helicopter—the Air National Guard takes on the mission.

The wind was blowing spray across the sea at such a velocity and in such volume that a roaring cloud of water particles rose two thousand feet, and when McKay peered out the window, he could see nothing of the waves below, just the blanket of spray, which looked entirely peaceful from the copter's altitude, but which McKay knew to be an utter ruse.

The copter crew and the PJs were all wearing headsets. The pilot, Ross Macklin, said, "A thousand feet is usually the best altitude for spotting things on the sea, but I can't get down that low because it'd be in the spray. We can't see a thing from up here, and we won't be able to see a thing down there."

Night vision goggles were on Macklin's helmet, up in the stowed position. Also on his helmet was a boom microphone with an NVG compatible lip-light. On his chest was a HEEDs, a helicopter emergency egress device with three minutes of emergency air. He and the copilot were also wearing knee pads because their legs took a beating in the tight cockpit on a rough flight. Knives were in their boots.

"Do we have the call yet," McKay asked. He could hardly hear the pilot over the whine of the copter's gear box.

"I'm still waiting on it. Our destination is something of a guess right now."

A Hercules search-and-rescue plane was far ahead of the helicopter, zeroing in on *Victory*'s emergency beacon, and would soon try to make visual contact with the sailboat. *Victory*'s EPIRB had led the Hercules to a general area, but spotting a boat in these seas would be chancy, with the breaking waves and the spray. The Hercules would fly a ladder pattern, its crew trying to make visual contact with *Victory*. Once the crew had found the sailboat, the Hercules would then circle the boat, and the crew would monitor *Victory*'s condition until the helicopter arrived.

The dense layer of spray was below, and from the dark clouds above came thick billows of sleet. Visibility was half a mile. The helicopter sank and rose as the wind threw pockets of air at it. Macklin had to crab the Pave Hawk, the helicopter's tail fifteen degrees to the side to make up for the wind.

The copter's range was 440 miles. It was built by Sikorsky, and was propelled by two General Electric engines. Pave Hawks used for other missions are equipped with two 7.62-mm miniguns. This one had body baskets instead of guns. The copter's rotors and windshield were deiced electrically.

The Pave Hawk was flying into headwinds, which at times made the copter feel as if it were suspended in the sky rather than flying forward. Ross Macklin strained against his safety belts, leaning forward to peer out of the sleet-blown window. The copter's controls were alive in Macklin's grip—one hand on the collective, the other on the joystick—and they seemed to be fighting him.

Jess had noticed a long time ago that they all had odd ways to fight their anxiety. Jess's was one of the oddest. During a summer when he was in college he had worked on a wheat farm in eastern Washington, driving a combine and a truck during the harvest. He would occasionally reach into the combine's bin or the truck's

bay and lift out fifteen or twenty kernels of wheat. He
would chew the kernels—which were raw and full of the
gamy taste of the earth—down to a dough, then chew the
dough until it disappeared, which might take ten minutes. So now he would occasionally visit a bulk health
food store and buy a bag of wheat kernels. Before a mission, he would put several handfuls into a pocket. He
was chewing wheat kernels as he rode in the Pave Hawk,
his jaw working aggressively, snapping away at them.

The helicopter flew into a vagary of wind, a pocket
of air that was flowing downward, and the Pave Hawk
fell as if an enormous hand had grabbed its tail and
thrown it toward the sea. McKay's innards rose up to
his Adam's apple, and he was straining against his
safety straps, floating in the air. Flight manuals
jumped around the cockpit. Macklin went full collective, and when the helicopter's blades found purchase
again, McKay fell back into his seat.

"I can't see a damned thing," Macklin said from the
pilot's seat.

Ramirez said, "How about giving us only the good
news, Ross."

Macklin said, "Up here in the cockpit, we're all cool,
calm, and collected."

McKay chewed his wheat kernels. The helicopter
sped into the storm.

Rex Wyman had been sending *Victory*'s GPS readings
over the radio to Lonnie Garvin. The big crab trawler
pushed through ramparts of water, sailing north from
Dutch Harbor. *Hornet* was traveling against the seas,
and the waves came at the boat from its port quarter,
often breaking over the gunwales and flooding the
crab deck, covering the entire aft end of the boat in

chaotic white water. The boat would muscle itself from under the crushing sea, the water falling away to the sides, and then it would struggle up the next wave.

The skipper had taken a turn with the bat out on deck, Bang The Drum at the wheel. Now Garvin was back at the helm, his eyes straining through the sleety window, then dropping to his gauges, then back up to the window. His target, *Victory*, was close, maybe within sighting distance, but ropes of foam torn from wave crests by the wind and sleet falling in thick folds obscured everything beyond the edges of his boat. Occasionally the wind would open a view, and Garvin could see the ranks of waves ahead of him. Mostly he was sailing blind.

The engines had drawn down the starboard tanks some, and the boat wasn't so imbalanced, but he was still worried. A TV screen on one side of his console showed a closed-circuit, black-and-white view of his engine room. Bang The Drum was below, trying to thaw several feet of pipe, which would allow transfer of fuel tank to tank. He was using two space heaters, but Drum had reported half an hour ago that he might as well be spitting at the pipes for all the effect he was having. Garvin again glanced at the engine room monitor, then at his oil and temperature gauges. Everything was normal down there.

Ollie Nordquist was on the crab deck, scraping off ice—some of it sheets two feet thick—with the deck crane's hydraulically powered arm. Nick Summers was batting away ice built up around the hatches on the superstructure.

The VHF radio crackled into life. "Garvin, here's our latest position." It was Rex Wyman's voice, sounding breathless and strained even over the radio. Wyman read the coordinates.

Garvin lifted the overhead microphone. "We're right

on you, according to our GPS reading. I can't see you yet, though. You've got to be within a hundred yards."

"My gear is on," Wyman radioed, "and I'm ready to go topside to receive a line."

"Let me find you first," Garvin replied. "I'll let you know when to go out." He hung up the VHF handset, then pressed the intercom button. "Bang The, I need another pair of eyes up here."

Then *Hornet* and *Victory* crested waves at the same moment, and suddenly the huge crippled sailboat was right in front of Garvin, four or five rollers away. The trawler dropped down the back of a wave.

Garvin snatched the handset and dispensed with radio formalities, "Wyman, you're right in front of me. Get out on deck, and go forward to your samson post, and we'll get the line to you."

The crabber skipper guided *Hornet* forward, the two boats playing hide-and-seek as they crested and descended the waves. For a few seconds, when the curtain of sleet opened and when *Victory* reached a wave top, he could see the big boat, nearer and nearer. Then the boat would disappear in a wave or behind the blast of sleet. The crab boat worked itself upwind, so *Victory* would be in its lee. Usually this maneuver would calm the expanse of water between the boats, allowing a flatter staging area, but in this storm Garvin doubted *Hornet*'s wind-blocking effect would be noticeable at all. At least his crew would be working with the wind to their backs.

When Garvin judged his boat was sufficiently upwind, he spun the wheel as *Hornet* was climbing a wave, and the boat turned as it crested the wave and as it fell down the backside, rolling wildly. Now *Hornet* was upwind, and the sea was chasing the boat, coming at it from its stern.

Garvin pulled back *Hornet*'s throttles, then pressed an intercom button, connecting himself with the crane platform. "Ollie, you and Nick move aft. Get ready with the line."

Hornet bore down on *Victory*, but it was a patchy business, as the two boats soared up waves and then skidded back down. The crab boat was now so close that Garvin could see the mess on *Victory*'s deck, the low, jagged stump of the mast, and rigging littering the deck and hanging over the sides. Garvin began playing with the throttles, powering up the engines on a rising wave, fluttering them on the down side.

The windshield wiper beat back and forth, and was beginning to build up ice again. He leaned forward over the wheel. He could see Wyman moving forward on *Victory*'s deck. The billionaire was half-crawling, half-walking, keeping both hands on the boat. His weather gear was traffic-cone red, and it stood out against the green furor of the waves. A comber broke over *Victory*'s deck, and for an instant Garvin thought Wyman might have been swept away, but the water receded, and Wyman was still making his way forward.

Ollie Nordquist was carrying a hand-held radio, a little Motorola that could send a signal two miles, another item purchased with Wyman's money back in Dutch Harbor. The radio's twin was on the pilothouse console.

Over the radio came Nordquist's voice, "We're on the aft rail, behind the pots. We're hitched up, but we're plenty wet."

Garvin acknowledged the message. *Hornet*'s props whirred as the stern lifted into the air on a crest. The sailboat was within a hundred yards. Garvin had seen photographs of *Victory* taken during its launch. The sailboat had once been a gallant and proud vessel, imposing in every respect, and mysterious, with new hull angles and curious machinery on deck. The glittering boat had strutted out of San Francisco Harbor, and on its way north *Victory* had dominated the sea, as if sailing were child's play. Now, stripped of its mast and boom, its rigging tangled on the deck, helplessly riding the waves and entirely at their mercy, *Victory* looked pitiable.

Hornet was swept forward by a wave, then rose to a peak. Now *Victory* was below the trawler, reeling in a wave trough. The trawler careened down a wave, nearer to the sailboat. Garvin was light on the throttles, letting the waves propel him toward Wyman's boat. As another wave lifted the trawler, he gunned the engines, gaining on *Victory*. As the crab boat fell down the wave, Garvin could feel the breaker drag down the aft end of the boat. He knew Ollie and Nick wouldn't be able to last long out there, not with wild water pouring on them. Garvin needed to corral *Victory* on the first pass.

A cross wave met *Hornet* in a trough, and foam enveloped his prow and the boat bucked. He moved the throttles as the trawler was carried up the next wave. Lifted by a massive roller, *Victory* suddenly appeared, startlingly close to *Hornet*. The two boats bobbed together, less than fifty yards separating them, the wind-whipped spray making the air between them opaque. Then the boats fell off the same wave, down toward a trough.

In those few seconds of relative calm, Garvin punched *Hornet* into reverse, backing the trawler toward *Victory*. A new wave lifted them both, and they rose in harmony. Then down they went again. *Hornet* rolled, and Garvin had to brace himself with the wheel.

"Back farther," came over the Motorola. Nick Summers's voice. He would be handling the radio while Ollie Nordquist had the coiled end of the line in his hands. "A dozen feet. The guy is out on *Victory*'s bow, ready to catch it. Give us a dozen feet, skipper."

Up both boats went. Garvin prayed that a cross wave wouldn't knock the boats out of alignment with each other. He tapped back the throttles. Again he looked at the crab deck TV. Nothing to be seen, because Nordquist and Summers were behind the pot stack.

"Give us a couple more," Summers called over the radio again. "Almost there."

Garvin nudged back the throttles. He waited five seconds, ten seconds, the next wave rising off his starboard side, dwarfing *Hornet*.

"He's got it," yelled Summers. "Wyman has our line. He's bent down now, tying it to his samson post." The storm's howl almost drowned out Summers's voice over the radio.

"Tell him to hurry the hell up," Garvin said to himself.

For those moments, *Hornet* was broached to the incoming sea, lying at right angles to the run of the sea, a hazardous position he would never otherwise put his boat into. And he was in an unbalanced boat. The trawler rolled to starboard, to the side where his fuel lay, but lumbering and hesitating and lifted by the next wave, *Hornet* slowly righted itself. Garvin breathed in through his teeth. God, he hated being afraid out here, because that meant he had committed a grave error. He didn't believe in bad luck, not out on the water. A sailor who says he had bad luck is confessing that he wasn't prepared or didn't have skill.

"Lonnie, we've got it secured." This time it was Ollie Nordquist hollering into the radio. "Wyman signaled us that it's tight. Now's he is crawling back to *Victory*'s hatch. Let's go, Lonnie. We're coming back in."

Garvin slowly pushed the throttles forward and spun the wheel. The trawler turned toward the next incoming wave, riding up its front side as the comber broke over the prow. Seething white water gushed along *Hornet*'s deck on both sides of the wheelhouse, then spilled aft onto the crab deck, and for a moment only the superstructure was above the water. Then the water fell away and the trawler crested the wave, then slid down the backside. The line connecting the two boats sank into the wave and grew taut. At that same instant, a cross wave lunged at *Victory*, staggering the sailboat.

Victory's hull and its samson post had been engineered to rigorous standards. But not to Bering Sea standards, not to force 12 wind and sea standards. The trawler had been so engineered, and so had the cable connecting the two vessels, so if anything were to give way, it must be the sailboat.

When *Hornet* sped down the wave, and when at the same time the cross wave smacked against *Victory*'s hull, the sailboat's prow—the front four feet of the hull—was wrenched from the boat. Suddenly, where there had been sparkling chrome and lovely lines were now twisted metal shanks and ragged fiberglass splinters framing a gaping hole.

Victory was open to the sea.

Gwen Weld was in *Victory*'s salon, clinging to the table. She had thought that the storm's noise was as loud as anything could be, that the sound was the limit of what the laws of physics allowed. Nothing in the universe could be louder.

Except this. Her head snapped toward the new sound, a grinding tear coming from the bow, sounding clearly above the storm. She had no time to wonder about it. A geyser of water shot through the forward companionway. Gwen saw it coming, but had no time to react as it soared into the salon. A scythe of water cut Gwen's legs from under her and swept her aft. Lost in the turmoil, she bounced off the furnishings and gear in the salon as if she were inside a pachinko game.

The water released her as the boat rolled, and she found herself beached near the table mount. The water's retreat was only temporary. It continued to gush through the forward hatch with the force of a broken main.

Over the past few days, Gwen had ridden *Victory* through every motion the Bering Sea could inflict on the boat. Had she been asked, she would have sworn that all the sea's influences during that time added up only to chaotic motion, that there was no pattern to it, and that she had gained no new knowledge of the sea or the boat. But even with *Victory* pitching and rocking, Gwen could now tell the bow of the boat had taken on a new motion, a restraint in rising, a new leadenness. The bow was lower in the water. Lying there shivering violently, new bruises covering her, she knew *Victory* was sinking.

The boat rolled, and the chilled water—only four degrees Fahrenheit from ice—swamped her again, rolling and rolling her. She banged against the bulkhead, and now two feet of water were in the salon, and no part of the deck was above water. She crawled like an amphibian downhill toward the hatch separating the berths, sail lockers, and tool room from the salon. The boat yawed in a cross sea, and the water

kicked her sideways. When she slid into a bench, the
wind was knocked out of her. Her lungs pumped
windlessly, and when she could finally inhale again,
the inboard sea came again on a roll, pitching her
again against the bench. She righted herself and
crawled down the increasing slope toward the bow.

Water rushed into the salon. The room was lit only
by emergency electric lamps, and the water gout was
spectral in the dim light. Gwen crawled on the deck,
then kicked through water to the hatch control. Her
fingers touched the wheel, but the boat rolled again,
and she lost the grip. Water was waist-deep at the forward bulkhead. Her hands searched for the wheel.
Her fingers were numb from the water. She found the
metal circle. As the boat pitched forward on a cross
wave, the mass of water in the salon pushed against
her, shoving her against the bulkhead. She willed her
hands to work, and she cranked the hatch wheel.

The steel hatch moved slowly, just three inches,
then a few more as she yanked on the wheel. Gwen
repositioned herself to one side of the crank so she
could put her back into the work, a new swell of water
lifting her off the deck. She was floating *inside* a boat.
The idea troubled her, but only vaguely. Her mind was
incapable of anything more.

Except knowing she had to yank. This much she
understood. She savagely pulled on the hatch wheel,
then again and again. The hatch slid, pinching the
incoming stream. She pulled and pulled, feeling nothing in her fingers. The door rolled on its bearings,
squeezing the water flow. She heaved again, and once
again, and the edge of the door slid into the frame,
choking off the sea water.

She was so cold her legs wouldn't obey. She had to
coax them. She half-swam, half-walked up the deck.

The new water inside *Victory* was acting as ballast, the boat's flooded bow well under the sea's agonized surface. The boat was marginally more stable with the new weight.

She climbed unsteadily up the deck, looking for somewhere dry. The water inside the boat sloshed back and forth, carrying cushions and clothing and wood spoons and paper and bottles.

A rush of bitterly cold air whipped into her. She looked up and aft, toward the cockpit hatch that had just opened and closed. Rex Wyman stood in the companionway, water pouring off his heavy-weather gear.

Gwen was now inside the boat with all that frigid and tossing seawater, and with a murderer.

Sandy Ramirez had vomited into a bag, but nobody was dogging him about it because they were all fighting their stomachs now. Jess McKay chewed his wheat kernels with mechanical efficiency. Though none of the PJs could see the plane, they knew that the helicopter was approaching a C-130 Hercules for refueling.

Ross Macklin often eased his own tension by giving a sportscaster's play-by-play over the intercom. Now he was silent as he guided his helicopter closer and closer to the belly of the refueling plane.

The Hercules above the helicopter was a rugged piece of equipment, and its principal mission was tactical and intratheater airlift. The plane was first deployed in 1955, but has been upgraded so many times that only its original profile is recognizable today. It is powered by four Allison turboprops, and the crew of five consists of two pilots, a flight engineer, a navigator, and a load master. With a twenty-ton payload, the Hercules can fly at thirty thousand feet for two thousand miles.

Ross Macklin said over his radio, "Visual contact with the left drogue."

This was the second refueling of the helicopter on this mission. The feeder hose—the drogue, which is shaped like a parachute—hung from the Hercules. The coupling mechanism attached to the end of the drogue required 150 pounds of pressure to clasp the helicopter's fuel intake valve, which meant the copter probe had to bump the drogue.

"The Hercules left drogue has fouled, so I'm going in for the right one," Macklin said. "It's a lot trickier because the probe is attached from the right side of the cockpit, so I've got both the drogue and the probe on the right side. Makes it tough to see the coupling."

McKay knew the Pave Hawk pilot was easing his nerves, acting as if he were gossiping over a telephone. The PJs also knew that in this storm the helicopter was doing things Macklin had no control over, that it was jumping around, and that the pilot was fighting his controls, that his knuckles were white and that his back was drenched in sweat.

"Oops," Macklin called.

"Damn it, Ross, will you kindly not say 'oops' when you're driving a helicopter with me on board," McKay said into his mike.

"I missed the drogue," the pilot said. "Here we go again."

The drogue was filled with air to hold it rigidly.

"See, the problem is, I don't want to overshoot the drogue and rip off the Hercules's rudder. Then we'd all—plane and copter—fall into the sea in flaming balls."

McKay reached for more wheat kernels.

Macklin went on, his words slowed by the intense concentration required to guide the copter in close quarters, "And with the left drogue gone, I have to get really up close to the Hercules's fuselage to get to the right one."

McKay closed his eyes. Maybe he could sleep. His six hours of shut-eye hadn't done anything for him, seemed like. The copter bounced in the wind, and McKay grabbed his seat frame. No, there'd be no sleep on the Pave Hawk.

"Missed again," Macklin said, then spoke over the radio with the Hercules pilot.

Ramirez held out his hand. "Pass me some of those wheat kernels, will you, Jess?"

McKay reached into his pocket.

Macklin said over the intercom, "The drogue flaps around a bit under the plane—prop wash and wind and all—and what I'm trying to do, see, is to keep my eye on the Hercules's wing flaps, and to guess the drogue's next move."

The copter bounced in rough air, and Macklin took it down a hundred feet to get clear of the plane. Then he brought the Pave Hawk up again.

"We've got ten minutes of fuel left, no problem," Macklin said.

The engines and gears and the passing wind filled the copter's bay with a steady blare.

"Got it," whooped Macklin. "The drogue and the probe are connected." Macklin again spoke with the Hercules pilot, then its load master. Next he said into the intercom, "We're fueling."

Jess leaned forward to look out the waist hatch. All he could see were roiling purple and black clouds above and below. McKay ground away at his wheat kernels.

CHAPTER 21

Hornet had undergone a stability test shortly after it was launched. At an Anacortes pier, a dockside crane placed concrete blocks onto *Hornet*'s deck, one at a time. Then the crane switched the blocks around to many different locations, adding and subtracting weight. After each new block was added, a naval engineer recorded the effect on a plumb bob that had been hung on the deck. The hull would lean to one side with each added block, and the plumb bob would show the angle of the incline, and then *Hornet* would slowly right itself. This test set the boat's baseline stability, showing how far the trawler could heel over and then right itself, carrying certain loads in certain locations on board. At the end of the testing, the naval engineer issued a stability letter, which set forth the best manner to trim *Hornet*—to balance the boat—in various weather conditions, including storms where ice built up on the deck and superstructure. *Hornet*'s danger point was a generous forty degrees.

Lonnie Garvin knew more about trimming his own boat than any naval architect ever would. Still, all his hard-won knowledge and all his skipper's instincts were suddenly for naught when Ollie Nordquist opened the hatch to the cockpit and yelled over the bellow of the storm, "Lonnie, the deck's not clearing."

Garvin looked at his work deck monitor. The deck between the crab pot stack and the superstructure was under water.

And only then was Garvin struck—fully struck— with the foolishness of his mission to rescue *Victory* and to save his own boat and crabbing career with Rex Wyman's money. The boat was so low in the sea that water wasn't draining off the work deck. It meant that *Hornet* was being claimed by the sea.

Just a moment ago, Garvin had felt the tow line break loose. He had not seen whether *Victory* was damaged, and he had been considering circling for another attempt at linking the two vessels. But now he threw his throttles forward.

He shouted, "Can you get any ice off the deck, Ollie?"

"The boat is making ice faster than we can get rid of it."

Nick Summers pushed into the wheelhouse. Water slid off his coat.

Garvin said, "All, right, let's—"

He didn't have time to complete the sentence. A three-story breaking wave caught *Hornet*, and the exaggerated incline of the wave front combined with the sledgehammer impact of the breaking crest, and tons of water soared across the trawler's deck. The crab pots—secure in any other sea on any other day— broke their chains. The torrent of water crossing the deck swept the tarp-wrapped stack to the starboard rail as easily as if the stack were on rollers. The shifting stack sliced off an eighteen-inch vent pipe to the engine room.

Already out of trim to starboard due to an imbalanced fuel load, and already low in the water under the weight of ice, *Hornet* now listed mortally. The boat's righting arm—the angle at which it could roll and then recover—had been surpassed. Heeled to leeward, the crab pots against the starboard rail, *Hornet* was doomed.

And Garvin knew it immediately. Still hanging on to the wheel, as if it could do anything now, he shouted, "Get into survival suits, both of you."

Nick Summers said, "But don't you think—"

"Do as I tell you, Nick. Get into it right now. We're going into the water."

Garvin grabbed his VHF handset, then reached up to switch to the emergency channel.

"Mayday," Garvin said into the microphone. "Mayday. This is the crab trawler *Hornet*. Do you read me? Mayday."

A voice returned on the radio immediately. "This is the United States Coast Guard Com-Sta Kodiak. We read you, *Hornet*."

"The boat is rolling." Garvin wondered at the calm in his own voice. "About to go under."

The Coast Guardsman said, "Give me your coordinates."

Garvin looked at his GPS. "Latitude 56 degrees 32 minutes north, longitude 167 degrees 22 minutes west."

After a moment, the Guardsman asked, "Is this the *Victory*?"

"No, hell no. It's *Hornet*, a crab trawler."

"The Air Force National Guard has an operation going in your area—right in your area—right now. What are you doing out there?"

"I'm losing my boat, is what I'm doing," Garvin shouted. "Can we get to business?"

"Describe *Hornet*."

"A hundred feet long. Superstructure forward. The superstructure is white. Large crab deck aft. Large pot crane on the deck."

From the radio came, "What color is the bottom of the hull?"

A moment passed before Garvin understood what the dreadful question implied. Then he said, "It's blue." He added weakly, "Royal blue." God, he loved that color and he loved this boat.

"I'll pass it on to the search and rescue team. Are you in survival suits?"

Garvin barked, "I don't need to be walked through abandoning a boat, Admiral. I know damn well what to do." He was about to throw the handset down—he would never need it or ever see it again, same with the rest of his boat—but Garvin was polite to his soul, always had been, so he put the handset back to his mouth. "Sorry, Coast Guard. I'm under a bit of stress out here."

"I fully understand, *Hornet*. Rescuers are on the way."

With *Hornet* lower in the water and leaning more and more, its superstructure was now more exposed to the breaking waves. An enormous tumbling breaker smashed the wheelhouse and punched out a so-called stormproof window. The water shot through the opening and churned the contents of the wheelhouse—human and equipment—as if in a mixer. Garvin and his crew were thrown to the deck and were rolled toward the hatch. *Hornet* leaned more.

Garvin pushed himself to his feet. He yelled, "Get into your suits. Now. Do it."

The water drained away. Garvin tore open the long vinyl bag and pulled out the suit. He glanced around at this beloved place. His electronics were scattered about the wet deck. Charts were everywhere, some rolled in tubes, some loose. Radios hung from the ceiling, swaying back and forth on wires. Two monitors had been ripped from the console and were lying on the deck near his chair. They slid toward Garvin when the boat rolled. Each time *Hornet* listed more, it didn't quite make it as far upright as the prior time.

"Hurry, Nick. Get into your suit."

A survival suit is donned by lying on the deck. Garvin and his crew wiggled into their suits. The suits were orange, and whistles hung from the front. Along sleeves and across chests were strips of reflective tape. Boots, gloves, and hoods were built into the suit.

Garvin yelled over the storm's noise, "Make sure the purge valves on each leg are closed. You need some help, Nick?"

"No," he called quickly. Summers was shaking with the cold. He wriggled into the suit.

Ollie Nordquist said, "You owe me a beer when we get back to port, Lonnie." He closed zippers and pressed Velcro strips together.

"Nick, cinch your hood tight, zip it high," Garvin called as loudly as he could, even though Summers was less than six feet away. "You don't want any water coming in there."

In his survival suit, Garvin crawled across the deck to Nick Summers, checking the kid's suit. "All right. Let's go."

Then the numbers hit Lonnie Garvin. There were only three people in the pilothouse.

"Where's Bang The?" he yelled. "Ah, hell." He grabbed Nick Summers by the shoulders and turned him toward the hatch. "You two get out on deck and throw the life raft canister overboard, but make sure it's

secured to the hull first. Then into the water you go.
Bang The and I'll be there in a minute."

Garvin waited until Summers had opened the hatch
and stepped out onto the heaving gangway.

Then he shouted into Nordquist's ear. "There's a
knife in the life raft. Get it ready. If the boat goes down
before I'm there, you make damned sure to cut that
line between the raft and the boat."

Nordquist nodded, the movement almost lost in the
bulk of the survival suit.

"But don't cut the raft's sea anchor line by mistake."

Nordquist looked morosely at his skipper. "I hadn't
thought about that, but I will think about it." Then he
went through the hatch.

"Hell, I don't want to do this," Garvin said to himself.

Hornet lurched to starboard a few more degrees.
He scrambled down the companionway toward the
galley and crew quarters. An ominous draft rose from
below. Air was being displaced below decks. He
glanced into the galley, then stepped down into the
engine room. Waves hurtling against the exposed hull
sounded like a cannon fusillade.

"Bang The, you there?" he called.

The boat answered, not Bang The Drum, and did so
by dousing the lights. *Hornet* was abruptly without
power, shorted out. Garvin was now in a black cata-
comb. The companionway steps no longer went
straight down, they traveled at an angle as the boat
leaned. Garvin gripped the rail with both hands and
felt his way sideways and down toward the engine
room. The bulky survival suit made him clumsy, and
the thick gloves made it hard to feel his way along.
When the boat listed a few more degrees, *Hornet*
groaned—a fearsome, throaty sound—as weight was

shifted throughout the boat and welds and metal
plates were tested. Chain moved in the anchor locker
and rattled against the hull.

"Bang The, where are you?" Garvin shouted.

The skipper could see nothing in front of him, only
black on black. The air coming at him smelled of fish
and fuel and bilge. He underestimated the boat's list, and
smacked his head on a partition. He maneuvered lower
on the steps, then came to flowing water. He jumped
down into it, onto the sloping engine-room deck.

He could see nothing, but the sound of water coming into the engine room told him all he needed to
know about *Hornet*: it had four or five minutes left on
the surface. Water was shooting into the engine room
from electrical conduit pipes and vent pipes. Seawater
was up to his chest and rising. He pushed forward into
the room, slipping on the incline.

"Drum, you here?"

Then he noticed a sharp chemical scent in the air.
He breathed it in again, testing it.

"Ah, hell. Drum, where are you?"

Garvin didn't know for sure, but the scent was
probably caused by batteries exploding when seawater had hit them. Battery casing would act as shrapnel.

He moved his arms back and forth, groping in the
black water. The boat's moan increased in pitch.
Waves against the hull created a steady roar. He knew
the ceiling was crisscrossed with pipes, but he
couldn't see them. He bumped against a generator,
then worked his way alongside it to a main engine.
The water hadn't reached the top of the diesel engine,
and it was still warm from its work.

"Bang The? Answer me."

In the blackness, Bang The Drum floated into Garvin,
startling him. As Garvin reached for the crewman, the

boat shifted in a wave, and Drum drifted away. Garvin stepped deeper into the room after Drum, grabbing at the crewman's coat, then at an arm. Garvin was floating face-up, his booted feet dragging on the deck below.

With one hand, Garvin felt his way forward, and with the other hand he pulled Drum toward the companionway. Burdened by seawater flooding the crab tanks and storage lockers, *Hornet* heeled several more degrees, and now the boat's groan lifted to a pathetic whimper. Garvin tried dragging Drum up the steps toward the galley, but didn't have the strength.

"Come on, damn you." Then the skipper added, "I'm afraid for both of us, Bang The. Really afraid. We've got to get out of here."

From the galley came the sounds of bowls and bags and boxes falling out of their lockers as the boat listed.

Garvin gulped a lungful of air, then ducked under the water, going down to his knees. He floated Drum across his shoulders. Then the skipper stood, his legs shaking inside the survival suit. He climbed up, one step after another, out of the water. The companionway was narrow, and Drum's head slid along the metal partition. Garvin struggled upward, the steps at a slant.

He breathed, "You'd better be alive after all this, Bang The."

With Drum on his shoulders, the skipper came to the tilted galley deck. He glanced aft, at the steel hatch out to the crab deck. Water was shooting through leaks in the hatch's seal. Through the circular window, Garvin could see seawater. The aft half of his boat was under water.

Garvin was breathing like a runner, and his shoulders ached and his legs were trembling from his effort. Carrying Drum like a stevedore, Garvin negotiated more steps, up toward the pilothouse, and the boat was now heeled over so much that he had to lean against the partition and slide on his shoulder and hip, slipping Drum along with him. A loud crack came from below, something giving way under the pressure. The noise of the storm—an unending blast—pressed down on him, adding weight to Drum's slack form.

His leg buckled, and his knee slammed against the edge of a step. Garvin grunted in pain. He forced himself off the step, forced himself upright, then planted one foot on the next step, and then Garvin concentrated, one step at a time, Drum seeming to gain weight with each step.

The skipper reeled up into the pilothouse. He tried to slip Drum off his shoulders, but they both fell to the steep deck. Drum's forehead was bloody. A two-inch gash was still spilling blood. Garvin pulled out another survival suit and started cramming Drum into it, which was like pushing a rope. He prodded and pulled.

When Drum groaned, Garvin said, "At least you're alive."

Forced from below deck, air hissed up the companionway. The boat rolled, and didn't recover more than a few of the degrees.

"Come on, Bang The. Come on."

Garvin zipped up Drum's suit, then tightened the fittings around his wrists and face. The trawler lurched, and Drum began sliding along the inclined deck. The skipper grabbed Drum's survival suit at the shoulders and slid him toward the hatch. *Hornet* was sinking stern first, and was listing to port at the same time.

Garvin yanked open the hatch. Frothing seawater was up to the deck outside the hatch. Only the superstructure and the forward hull were now above water. Garvin looked out into the sea. He couldn't see the life raft. The boat sank under him. Seawater rushed up the deck, but he knew it was an illusion. The deck was going under. Pushed from below, air rushed out the hatch. He looked out at the Bering Sea. He was in a canyon of water, water in every direction except straight up.

He didn't have time for one last look at *Hornet*. Didn't have time for a goodbye. His trawler was sinking beneath his feet.

Garvin balanced Drum on the rail, sat on the rail himself, then dragged Drum over the side. They fell into the bounding sea.

Gwen Weld pressed herself against the bulkhead in *Victory*'s control room, staring at Wyman, deathly afraid of him, and wanting away from him. But *Victory* lay low in the water, its forward compartment flooded and sealed off, Roger Hall's body wrapped in a sail and enduring a premature burial at sea. *Victory*'s salon was half-filled with chilled, sloshing seawater. The stern third of the boat was almost out of the sea, lifted by the waterlogged front end. The control room was the only place on the sailboat still habitable.

So she was finally alone with Wyman, and had his complete attention, with no business distractions, something she had fervently desired for months, and had she the strength, she might have thought it funny.

"It was Toby all along," he said. "Toby did it all, one thing after another to ruin me. I never saw it coming."

Wyman was in her chair, talking to a black monitor screen, not to her. He was speaking in short bursts, a few words on each ragged exhalation. His elbows were on the table, and his head was in his hands. He might have been weeping, she couldn't tell. She kept her back to the bulkhead, watching him. She had just seen her boyfriend—a man she had been subtly inveigling to make a commitment to her—kill someone, just out-and-out murder Toby Odell.

She couldn't distinguish her fears, didn't know where the greatest danger lay, with the boat or with Rex Wyman. She was so exhausted that her thoughts were weak pulses. She could focus on only one thing, and on that only dimly. She had to get off this boat, but she simply couldn't figure out how. Her mind wouldn't take her to the solution. It only allowed her fear.

Victory was a floating hulk, destined for the bottom of the Bering Sea, she was sure. She was trapped in the boat that was trying to kill her.

She looked over Wyman's shoulder at the hatch from the control room to the companionway. She breathed quickly, trying to control her fear. The past few days had physically transformed Rex Wyman. His boyish good looks and his gloss of urbanity had been stripped away from him and replaced with axe-hewn features. She knew it couldn't have happened, a face growing new angles and knobs, but Wyman's brows seemed lower and his eyes deeper in his face. His cheekbones were newly blunt, and his jaw bonier. He had not been able to shave, or to eat much, and his cheeks were newly sunken and shadowed. She stared at him and blinked, thinking she might flick away an illusion, but there he still was, his face still newly primitive.

He glared at her, and had to shout over the hiss and rush of the storm. "Toby was the first of the hackers, did you know that? He might've invented hacking. He started that crap back when we were in college. He always liked doing little crimes on his computer, and even after he left WorldQuest with all his billions, he was hacking."

"Rex, listen to me. We are being locked down here. We have to go topside. We can talk about this later."

He might not have heard her. "One of Toby's new businesses was called the Wayward Souls, I just found out from Ted Landers. A bunch of twenty-year-old hackers, brilliant, all of them, Landers said. At Toby's direction, much of what they did was aimed at WorldQuest and at *Victory* and at me. Toby spent millions and millions of dollars on his sabotage. He had a whole crew working on it."

Wyman tugged hard at one of his ears, an odd, muscular motion, as if he were trying to pull apart his face.

He was so angry his voice crackled like electric sparks. "Landers caught one of Odell's hackers, a kid named Brady Lane, caught him at a skateboard park. Lane had been bragging online about his job and all his hacking accomplishments. Ted Landers tracked him down and questioned him, and Landers knows how to do it, and within a few hours Lane was telling everything he knew about everything."

She looked over his shoulder, measuring an escape. It was hopeless. In the tiny control room, he entirely blocked the way to the hatch.

He spat, "Toby began his sabotage operation on *Victory* the very damned day I ordered the boat from the shipyard. And his crew worked as hard on planting the bugs as you and your crew worked on designing the boat's software systems."

He had been raging, but he caught himself, shuddering with the effort. He looked demented, his hair matted and tangled and his eyes glowing as if from within.

Victory rolled, leaning one way, then back. The waves relentlessly hammered the hull, rocking it with blow after blow, and the control room swayed madly. Only emergency lights were working, not the heating system, and the air below deck was chilled. Every piece of Gwen's clothing was wet, and she was shivering. She seemed melted away, nothing left of her that was human. She was a hulk, just like *Victory*. She wanted to sink to the deck, fold herself up, and sob. Instead, she gazed at Wyman. He seemed so detached from their plight on board—so unaware of the pitching boat, low in the water, and the storm outside that was determined to crush them—that he was unwittingly helping her. Staring at him and trying to make sense of his words was an appalling diversion.

Wyman breathed through his teeth. "Toby controlled it all, from the timing of the boom's swing that vaulted Jeff Chapman off the boat, to the power outage, and all the rest. *Victory*'s ignorance of the incoming storm was Toby's work, all of it."

She hugged herself. She was trembling violently. The boat rocked, and he slammed into the table edge. He didn't seem to care.

He said, "The Wayward Souls was funded by Toby. Eight or ten professional hackers were conspiring against me."

His words washed in and out of the storm's ferocious noise. The clamor was unending, as loud as a locomotive.

"And the downward pressure on WorldQuest stock, that was mostly Toby." Wyman's hands went to his head, and he pressed his temples with his fingers, as if testing for bruises. "Over the years Toby had sold much of his WorldQuest stock, but it turns out he was selling it to dummy corporations, all controlled by him. The Wayward Souls created a maze of ownership, impossible to trace. Toby directed a massive selloff of WorldQuest stock over the past year, and this caused a panic among smaller holders, so WorldQuests' stock lost almost 90 percent of its value, all Toby Odell's work."

She closed her eyes.

He said, "And some other stuff, like ruining my

investment in a building in Malaysia. And a Caucasus pipeline investment. He made me lose that, too. Toby Odell has cost me billions and billions of dollars."

Wyman abruptly seemed reasonable. His face lost its harsh angles. "He was the code guy and I was the business guy. After WorldQuest got going, I could hire a hundred, a thousand code guys. I forced him out, and he didn't go quietly. It was a battle, and he kicked and screamed the entire time. But we kept it quiet, because a rancorous breakup always turns a stock down. We issued a bunch of PR stuff about Toby resigning to spend more time on his other interests, the usual smokescreen."

Wyman lifted the radio and called *Hornet* again. There was no answer. He threw down the handset. His face screwed up, and he shook his head. "But Toby and I patched it up. We became friends again after a couple of years. But now I know it was all a ruse on his part. He was just lying in wait, setting all his traps, and they all came together during this race."

Her exhaustion was a fog. She pushed herself upright, her stance wide against the roll of the boat. She was going to try to get out of the boat.

Wyman said, "I've got to admire the guy, really. He set out to ruin me, and he has."

Then he turned to her and saw that she was trying to get past him. He lifted himself out of the chair and viciously shoved her back against the bulkhead. The back of her head hit the bulkhead. She slid down to the deck.

"Don't worry about it, Gwen." He returned to his chair without offering her a glance. He knotted his hands together, then he gripped the chair arms, his knuckles white, and then he abruptly rose from the chair and moved toward the hatch, leaving her in the control room. "I'll figure it out. I always do."

CHAPTER 22

The sea and the storm, fearsome from the wheelhouse of a trawler, were beyond understanding when the point of view was a few inches above water level, which was where Lonnie Garvin found himself. He hugged Drum to him. Garvin was cold, but the cold didn't seem to be killing him, not yet, anyway. The suits were self-floating, and he and Drum bobbed in the wild water, waves rising on all sides of them. Drops of water leaked under his cheek flap and dribbled down his neck, so cold he felt as if it were burning him.

Garvin kicked his legs, trying to swim away from *Hornet*, which had rolled onto its side so that antennae on the pilothouse were pointed at him. A comber burst over the hull, rolling the boat more, and it slid lower in the water. Garvin churned the water with one hand and kicked his legs, tugging Drum along. The trawler loomed over him, and he swam frantically, his legs bouncing off Drum's legs. A wave lifted them swiftly, and as they neared the peak, it broke over them, submerging them in white water. They popped out of the wave on its backside. *Hornet* was far above them on the crest of the wave, and it followed them down. The searing wind filled the air with spray. The waves kept trying to pull Drum away from him, but Garvin held him close. The sea had beaten him, had outsmarted him at every turn, but it wasn't going to do this one last thing, to drown Ben Drum without Garvin having a say in it. He hugged Drum tightly.

The trawler slid further under, and now only its forward quarter was above the water, and the pilot-house was no longer visible, just the forward deck. Garvin watched his boat, and there was less and less to watch. Only the stem remained, that lovely prow that had anchored Garvin's view of the sea when he was in the pilothouse gazing out the windows. Then it, too, went down, slipping below the surface, until the boat disappeared. Garvin stared at the sea where *Hornet* had been, thinking that the unfettered wave that rushed over the spot was a poor memorial for his beloved trawler.

"I'm right here in the sea, aren't I?" Bang The Drum said, his first words since Garvin had carried him out of the engine room. "What happened to the engine room?"

"We're in a fix, Bang The."

"That you, Lonnie?" Drum tried to turn his head to look over his shoulder.

Seawater had washed blood from the gash in Drum's head, which had been cut to the bone. Another wave poured over them, and when they broke the surface, Drum coughed violently. The two men's horizon was limited by the slopes of waves, and within that small area the sea was tossed to white. Icy spray swept across the water.

Garvin kicked the water, keeping Drum close. He said, "You've got a bad cut on your forehead, Bang The."

"I can't feel it." Drum spit salt water from his mouth. "I suppose we're going to die out here, Lonnie. Is that what's happening to us?"

"Maybe," Garvin replied into his ear. "But you and I'll take a lot of killing, and we're still breathing. That's the main thing. If we can keep breathing, we won't die."

"You always made a lot of sense," Drum said. "That's why I've always favored crewing for you." Drum brought a hand out of the water. "What's that?"

Garvin stared through the spray, an impenetrable, wind-whipped barrier. He couldn't see anything but spray and a glimpse of wave behind it.

"It's nothing, Bang The."

"I thought I saw something."

A mammoth wave lifted Garvin and Drum, and they soared toward the black clouds overhead. Garvin peered into the blind white of the spray.

"You afraid?" Drum asked.

"We've got quite a bit of time in these suits, Bang The. We sent a Mayday. There's people looking for us. I'm hopeful, is what I am." Hell yes, Garvin was afraid.

"There it is again," Drum said.

"You're hurt worse than you think, Bang The."

But in a fissure in the spray appeared a flash of orange, there and gone in a blink. Garvin wiped his face with a hand. Then he might have seen it again, a slight smudge in the white spray.

"It's the life raft, Bang The," Garvin hollered jubilantly.

Garvin searched under the water for the whistle, fumbling in his thick gloves. He brought it up to his mouth and blew. His mouth was numb with cold and he couldn't feel the whistle. The shrill note was swallowed by the peal of the storm.

The raft was gone. Then water swallowed Garvin

and Drum, a vast tumult of churning green-and-white foam. When they emerged from the surf, the raft was right in front of them, thirty or forty yards away. Ollie Nordquist was leaning over the inflatable tube at the hatch, using a paddle, trying to get closer, paddling furiously. The canopy caught the wind, and the raft strained against its sea anchor. Garvin kicked toward the raft. The sea tossed the swimmers and the raft, lifting and dropping them.

Nordquist passed the paddle to Nick Summers, whose head came into view in the hatch. Summers worked the water with strong strokes, Nordquist holding his legs from behind. The raft's canopy flapped tightly in the wind.

The wind carried the raft away from Garvin and Drum on the crests, but Summers paddled hard in the troughs. Garvin used his free arm to stroke, but doubted he was making any headway. Drum tried to help, but he couldn't put muscle into it. Blood leaked down his cheek.

A wave broke against the raft, and scooted it closer. Summers was a demon with the paddle, ignoring the foaming water that enveloped his head again and again. The current and the wind were flowing in the same direction, rather than pulling the swimmers and raft apart, and the raft drew closer.

Garvin could make out Summers's face now, the eyes above the flap. The kid was usually eager but a bit vacant. Garvin had never seen such fierce determination on the boy's face. Summers had finally found something on a boat that he was good at. He fiercely dug the sea with his paddle. The raft was pushed away and then pushed near by the breaking waves. It was above Garvin, and then it was under him. Nordquist was inside the raft, behind Summers's shoulder. Garvin could see the grin on Nordquist's face.

And then the raft was close enough for Summers to
extend his paddle. Garvin gripped it and was pulled to
the tube. Nordquist and Summers grabbed Drum first,
and hauled him up and through the hatch. Then they
pulled Garvin up and in. Nordquist sealed the flap
over the hatch.

The raft shot up the side of a wave, then glided
down the back. The sea anchor, a parachute trailing
the raft on a line, gave the raft a survivable ride. Six
inches of seawater were on the raft's fabric deck, and
it moved back and forth. Nick Summers collapsed
against a tube, breathing in huge gulps. Everybody in
the raft was grinning, even Drum, though his smile
looked slightly addled.

Garvin roughly patted Nick Summers on the shoulder. "See what you would've missed, had you stayed
in college this quarter?"

"We're at three thousand feet," Ross Macklin said over
the intercom. "Looks like snow down there."

McKay leaned forward to peer out the hatch. The
surface of the Bering Sea was hidden by a layer of
wind-driven spray. No waves could be seen below the
spray. The sea seemed smooth and soft, and with the
steady engine, gear box, and rotor noises, McKay
couldn't hear the wind. The storm was entirely hidden
from him, he knew.

"The boat is below us somewhere," Macklin said.
"The Hercules can't get a better fix with the boat's
beacon. . . . Hey, I've got a signal."

The PJs in the helicopter's bay had been listening
to Macklin and the copilot, Joe Junius, communicate
with the Hercules high above them and with the
Kodiak Coast Guard station. Macklin was putting the

radio feed through the intercom. The chatter helped keep McKay's mind off the rough ride. McKay hadn't heard the new signal. He pressed his ear cup more tightly against his head. He heard only static.

"It's scratchy," Macklin said. "Too much static. I'm going to cut out the squelch."

The static abruptly faded, and McKay heard Gwen Weld's voice, "Mayday. This is the sailing boat *Victory.*"

Macklin said, "*Victory*, we are somewhere overhead, but we can't make you out on the surface. Do you copy me?"

"Yes, I can hear you. This is *Victory*."

McKay wondered how much of the hollowness in Gwen Weld's voice was caused by the radio transmission, and how much was fear and fatigue.

"We need help. We're sinking, and I've been injured and Rex is out in the salon and I don't know what he is doing. I can't . . . I can't . . ."

Macklin said, "I'm going to use a radio direction finder on the copter. I want you to count to ten twice, and keep your radio button pressed down. Count fast to ten, and then count slowly to ten. You copy?"

"Yes. I can do that." Her tone indicated she wasn't so sure. She began a count.

Macklin said over the intercom. "The needle is jumping around, damn it."

Junius said, "Switch it off and then back on. That sometimes works."

"Off and on," the pilot said. "Good. I've got a heading on the RDF. South twenty degrees."

McKay said, "Where's all your chat, Sandy? Usually you're talking my ear off."

"Yeah, well, I've got bigger things to think about. I've never seen a sea like that before. Looks like mayonnaise down there. I can't even see the water, just the spray."

To all sides of the helicopter, the horizon was close,
and was a narrow strip of ochre green and sulfurous
yellow, a menacing haze. Above were the smudged
black clouds, so low they appeared to touch the helicopter's rotor.

"Keep counting, *Victory*," Macklin ordered. "Count
to ten six more times. Fast and slow."

McKay could hear Gwen Weld count. He looked out
the window again. She was somewhere below, maybe
within a mile or two.

"Now the signal is behind us, Ross," the copilot said.
"So we passed over her a few seconds ago."

"The hell?" Macklin exclaimed. "I can't turn the
copter, can't bring around the tail rudder. It's being
overpowered by the wind."

"Some of this chat," Ramirez said into the intercom,
"I wish Ross would keep to himself."

"I'll lift the main and take us back," Macklin said.

"The needle just jumped through one-eighty.
Victory is right below us."

"I'm going to take it forward a hundred yards. Man,
my wind-speed indicator reads eighty-three miles per
hour, and the ground-speed indicator reads ten miles
per hour."

"The needle jumped forward," Junius said.

"Mark the coordinates," replied the pilot. "Get a
floating EPIRB ready. I'm taking it down slowly, real
slowly." He added needlessly, "You PJs get ready."

Macklin's voice was strained, despite earnest
attempts to sound entirely composed and thoughtful.
He was grappling with the controls, and the wind was
tossing the Pave Hawk in all directions. Pencils and
notebooks flew around the cockpit. In the cabin,
McKay gripped his seat. A vomit bag was pinned
under his thigh. He prayed he wouldn't have to use it,

but if he had to, he wanted it within quick reach. If a PJ blew lunch on Macklin's ride and missed the bag, the PJ cleaned it up back at the base, using a toothbrush, Macklin pacing and glowering the entire time.

The helicopter descended slowly, thrown around by the wind. The layer of spray seemed to grow up toward them. The copter dipped into it, and suddenly all that was visible outside McKay's window was a dense whiteness, as if the window had been painted.

"My altimeter is juking around because of the waves," the pilot said. "Get the door open. I need visuals from you guys back there."

McKay braced himself next to the door, then attached a safety harness to a bolt. He and Ramirez slid open the door. The blast of frigid air was like a body blow. It instantly chilled the copter's cabin. McKay was enclosed in an heavily insulated state-of-the-art immersion suit, as warm as a human body can be in such conditions, and still he was cold. His equipment included a camelback water pack and tube, a PRC-90 radio and beacon, a survival strobe with an infrared lens, seven low-altitude flares, ten colored smoke flares, a first-aid kit, a single-handed chem light, a survival knife, and other tools of the trade. He was also wearing a mini scuba set. Ramirez and the other PJs were similarly loaded.

"I've just turned on the midnight sun," Macklin said. "That help?" This was a powerful spotlight.

McKay said into the helmet intercom, "It just turns the foam yellow. I can't see a thing. Get lower."

"Yeah, I'll get lower," Macklin said, "but you know what happens when rotors hit water."

The main rotor was spinning at eight thousand rotations per minute. If the blades bit into a wave, they would shatter like icicles.

Secured by his safety line, Ramirez readied the hydraulic winch alongside the copter's door, securing a basket to it. Below was nothing but white. Frozen spray whipped into the cabin. The copter bucked and sagged in the violent wind.

"Is it cold out there or what?" Ramirez asked into his microphone.

"See anything yet?" Macklin asked.

"Nothing," McKay replied.

"Keep your eyes down. I've got to know where the damned water is." Windows at the pilot and copilot's knees allowed an angled view downward, but Macklin and Junius were piloting the helicopter in instrument conditions.

"Wave crests visible now," Ramirez called into the intercom. Then he added, "Jess, will you look at that? We'll be earning our paychecks in a few minutes."

Across that patch of sea visible to the PJs rolled white-topped parapets of waves, the troughs far below the crests. The wind had beaten the wave surfaces almost flat, and the waves were strangely glassy. When a wave broke, the wind would sweep its foam into the air and send it across the surface.

McKay worked with the belaying line. The two other PJs, Mercer and Ridley, would remain in the copter in reserve, and would be handling the lines and winch. They gathered at the hatch, fastening their safety lines.

"You see the boat?" Macklin called.

"No, nothing but water."

"There it is," called the flight engineer, Lance Urban. "Quarter click south."

After a moment, *Victory* came into view below McKay.

"That's it?" Ramirez asked. "Looks like an iceberg."

Victory was not recognizable as a boat. The aft half

of the vessel was above water, inclined so that the stern was six or eight feet into the air. Ice completely covered the vessel above water. The cockpit and features on the deck were visible only in a vague white outline. A breaking wave rolled across the boat, submerging the entire boat. *Victory* seemed to shake it off.

Ramirez said, "The cockpit hatch is sealed shut, Jess. You got a heavier tool? Your knife isn't going to pack it."

Kurt Ridley passed McKay a ball peen hammer from the copter's tool kit. McKay fit it into his harness.

The Pave Hawk was capable of allowing four PJs to lower themselves by ropes at the same time, but here only one would descend first. Macklin didn't want four of them dangling under the copter, perhaps smashing into each other in the wind. The Pave Hawk's rotor wash stirred the water's surface, but fully fifty feet downwind of the copter, blown by the storm.

McKay set his belay, and Ramirez doubled-checked it.

Then Ramirez grabbed the throat of McKay's suit and brought McKay's face right up to his, right at drill instructor distance. Ramirez shouted, "Jess, you've been taking risks with yourself for weeks. Don't do anything down there that's not in the damned manual. I'm going to personally kill you when we get back to land, you do any of that crap. You got me?"

McKay grinned under his mask. "I got you, Sandy."

McKay stepped off the ledge, and down into the storm he went.

Gwen Weld pushed herself off the deck. The back of her head pulsed with pain. The control room rolled under her feet, but the boat wasn't swaying as it had been. The storm still pummeled the boat, yet *Victory* was lethargic, no longer responding fully to the punishing waves. The vessel was low in the water, its bow submerged.

The control room was off kilter, with the deck slanted to forward and leaning to port. Rex Wyman was again in her chair, his fingers on a useless keyboard. He stared at a monitor's black screen, studying his dark reflection. He shook his head several times, a quick movement, like a tic. He was blinking repeatedly. His mouth opened and closed.

Gwen was unsteady on her feet, and was bruised everywhere from rolling around the deck, and from Rex ramming her into the bulkhead. She took a step toward him, toward the hatch out to the lockers.

"We'll be okay," he said tonelessly. "The watertight hatches are closed. We aren't taking on any more water. We'll float."

"I'm getting out," she said dully. "We're being iced in."

He started to rise from his chair, started to hold up a hand to stop her again.

She was faster. She lifted a keyboard from the table and used both hands to hit him with it, a solid blow to the side of his head. The sound of the blow couldn't be heard above the storm outside the hull, but she felt it to be solid. He slid back down into the chair and leaned forward over the table, groaning.

She squeezed by the chair, then moved out of the control room and to the aft hatch, passing equipment lockers, walking uphill on the inclined deck. Behind her, the aft watertight hatch was closed, and she knew the forward hatch was also closed. She was shivering. From a locker she pulled out a bag containing a survival suit. She had never put one on. Wyman hadn't insisted on drills, so she hadn't bothered, the foolishness of it now bruising her anew. She rolled it out and instinctively knew that she had to get down on the deck to put it on. She sat down, putting her feet into the suit. She struggled with it, tugging and pulling, wiggling into it.

She forced herself to concentrate. She wanted to lie back on the deck and take a nap, maybe forever. She had no energy left, and she had no idea why her hands and feet were still moving in something of a coordinated manner. More than getting off the boat, more than returning to dry land, she wanted to sleep. And she knew, from somewhere in a far corner of her mind, that she had to fight sleep, fight the overwhelming urge to simply lie down where she was and close her eyes.

She glanced aft, watching for Wyman. She fit her hands into the gloves, then zipped up all around. She stood, the deck moving under her. The survival suit was bulky. She shuffled aft to the hatch out to the cockpit. The narrow corridor was dimly lit by backup batteries.

"Gwen, we're okay," came from behind her.

Wyman was on his feet, staggering against a locker, his hand at his temple. He bent over as if trying to catch his breath, pressing his head where she had sent the keyboard at him.

"We're floating." His words were more a groan. "We'll be okay."

But they weren't okay. Dead and in a watery grave, Toby Odell was not done with his ex-partner. At that moment, another bit of deadly mischief was under way. Perhaps it was a coincidence that it happened now, just another of Odell's viruses, happening whenever it happened, or perhaps Odell had somehow timed it to occur now, when they needed the boat's safety features most.

Gwen heard a mechanical sound, a low grinding, the first noise the boat had made on its own since the main power had gone out. She looked forward, beyond Wyman to the watertight hatch.

The hatch was opening slowly. Several feet of seawater were in the salon behind the hatch. And further forward, the first watertight hatch was also opening. The emergency electrical system was powering the doors as they opened, another bit of brilliance from the Wayward Souls.

Wyman gazed stupidly at the hatches, his hand still pressed onto his head. Seawater was bubbling through the forward hatch, beginning to fill the salon.

She turned to the cockpit hatch, the only way out of the *Victory* now. Other hatches were below water. She worked the handle, then yanked on it. The hatch was sealed shut with built-up ice.

She looked at Wyman, then at the hatch again. She and the billionaire were sealed inside *Victory*, and the boat, a hole in its prow, was settling lower and lower into the sea.

CHAPTER 23

n the spray-filled air, McKay couldn't see the surface of the water until he was almost into it. Ice particles pummeled him at buckshot velocity, it felt like. He belayed down, the Pave Hawk keeping him fifty yards from *Victory*. He wanted to board *Victory* on his own terms, not the Bering Sea's terms, a comber slamming him into the hull.

He spoke into his helmet microphone. "I'm twenty feet above the wave crests. Get me closer to the boat, Ross."

When the copter bounced in the wind, so did McKay, and he felt as if he were hanging on to the end of a whip.

He asked, "You trying to shake me off the line, Ross? Take it easy up there."

It was a useless, unprofessional crack, and Macklin didn't respond. The wind was so fierce that McKay couldn't feel the copter's downdraft, just the unending rush of northwesterly wind and frozen spray. The line was a three-inch fastrope.

"Closer, Ross."

McKay swung side to side as the wind played with

him. He looked above, but could see only an opaque outline of the helicopter. He might've seen Ramirez, his head out the door, peering down. Below, *Victory* resembled a shelf of ice, something broken off an iceberg, a growler, fishermen call them.

"Get closer, Ross. I can't see the hatch in the cockpit. It's under ice."

With the seas heaving and falling, McKay didn't want to drop directly onto the boat, because a four-foot drop might suddenly become a forty-foot drop. He was aiming for the water alongside *Victory*. Nor did he want to hit the water too far from the boat, because large objects drift at a greater speed than small ones. *Victory* might move away from him.

Kurt Ridley said over the radio, "The boat's getting lower in the water, Jess."

Progress was unsteady, closer, then farther away, then even closer to the boat as the storm did its work on the helicopter and the boat and McKay. He lowered himself several more feet, until breaking waves were ten feet under him or so, he couldn't be sure because of the lack of perspective. A scuba regulator was hanging in front of his mouth. The wind was so strong that he had to position his diving fins so they would catch less air and pull him out of line.

McKay stared at the water, timing his release. *Victory* was no longer riding the waves, but was anchored by its own weight, no longer lively in the sea. He turned his head to grab the regulator mouthpiece in his jaw.

Then the boat was directly under him, and then he swung away from it, and then he released the belay and the fastrope and fell into the water.

Blue and green and white were all around, and then McKay surfaced on the front slope of a wave, a comber breaking above him. He let himself sink, the water below the surface almost placid. When he emerged, *Victory* was thirty yards away. He kicked toward it, his breath through the regulator, usually loud, lost in the storm's noise. He was above the boat, then he was below it. *Victory* was a moving target.

A comber punched him forward, and then on the next wave he skidded down some of the incline, and then he could touch *Victory*'s hull. He swam forward along the hull, both him and the boat rising on the next wave. He came to the point where *Victory*'s deck entered the water. So much of the boat was now below the surface that he could not see the mast stump. He glanced overhead at the Pave Hawk. A flickering window in the spray allowed him to see Sandy Ramirez push himself out of the helicopter.

McKay kicked his legs, swimming onto the sailboat's deck. Then he scrambled upward toward the stern, his feet slipping, and his hands unable to find a hold that wasn't ice. The wind ceaselessly pushed him, trying to carry him off the boat. Fallen rigging was below a layer of ice. He kept low, almost a crawl, and he came to the cockpit. Here in the well of the cockpit he could brace himself with his legs, standing in water that could no longer drain. A wave broke over the boat's stern, and he and all of *Victory* were under water. He rode the boat through the comber. Then he pulled the hammer from his belt. He could see the outlines of the hatch in the ice.

He hammered frantically, chipping away at the sheet of ice covering the entryway. He looked forward. More of the boat was under water. The sea was almost to the cockpit. Then he hammered angrily, ice slivers flying. He spit out his mouthpiece so he could draw more air, which was raw in his throat. A wave sent *Victory* toward the sky, and then dropped the boat to a trough. McKay hammered and when his right arm gave out, he switched to his left. He couldn't tell if he was making progress against the ice. The hatch seemed no closer, the ice still thick over it.

His arm burning, McKay cried out in frustration, maybe her name, maybe just a primitive call. He hammered and he hammered more, and his arms were weakening.

Sandy Ramirez appeared next to McKay. He was carrying a tool of some sort, something from the helicopter, something McKay didn't recognize, not a crowbar but similar, with a flange at one end.

Ramirez motioned McKay to one side, and then he lit into the ice with the bar. Shards of it flew away. Ramirez became a machine, a terrible blur of motion. Quickly some of the hatch was exposed, then more. A wave churned the cockpit, and Ramirez didn't even try to lower himself out of its way. He shattered ice and he did so quickly. Water spilled into the cockpit from the deck. Only the boat from the cockpit aft remained above the surface.

"Try it now," Ramirez shouted, lowering the tool.

McKay savagely kicked the hatch cover. It didn't move. He stepped aside, and Ramirez began again with the bar, lower on the hatch, clearing away the ice with vicious blows. Another wave rolled across the cockpit, and McKay and Ramirez had to duck. Much of the rampaging wave coursed over their heads.

A dozen more blows, then Ramirez stopped again. Now the hatch handle was above the ice. He turned it, then kicked again, then again.

The hatch cover flew open, falling inward. Gwen Weld was just inside the hatch, only her wide eyes visible under the survival suit. McKay reached down for her, but another wave shot across the cockpit, dump-

ing water down through the hatch, and blowing Gwen
back down into the boat.

Ramirez screamed above the storm, "Jess, don't
you go into that boat, damn you."

Ramirez moved to block his partner, but he was big
and McKay was quick. McKay fell through the opening into the interior of the boat.

Under the water, inside a boat in the rocking sea,
McKay was disoriented, unable to tell which way was
to the surface. He kicked once, guessing, but then a
hand grabbed his arm, pulling him up. He came to the
surface next to Gwen. The boat's interior was dark. He
shoved his mouthpiece back in.

Above him, Ramirez was framed by the hatch opening. He reached down for her, but a wave washed
across the little of *Victory* still in the air, and seawater
poured through the hatch, roughly pushing Gwen
Weld and McKay back down, and almost toppling
Ramirez into the cabin.

Ramirez righted himself, glanced anxiously at the
surrounding sea, then yelled something McKay couldn't
hear. Ramirez leaned through the hatch again. Something bumped McKay. He turned his head to see Rex
Wyman next to him. Four feet of air space remained
below deck.

His face twisted with horror, Wyman kicked the
water and reached for Ramirez's hand. Ramirez slapped
it aside, grabbed the woman, and lifted her up through
the hatch.

Water poured through the opening, now steadily,
not a wave but rather the mass of the sea.

"Get ready," McKay shouted at Wyman, water falling
on them from the hatch.

McKay positioned Wyman, trying to hoist him up,
but McKay's legs couldn't find anything to brace him-

self on. More water came through the hatch, a steady and increasing stream.

Back down came Ramirez's arm. Wyman reached for it.

Ramirez swatted aside Wyman's arm and grabbed Jess McKay by his survival suit's hood. Ramirez dug his fingers into a space between McKay's hair and the fabric. He yanked mightily, lifting McKay. Then when McKay's head was out of the cockpit, Ramirez hooked McKay's arm and pulled him up and through.

Wyman's arm appeared in the hatchway. He might have been screaming, but the sound was overwhelmed by the storm. White water poured into the hatch, sending him back down into the boat.

Ramirez threw McKay out of the cockpit into the Bering Sea, seized Gwen Weld by an arm, then stepped over the rail and walked into the sea, dragging her behind him. *Victory*'s stern disappeared beneath the surface and the boat was gone.

EPILOGUE

Jess McKay sat awkwardly on the chair, not knowing what to do with his legs, which he crossed and uncrossed, nor with his eyes, which watched her for a while, until she opened her eyes to watch him, and then he would look away.

Behind her bed was a headwall with an examination light and outlets for oxygen, nitrous oxide, and medical air. A blood-pressure gauge was on the wall, and an IV stand and bag were near her shoulder, the tube running to her right arm. A tray of untouched food was on a rolling table as were a bottle of wine and two glasses McKay had snuck in. The room at Alaska Regional Hospital had a big plate-glass window looking out onto DeBarr Road in Anchorage.

"This isn't where I was hoping to have our glass of wine together," Gwen said.

"How long have you slept?" McKay asked.

"Twelve hours, and I'm still tired." She continued to stare at him. "You look better without the helmet and goggles and face mask you were wearing in the photo you emailed me. You're a blonde, Jess." She grinned at him.

"I was blonder when I was a kid." What a moronic thing to say. "I was shorter, too, back then."

"And you are real." She reached out with her left hand and touched his ear, then moved her fingers along his jaw, hesitating, letting her hand rest on his cheek a moment. "So many times when we were emailing each other, me on the boat and you here, I had a frightening idea that you didn't exist, that my email conversations with you were generated by the boat somehow, to trick me. Maybe the Voice had decided to email me instead of using the speakers. But you are really you." She let her hand fall away.

"What's the Voice?"

She shook her head, a small motion that appeared to tire her. She inhaled deeply.

McKay pulled a corkscrew from his pocket and clumsily fit it to the bottle's cork. "Most things I drink have pop-tops."

He turned the corkscrew, then said quietly, "You are staring at me."

"Yes."

He cleared his throat. "I'll pour you some wine."

McKay half-filled a glass, then passed it to her. His own glass was to his mouth before he realized she was waiting for a toast. He smiled, then clinked her glass.

"Here's to dry land," he said, raising his glass.

She still stared at him, and then she smiled, and to Jess it was a knowing smile, but he didn't know what she was knowing. She raised her head and wet her lips with the wine. On the pillow, her black hair framed her face. Her cheeks were sunken, and her neck was thin. The doctor had guessed she had lost ten pounds on board *Victory*, and had added that she hadn't had much poundage to spare. Her right forearm was bruised to purple from one of her rolls across the boat's deck, one of many contusions, but other than those she was all right, the doctor had told McKay.

Gwen said, "Are your eyes blue or gray or green? I can't tell."

"It says green on my driver's license, but I'm not sure. Depends on the light."

She smiled again. "Your nose is bigger than I had imagined."

"It works well enough, though." He sniffed loudly. "Smells like a hospital in here." He wondered what she was doing, inventorying him.

Sandy Ramirez walked into the room. He was grinning, and he went over to the bed to plant a kiss on Gwen Weld's forehead.

"I'm the other guy, behind the other set of goggles," he said. "Me and Jess, we do things as a team, me leading, Jess following."

McKay introduced Ramirez, who found a chair and spun it around so he could lean forward on the seat back.

"Good news regarding *Hornet*'s crew," Ramirez said. "Craig Cheney and his crew picked them up." Cheney was a Pave Hawk pilot. "They've all been checked out, and they're fine."

"Why was *Hornet* out there?" McKay asked. "You'd think a crab skipper would know better."

"Money. I spoke with *Hornet*'s skipper, Lonnie Garvin. He and his crew spent a couple hours here at the hospital and have already been discharged. Wyman offered Garvin half a million dollars to attempt the rescue of *Victory*, and another half a million if Garvin were successful."

McKay asked, "How is Garvin going to get his money for the rescue attempt, now that Rex Wyman is dead?"

"Wyman paid up front. Garvin had half a million in his bank before he left Dutch Harbor. And *Hornet* had an all-risk policy on it, so Garvin will be reimbursed the cost of his boat. He doesn't know whether to kick himself for risking himself and his crew, or to celebrate because he's got no financial worries. When I left him, he was dialing up his wife down in Seattle, and Garvin was grinning, waiting for her to answer the phone, so I suppose he'll mostly celebrate."

"I'd mostly celebrate surviving, if I were him," Gwen said. "Same thing I'm celebrating, lying here in a hospital bed."

Ramirez asked, "So what are you two planning?"

McKay felt the blood rise in his face. "We are planning to drink these glasses of wine. Why don't you join us?"

"You two aren't planning anything?" Ramirez asked, pouring wine into a hospital glass.

McKay said, "Gwen has a flight back south to Boise. If time allows, we're going to have dinner somewhere before she goes. You aren't invited."

"I just thought of something." Gwen's voice was soft, little above the sound of air coming through the heating duct. "Except for the last few days aboard *Victory*, this is the first time in six years that I haven't looked at WorldQuest's stock price every thirty minutes, to see how the company was doing, and how I was doing. It's wonderful, lying here, not thinking about that, and not knowing anything about it."

"It's up nine dollars today," McKay said, then frowned at himself for bringing it up.

Ramirez laughed. "You are ruining this nice romantic hospital mood, Jess."

McKay glanced at Gwen. "Yesterday Microsoft offered to purchase two of WorldQuest's four divisions. Big news all around the world. WorldQuest's board will probably accept the deal, the analysts say. The other divisions will be folded."

"I'm still not going to think about it," she said.

Ramirez threw back the wine and then placed his glass on the table. He lifted himself from the chair. "I'm due at the gym." Ramirez blew Gwen a kiss.

He left them alone in the hospital room. When Jess looked again at Gwen, her eyes were half-closed. "I'm still tired, Jess."

He nodded, holding his wine.

Her eyes opened, and again they gazed at him. Her eyes were intense and candid, and bright with emotion and very blue. He looked away, and when he could look back, those eyes were still on him. She reached for his hand, and brought it to her side, and she held it. Her eyes closed again.

They held hands, and just before sleep she said, "I don't have a flight back south, Jess."

Visit
❖ **Pocket Books** ❖
online at

....

www.SimonSays.com

....

Keep up on the latest new
releases from your favorite
authors, as well as author
appearances, news, chats,
special offers and more.

SIMON & SCHUSTER
A VIACOM COMPANY
www.SimonSays.com

Pocket
Books

2381-01